ALSO BY PAUL GOLDSTEIN

A Patent Lie

Errors and Omissions

HAVANA REQUIEM

HAVANA REQUIEM

PAUL GOLDSTEIN

FARRAR, STRAUS AND GIROUX

NEW YORK

Farrar, Straus and Giroux
18 West 18th Street, New York 10011

Distributed in Canada by D&M Publishers, Inc.
Printed in the United States of America
First edition, 2012

Library of Congress Cataloging-in-Publication Data
Goldstein, Paul, 1943–
    Havana Requiem / Paul Goldstein. — 1st ed.
      p.   cm
    ISBN 978-0-8090-5393-3 (alk. paper)
    1. Cuba—Fiction.   I. Title.
PS3607.O4853H38 2012
813'.6—dc23
                                    2011024570

Designed by Jonathan D. Lippincott

www.fsgbooks.com

1   3   5   7   9   10   8   6   4   2

FOR LIZZY

"You are saved," cried Captain Delano, more and more astonished and pained; "you are saved: what has cast such a shadow upon you?"

"The negro."

There was silence, while the moody man sat, slowly and unconsciously gathering his mantle about him, as if it were a pall.

There was no more conversation that day.

—Herman Melville, *Benito Cereno*

HAVANA REQUIEM

1

The man could have climbed from the frame of an ancient newsreel: a sharecropper escaping the Depression-era South with the last scraps of his possessions; a skin-and-bones survivor fleeing yet another sub-Saharan catastrophe. His suitcase, scuffed and worn, was a cardboard imitation of tweed and leather straps, but the way the old man clutched it to his chest, the valise held his most precious belongings. Black but light-skinned, erect as a recruit, he waited inside the office doorway, intelligent eyes darting about, undecided between entering and escaping. Was it apprehension that Michael Seeley detected, or just curiosity? Fear that Seeley wouldn't take him as a client, or that he would?

Seeley rose and glanced a second time at the yellow message slip on the corner of his desk. *Héctor Reynoso. Musician. Havana. Ref'd by H. Devlin.*

"Mr. Reynoso."

The trim straw hat was a shade or two darker than the suitcase, and Seeley waited while the musician carefully set it on the bookshelf before extending his hand. Reynoso's gray hair was cropped close and the fingertips against Seeley's palm were callused.

"Mr. Herbert Devlin said that you can provide me with legal assistance." The inflection, measured and serious, gave no sign of indecision. Whatever doubts Reynoso had in the doorway, he had made up his mind.

Seeley indicated the client chair and dialed the number for Elena Duarte, one of the three young associates assigned to him. He had asked her to come to the meeting in case he needed translation. Her Spanish was perfect and, he now thought, her good spirits and lively mind might put Reynoso at ease.

Even seated, Reynoso held on to the handle of the suitcase. The musician wasn't so much thin, as Seeley first thought, as he was narrow: his wrists were sturdy, like a farmer's, and, in his neatly pressed cotton jacket and khaki pants, he looked taut as a cable. Repeated laundering had worn the jacket white at the seams. The pants had a razor-edge crease and the starched white shirt, tieless but buttoned to the top, was frayed at the collar.

Elena didn't answer, and Seeley replaced the receiver. "How did Mr. Devlin say I could help you?"

Green eyes measured the office from wall to wall, floor to ceiling. The beginning of a small smile played at the corners of the musician's mouth. "*Muy caro*," he said.

Seeley guessed at the meaning of the phrase, and wondered what Reynoso saw. The furniture was either rented or borrowed, and the office wasn't half the size of the one, a floor above, that he had occupied for years, before the partners at Boone, Bancroft, & Meserve forced him from the firm. It was only five months since they'd readmitted him to the partnership, and following Reynoso's admiring gaze as it traveled around the small room gave Seeley the same feeling as when he stopped drinking more than a year ago: that his life had become infinitely precarious.

Reynoso's eyes stopped at the empty picture hooks on the opposite wall, then dropped to where three frames rested against the baseboard, images facing the wall. The pictures were black-and-white still lifes of apples and pears that the artist had fussed up with garish pastels. The stagy colors weren't the only reason Seeley had turned the pictures to the wall; it was the very idea of ruining a perfectly acceptable photograph that way. When Seeley looked at Reynoso, the old man winked, as if to communicate that he sympathized with Seeley's taste. Was the wink a feint, or just a tic? Without seeing the pictures, how could Reynoso possibly know why Seeley had removed them?

"Very rich," was Reynoso's final appraisal. "Mr. Devlin informed me that you represent artists with not so much money . . . how do you say . . ."

"Pro bono publico," Seeley said. "But I haven't done that for a long time. Not now."

Seeley once represented as many impoverished artists as he did paying clients. That wasn't why his partners fired him, but the dwindling billable hours hadn't helped. Since his return to the firm he had stayed close to the arts, taking an art gallery to court for gouging on its commission to a painter and suing a corporate collector that thought that owning a painting entitled it to reproduce the work on the cover of its annual report. He settled a case for a screenwriter, forcing a film studio to change the way it shared profits with writers. But these were wealthy clients, and they paid six-figure fees and more for Seeley's time. Today if an artist seeking free legal representation called, Seeley would plead overwork and refer him to one of the volunteer lawyer organizations in the city. In the increasingly frequent moments when he let himself think about it, the absence of these struggling artists from his life felt like missing a limb.

"Herbert Devlin said that you are the right man to be our lawyer."

"Well, he was wrong," Seeley said. He resented Devlin for setting up two people for disappointment, Reynoso and Michael Seeley himself, and mentally scrolled down a list of other lawyers who might help Reynoso. In twenty minutes he had to be across town to give a lunch talk to Volunteer Lawyers for the Arts. There would be dozens of lawyers there glad to represent Reynoso. But they would want to know why he needed a lawyer. "You didn't tell me what your problem is."

"Not a problem. Mr. Devlin said it is an opportunity." Reynoso let go of the suitcase handle. He tilted his head and clapped his hands once. "We know each other for many years. Before Fidel. Mr. Devlin came to the clubs where my friends and I played. Always he had a good-looking woman on his arm." Reynoso's smile revealed stained but even teeth. "No women today. Only business and music. No *americano* loves our music like he does."

Why would Devlin risk his law license by traveling to Cuba? And how had Reynoso contrived not only to leave Cuba but to enter the United States?

"Mr. Devlin promised you would help us."

Seeley glanced at the phone. Elena was never late for a meeting, but he was glad she wasn't here. Difficult as it was to turn down the musician, if Elena were here it would be even harder. Twenty years apart, she and Seeley had studied with the same professor at Harvard, the legendary Felix Silver, and although Elena had her pick of New York law firms when she graduated, Silver told her to take Boone, Bancroft's offer. He told her that she would have her choice of partners, too, but that she should grab onto Seeley and not let go. Elena hadn't yet complained that in her time working with him Seeley had not taken a single pro bono case for a hard-pressed artist. But if he didn't represent one soon, Seeley knew that she would find a partner, or a firm, more promising.

Reynoso hadn't answered his question. "What kind of help do you need?"

The musician lifted the suitcase to his lap. Where the varnish had worn away and the tweed print faded, the cardboard pilled like an old sweater. Again the musician pressed the suitcase to his chest.

Seeley said, "Unless you're carrying body parts in there, you might as well open it up and show me what you have." If there were legal documents that needed translation, they would have to wait for Elena. Seeley corrected himself: they would have to await another lawyer and another firm.

It took almost a full minute for Reynoso to decide. He set the valise on the desk, carefully squared it with a corner, snapped open the old-fashioned locks, lifted the top, and tilted the case so that its contents spilled out: sheaves of sheet music; a bursting collage of spidery staves, bars, notes, and clefs; packets of staff-lined pages, some tied with faded ribbon, others with fraying twine; CDs and tape cassettes; even a dozen or so black vinyl 45s with their donut-center holes. There was a vague tobacco smell, but Seeley didn't know if it was from Reynoso or the accumulated scent of the contents. From the bottom of the suitcase, the musician took a manila envelope that had suffered a lifetime of foldings and unfoldings, but he didn't undo the brown shoelace tie or add the envelope to the pile on the desk.

Long musician's fingers slid over the pages. "My friends and I made this music in the nineteen forties and fifties," Reynoso said. "We were just street musicians in Havana. We played in restaurants and clubs for tips when they let us. These were black clubs, not where the American tourists went."

The two decades, the forties and fifties, were the giveaway. Seeley instantly understood what Reynoso wanted. The musician and his friends had signed away their rights long ago, and now they wanted the music back. For that instant, Seeley felt trapped, and adrenaline pounded through him. He could do this. He had to. He, not one of the volunteer lawyers. Seeley caught himself. This was always how he got into trouble. He remembered the conditions on which his partners had taken him back into the firm. Seeley said, "There are a dozen other lawyers in New York who can get your songs back for you."

"Mr. Devlin said you are the best."

"For this kind of work, best doesn't matter." Any competent copyright lawyer could draft, execute, and record the necessary termination documents for Reynoso and later negotiate with his American publishers. "I'm sure there are Cuban lawyers who can do this."

"No. Mr. Devlin said it must be you. My friends and I trust him. In those days, you didn't see whites at the black clubs, but Herbert

Devlin was always there. He told us we were not just musicians. He said we were *composers*." The words tumbled out, as if opening the suitcase had released a catch inside Reynoso, too. "None of us wrote music, so Herbert Devlin brought a man from New York to write out the music for us. He arranged for American publishers to buy our songs. Record labels to record us."

Devlin was Harry to everyone Seeley knew, but the name on the Los Angeles lawyer's doorplate was in fact Herbert, and it seemed natural for Reynoso, so formal in manner, to refer to him by his given name.

Reynoso stopped to catch his breath, but instead of then continuing he moved away from the desk and adjusted his shoulders as if to take a blow.

Seeley said, "You didn't have to bring all of this. A list would have been enough."

Reynoso swatted the observation away like a bothersome fly. "Mr. Devlin said you are not afraid to fight big companies."

Seeley pushed the tapes, CDs, and 45s to the side and, untying the ribbons and twine, sorted through a packet of sheet music. The paper was fragile, almost crumbly, and behind the tobacco smell it had the musty, closeted odor of old books. The titles were from another world. "Cara a Cara," "¿Por Qué Me Siento Triste?" "¿Dónde Estabas Anoche?" "Somos Differente." So were the names of the composers—Rubén Fornet, Justo Mayor, Onelio Bustamante.

Seeley put down the music. "Buena Vista Social Club." Seeley had seen the movie when he was still married. Clare had loved the music, he the musicians.

"Buena Vista is good," Reynoso said, "if you like tourist music. This"—his gesture took in the haystack of paper and plastic—"is not for tourists. It is more than music. But do you know what they do to our work in America? Frozen tacos! They use our music to sell frozen tacos. Mexican food!" The dark fingers scrambled through the paper sheets until they stopped at a yellowed folio. "My friend, Justo Mayor. This is his work: 'Tu Mi Delirio.' A work of art. Do you watch television?" Anger flared behind the thought-ful eyes. "My niece who lives here says, day and night, they play 'Tu Mi Delirio.' For what? To sell shaving cream!"

"And the reason you want your music back," Seeley said, know-ing that it would inflame Reynoso, "is that these people, these taco sellers, aren't paying you enough."

Reynoso's hands went to the pile on the desk, as if to protect it. "This is not about money!"

"Then what is it about?"

Reynoso looked up and past Seeley's shoulder.

Seeley turned. Elena was at the door, flushed and out of breath, her arms around a stack of binders, yellow Post-its beetling the pages like feathers on a boa. The deposition transcripts for Seeley's trade secret trial in Boston in two weeks. Seeley shook his head to let Elena know this wasn't the time to explain why she was late, then introduced her to Reynoso, who gave a courtly bow.

She nodded in return. "*Mucho gusto.*"

Reynoso said, "*Es un placer conocer a una mujer tan encanta-dora.*"

Seeley didn't understand the words, but he was certain that Elena's flush deepened. To Reynoso he said, "If it isn't for money, why do you want your music back?"

Reynoso stared at them, not blinking, as if he didn't under-stand the question.

"*Por favor,*" Elena said to him, "*es necesario que nos diga, para que le ayudemos mejor,*" and, to Seeley, "I told him that we must know if we are to help him." Elena's English had no accent, but when she spoke Spanish, even just a word or a name, she turned it into something exotic. The effect matched her looks. She was small and fine-boned, and her hair was as black and thick as a wild woman's.

The air in the office grew still. Finally, Reynoso said, "This is about history. My people's history. I cannot explain it to you."

"Then explain it to Miss Duarte."

"No. It is not the language. You must be a Cuban to under-stand. This is about *la cultura*. Mr. Devlin will tell you."

"He will tell me the reason?"

"No," Reynoso said. "He will tell you why it cannot be explained."

The composer's expression was contrite, and a glance from Elena told Seeley to let it go. Seeley opened a second packet of music, then another, as if the answer to his question might be secreted among the brittle pages. In the fourth packet, all of the folios had Reynoso's name in the upper-right corner of the cover page.

"Mr. Devlin said there is little time."

The composition on top, "Ron de la Habana" was published in 1950. Even if Reynoso was twenty when he wrote the song, that would make him more than eighty today, at least a decade older than he looked. Seeley made a quick calculation. "You have six months, maybe a year, to get your music back."

Reynoso said, "But you can do that? For my friends, too?"

Elena watched Seeley expectantly.

Seeley paged through another handful of compositions. Publication dates spanned the early 1940s through the late 1950s. "For some of the music, yes, it is still possible for a lawyer to get your rights back for you. Maybe most of it. But, for the music before 1950, it's already too late."

Under lizard eyelids, the intelligent eyes sharpened. "But you can fix that." Reynoso looked at Elena for support, but she shook her head.

"No," Seeley said. "The law says that for those songs it is no longer possible to get back your rights. No one can fix it." He checked his watch. If he left now, he would miss the Volunteer Lawyers lunch but still get there in time to give his talk. The hypocrisy of entertaining a crowd of morally ambitious young lawyers with war stories about the great cases he won for struggling artists depressed him.

Seeley looked again at the cover page of Reynoso's "Ron de la Habana." The publisher was Ross-Fosberg Music, a longstanding client. When sorting through the songs of the other composers, he recognized the names of other publishers, too. Several were small family companies that had liquidated years or even decades ago, their contracts taken over by one or another of the large American music publishers still in business. Even if he decided to take on Reynoso as a client, any one of those publishers could object to his working for him.

"Your publisher is one of my clients. So are some of the others. We have a rule in America about conflicts of interest."

"Yes. Of course. Mr. Devlin said you would have this conflict of interest. He has this conflict also. That is why he cannot help us. But he said your clients will trust you." Reynoso clapped his hands. "And my friends and I trust you. So, you see, there is no problem."

Seeley still had his partners to appease, but what if a publisher client, just one in a weak moment, waived the conflict and let him represent Reynoso and the others? The possibilities opened like an unfolding parachute. "I'll talk to the publishers and see if they'll waive the conflict—"

"What does this mean, 'waive'?"

"I'll see if they'll let me be your lawyer." The publishers were loyal clients, but they were demanding, and none had a good reason to let him represent an adversary in negotiations over their rights to the music. Still, if there was even the smallest chance that one of them would give him a waiver, he would never forgive himself for not asking.

"You are a good lawyer," Reynoso said, not moving. "You will explain to the publishers why it is right for you to help us."

"Let's see," Seeley said, even as he regretted raising Reynoso's hopes. "I need a list of your friends if I'm going to ask for waivers."

Beaming, Reynoso handed Seeley the much-folded manila envelope that he had taken from the bottom of the suitcase. Inside were sheets of paper neatly ruled in pencil, and on each line, also in pencil in a plain but elegant hand, were the names and addresses of the composers and, for some, a telephone number. Behind Seeley, Elena picked through the pile of sheet music.

One name on Reynoso's list had no address. "What about Maceo Núñez?"

Reynoso hesitated. "He is in prison. It is not always possible to speak with him."

"What does a composer have to do to get himself put in prison?"

"I am sure that he wants his music back."

Seeley waited. Reynoso's English was too good for him to have misunderstood the question, and the old composer's evasions were beginning to wear on Seeley. Reynoso looked away. "He played his music. He performed it in public."

"Do you still perform?"

"Not for many years." The smile faded. "I used to play some guitar, bass, piano."

Sooner or later, most of Seeley's clients lied to him, but few about something so unimportant. If Reynoso had stopped playing, the calluses would have disappeared from his fingertips in a month or two, not years.

"Are you sure the other composers want their music back?"

"Some of them think it is wrong to break a contract. They think, once you sign a contract, you must honor it." Reynoso studied his fingernails. "Herbert Devlin said you could come to Havana and explain to them why this is not a wrong thing to do. That in America this is the way business is done."

"Oh my God!" It was Elena. Her hands rapidly sorted through the music. "I don't believe this."

Seeley shot her a hard look and turned back to Reynoso. "Even if the publishers waive the conflict, there is no way I can go to Havana. I told you, a Cuban lawyer could do this work. You didn't have to come here."

"You are afraid to leave this fine office of yours."

"You couldn't find a Cuban lawyer who would do this, could you? There's someone in Cuba who doesn't want you and your friends to get your music back."

Reynoso brushed the words away, and Seeley glimpsed anger as well as bravado in the dismissal. The gesture drew Seeley's eyes to the straw hat on the bookshelf. A neat pucker creased the crown and the front of the narrow brim was snapped down gangster-style. The hat was as plain as the rest of the man's clothes, except for a bright madras ribbon around the base of the crown that could have been plucked from a young girl's hair.

Elena was arranging the sheet music into two piles, one taller than the other.

"Mr. Devlin said it must be you who represents us. No Cuban lawyers."

"Is it your government that doesn't want you to get your music back? Are you in danger, just coming to see me?"

Reynoso's smile was sly and followed another wink. "There is no danger. Mr. Devlin says we are so old that we are ghosts more than we are flesh and blood. He says we pass through buildings and airports and no one sees us—they only feel a cold wind."

Of course. That's how the two of them crossed illegal borders so easily. They were ghosts. "It's my job to help my clients, not to make their situation worse." I have ghosts of my own, Seeley thought, and again regretted his promise to ask the publishers for waivers.

"I made a mistake," Reynoso said. "I am sorry to take your time. Herbert Devlin told me you are someone who fights for artists. But I suppose he was wrong."

The attempt at manipulation was so obvious that Seeley felt embarrassed for Reynoso. Elena, absorbed in her sorting, didn't hear. He looked at Reynoso's list. "Is your telephone number here?"

Reynoso rose. "My niece has a telephone."

"In Cuba?"

"No. New York. *Queens*." Pride lit Reynoso's eyes. He had a niece who lived among royalty. The musician fumbled a stub of pencil from an inside jacket pocket and, on the legal pad that Seeley handed him, wrote his name and a telephone number with the same easy strokes as on the list of composers. "I am staying with my niece."

Seeley began placing the spilled contents into the suitcase, and nodded to Elena to do the same.

"No," Reynoso said. "You keep this. You are our lawyer now. That is why I brought it." He nodded in the direction of the suit-case. "This music is older than the revolution. My friends and I trust you to keep it safe."

Safe from what, Seeley wondered.

Reynoso's smile opened to a grin and he patted Seeley lightly on the arm. "It is hotter on your streets than in Havana, and your client is an old fellow. You don't want to send him out like a mule with a pack, do you?" He drew closer and with a darting gesture reached up and twisted Seeley's ear. "I know you are go-ing to take good care of Héctor."

The movement was so unexpected, yet so astonishingly famil-iar, that if not for the tingling left by the callused fingers, Seeley would have questioned that it happened. He led Reynoso to the door and asked his secretary to show him to the elevator, then went back to his desk to collect the notes for his lunch talk. He unclenched his jaw. The last half hour hadn't been a client inter-view. It was more like the cross-examination of a difficult but life-or-death witness.

From behind the piles of sheet music, Elena said, "Do you know what this is?" Her breathlessness was that of an excited child.

"I don't have time." Seeley started out the door. "I was sup-posed to be at Volunteer Lawyers ten minutes ago."

"The music in this pile?" Elena lifted her hand from the shorter stack. "Every one of them is a standard. The classics they play on all the Spanish-language stations. All the Latin groups today re-cord them. Los Van Van, Orquesta Melaza, Los Tainos. You can't turn on the radio and *not* hear these songs."

"Or buy a frozen taco," Seeley said, "or lather up your cheeks with shaving cream."

"This is your case, right? I want to work on it."

"It's not a case," Seeley said.

"Then what is it?"

"Nothing. There's a conflict with our publisher clients." Seeley added numbers in his head. If Elena was right, between performance royalties and advertising licenses, Reynoso and his friends' songs were bringing in millions of dollars a year, and would continue to do so for the next thirty or forty years. With that kind of money at stake, there was no chance that the publishers would let him represent Reynoso. If anything, the publishers would want to hire him to find a way to stop the Cubans from reclaiming their music.

Elena said, "But if they waive, I can work on it?"

Seeley nodded, just to be able to leave.

Elena said, "Héctor looks like he'd be fun to work with."

Seeley thought back over the last forty minutes of feints and evasions, winks and handclaps. "Sure," he said on his way out the door, "like juggling razors."

2

Seeley pushed Reynoso to the back of his thoughts so that he could concentrate on the black ball coming at him off the brilliant white surface, but the composer elbowed his way forward. Why in fact did Reynoso want his music back? Why couldn't he get a Cuban lawyer to represent him? At the last possible moment, Seeley stepped back and swung at the ball. Had he put Reynoso at risk just by meeting with him? By letting him leave the music-filled suitcase in his office? Was he so desperate to retrieve his old practice that he would take an engagement at a client's peril? When the hubbub in Seeley's head gathered momentum like this, alcohol was the only off switch that he knew. An abstinent year had won him back his partnership, but this wasn't the first time that he questioned the wisdom of the exchange. And what was Reynoso hiding?

Seeley shifted, spun, spooned the ball off a side wall and lobbed it overhead.

Nick Girard took the lob without a bounce and stepped back to center court. He was as tall as Seeley's six feet, but thicker around the torso, and the tiny sports goggles gave him a froggy look. Girard said, "Did you know Clare's wedding is Sunday?"

Months ago, Girard told Seeley that his former wife was remarrying, and Seeley knew that his partner had timed the latest news to distract him from his game. Seeley gripped the racquet tighter and calculated where the ball would zigzag next. "The mailman must have lost my invitation."

Girard grunted.

It was Girard and his wife, Maisie, who had introduced Seeley to Clare, and, though Girard never said so, Seeley knew that the two blamed him for the failure of the marriage. "Wish her luck," Seeley said. The words didn't come out as casually as he wanted.

"You mean, better luck than last time."

Seeley bit back his lower lip, the ball landed in a dead spot, the volley ended, and he lost the point.

Girard served before Seeley returned to position, forcing a lunge for the ball and a flailing, easily destroyed return. The two had been playing for forty minutes and, although Girard barely moved about the court, his shirt was soaked through and his breath came in gasps.

"You know," Girard said, exertion strangling the words, "Hobie's going to make you drop your Cubans."

It was another distraction, but this time Girard also positioned his bulk to block Seeley's path to the return. Seeley stepped forward, shot a hard elbow to the base of his partner's spine, staggering him, then slammed the ball home. His point.

Hobie's interest in the Cubans surprised him. Seeley had no hope that the publishers would waive the conflicts, but since he'd promised Reynoso, and himself, that he would ask, he had filled out the standard new-business memo. Hobie—Hobart—Harriman, the head of the firm's litigation department, had apparently seen the memo. "It's me Hobie doesn't want at the firm. He's pissed that my old clients are leaving him to come back to me."

Hobie had joined Boone, Bancroft soon after the partners forced Seeley out, inheriting Seeley's entertainment and publishing clients. He had been in and out of government service, mostly in the State Department, through Republican and Democratic administrations and was never more than an intermediary or two away from the secretary's ear. According to rumor—which he did nothing to suppress—Hobie regularly served as liaison between State and the CIA. Between government posts he'd worked at Wall Street law firms, but never returned to the same one. The partners on Boone, Bancroft's executive committee thought that Hobie's political and social connections could bring more Fortune 500 clients to the firm, as well as lucrative work from the downtown investment banks, and had agreed to consider him to head the firm when the current chairman stepped down. In the meantime, the committee made Hobie head of the litigation department even though, so far as Seeley knew, he had never tried a case.

When Girard saw that Seeley was holding his serve to let him catch his breath—penance for the elbow a minute ago—he said, "Hobie thinks you're gunning to take his office away from him."

"Give me one reason I shouldn't have my old office back."

That office had been the war room from which Seeley orchestrated hundred-million-dollar intellectual property lawsuits, trying them back-to-back with his pro bono cases, finishing one trial on a Friday, starting the next on Monday, using alcohol to lubricate the passage between. The office had belonged to founding partner Ed Meserve, a lion of the New York trial bar, before he retired and handed the office over to Seeley, its wet bar still fully stocked.

"That was my deal with Daphne when I came back. I build up my billable practice again and the firm gives me back my office. I've held up my end." The office was the last piece of his old life that Seeley had not regained, and the craving for it was visceral.

"You're forgetting there was another part to the deal. Your work for the deserving poor. You might want to think about dropping the Cubans."

"They'd be paying clients."

"Well, paying or not, Hobie put them on the executive committee agenda for this afternoon."

"Then I'll have to be there," Seeley said. He served, and for a while the two men rallied easily, friendly rivals, Girard placing his returns precisely, off one, two, three walls, forcing Seeley into constant movement, the graceful but animated marionette of a fiendish puppeteer.

In Seeley's year away from New York, the University Club had renovated its squash courts, and the turpentine snap of fresh paint in the boxlike room mingled with a funky bouquet of floor wax, stressed rubber, and old sweat. For as long as they had known each other, Seeley and Girard played squash two or three mornings a week, first when they were young lawyers in Buffalo, and then, when Seeley moved to New York and Girard followed for partnerships at Boone, Bancroft, at the University Club, off Fifth Avenue. But this was only the second time they had played since Seeley's return to the city.

"You don't want to push Hobie away." Girard returned an easy lob. "Remember what Michael Corleone said."

For a confused moment, Seeley tried to place the name among the firm's lawyers.

"Keep your friends close, but your enemies closer."

"That was Sun Tzu."

"Oh." Girard slammed the ball across court, forcing Seeley to circle around him for the return. Girard had played since prep school, and Seeley only picked up the game after starting out as a lawyer. A quarterback in high school and college, Seeley was the better athlete, but he'd learned that mastery of squash started not far from the cradle.

Seeley's next return was hard and, he thought, well placed, but Girard scooped up the ball and, for what seemed like a full second, willed it to a dead stop on the face of his racquet, then tipped the sleeping missile into a corner so that it rolled lazily across the floor.

The game was over. "I have a City Bar meeting downtown," Girard said. When he lifted his goggles, his eyes were red from strain. "I won't be able to run interference for you with the executive committee."

"I can handle it," Seeley said. They were at the dollhouse-sized

door in the back wall of the court. Along with the mechanical whir
of the ceiling fans, the echoes of play from other courts bounced
about the white room.

Girard said, "Hobie's trying to build his own practice. Banks,
investment companies. Big retainers, lots of billings, long-term
work. He thinks your street people are going to set the wrong tone
for the firm."

"Fourteen penniless musicians are going to scare off an investment bank?" Seeley toweled his hair. "Who wins when the two of
you play?"

"What do you mean?"

"You and Hobie." Why did Seeley assume that the two played
squash together? "He beats you, doesn't he?"

Girard looked around the court, as if he might have left something behind. When his eyes returned to Seeley they were veiled;
Seeley couldn't read them.

"Hobie's strategic." Girard swatted his racquet back and forth.
"He plays the long game. He'd play with knives, if he could. That's
why you want to be careful with him. Keep the peace. Get someone else to represent these people."

"Fifty years ago, the American music publishers ran over them
like a truck. They paid them a few bucks a song."

"And now Michael Seeley has appointed himself to be their
savior." Girard swatted the racquet again. "I hope this doesn't turn
into a train wreck like the last time, with that Chinese girl . . ."
He let the rest of the sentence hang in the air between them.

"This is different."

"Why, because you're not drinking?"

"That's part of it."

"You think you can make up for what you let happen to her."

"Like you did when you got the partners to take me back?" In a
firm of 650 lawyers it is easy to get lost, and in the weeks before
the partners forced Seeley out, Girard disappeared. Squash dates
were canceled by a secretary and phone calls were not returned.

And, when the decision was finally made and Daphne Hancock, the firm's chair, gave Seeley the news, Girard was in France, on vacation with his family.

"No, taking you back was just business." Girard pulled open the door and Seeley ducked to go through. "We always need good lawyers." When Seeley turned, Girard's eyes met his and he was the hearty friend once again, "Sober, you're the best lawyer I know. I want to keep you here."

They were in the narrow corridor leading to the showers before Seeley said, "How long is my probation going to last?"

"Do you really think the partners are watching you?"

"No." Seeley walked in the direction of his locker. "Only when I breathe."

Three columns divided the sheet that Elena handed to Seeley. In the first column were the names of the composers, with Reynoso's at the top, and under each name an address in Havana; for a few, there was also a telephone number. Across from the composers' names were the titles of their compositions and the publisher that today owned the rights to each song. It must have taken Elena hours just to trace the chain of ownership from the small publishing companies, now defunct, to the larger and then still larger firms that had gobbled them like fish in a food chain. In all, seven publishers presently owned the Cuban composers' songs. Five were Seeley's clients.

Seeley nodded at the pile of deposition transcripts for the Boston trade secrets trial tabbed with Elena's yellow Post-its that was still on the corner of his desk, unread. "How do the depositions look?"

"Our witnesses are solid," Elena said. "A lot better than theirs. I marked the weak points for attack on cross."

"That's good," Seeley said, "because I just talked to our client. They're rejecting the other side's last settlement offer."

Their client was a medical device manufacturer in Boston, one of the world's leading developers of vascular stents. The company had been hosting a delegation of scientists from Beijing at its research facility in Waltham when a security guard found two of the Chinese visitors in a restricted area. The company's general counsel moved quickly, calling Seeley within the hour. Seeley, too, wasted no time, and the next day, while the two researchers were having drinks in a departure lounge at Logan Airport, a process server handed each a subpoena and a hastily drafted complaint for trade secret theft. After the investigators Seeley hired returned from Beijing and reported their findings, he amended the complaint to request an award of $100 million damages to compensate his client for its loss.

Seeley said, "You can tell the other partners you work for that you'll be in trial in Boston starting August third."

A dazzling smile lit the serious face. After months of library research and document review, poring over depositions and interrogatories, this would be Elena's first trial. Seeley didn't like to overstaff his cases and, in addition to Elena, he had assigned only a younger partner and a litigation paralegal to the team. Lawyers from the Boston firm that was acting as his local counsel would provide whatever backup Seeley needed.

"That's what you wanted, isn't it?" Like Seeley, Elena had gone to a blue-collar college on scholarship and then to Harvard Law, taking loans and part-time jobs to get through. And, like Seeley, she wanted nothing more than to be a trial lawyer, even for a medical device manufacturer, if that's what it took to pay the firm's overhead and keep her skills sharp for the pro bono clients who really mattered.

She said, "What about Héctor?"

Seeley took her list off his desk. "I'm calling the publishers now."

Ross-Fosberg Music owned the rights to Reynoso's compositions, as well as those of three other composers on Elena's list. Seeley dialed the number for Joel Simkin, the company's general counsel. A year ago, Seeley would have told the publishers to give him the waiver or to find another lawyer to do their work. Today, he didn't give ultimatums to paying clients, but while he waited on hold, Seeley considered what he would do when Simkin refused to waive the conflict. I should cheer, Seeley thought. Celebrate my release from a doubtful client who, he guessed, needed a bodyguard more than a lawyer.

Simkin came on, but he wanted to complain about Hobie. "I know he's your partner, Mike, but he doesn't understand the first thing about our business."

"Give him a chance. He's learning."

"Then he can pay me for my time, instead of me paying for his."

Seeley said, "I want to know if you can waive a conflict for me—"

"As much as I love you, Mike, you know our policy on waivers."

Seeley said, "I have four of your writers who want me to terminate transfers for them."

"You mean it's not an Internet case? No file sharing? No pirates?"

Seeley's heart skipped as it occurred to him that Simkin might actually waive the conflict. "They're Cubans. There's not a pirate in the lot."

"Who are they?"

"Héctor Reynoso," Seeley said. He glanced at Elena's list. "Justo Mayor. Onelio Bustamante. Jorge Garcells." He liked the sound the names made, the rhythm of vowels and soft consonants.

There was a silence at the other end, then Simkin said, "Sure, why not?"

Simkin was a brusque man whose pride thrived on his ability to make quick decisions, but Seeley didn't know if he was joking. "Can't you give me a quicker answer?"

"What's to think about? We don't have a problem here. We love our composers like family. Any one of them you want to represent, we'll waive the conflict. You just have to give us first crack at negotiating a new deal with these boys."

For someone to call Reynoso a boy amused Seeley, but he distrusted Simkin's casualness in giving him the waiver. "I know every one of your weak points, Joel. Don't think I won't exploit them when I'm negotiating with you for my clients."

"You're forgetting," Simkin said, "I know your weak points, too. Maybe that's why I'd rather negotiate with you than someone I don't know."

When Seeley didn't respond, Simkin said, "Look, Mike, the publishers fought this thing in Congress decades ago, and we lost. If we have to deal with these notices, I'd rather have you representing the composers than some amateur. But no free rides. Your clients already missed some deadlines. I don't know what you did to get the judge to push back the date in your case for that science fiction writer, but if you try that with us, we're not going to roll over."

Seeley had represented the writer's estate in the first lawsuit after Congress changed the law to let authors get their works back decades after they first sold them. The estate's lawyer had overlooked the statutory deadline and filed the termination notice three weeks late. Seeley won the rights back anyway, convincing the judge that Congress meant the change to protect authors and not to penalize them for failing to comply with formalities.

Seeley said, "How much do the songs earn?"

"Our whole Cuban catalogue?" The wariness in Simkin's voice was what Seeley expected to hear earlier, when he asked for the waiver. "Latin's big these days. All in all, I'd say maybe fifteen to twenty million."

Seeley's earlier estimate had been too conservative. "How much do you send Reynoso?" The composer may have disclaimed any interest in money, but if a publisher sent him a large check every six months Seeley didn't think that he would send it back. And since the money would keep coming until the copyrights expired, for the Cubans and their families it would be like winning a good-sized lottery.

This time, Simkin made no effort to hide the edge in his voice. "Ask your client if you need to know."

"Reynoso's clothes looked as old as his music. Do you know if he's even getting your royalty checks?"

"I'm waiving a conflict for you, Mike. That doesn't mean you get to see our books." Simkin couldn't have made the point more clearly. If Seeley continued to press he'd take back the waiver.

"I have a trial in Boston, but I'll get you the termination notices in a week or two."

Elena looked up from her computer keyboard when Seeley came in. Behind her, as elegant as a tapestry, a gold, blue, and red striped banner with an elaborate medallion at the center covered one wall. The flag of Ecuador, where her parents were born. Although she and Seeley both came from immigrant families and paid their own way through school, the most important fact about their origins couldn't have been more different. Through her four years at college, Elena lived with her parents in their apartment in Washington Heights at the northern tip of Manhattan. When Harvard and Columbia offered full law school scholarships, her parents had to plead to get her to make the move to Cambridge. Seeley had abandoned his parents' house at fifteen and never returned.

Seeley said, "I don't know why, but the publishers are going to waive."

After talking to Simkin, Seeley reached the general counsel at two of the other publishers, and the conversations went much like the first. No waivers for Internet pirates, but for Cuban composers, why not? Seeley was certain that when the last two publishers returned his calls, they, too, would waive the conflict. He was skeptical when Simkin said that he'd rather deal with him than with an amateur, and when the others gave the same reason, he disbelieved them all. And, like Simkin, neither would say where the tens of millions in royalties and license fees were going. These were lawyers who rarely agreed on anything. If one said that the music industry was dying, another would say that it was already dead, and the third would argue that it was on the brink of a renaissance.

Seeley glanced at the stacks of files on the floor. "What's your workload like?"

"I still have to mark up the party depositions for Boston, and I have a couple of small projects for Barry." Unlike the other young associates at the firm, Elena wasn't self-conscious about calling even the most senior partner she worked for by his first name. Also unlike the others, she ignored the casual dress code and was always in a skirt and heels. She pushed back from the desk. "But if something needs to be done for Héctor, I can do it."

"I don't know how good the mails are in Cuba. See if Reynoso can get you phone numbers for the rest of his friends."

"I already tried. I called his niece in Queens, but she hasn't seen him since yesterday morning."

Seeley said, "There should be a blank termination form in the copyright files. Translate it into Spanish and then make copies and start filling them out." Elena flipped the densely filled page of the legal pad on her desk and continued on the reverse side. In twenty-four years of practice, Seeley had never seen a lawyer write on two sides of a page. "Also, translate one of our retainer letters. I don't want anyone complaining that Reynoso and the others didn't know what they were signing." Seeley glanced at his watch. In less than two hours, he would have to persuade the executive committee to override Hobie's objection to the Cubans, but now that he had the waivers he was sure he would prevail.

"Let's call our client and tell him we're working for him."

Elena took a file from a desk drawer. Stapled to the inside was the start of a phone list. At the top, Seeley saw his office extension and the telephone number for his rooms at the University Club. Below that was a number for Dolores Moncada, Reynoso's niece. Elena dialed and handed the phone to him. A machine answered with a scratchy recording in Spanish, giving what sounded like a standard message. The message ended, and Seeley was about to hang up when the same woman's voice came on again, but louder and more urgent, the Spanish words colliding like tenpins, Reynoso's name among them.

Seeley pressed the redial button and handed the receiver to Elena. After listening to the two messages she put down the receiver. "The second message said, 'If this is Uncle Héctor, please leave me a message. Your niece loves you and she is worried about you. Where are you?'"

3

A single page of a deposition transcript contains no more than twenty-five triple-spaced lines of witness testimony, but after ten minutes on Seeley's lap, the loose-leaf binder lay open to the same, unstudied page. I have a client who's disappeared, Seeley told a *New York Times* reporter for whom he had done favors in the past, asking him to inquire around about Reynoso. My client is missing, he told an acquaintance at the *Post* whose beat was in Queens. This was one of the rare times Seeley regretted not having friends in New York's police department. Disappeared. Missing. In Seeley's mind, the words engulfed Reynoso like amber embedding an insect.

A shadow crossed the page.

"I thought we might have a word before the executive committee meeting." The voice was gravelly, a smoker's rattle, and went with Hobie's thinning hair and drooping, hangdog features. The light summer suit with a white handkerchief in the breast pocket was hand-tailored. There were working buttonholes on the sleeves and delicate pick stitching on the lapels, but the suit was as rumpled as the man himself. Hobie's manner and dress were, Seeley knew, a deceit. It is an old ruse among lawyers to affect neglect in order to lull adversaries into complacency.

Hobie said, "I didn't want you to think there was anything personal about my objecting to your Cubans."

Seeley said, "I hadn't considered that." He swung his feet off the desk and gestured for Hobie to take the chair across from him. The desk was old, but not antiques-shop old, and from the vague lemony cloud always hanging over it, Seeley guessed that the cleaning crew waxed it nightly in an effort to revive the patina. "What's your problem with my clients?"

"You may be a fine lawyer," Hobie said, "but you don't understand what it requires to shape and steward the image of an institution. This law firm is not going to move into the top tier if our idea of business development is to take on every ragtag musician who asks to be our client."

"Is your problem that they're poor, that they're black, or that they're musicians?"

If he heard the words, Hobie gave no sign. "There's also a question of loyalty to your country. Right now, the revenues from that music are contributing to our economy—"

"What do you know about where the money is going?"

Hobie hesitated, but Seeley was sure he didn't know.

"Well, to the American publishers, I would think. They're the ones you're trying to take the music away from, aren't they? If you break these contracts, that money is going to disappear down the rathole of a Third World country."

Seeley didn't question Hobie's shrewdness, but he was as bored with him as he would be with any politician.

"Some of these publishers are our clients," Hobie said. "Do you have any idea how embarrassing it would be for us to ask them for waivers so we can represent this rabble?"

Seeley watched Hobie for the effect of what he was about to say. "The publishers already waived the conflicts."

"Waived?" He lifted his hands as if to defend against a blow. Confusion clouded the pale blue eyes. "All of them? They gave you written waivers?"

"They're clients of the firm. If they tell me they'll put it in writing, I trust them." The last two publishers still hadn't returned

Seeley's call but, mystified as he was by the publishers' collaboration, he knew they wouldn't be a problem.

"I think we'll keep this on the committee's agenda anyway." Hobie's voice had a fateful quality to it that gave the impression of encompassing all possible outcomes. "On a steady ship, no one falls overboard."

Seeley remembered that Hobie was a weekend sailor. "I'm sure," he said, lifting the deposition transcript onto his lap and turning the page.

"You know," Hobie said, "I was on the phone this morning with an old friend at the State Department." He leaned forward, grasping the corners of the old desk as if it belonged to him. "The subject of your Boston trial came up."

"Just like that?"

Hobie lifted his hands from the desk and examined them. He rubbed his fingers together, then took the handkerchief from his breast pocket and delicately wiped the lemony residue from his fingertips. "My friend at State was asking how I liked running the litigation practice here, and I suppose I mentioned that you were one of our stars—"

"And this old friend of yours had some views on my trial in Boston."

"In a manner of speaking, yes, I suppose you could say that." Hobie leaned back in the chair again, but looked uncomfortable, as if he realized for the first time that the conversation was going to end differently from what he and his friend in Washington had planned. "My friend was just thinking, out loud, you know, how since the Olympics China has become even more concerned about its public image. Human rights. Pollution. Foreign exchange rates. Industrial espionage. But China also owns most of our nation's debt, and that means our relationship with them is . . . well . . . fraught. If we can do them a small favor from time to time . . ."

"What's your point?"

"Your industrial espionage case in Boston is going to give the Chinese a black eye."

"Do they do that a lot in the State Department?"

"What's that?"

"Think out loud?"

"We understand that there was a generous offer of settlement on the table—"

"My client already turned it down." Seeley's client hadn't talked to Hobie or to anyone else. That meant the State Department got its information from the Chinese government or from the Chinese company's lawyers.

Hobie said, "I'm sure that if you revised your estimate of the chances for success in the case, your client would want to reconsider its decision not to settle."

"Why would I do that?"

"Because, like dropping the Cubans, it's the right thing to do for your country."

"You mean the right thing for your friends in Washington," Seeley said. "But not for my client in Massachusetts. *Our* client. We work for this law firm, not the State Department."

"How carefully have you considered the merits of your case?" Hobie's hands moved toward the desktop, but abruptly drew back. "A jury looking at this might think the conduct of these two Chinese researchers was entirely innocent. What they learned in your client's factory—"

"It's not a factory. It's a research and development facility—"

"There's an old Chinese saying," Hobie said. "'Two men can keep a secret so long as one of them is dead.' In one or two months everyone will know your client's secret anyway."

This was going to be the Chinese defense in Boston, that no technology can remain a secret for long. "More like two or three years," Seeley said. "That gives our client a head start on its competitors. The Chinese got their device onto the market as soon as they did because they stole it from our client."

"And you're going to try to convince a jury that this is unfair? For a developing country like China to try to lift itself up by its bootstraps is unfair?"

"Convince a Boston jury? Sure." Hobie's claim was so preposterous and his expression, eyebrows drawn into an angle of earnest concern, so melodramatic that Seeley wanted to laugh. He didn't know whether to despise the man for his amorality or to envy him.

"Even if you burn through your client's retainer and win a judgment, where's the client's payday? Two Chinamen aren't going to pay a hundred-million-dollar judgment. That's what you're asking for, isn't it? They don't have enough between them to cover your client's court costs."

Hobie had discovered the single weak spot in Seeley's case. Although Seeley's complaint named as defendants not only the two trespassing researchers but also the billion-dollar Chinese conglomerate that employed them, the employer had filed a motion for the court to dismiss it from the case, claiming that the two men had acted entirely on their own.

Seeley said, "The judge will keep the Chinese company in the case."

"How can you be sure of that?"

"Whatever risk there is, the client's willing to take it." When they discussed the settlement offer, Seeley had explained to his client's CEO the possibility that the judge would drop the Chinese company from the case and, with no prodding from him, the CEO told Seeley that the principle of protecting hard-earned technology from freeloaders was too important to settle.

Hobie leaned in, confidentially. "You know, if we could give our friends in China some evidence of our good faith in this matter, they might be willing to help you with information about that client of yours, the woman journalist who disappeared."

So Hobie, too, knew about the final disaster that led to Seeley's expulsion from the firm. Had a partner told him, or someone at the State Department? The State Department, Seeley decided. "No deals," he said. "I represent one client at a time."

"Apparently you also lose them one at a time." Hobie jammed his hands into his pockets. "If they told you where she was, you might be able to apologize to her. Who knows, she may even forgive you."

"This isn't just about the Chinese, is it? Your friends in the State Department have an interest in my Cuban clients, too."

Again Hobie hesitated, and he shifted in the chair. "As you said, one client at a time. Every ship on its own bottom."

"Then why is it so important to you that I not represent the Cubans?"

"To me? Not at all. The importance is to the firm. It's only the firm that I'm thinking about."

"Just keeping the ship of commerce steady," Seeley said.

"So," Hobie said, "you understand." There wasn't a trace of irony in the gravel voice.

When Seeley came into the conference room, Daphne Hancock was already there, clearing away paper plates and napkins from an earlier meeting. "If they can't bus themselves, you'd think they'd get one of the staff to clean up."

Almost as tall and broad-shouldered as Seeley, Daphne was in a fashionably cut suit and one of her bright silk scarves. In the time that Seeley was away from the firm, she had begun knotting the scarf in the French style, on the side. No one would call Daphne beautiful, or even handsome, but, widely traveled, she had learned to carry herself well. The first woman to head a large New York firm, she insisted that people call her chairman, not chairwoman, or even chair.

Seeley took a seat at the long table next to Darryl Valentine, the head of the firm's trusts and estates department. Valentine was trim, athletic, and black, and his melting brown eyes were a source of comfort, if not joy, to the well-heeled widows on Boone, Bancroft's client list. Seeley noticed that of the hundred-dollar bills at each partner's place around the table, Valentine had already pocketed his. The bribe was Daphne's invention. Department chairs might have crowded schedules and annual incomes of two to three million dollars, but Daphne had guessed, shrewdly, that a crisp new hundred-dollar bill, for which they were accountable to no one, would ensure their presence at these meetings.

"I put you first on the new-business agenda." Daphne sounded tired. "We're not going to have a problem, are we?" She spoke to Seeley, but her gaze took in Valentine, checking for his reaction. "No more messes for me to clean up?"

Seeley said, "I hear you're going to retire."

"Only from management. I'm keeping my practice. Let someone else see what fun it is to be overhead."

The conference room had been redecorated since Seeley was last here. The hard chrome and glass edges had disappeared, replaced by a clubby abundance of leather and wood. The surface of the conference table was of animal hide, discreetly stitched and stained dark green, and the framed prints on the wall were from the same portfolio of painted-over black-and-white photographs that Seeley had taken down in his own office. He wondered if the firm's decorator got a volume discount on the prints; a kickback seemed more likely.

The department heads of tax, bankruptcy, municipal bonds, and real estate came in and took the places marked by the hundred-dollar bills, some of which got folded and tapped on the table while others quickly disappeared into pockets. Not a single lawyer was unembarrassed by the bribe. What did Seeley really know about his partners, other than Girard? Jack Reitz, the head of the bankruptcy department, who took the seat to his right, was on his third marriage. Next to him, Thatcher Burleigh, from municipal bonds, had an autistic adult son. Jim Talcott, the head of real estate, maintained a precisely scaled replica of the New York subway system in the basement of his home in New Rochelle. That was the sum of Seeley's knowledge of his partners' personal lives.

Hobie arrived last, surveying the available spaces as he made his way around the table, touching one partner's shoulder, whispering in the ear of another. Like Girard, he had the easy sociability of people who, wherever they find themselves, know that they belong. Pointedly, he avoided the last place marked with a bill and instead, after making a full circle, took the chair next to Daphne at the head of the table. He rubbed his pink freckled hands briskly, as if he were preparing for a hearty meal.

While Daphne reviewed old business with the partners, Seeley studied Hobie as he would a puzzle. The basset head was too large for the slender, potbellied frame and, even seated, the lawyer held himself delicately, as if the conference room furnishings might injure him. Alone among the men at the table, Hobie kept his suit jacket buttoned, and the result was that the back of his jacket gaped two or three inches from his shirt collar, giving him a strangled, off-kilter, aspect. Seeley could imagine the pouchy eyes that now stared at the wall over Seeley's shoulder scanning some watery horizon. When Hobie looked down, his eyes caught Seeley's staring at him. Mildly startled, they seemed to ask, as they had from the first time they met: *Who are you? And, remind me, what was your name?*

Daphne said, "Nick has a City Bar meeting and can't be here. But he asked me to let you all know that if he were here he would support Michael on this."

Seeley hadn't expected that. Maybe Girard was still atoning for when the partners had fired him. Or maybe he actually believed that Seeley was doing the right thing.

Daphne nodded at Seeley. "Tell us what you want to do for Héctor Reynoso."

The casualness in the way she referred to Reynoso, as if he were already a client, surprised Seeley. He quickly described how copyright transfers got terminated and the work that this would entail for the firm: completing and delivering the termination notices, researching and resolving any objections from the publishers, negotiating the resale of the music for the writers.

At regular partner meetings, Daphne spoke first, letting the others know where she stood on the issue before them, shifting to the partners the burden of proving her wrong. But this time, still watching Seeley, she said, "Hobie?"

Hobie rose. "If you heard what its proponent has just described to us, this is a very minor matter for a firm of our size and, more important, for a firm of our aspirations. It's hardly worth the expense of opening a file."

Seeley wondered if Hobie had any idea how much money the Cubans had coming to them.

Hobie continued. "But, large or small, it is the quality of our clients and the nature of our work for them that signals to the world the direction in which this firm is headed and the kind of clients it hopes to serve." Hobie's voice was determined, his look, as his eyes circled the table, convincing and consequential. The gap between jacket and shirt collar had shrunk an inch. "Going forward, I am sure you will all agree that the only law practice worth devoting our careers to, the only law practice deserving of the individual sacrifices that we make daily, is a global law practice, and that means serving multinational clients with the most sophisticated projects, drawing where appropriate on our good relations with interested governments at the highest level . . ."

As Hobie rattled on, Seeley saw that the lawyer's visit to his office had been as carefully plotted as a diplomatic meeting between a great and a small power. Hobie had been testing out his argument on Seeley, while reminding him of the sources of his influence. In raising the question of the Chinese trade secret case, and then of Jun Wei, the Chinese journalist, Hobie had a second purpose as well: to let Seeley know that he had powerful allies in Washington, and probably elsewhere, and to warn him that if he persisted in representing the Cuban composers, they would throw obstacles in his way. But, Seeley asked himself, to what purpose?

"This means we should not be taking on small clients of no particular substance, and it certainly means we should not be taking on clients for the sole purpose of breaking their contracts—"

"Hold on a minute, Hobie." It was Reitz, the bankruptcy lawyer. "That's what I do. Renegotiate loans, get clients out of leases—"

"Well of course," the low voice remained firm and the pale eyes skipped over Seeley as they moved around the table. "The reorganization and restructuring of multinational companies is as much a part of a global practice—"

"How does someone do that?" It was Valentine. Behind the trust lawyer's amiable appearance was a skeptical and edgy mind. "How does a composer sell his rights and, just like that, whenever he wants"—he snapped his fingers—"he gets them back?"

Seeley waited for Hobie to answer and, when he didn't, it occurred to him that the head of litigation had not the vaguest idea of how the copyright act worked. Seeley said, "It's not just snapping your fingers." As he explained the steps required for the composers to get back their music, Hobie nodded impatiently as if he already knew. Seeley said, "This is how the guys who created *Superman* got their rights back from Warners."

"That's exactly my point," Hobie said. "This firm's future lies in representing companies like Time Warner, not the two-bit cartoonists who sue them."

Girard was right; it would be a mistake to underestimate Hobie. Hobie knew what the partners on the executive committee wanted, and they understood that when they elected him the firm's new chairman, he would know how to return the favor. A corner office. Seats for them and their clients in the firm box for Yankees and Knicks games. Conflicts resolved in their favor rather than another partner's. Hobie was the force that brought people together with the trappings of power and pleasure.

Seeley said, "Who's going to represent this kind of client if we don't?"

"They can go to Legal Aid."

"Not in this economy." Seeley considered pointing out to the partners that the Cubans would be paying clients, that in fact the engagement would involve many millions of dollars, but decided that he wanted his partners to commit to the principle of representing, free, people who could not afford them. "Most of the legal service storefronts have shut down."

Again, Hobie looked around the table. "Unless someone misled me, I didn't join a firm that takes on every small-time musician who wants our services."

"No one's asking us to," Seeley said. "We also can't take on every multinational that wants to hire us."

Daphne's fingers tapping on the table said that she wanted to move on, but Valentine ignored her. "Is he black? This musician you want to represent."

"Light-skinned," Seeley said. "Why would that matter?"

Valentine rapped the table lightly for emphasis. "It always matters."

Daphne said, "Do you have waivers from our publisher clients?"

Seeley nodded. Daphne had recruited him to the firm even before she became chairman; had fired him; then, at Girard's urging had rehired him. Seeley couldn't imagine her as anything but chair of the firm and, although his lifelong instinct was to resist authority, the thought that Daphne was going to retire saddened him.

"It's not technical conflicts with present clients I'm objecting to," Hobie said. "What I see here is a more profound conflict with the future of this firm."

Seeley said, "What room does this future of yours have for our pro bono practice?"

"The partners here do more than their share of pro bono," Hobie said. "The Philharmonic. The Met. The Museum of Natural History. Pro bono doesn't have to mean riffraff."

Again, Daphne's fingers tapped, and Chuck Vogel, who ran the tax department, leaned his bald head into the silence. He was a man of constant smiles and snappy one-liners that only he laughed at. "Why didn't this go to the pro bono committee instead of us?" Behind the smile, a horse laugh was ready to erupt.

"Because," Seeley said, "it's not a pro bono matter. They're paying clients. The work is all billable."

"Billable, sure." Vogel cocked his head in a New York way, lips pursed. "But, at the end of the day, how are we getting paid?"

Seeley regretted straying from the pro bono principle but, right now, he just wanted to represent Reynoso and the others. "We'll defer payment of our fees. When we renegotiate the contracts with the publishers, we'll take our fee off the top." The arrangement was customary and fair, and Seeley didn't expect Reynoso or his friends to object. "But you're missing the point. We should be taking these engagements whether they're billable or not."

"There are plenty of deserving poor out there." Hobie gestured toward the window behind him. "And their interests don't conflict with the interests of our clients. But these Cubans haven't done anything to justify our support—"

Seeley thought Valentine tensed at the word *deserving*, and he saw an opening.

Vogel said, "We need to back Hobie on this. He's head of litigation, and that makes this his call."

"No," Seeley said, "that's not good enough."

"Why not?" Vogel was not going to let up.

"Because these people are artists, and art is as important— more important—as any multinational business deal this firm will ever work on. Without art, we're no better than cows grazing in a field."

Seeley paused, as he would with a jury, to count who was with him, who against; who wanted him at the firm for his billables, and who wanted him here for what he believed in, even if that sometimes had a cost. Valentine was for him; Hobie and Vogel surely against. And the others? As with a jury, he could only guess. "The question," he said, looking first at Hobie and then at Valentine, "is not whether these musicians deserve us. It is whether we deserve to work for them." He turned to Vogel. "Do you have any idea how empty your life would be without music, without movies, books—"

"Not me." Vogel's laugh was a harsh squawk. "I'm a bridge player."

No one joined in Vogel's laughter. They all watched Seeley, who was thinking about the question he asked himself this morning while he waited for Simkin to come on the line. Would he have taken Reynoso on as a client even if the publisher had turned down his request for a waiver? Would he do the same now if the executive committee turned him down?

Daphne leaned into the table, her signal that discussion was over. "Are there any other comments?" Her tone invited none. "Good. I think Hobie's observations are right on the mark about where we should be heading as a firm, and what it will take for us to get there."

Hobie's features resolved into an expression of entitled vindication.

"At the same time," Daphne said, looking directly at Hobie, "our young associates also represent the future of this firm, and we always need to make room for the kind of interesting work that attracts these young people." Her gaze widened to take in the entire table. "Have any of you ever heard Héctor Reynoso's music?"

Everyone but Hobie smiled. Once again, Daphne was going to surprise them. "It's been years since I heard him play a New York club, but I have his recordings. Héctor Reynoso is a fine musician. A fine composer, too." She winked at Seeley. Hobie, sitting next to her, couldn't see it, but Valentine did and gave Seeley a sidewise smile. Daphne's knowledge of Reynoso's music startled Seeley as much as the others. So did her support. She wanted her legacy to include positioning Boone, Bancroft as one of the great global law firms of the twenty-first century, and Seeley knew that if he ever truly got in the way of that legacy, he would immediately lose her backing.

Daphne looked at Seeley. "Is Reynoso still in New York?"

For some reason, it was the weight of Hobie's eyes on him that Seeley felt, not Daphne's. This wasn't the time to report Reynoso's disappearance. "He's staying with his niece."

Valentine said, "If Mike thinks it's important for us to represent these composers, then I think we should take them on and be glad to do so."

"I agree with Darryl." It was Burleigh. Seeley expected Valentine's vote, but hadn't counted on Burleigh, and didn't know if the bond lawyer was supporting him or Valentine. That left Vogel, Reitz, Talcott, and Daphne. Girard's announced support was fine, but a partner had to be present to vote.

"I'm in," Reitz said.

Vogel shook his head. "Not me."

Talcott said, "When you go down to Cuba, make sure you bring me back a box of Cohiba Espléndidos."

"Don't get lost down there." It was Burleigh. "I read that they threw an American in jail for handing out laptops to dissidents."

Seeley said, "No one's going to Cuba—"

"Of course you can't go." It was Daphne. "You have an important trial in Boston."

"We'll prepare the notices here," Seeley said, "send them to Cuba for signature, and then do the negotiating from here. All the publishers are in New York."

Daphne said, "So long as the publishers have waived, and so long as taking on this work won't upset an important client—"

"What about United Pictures?" Hobie started to his feet, but changed his mind midway. Although Daphne was still United's principal outside counsel, Hobie had in Seeley's absence overseen the motion-picture studio's licensing work.

Daphne looked at him. "What about them?"

"We were just told by"—Hobie thrust a hand in Seeley's direction—"we were just told that these terminations were a problem for Time Warner. Why would United keep its business here if we get a reputation for taking works back from their lawful owners?"

"If we were terminating a movie company's rights," Daphne said, "I'd consider backing off. But we're not, and—"

"But United is my client—"

"United is not your client, Hobie, and it is not my client either." For the first time, Daphne's voice rose. "No partner at this firm has his own clients. United Pictures is a client of this firm, just as Héctor Reynoso and Michael's other Cuban composers are going to be clients of this firm. I'm sure that if United asks, I will be able to persuade them that this is the right thing for us to do. Now let's move on."

Hobie cleared his throat for attention. "Even—and I believe it's a mistake—even if we put United aside, there are other large clients I'm working to bring on board, and they may find the Cubans to be a problem."

"Well," Daphne said, "if and when you bring these clients in, we'll see if they have a specific conflict and we'll deal with it then."

The blue eyes filled with misery and Hobie brushed an imaginary speck off his sleeve. "I truly deplore having to raise this, but is anyone here concerned that our partner will once again embarrass himself—and this firm—the way he did with that Chinese journalist?"

"Water under the bridge," Daphne said. "A sailor should understand that, Hobie."

One or two of the partners nodded. The others looked stunned by the exchange.

Seeley was glad for the partners' support, just as he was glad to be able to represent Reynoso. He liked winning battles of principle, and had since his high-school football days when the only principle was that winning is better than losing. But Seeley never forgot that his opponents disliked losing even more than he liked winning, particularly when, as now, the loss was a humiliating one, in front of friends or colleagues. If, as Hobie told him before the meeting, there was nothing personal in his opposition to Seeley's working for the Cubans, that surely was no longer the case.

•

Seeley stopped at Elena's office. "Have you found our client yet?"

She looked up from the document she was marking. "The executive committee said yes?" When Seeley nodded, she said, "I talked to Dolores an hour ago. His niece. She still hasn't heard from him."

First his Chinese journalist, now Reynoso. How easy it is to disappear in a city the size of New York. Who would notice if at 2:00 in the morning someone hustled an elderly Cuban into a sedan on one of Manhattan's side streets?

"Does Dolores know who his friends are here? Did she call them?"

"I don't know. She says Héctor's a free spirit, but he always checks in with her." There was a child's quaver of worry in her voice.

"Call every Latin music club you can find in the city. The boroughs, too. New Jersey. Ask if anyone's seen him. One of the booking agencies should have a list of clubs."

Elena wrote notes on a fresh pad.

"Did he have any reason to come to New York other than to talk to a lawyer?"

"Dolores said he's been trying to put together some kind of festival of Cuban music here." Anxiety rushed her words, disengaging them from the natural rhythm of her voice. "The last time she saw him, a couple of months ago, she thought he'd changed. He never talked about politics before, but this time every other word was about the government."

Seeley bit down on his instinct to expect the worst. He should have pressed Reynoso harder, not accepted his evasions; he should have asked better questions. "We just have to wait."

"Did you see the dates on the music? He has only a couple of weeks to sign the forms for some of them."

The question failed to mask Elena's real worry, for the composer, not his music, but Seeley admired her for trying to make the concern sound professional.

"We're just his lawyers, Elena, not his babysitter." Again, he felt that he had let her down. He could only guess what Felix Silver had told her about him. Seeley hadn't been in contact with his Harvard Law professor for years, but if Silver knew what had become of him, he never would have told Elena to work for him. "Harry Devlin may know something. The lawyer who referred him to us. I'll call him. You stay in touch with Dolores. Let me know when Reynoso shows up."

"And if he doesn't?"

"Let me know that, too."

4

Starting with his name (Seeley later learned that Silver's parents named him Felix after the Supreme Court Justice Felix Frankfurter), Seeley had never met anyone like Felix Silver, his first-year civil procedure professor at Harvard. Among the aggressively cerebral, self-absorbed law faculty, Silver's uncapped brilliance thrust him out like a refugee from an alien culture. He was gaunt, even cadaverous, his eyes set so deep that it was impossible at any distance to discern their color. No stodgy podium dweller, more quicksilver than silver, he restlessly paced the vast lecture hall, carriage ramrod, his hands always in motion. What distinguished his intelligence was that it fastened not on ideas, or even law—the standard Harvard grist—but on practical things. If you master civil procedure, he preached to his students, if you learn every entrance and exit to the Federal Rules, the trap doors and secret passages that lie hidden in its corners, then you will have mastered the federal judicial system, the supreme battlefield of legal warfare.

When in the autumn term of his second year, Seeley saw a notice posted on the placement board in Harkness Commons advertising for six volunteers to help Silver on a case, he knew before he finished reading it that he would sign on, even though his schedule was already filled with the part-time work and tutoring jobs that supported him along with loans and scholarship funds.

Silver's client was a writer who for eight years had struggled to assemble the first unauthorized biography of Peter Kirby, a Los Angeles industrialist whose pathological craving for privacy had obstructed the efforts of previous writers. Kirby's family and business associates, even his ex-wives, had refused to talk, but Silver's client had gathered enough scraps of information from magazine and newspaper articles, as well as Kirby's correspondence with politicians and business competitors, to compile a slim but revealing book. His publisher was about to go to press when a Kirby-owned company that over the years had bought up the copyrights to every newspaper and magazine article ever written about the industrialist, as well as his correspondence, filed a copyright lawsuit to stop the biography's publication.

Silver knew that only in rare cases will a court hesitate to enforce a copyright. His strategy was to show that this was one of those rare cases by proving that Kirby had acquired the copyrights for the sole purpose of suppressing publication of his biography. As part of his pretrial discovery in the case, Silver required Kirby's company to produce every document in its possession—letters, memos, telephone notes—that had any connection to the company's acquisition of the Kirby copyrights. When the requested papers finally arrived, there were twenty industrial-sized bins of them, all unsorted. The haystack of papers triggered Silver's call for volunteers.

On one of Silver's regular visits to the warehouse where Seeley and the five other students reviewed and sorted documents in shifts around the clock, Seeley asked the professor if his revered Rules of Civil Procedure didn't in fact require documents to be produced in an orderly, catalogued form. Silver answered that it is one thing for the rules to prohibit parties from dumping documents on their adversaries as Kirby had done, but another thing entirely to get a court to enforce the prohibition.

Barely in time for Silver to file his motion to dismiss Kirby's case, the students found three memoranda and two letters that clearly revealed the industrialist's intention to buy up the copyrights solely in order to shut down unauthorized biographies. A month later, the court granted Silver's motion and, when the biography was published, it included an afterword about the lawsuit and an appendix reproducing the damning letters and memos that the students had discovered in the barrels; confidentiality had cloaked the discovery process, but somehow the documents found their way into the biographer's hands.

Seeley took Silver's class in copyright that spring term. The course was a revelation. Seeley's love affair with art had begun in grade school, with a class trip to Buffalo's single art museum, the Albright-Knox Art Gallery, but he soon made visits on his own to escape from his violent household. At first he thought that he went to the museum for the quiet inside the high white walls, and only after a time did he realize that he had been studying the pictures all along. Insistently, the Kandinskys, Klines, Pollocks, and Rauschenbergs kept bringing him back. But if art was the one safe place that Seeley knew, here in Silver's class was a body of law—copyright—custom-built to protect that sanctuary and the artists who created it. He received the second-highest grade in the course but, for reasons known only to Silver, it was Seeley the professor invited to be his research assistant for the following year.

It seemed like Silver was away from Cambridge that year more than he was present, but until he took on the Russian cases, he always managed to return to meet his classes from Chicago, or San Francisco or Los Angeles, or wherever he had been arguing an appeal or seeing his artist or writer clients. Nor did he ever leave Cambridge without giving Seeley a fresh list of research projects. Although the assistantship paid poorly, and Seeley needed money, he dropped his part-time jobs and tutoring, as well as most of his coursework. When he wasn't in the library, he was at his desk in the small alcove across from Silver's office on the third floor of Langdell Hall. Silver's secretary, Mrs. Lippincott, a woman as phlegmatic as Silver was animated, would occasionally look up from her typing, glance at Seeley, shake her head and return to the keyboard.

The Russian cases colored that entire year in dull shades of brown and gray. Silver's clients, the writers Trafimov, Babenko, Gortikov, and Gennadiev, were Russian dissidents, and when friends smuggled their writings to the West, the Russian government responded by seizing ownership of the works and filing copyright lawsuits in the United States to halt their publication. Two of the cases were in Washington, D.C., two in New York City, and Silver was on the train every week, shuttling between his classes and hearings in the two cities. The research tasks escalated, taking Seeley well beyond the boundaries of copyright law, into doctrines of international law, expropriation, sovereign power, and the countervailing constitutional forces of free speech and press. The names *Trafimov, Babenko, Gortikov, Gennadiev* repeated endlessly in pleadings, briefs, and research memos, as well as notes in Silver's indecipherable hand, became in those bleak winter days the words of a Russian folk song; Seeley even composed a private tune for them.

One night in late February, Seeley looked up from work in his alcove to see Silver across the way, feet up on his desk, watching him. When their eyes met, the professor waved him in. "We lost two of our motions to dismiss," Silver said after Seeley had taken one of the hard wooden chairs across from him. "We're going to lose the other two when Judge Moffat in D.C. gets around to ruling."

"But you're going ahead with the cases."

"*We're* going ahead with them. Of course." Silver's accent was a blend, unusual anywhere but in Cambridge, of skewed New York vowels and New England's softer inflections. Law school rumor was that Silver and his socialite wife lived in an elegant town house on Louisburg Square. His wife was also reported to be movie star gorgeous. But Silver wore no wedding band, and for all that Seeley knew, he was unmarried and lived on the Metroliner.

"I have to go to Russia to see our clients. They're all over the country. Novgorod. Kaliningrad. Volgograd." Silver reached into a bottom desk drawer and lifted out two squat crystal tumblers, then a clear bottle with a white label and the name Dewar's above a bagpiper in kilts.

Seeley, the son of a brutal alcoholic, a wife- and child-beater, had never taken a drink, not even a beer with his football team-mates after a game. He knew no more about how his life would turn out than any other twenty-five-year-old, but he had long ago resolved that he was not going to be a drunk like his father.

Silver splashed an inch of whiskey into each tumbler and pushed one across the desk to Seeley.

In the incandescent glow of Silver's office, the whiskey at the bottom of the glass looked, if not innocent, then inviting. The mystery of it absorbed Seeley: that in his father's glass this liquid threatened a ferocious, all-destroying violence, while in Silver's it seemed to promise easy friendship, even intimacy. If this is not a safe place for me, Seeley asked himself, what will be? To his astonishment, the Scotch tasted like an unpleasant medicine. It took less than a minute for the warmth to unfold like angel's wings inside him, and for Seeley to understand his father.

Silver read Seeley's silence as disapproval of his travel to Russia. "If we're going to take this case forward and into trial, I need to talk to my clients."

"You could write," Seeley said. "I'm sure they have telephones in Novgorod, Volgograd . . ."

"And Kaliningrad. Yes I'm sure they do."

Seeley did disapprove. If Russia's secret police silenced writers and imprisoned them, why would they not do the same to their lawyer?

Silver said, "With all the facts about repression in Russia that are going to come out at trial, our clients' lives will be in jeopardy. I need to sit down with them and be sure they understand the risk before I can let that happen."

"And your classes?" Seeley's worry wasn't for Silver's classes. He was still thinking about his mentor in a Siberian labor camp.

"That's why I want to talk to you. You know the material. You can teach the copyright class until I get back."

If you get back. "Are you sure—"

"As I hope your career will teach you, Michael, one of the great luxuries of choosing your clients carefully, of making certain not only that they are right, but also that they are truly victims, and of being sure that your adversary is not just wrong but evil, the great luxury of this is that it frees you to do anything, to violate every ethical canon there is, if you must, to lie to your adversary and even to the court if you have to. You can—"

"—go to Novgorod, Volgograd, and Kaliningrad, if you must." The alcohol, just two fingers, had made Seeley giddy. "But how do you know which is the right side?"

Silver, God bless him, took the question from his half-drunk assistant seriously. "If you are honest with yourself, you will always know. If you are honest, you will at least know if your client is on the *wrong* side." The professor added Scotch to his own tumbler, considered Seeley's, then returned the bottle to the drawer. "We are representing four writers who dared to stick out their necks to criticize their government. Can you imagine the lies that our worthy adversaries, the American lawyers who are representing the Russian government, have to tell themselves just to get out of bed in the morning?"

Outside, snow fell. Seeley was a larva inside a cocoon. It was as if Silver had reached with surgeon's fingers past Seeley's thoughts and feelings into his raw experience, his very being; he had plucked out his soul and given it a name. Seeley did not want the night to end.

Silver flew to Moscow the next day, and Seeley took over his copyright class. He discovered that although he didn't have anything like Silver's style, he did have a vocation for performing before intellectually critical minds. But in truth he yearned to be in

Russia, at Silver's side, talking to the writers. As he left his second class, one of the associate deans waited just outside the door.

"You're teaching this class?"

"While Professor Silver is away. Yes."

"He can't do that," the associate dean said. "You can't. We can't have 3Ls teaching our classes."

At age fifteen, Seeley had aimed a loaded gun at his father's heart, so to him the encounter with the associate dean meant nothing. He understood the man's objection, and at once dismissed it. But he also knew from his youthful experience not to argue. He continued teaching Silver's class and the associate dean did not return.

The second week Silver was away, two gray-suited men who said they were from the State Department were in the office suite when Seeley entered. They asked Seeley where Silver was and whether he had heard from him, and behind their backs Mrs. Lippincott shook her head, somewhat more vigorously than in the past. Seeley said he didn't know where Professor Silver was, nor had he heard from him. And no, he had no idea when he would return to Cambridge, if in fact he was gone.

Silver returned the following week. He looked thinner than before, if that were possible, his eyes sunk even deeper beneath his narrow brow. He resumed teaching his classes and shuttling once again between Cambridge, New York, and Washington. The Russian cases never went to trial. Instead, as in the case of the Los Angeles industrialist, Silver filed for summary judgment, attaching to his motion papers affidavits that he had obtained from the writers when he was in Russia. That was enough for the trial judges. The New York judge had harsh words in his opinion for the Russian government; the judge in the District of Columbia was milder. The Russian government did not attempt an appeal from its total defeat.

In retrospect, that whole year swirled around Seeley as if under a magician's cape. At the center of it was the folk tune of Russian cases—*Trafimov, Babenko, Gortikov, Gennadiev*—and the memory of that one cloistered conversation in Silver's book-lined office, the snow falling outside in the Cambridge night. Seeley never acquired a taste for Scotch. (Gin was his downfall, and he sometimes considered whether his life would have turned out differently if he had stuck with Scotch; wondered whether, like Silver, he might have drunk like a gentleman.) But other than that, he bought everything that Silver said, did, and was; he bought it whole.

Harry Devlin was a man who would, unless Seeley was constantly vigilant, climb right into his skin like a second conscience. Gruff but infinitely charming, he would tell Seeley where he was wrong and what he needed to do, and only days or months later would it occur to Seeley that this companionable man trying to order him about did not have a shred of moral authority that he hadn't manufactured himself. Seeley knew that he would get what he wanted only if he gave the old lawyer no room to maneuver.

"Why didn't you tell me Reynoso was in trouble?"

"Well, perhaps that's because I don't know that he is." Devlin was close to ninety, but the easy baritone on the telephone had lost none of its honey. "I'm glad the two of you got together. I thought you'd get a kick out of helping him."

"You didn't hear me," Seeley said. "He's disappeared. His niece told me he always checks in with her. She thinks something's wrong."

"There's nothing for you to worry about, Michael. Héctor's not very good at remembering appointments. Keeping track of time, either. And don't let that gray hair of his fool you. I wouldn't be surprised if he's shacked up somewhere."

"Or in a Cuban prison, like Maceo Núñez."

"Ah, so he told you about Maceo. Poor fellow's like a good number of their countrymen who don't know enough to keep to themselves. Have you listened to their music? You must. I'm glad you're helping them get it back."

"Why can't a Cuban lawyer do this?"

"A Cuban lawyer? How many *American* lawyers do you know who can do this?"

"It's just filling out a form and getting it signed. For some reason, the lawyers down there are afraid to touch this." For the first time, Seeley realized that the simple mechanics of getting the forms signed would require someone to travel to Cuba. "What kind of politics is he involved in?"

"This isn't about politics. Héctor and the others want their music back because they don't want to hear it in television commercials. That's why I sent him to you. I remembered how much you care about artists' rights. If Héctor were in political trouble, how do you think he gets to travel in and out of Cuba? I promise you it's not on a raft."

No, Seeley thought, he wafts through airports like a ghost, like Devlin himself. "And you can travel back and forth because—"

"I occasionally do some work for the Cuban government."

Devlin had started out as a lawyer in Upstate New York in the 1940s, representing small-time union gangsters. When he moved West, he climbed up a rung to represent Hollywood screenwriters, and then another rung to work for directors, movie stars, and studio executives. Seeley first met him when he needed help finding a blacklisted writer Devlin had represented during the communist witch hunts in the 1950s. If the old-time mobsters were why Devlin went to Cuba in the 1940s, the blacklisted writers would explain why a communist government would accept him as its lawyer today.

"What kind of work?"

"Trademarks. Brand names." Devlin polished the words as if they were jewels. "Officially, there's still no private property in Cuba, but they understand how markets work. The great irony—you'll love this—is that it took a communist revolution for the Cubans to recognize the power of a brand. I helped them stop Bacardi from using 'Havana Club' on rum."

"Only after Castro stole the name from the family that owned

it." The Havana Club case was famous. "I wouldn't expect someone of your high moral standards to help the state steal property
from its citizens."

"I've found that who's the thief and who's the victim depends
on your point of view. Do you know that photograph of Che? *Guerrillero Heróico?* We make companies pay to put it on their prod-
ucts. Not just T-shirts. Anything from candy to condoms, anywhere
in the world. Castro turned Che into an icon. Billboards. Posters.
The portrait covers an entire side of the Ministry of Interior headquarters. How many countries have a brand like that? A brooding,
romantic revolutionary. What do we have—Uncle Sam? Mickey
Mouse?"

"And before the revolution?"

"I helped Americans with legal problems in Cuba, Cubans
with problems in America. I lined Héctor and his friends up with
some music publishers."

"You gave the publishers a good deal."

"It was fifty years ago. No publisher paid a writer anything
back then. You didn't have to be Cuban to get screwed. Americans, Frenchmen, all any of them got was pennies."

"I meant today. Who's getting the money today?"

"You would have to ask Héctor's publisher."

"I did," Seeley said.

Devlin said, "Then you know what the music's worth."

"That's why I'm surprised you're not representing them."

"Didn't Héctor tell you I have a conflict?"

"With who?" It surprised Seeley how easy it had been to blind-
side Devlin. "It can't be the publishers, because I represent them."

"Conflicts come in all sizes." If Devlin felt trapped, his voice
didn't reveal it. "Surely you understand that."

Devlin either had a conflict or he didn't, but he wasn't going to
give Seeley the details. Seeley said, "Your client must be very important if you won't help this old friend of yours out of whatever
trouble he's in."

"You're repeating yourself, Michael. I told you, neither of us knows that Héctor is in trouble." Devlin's sigh was theatrical. "I hope you're not planning to go to Havana."

"You're telling me that's where Reynoso disappeared. Cuba."

The sudden silence at the other end of the line told Seeley that he was right. And if the old lawyer knew where Reynoso was, he also knew why. It was good for a change to have Devlin off balance.

Seeley said, "I promised Reynoso that I'd help him if the publishers waived the conflict."

"Did you promise that if he took off, you'd go chasing after him?" When Seeley didn't answer, Devlin said, "I didn't think so."

"I've never broken a promise to a client."

"Maybe this is the time to start. Havana's not a safe place for you. Remember what happened last time—"

Seeley steeled himself for Devlin to remind him about Jun Wei.

"That time when you went off to find that blacklisted writer? When I told you not to go? How many people got hurt?"

"Unless you're losing your memory," Seeley said, "none of that would have happened, except for what *you* did."

"I didn't say you were responsible. What I'm saying is that when you go charging off to places you don't belong, bad things have a habit of happening." Devlin stopped for a breath. "What can you do in Havana? Do you know the city? Do you speak the language? I bet you've never even been there."

Until now, the thought of going to Cuba hadn't seriously occurred to Seeley. "All I need is to get some people to sign some forms."

"What were you planning to do? Go door to door collecting signatures? The security police snap open their holsters if they see three Cubans talking on a street corner. How do you think they're going to react to an *americano* pushing legal papers at the locals? All you're going to do is stir up problems. The past. Let me tell you, in Cuba you don't want to be a person who gets in the way of history."

"Then why did you send Reynoso to me?"

"I didn't know he was going to disappear." Exasperation muddled the honey.

"So you admit that he's disappeared."

There was another sigh, as if the last of Devlin's will was escaping. "All I know is what you've told me."

5

Girard crowded Seeley's office the way he did the squash court. "Do you know a banker at Evernham's named Dwight Butler?" When Seeley shook his head, Girard said, "He goes by 'Ike.'"

"I'm sure he does."

"Well, he knows you. Or of you. He wants to talk to you about representing their entertainment clients."

Private banks like Evernham & Company have clients, not customers. Seeley had handled litigation for large New York investment banks when their publishing and entertainment investments ran into legal problems, but not Evernham's, which was in a category by itself. The small bank was the oldest in the city and occupied its own landmark building, set like a precious stone in the tangle of alleys around Wall Street. The bank was rarely mentioned in the news, even in the business press, but Evernham's had a reputation for plying its financial and political influence to help large fortunes, domestic and foreign, grow larger. Seeley had no greater objection to working for banks than for any other corporate client, but there were moments—like when he thought that he might represent Reynoso even if Simkin didn't waive the conflict and even if the executive committee didn't approve—when he realized that his law practice had turned a corner. The sensation was like an unshackling, a reprieve. "I'll pass on this."

"Butler specifically said he wants you." Girard swung an imaginary squash racquet as if it would swat away any objections. "Look

Mike, I've been pitching Evernham's for M&A business for years. Butler's already talked to Reitz and Talcott."

"And you?"

"I met him for drinks yesterday. Evernham's clients can grow this firm in the right direction." Girard gave the invisible racquet a half swing.

"What aren't you telling me?"

The racquet stopped mid-swing. "What do you mean?"

"You only do that"—Seeley nodded at the imaginary racquet—"when you're trying to avoid something."

Girard's racquet hand fell to his side. "All you have to do is go down there, chat Butler up, let him look you in the eye, and you've got the engagement, whatever it is. Just because the executive committee let you represent your Cubans doesn't mean Hobie was wrong about the kind of work you need to go after. The executive committee may not be so supportive the next time."

There was a knock at the open door, and Seeley waved Elena in. "Dolores Moncada called."

Seeley remembered his promise of help. "Tell her we'll call her back. I'll come to your office."

"She won't talk on the phone." Elena handed Seeley a yellow message slip. "She sounded really upset. I asked her to come here, but she won't leave her apartment. Héctor's in Cuba."

She might as well have said that he was in China.

Girard said, "This is about your musician?"

"His niece," Seeley said. "When does Butler want to see me?"

"Right now. He's at his office waiting for you."

The message slip had an address on it. Seeley handed it back to Elena. "Ask one of the receptionists to order a car to pick me up at Evernham's, downtown, at noon. I'll meet you at Dolores's."

After Elena left, Girard swung the racquet. "I hope this isn't the beginning of one of your crusades."

Seeley waited for the invisible black ball to take its final bounce off the office wall. "It's just a trip to Queens," he said.

On his way to the elevator, Seeley passed Hobie's open door. Oblivious to passersby, the lawyer was sprawled over his desk, elbows out, his nose inches from a legal pad, humming to himself as he busily wrote, an avid schoolboy at his homework.

It was a short, gritty walk from the Bowling Green subway station to the brass doors of Evernham & Company's offices at the foot of Broadway. Lights glowed behind tall quarter-paned windows, and the building, six stories of granite block, looked as invincible as a safe. Seeley's footsteps echoed in the vaulted lobby. Marble was everywhere: not only the floor, but the walls, columns, and cambered ceiling. Marigold and bloodred tiles framed the two elevators. The air was cool and smelled like stone.

"May we help you?"

The dark-suited attendant was at a wooden table in the shadow inside the doors, where the guard might sit in an old church in Italy. Seeley had already guessed that there would be no laminated passes or clip-on IDs at Evernham's. He gave his name and Butler's, and the attendant ran a narrow white finger, pale blue at the fingertip, down the open page of a black-bound ledger. He lifted the telephone, whispered a few words, and directed Seeley to the elevator. "You may press the button for the fourth floor."

The elevator opened directly onto the reception area. There was no marble here, just lots of dark wood, ivory walls, and worn Persian rugs on floors turned ocher from layers of accumulated varnish. An attendant, who could have been the twin of the one in the lobby, said that Mr. Butler would be out shortly. Seeley ignored his direction to take the tufted leather couch and instead examined the three oil portraits, murky and funereal, in ornately worked gilt frames. There were no labels, and Seeley supposed that they were generations of Evernhams, severe-looking men with pinched cheeks and eyes set a degree too close. The paintings needed cleaning.

Ten minutes passed before Butler came in, all busy movement, with no apologies for the wait, one hand outstretched—"I'm Ike Butler, thanks for coming down"—the other aimed at Seeley's back to steer him down the hallway. They passed a glass-walled conference room that looked out onto New York Harbor. Six or seven men in coat and tie sat around a table listening as another, standing, spoke. In the golden light, the effect was of an old Dutch painting, with the prosperous-looking bankers and clients in the foreground and behind them, through two high-arched windows, views of the sun-dappled harbor. An evenly tanned face in the foreground caught Seeley's attention, and he recognized at once the wattled, owl-like profile of a former secretary of state, as un-blinking as any of the figures in the reception-room paintings.

"Right in here," Butler said, holding open the door to a smaller conference room with the same framed view of the harbor and the Statue of Liberty. Across State Street, a line of tourists snaked through Battery Park, waiting for tickets for one of the tourist boats skimming like water bugs around the base of the statue. In the distance, loading cranes bobbed and nodded, giant Tinkertoy dinosaurs.

Butler took the chair at the round table that put his back to the view. The close-cut graying hair and the creases at the corners of his eyes put him in his mid-fifties. He was slender, with the rud-diness of an outdoors man, and he moved like an athlete. Fencing, Seeley thought, or some other sport with more grace than brawn. Even seated, the banker exuded vitality, and Seeley reminded him-self not to confuse that with acuity or even intelligence.

"Thank you for making the trip downtown."

"Nick Girard told me you have clients who want to retain us."

"Retain you, specifically. Evernham's would be your client to start. Over time, as they require your services, we would plan to send certain of our entertainment clients directly to you."

Butler's voice had an inflection that, Seeley knew from his three years in Cambridge, was defined by social class, not geogra-phy, an inimitable timbre more than an accent. In the blue-collar neighborhood of Seeley's youth it might have been mistaken for the beginnings of a whine. "What kind of entertainment companies?" This was why Seeley had resisted Girard's request to meet with Butler. Now that he had committed to taking pro bono cases again, he didn't want to be saddled with clients who wouldn't waive conflicts.

"Some Americans," Butler said, "but mostly foreign. We have a number of clients in Europe and the Middle East who are interested in acquiring entertainment properties."

"Do these clients have names?"

"As you can imagine, Michael—may I call you Michael?" Butler yawned, making no effort to cover his mouth. "As you can imagine, one of the services that we offer our clients is discretion." Condescension rippled through the words. "Confidentiality is part of that."

Seeley said, "I promise my clients confidentiality, too. But before I can do that, I need to know who my client is."

"For the present, why don't we just let the bank be your client. Evernham's."

Two oil portraits hung side by side on the conference room wall. They were less grand than the ones in the reception area, the gilt frames less intricate, but, like the others, the subjects were anonymous, as if the bank were saying, *If you have to ask who these men are, you don't deserve to know.*

Seeley said, "Lawyers get in trouble when they let an institution, even a fine bank like yours, act as a front for the real client." The words didn't come out as light as he intended, so he smiled and said, "*Especially* a fine bank like yours."

Butler yawned again, this time lazily putting a hand to his mouth. Seeley noticed that like Hobie, Butler didn't unbutton the jacket of his dark gray suit when he took his chair but, unlike Hobie's, the jacket draped elegantly. "That would only be a problem if our clients were engaged in illicit activities. I can assure you that would not be the case here." If Butler had any idea how absurd the conversation had become, he didn't show it.

Seeley said, "I know I came to your office, you didn't come to mine." He no longer cared if his tone was light. "But you requested this meeting, not me. You're acting as if I'm asking you to hand over the family jewels." He stared back at Butler. "Or am I?"

"Please," Butler said, the word like a scalpel. "Perhaps we got off on the wrong foot. Let me tee this up in a more positive way. Evernham's would be willing to give you—your firm—a substantial retainer, say two hundred and fifty thousand dollars for the first year. And our client would never ask that you drop an existing client."

Over Butler's shoulder, Seeley watched a tourist boat, pink and tiered like a layer cake, cross in front of the Statue of Liberty. If Butler's opening figure was $250,000, the final number would be closer to $500,000. "What do we have to do to earn this retainer?"

"For Evernham's directly? Some due diligence, I would think, perhaps help us evaluate an acquisition target or two for exposure to copyright liability. The Internet's changed everything, I'm told. And, of course, we would want you to keep yourself available to represent our clients as and when they need your assistance."

"And that will be the first time I get to know who they are," Seeley said. "Or are they going to come to my office with paper bags over their heads?"

"I'm sure there will be no problem identifying our clients once you commit to take on this engagement."

"Why me?"

"Because our clients are accustomed to having the best advice in their legal as well as in their banking matters."

Seeley wanted to laugh at the smug self-congratulation.

"Hobie Harriman specifically recommended you."

Evernham's was apparently one of the consequential, unnamed clients that Hobie told the executive committee he was chasing. Maybe the only one. If Girard had already met with Butler, he had to know that Hobie was responsible for the introduction. Why, Seeley wondered, didn't he tell me? "I'd think Hobie would want this work for himself. Why didn't you sign up with him?"

The question caught Butler by surprise, and the pink cheeks turned a deeper color. "Hobie and I prepped together at St. Paul's. Didn't you know that? Where did you prep, Michael?"

"St. Boniface," Seeley said. St. Boniface was a parochial school in the parish of Buffalo's old St. Bonifacius Kirche, and between it and St. Paul's lay more social strata than in a Dickens novel. Against his expectations, Seeley was enjoying himself. "You haven't told me why you're not sending your work to Hobie."

Butler leaned forward, as if sharing a confidence. "My first duty is to this bank's clients. As I have told you, we understand that in copyright matters you are the best lawyer in Manhattan."

Maybe it was the undisguised yawns, but Seeley expected Butler to be a better liar than this. "I still need to know who your clients are."

Butler's features collapsed into angry exasperation, and for an instant Seeley saw the mean glint that the banker probably reserved for servants. The expression quickly returned to a fencer's repose.

"They are all private companies."

"Of course," Seeley said. "But they have names. Who owns them?"

"Much as I'd like to help you, I can't give you anything more without my clients' authority."

"Call me if your clients decide to come out of the shadows, and I'll let you know if I can represent them."

"As I already told you, there will be no problem disclosing who our clients are once you commit to take on the engagement."

"And commit to turning away any clients whose interests would conflict with your clients'."

"Of course."

"No, thanks." Seeley rose. "I'll stick with clients I know."

"Don't make a decision now," Butler said, getting up from his chair. "Talk to your partners. Reitz. Talcott. Talk to the head of your business department. Girard, isn't it? He's been pitching your firm to us for years. I'm sure they'd all like to develop a relationship."

Relationship. What a fine, resonant word, Seeley thought. A husband and wife have a relationship. So do brothers and sisters. Friends. But a banker could have a relationship with a law firm, and a lawyer with a bank. If you thought about it, the possibilities were endless. What would a relationship with the plumber look like, or with the hot-dog vendor on the corner? Maybe this was his problem. He didn't understand the possibilities for relationships.

Apart from Kennedy Airport, Seeley had been to Queens only once, and that was by mistake when he got on a Manhattan subway heading east rather than south. From Wall Street, the leather-cushioned town car took him past tired-looking strip malls and stretches of vinyl-sided two-family homes that could have been the Buffalo neighborhood where he grew up. Dolores Moncada's address was a low-rise yellow-brick building on a wide but lightly traveled parkway. Children danced and shrieked under a sprinkler on the ribbon of lawn. The apartment was on the third floor, and Elena answered the doorbell. Her first words were "Héctor's in trouble."

"When did Dolores talk to him?"

"She didn't." Elena led him into a living room crowded with furniture. "A friend called her from Havana."

Dolores, a plump and pleasant-looking woman, stood between a sofa and a low coffee table, her hands fluttering birdlike at her sides. When Elena introduced Seeley and Dolores took his hand, Seeley guessed that the strained smile would be beautiful if she weren't so worried.

In the room, an anticipatory thickness of broken-off sentences hung in the humid air, thoughts still buzzing between the two women, as if they had been arguing, plotting, or both. An air conditioner buzzed and rattled in the window frame, and from the other side of a door an excited radio voice competed in Spanish with brassy music.

Elena said, "Héctor is famous in Havana. In all of Cuba. A baggage handler saw him at José Martí Airport. He told another worker, who told someone else, and the news got to a friend of Héctor's, who called Dolores."

Reynoso's ability to travel so freely between the two countries still puzzled Seeley. "Why would it be unusual for him to be in the airport?"

When Dolores didn't respond, Elena repeated the question in Spanish and the niece answered in a torrent that ended with the angry word *Minint*. "Two men were with him," Elena said. "There were no uniforms. They were in plainclothes. But the man who saw them knew they were security police. Dolores says in Havana everyone knows the security police. They are part of the Ministry of Interior. Minint."

"Did it look like he was in custody? Under arrest?"

While the women went back and forth in Spanish, Seeley looked around. The room could have been a secondhand-furniture shop. Along with the sofas were standing lamps, upholstered chairs, a television console and what looked like two more coffee tables but might be footlockers, draped in colorful fabrics. A corner of yellow bed linen peeked out from under a sofa cushion, and it occurred to Seeley that at night the furniture store turned into a bedroom for Dolores's family.

Elena took an overstuffed chair covered in stiff, clear plastic that crackled when she sat. "The man didn't say. But why else would the security police want Héctor?"

"When was this?"

"Last night. Dolores got the call this morning."

Seeley remembered the change in Reynoso that Dolores had earlier described to Elena. "How deeply is he involved in politics there?"

"His friend told Dolores that all Héctor did was talk to the others about getting their music back and holding some kind of festival in America. A tour. No politics."

Seeley supposed that, communist government or not, business and politics were as deeply interlocked in Cuba as they were in the rest of the world. "The one who called, who is he?" If Reynoso's escort was in fact the security police, his friend should have been as concerned about them tapping his telephone as he was about Reynoso's welfare. Elena asked Dolores, who frowned and shook her head before answering, her eyes darting from Elena to Seeley and back.

"Justo Mayor. He's on the list Héctor gave us. We have his address at the office."

When Elena spoke Mayor's name, Dolores moved to the edge of the sofa and again looked from her to Seeley. "You must help," she said to Seeley. The rest was in staccato Spanish directed at Elena.

"She thinks they have Héctor locked up," Elena said. "If Héctor can't get the papers to the composers to sign, someone else has to. She's worried that if they wait too long, they'll never get their music back."

Seeley could tell that Dolores didn't care about getting the forms signed—she was worried about her uncle. Elena had done the same in the office yesterday, covering her anxiety about Reynoso with a made-up concern that she thought Seeley would find more compelling, and Seeley suspected that the words were hers, not Dolores's.

Elena said, "I'm taking the forms to Cuba. I already translated them at the office. I have the names and addresses. I can deliver them to the publishers when I get back."

"You can't go." Seeley's response was automatic. "We have a trial in two weeks. You still have depositions to review. A motion to draft." What he was really thinking, but knew that he couldn't say, was that if anything happened to Elena, he would never forgive himself; the chatter in his head would never stop. He said, "Travel to Cuba's illegal."

"I'll fly from Toronto. I won't let them stamp my passport. Who will know? You? Dolores? Call it a vacation. The firm owes me the time. I haven't taken a day off since I started, and this won't be more than two or three days."

From the next room, over the racket of the radio, came the *beep, beep* of a video game. A small, dark head peered out from the doorway. Dolores rose and crossed the room, spoke a few words to the boy, went in, and closed the door after her.

Elena must have seen something in Seeley's expression, because her eyes widened. "You're afraid for me, aren't you? That's crazy! You promised Héctor we'd help him with this."

What Seeley heard was: *When I agreed to work with you, it was because you promised we would take cases for people like Reynoso.*

He said, "Of course I'm worried. The security police arrested Reynoso for organizing his friends to get their music back. What do you think they'll do to you if you start going door to door?" Seeley despised himself for repeating Devlin's objections, but what more did he have? He lacked the authority to order Elena not to go and, even if he had the power, he suspected that she was enough like him to quit her job rather than obey.

"That's silly," Elena said. "I'm an American citizen. I'm a lawyer. What can they do to me?"

Dolores returned to the room and to Seeley said, "*Tienes que ir a La Habana. Héctor necesita tu ayuda.*" Seeley didn't understand the words, but immediately grasped what was happening. Elena thought that by threatening to go to Havana she would give Seeley no choice but to go himself. This was what she and Dolores had been arguing about when he arrived, and the uneasy resolution between them was that Seeley should go looking for Reynoso, not Elena. And if Seeley didn't go, Elena would, whether or not Dolores or he approved.

Dolores lifted a fist from her lap and pumped her arm. "*Necesitamos que vaya un hombre, alguien con autoridad.*"

"What did she say?"

"She's thinks the old men, Héctor's friends, won't help me. She thinks someone with authority, a man, has to go."

Elena and Dolores had invested too much in their small entrapment for Seeley to tell them that he had decided to go to Havana even before he pressed the doorbell. He had made the decision when he rejected Butler's retainer; or perhaps he'd made it two days before when he told Reynoso that he would represent him; or maybe on that snowy night sipping scotch in Felix Silver's office in Langdell Hall. He could no more stay in New York than he could live one more day with the braying of the harsh chorus inside his head.

Seeley said, "I'll need someone to translate for me."

Dolores nodded, and this time, as Seeley guessed it would be, her smile was gorgeous.

"You're serious?" Elena's voice rose like a child's. "You'll really go?"

"If Dolores can get someone to translate for me."

"Me," Elena said. "I'll translate for you."

"I already told you. I need you here. If you want me to go to Havana, that's the deal."

Dolores said, "My friend in Havana speaks good English. She will take you everywhere you have to go." Seeley wondered how much more English Dolores knew.

He thought about the incomplete preparations for the Boston trial, which was to start in two weeks. Elena could research and write the first draft of the motion to keep the Chinese company in the case. But he still had to review the papers and organize the trial notebook. *"Dos dios,"* he said, raising two fingers.

Elena and Dolores glanced at each other and giggled. *"Dos días,"* Elena said. *"Dios* means *God."*

He was giving himself two days to meet with thirteen composers or their families while also looking for Reynoso. "Your friend," Seeley said to Dolores. "Can she take two days off work to do this?"

"Amaryll es una belleza," Dolores said. *"Todos los hombres están locos por ella, pero ella no quiere saber nada de ellos."*

"She says that Amaryll is beautiful, that all the men are crazy about her, but she has nothing to do with them. What she means is, a woman like that arranges her own schedule."

More unintelligible words rushed out, Dolores not stopping to breathe. Her eyes filled with tears.

"Amaryll is her best friend," Elena said. "In Cuba, there's something called the *bombo*. It's a lottery, except, it's not for money. It's for exit permits to leave the country. Last year, they both won the *bombo*, but because Amaryll wouldn't leave, Dolores almost didn't come. But Amaryll convinced her."

"Why would she do that?"

"Because she knew how much Dolores wanted to leave. So, of course, Amaryll will help you in Havana."

Seeley knew better than to ask why Amaryll would play the *bombo* if she didn't want to leave. Women were the one mystery that he would never penetrate. The secrets and silences, the deceptions as varied as their paints, powders, and fragrances, and as subtle as a small drama staged by two of them to convince him that it was his idea, not theirs, that he travel to an illegal country. Because he had never breached the periphery of women's lives, the injuries inflicted by a failed marriage and a few brief affairs were also no more than peripheral. At the end of them sometimes were patches of sadness, but nothing to turn him inside out the way it happened in songs on the radio. "Tu Mi Delirio" sounded about right, even though he didn't know what the words meant. Seeley felt from time to time that an essential element was missing from his life, but he was on the whole grateful for at least this corner of quiet.

6

Heedless of the suffocating heat, a girl skipped from tree to tree on the grassy median leading to the hotel. When Seeley's taxi drew up to the Nacional's entrance, the girl's face, sweet but intensely solemn beneath wiry brown spirals of hair, appeared at the car's side window and peered in, then disappeared when the doorman came out from under the portico to take Seeley's bag. Seeley wondered how a youth skipping so gaily could look so sorrowful.

Forty minutes ago, coming through the doors of José Martí airport into the taxi pickup zone, Seeley's first impression was of being sucked into a viscous boiling syrup. *Lava.* It wasn't just the heat, but the weight of the air, like a thick woolen blanket, and the reek of automobile exhaust that filled its stagnant folds. As the taxi moved out into the traffic, wisps of tepid air squeezed through the laboring air conditioner like pudding through a strainer. Around the driver's neck, a rolled-up bandana absorbed rivulets of perspiration.

Seeley lowered the window, but quickly raised it again. An oily haze hung over the tired-looking palms and tin-roofed warehouses. Here and there behind low clusters of trees nestled enclaves of what looked like trailers or tourist cabins. Giant black letters on white billboards declared, HOY COMO SIEMPRE MUJER ES REVOLU-CIÓN. ¡VENCEREMOS! One weathered billboard depicted beaming youths; another a tight-jawed portrait of George W. Bush. In black outline against fading red paint, the iconic Che, Devlin's *Guerrillero Heróico*, gazed heavenward above the legend HASTA LA VICTORIA SIEMPRE.

Seeley's second impression, as much a sensation as a thought, was This is a place that could defeat me. He followed the white-jacketed doorman into the Nacional lobby. A clerk was busy with a German-speaking couple, but when Seeley approached the reception counter, a silver-haired man in a dark business suit and tie appeared from behind a partition. Seeley gave his name and the man went to a low cabinet, stopping to examine the fingernails first of his right hand, then the left, before he pulled open a drawer and sorted through a row of vertical files. He found Seeley's reservation and placed a registration form on the counter for him to complete.

Seeley said, "Did someone leave a message for me? A woman?"

The clerk took a yellow slip of paper from the file. "No woman," he said. When he checked his fingernails again, Seeley observed that they were impeccably manicured under a gloss of clear lacquer. "Just a small girl." The man nodded in the direction of the entrance. "Of course, she must wait outside."

The solemn, skipping youth. Seeley handed the clerk Justo Mayor's address from Reynoso's list.

"This is in El Centro," the clerk said. "Central Havana. There is nothing you wish to see there. Only old buildings that will fall down on you if you even look at them." He brushed his fingers together as if crumbling a lump of sugar, and struggled not to admire his nails again. A map appeared from under the counter, and with a ballpoint pen the clerk pointed to a district brightly colored in yellow and green. The white ballpoint had a Heineken logo on its barrel. "La Habana Vieja. Old Havana. This is where you wish to go. Very touristic. The historic buildings have all been returned to new."

Seeley took back Mayor's address. "If I show this to the taxi driver, will he know where to take me?"

The clerk shrugged and looked across at the departing Germans.

"Our taxi drivers in Havana are knowledgeable, but they are not always, how would I say, not always so . . . careful. But of course you know where you wish to go." He disappeared behind the partition.

Seeley left his bag with a bellman. The girl was squatting under a palm tree across from the entrance when Seeley came out, but rose when he approached. She looked to be ten or eleven and her khaki shorts were spotless and neatly pressed, but with the same wear at the seams as Reynoso's much-laundered cotton jacket. The four profiles in bleached-out red on her white T-shirt belonged unmistakably to the Beatles.

"My name is Michael Seeley. Are you waiting for me?" If she didn't speak English, he hoped the doorman could translate.

It took the girl a moment to understand the meaning of Seeley's extended hand and, when she took it, hers was soft and moist. "I waited three hours for you. My name is Nilda." Her voice was as grave as her expression. "My auntie Amaryll sent me." She tapped her forehead with a plump index finger. "Auntie has *una migraña*. She sent me to help you."

Seeley signaled to the taxi at the head of the line of black Mercedes sedans and gave Nilda the paper with Mayor's address. "Can you ask him to take us there?" Nilda handed the paper to the driver, ordering him in Spanish, completely in charge. Seeley wasn't accustomed to having someone else speak for him, much less a young girl, and he had the uncomfortable sense of shrinking. He reminded himself, as he had during the flight from Toronto, how much better at this Elena would be.

After fifteen minutes, narrow streets and faded tenements replaced the busy commercial district around the Nacional. Laundry hung like pennants across grillwork balconies and gaunt dogs nosed about trash cans. On one corner, a scorched mattress straddled a car jacked up on cinder blocks. Here and there between the decaying colonial facades, a Soviet-era building of cast concrete shouldered its way out, squat, thick, perdurable. Seeley knew that there were whites in Havana, but they must live elsewhere, or they were all inside, for the colors thronging the sidewalks made up an Afro-Cuban rainbow, from light coffee to near black. The colors simmered in the heat, angrily it seemed, and the odd thought occurred to Seeley that the whites had gone into hiding.

The taxi was newer than the one from the airport, but, even with the air-conditioning, an odor of rot, as if from overripe fruit, clung to the interior, and Seeley's shirt stuck to the back of the vinyl-covered seat. This driver, too, wore a rolled neckerchief, and he dabbed at his cheeks with another cloth that had probably once been white. In the rearview mirror, his glance shuttled between Seeley and the girl. His eyes, when Seeley caught them, were filled with revulsion, and Seeley wondered what Nilda told him.

Nilda said, "Why did you come to Havana?"

Seeley said, "I suppose you'd rather be doing something else."

"I don't know."

Seeley didn't have much experience with young people, but he thought that they usually smiled more than this one.

Nilda said, "You don't speak Cuban, so I think you need me."

The Nacional desk clerk was right. From the looks of it, a hurricane gale would crumble Mayor's building like a lump of sugar between two manicured fingers, and the rain would reduce it to a sodden pile of plaster and lathing. Inside the tenement there were light fixtures but no bulbs, so that, cut off from the sun-baked courtyard, the maze of hallways was dark. Nilda stopped at a partly open door and called into the apartment, above the racket of a television game show. A woman's voice shouted back, "*Espera, espera.*" The volume dropped, Nilda and the woman had a brief exchange, and the volume rose again.

Mayor's apartment, Nilda reported, was on the third floor. The decrepit staircase at the other end of the corridor stopped at the second floor, where it was replaced by crudely carpentered steps, a ladder as much as it was a stairway. Nilda danced lightly up the stairs and Seeley stumbled after her. No one had told the carpenter, or perhaps he just didn't care, that risers should be evenly spaced.

Music and television noise filled the hallway along with the cries of children. There was the pervading odor of something burned, but the cooking smells were too foreign and densely layered for Seeley to identify any one. Nilda stopped at a bright turquoise door, knocked and, after a few seconds, knocked again. The door opened an inch or two, and part of a face appeared, a woman's, with wrinkles years older than the anxious brown eyes. An arched eyebrow asked, *What could I possibly have that you would want?*

Nilda said, "*¿Dónde está Justo Mayor?*"

The woman nodded toward Seeley. "*¿Quién es él?*"

"*Señor Seeley. El abogado americano de Héctor Reynoso.*"

The door opened wider, but the eyebrow remained arched as the woman's sharp glance took in the length of the hallway. After another exchange, Nilda said to Seeley, "You must go inside. Justo is downstairs with a friend. His wife doesn't want you standing in the hall. Her name is Lourdes." She turned and skipped down the dim corridor, calling back over the corridor noise, "Lourdes Gallindo."

Lourdes looked up and down the hallway a last time, then stepped aside for Seeley to enter the high-ceilinged room. In one corner was an ancient refrigerator and a steel-and-Formica table that, with its patched set of vinyl-covered chairs, could have first done service before the revolution. In a closet-sized alcove, a four-burner range sat atop a small oven next to the sink. Wherever the music publishers were sending their royalty checks, it was not to the composers.

Lourdes took four plastic tumblers from the cabinet over the stove. None was the same size or color as the others. "*¿Limonada?*" She set a quart bottle from the refrigerator on the table next to two squat, unlabeled jars containing what looked like homemade condiments, one a deep red, the other emerald green.

"No," Seeley said, to the offer of lemonade. "*Gracias.*" Had he ever spoken that word before? He had sidestepped Nilda's question in the taxi—*Why are you here?*—because the answer, which seemed so plausible in Dolores's living room, now seemed absurd. He would fail in his search for Reynoso; even in New York, he didn't know where to begin. Did Reynoso's disappearance worry the other composers as much as it worried him?

When the immigration officer at the airport asked him why he had come to Cuba, Seeley said, "Tourist," and that seemed to be enough. Seated behind the high counter, the officer studied the passport, glancing up from it to Seeley and back, then from beneath the counter raised an armature at the top of which was a device the size of a billiard ball. With hand gestures, he directed Seeley to step back and look directly at the center of the ball, where a blue light flashed on and off. The man held Seeley's passport up behind the instrument and glanced repeatedly from it to another device, hidden from Seeley's view behind the counter. Or perhaps there was nothing on the counter at all, and it was just an elaborate charade to intimidate a foreigner.

Finally, the officer swung down the armature and flipped through the pages until he found one that was blank. He held up a rubber stamp and observed Seeley from under girlish eyelashes. *Yes or no,* the eyes asked. *Do you want me to make a record of your illegal stay here, or do you wish, officially, not to be here?* The rubber stamp circled over the passport, like a bird deciding whether to perch. Seeley rarely gave much attention to decisions like these, and he wondered why this one seemed so hard. Patient, even serene, the officer no more than tilted his head; Seeley's dilemma was not his concern nor Cuba's.

"No," Seeley said. "Nothing."

The man put down the stamp, quickly selected another for Seeley's visa, and slid the visa and passport across the counter. A buzzer unlocked the metal gate.

The door to Mayor's apartment swung open and a slight, dark

man shuffled in, Nilda behind him. Mayor examined Seeley for a long moment before closing the door. Light from the room's single window raked the old man's features, revealing a seamed, almost fragile face and a day's gray growth of beard. Age had collapsed the narrow ribbon of flesh above each eyelid, giving the watery eyes a shrewd, almost Asian covertness. The jeans and sweatshirt were baggy on his thin frame and, improbably in this heat, Mayor had on a navy seaman's toque, its fold pulled down almost to his ears. He gave off the sweet, raisiny smell of rum.

"*Señor Seeley*—" Mayor started, but Lourdes's raised eyebrow and three or four sharp words stopped him. Lourdes indicated to Seeley where he should sit at the table and nodded for Mayor to take the chair next to him so that either man would have to turn if he wanted to speak to the other. She took the chair opposite and murmured a few words to Nilda, before pouring a glass of lemonade and handing it to her. Off to the side, a loft with a double-sized mattress rose on stilts above them.

To Mayor, Seeley said, "You called Reynoso's niece and told her two men took him from the airport." He waited for Nilda to translate and, when Mayor nodded, said, "I came here to find him. I also came to help you get back your music."

Amusement played in the old man's eyes even before Nilda translated, and it seemed to Seeley that the angle at which he tilted his head was to prevent Lourdes from seeing.

Nilda started to speak, but Lourdes put a hand on her arm and, to Seeley, said: "*¿Quien sabe usted del problema en que Héctor está involucrado?*"

"She asks what you know about the trouble Héctor is in," Nilda said, but Mayor answered before Seeley could. "Justo says Héctor is a dreamer and a fool."

Reynoso might be a dreamer, but he was no fool. "I don't know why Héctor is in trouble. But once you sign these forms, you will have your music back, and no one can take it from you."

Seeley didn't know what Mayor said to his wife next, but his voice was harsh. Nilda said, "Justo says Héctor is not in trouble. He says Lourdes doesn't know what she is talking about."

"What trouble does she think he's in?"

"Political trouble. He is with the security police." Nilda said, translating Lourdes. The words *security police*—La Seguridad— had startled Nilda, and for the first time Seeley thought he saw an edge of worry in the serious eyes. "It was the security police who took him from the airport."

Justo waved his wife's words away. "Justo says Héctor is probably with one of his girlfriends."

That had been Devlin's story, too.

"If Héctor isn't in trouble, why did Justo call Dolores?"

Justo shook his head even before Nilda finished.

"Does he have an address for these girlfriends? A telephone number?"

Nilda started to translate, but husband and wife, throwing words at each other, didn't listen, and Nilda became the referee, the plump, pacifying hand restraining Justo, then Lourdes, while she translated. From time to time, she sipped at her lemonade. "Lourdes says Justo should know better, that he knows what kind of trouble Héctor is in and he shouldn't go looking for trouble himself." Dark curls stuck to the girl's damp forehead.

For the moment, Seeley gave up on the search for Reynoso. He said to Nilda, "All I need is for him to sign the form. Can you ask him to do that?"

Nilda said, "Lourdes runs things here. White women are like that when they marry black men. If you want Justo to sign your paper, you have to stop them from arguing. Get him to talk about the old days with Héctor."

What did this young girl know about the old days, Seeley wondered or, for that matter, what it took to defuse domestic or racial tensions? Mayor, even though he hadn't spoken a word of English, smiled, as if he admired Nilda's shrewdness as much as Seeley did. Seeley said, "Did you and Héctor perform together?"

"*¿Tocaran juntos?*" Mayor's smile widened and the outpouring of words allowed only the most fragmented translation. Bruzón, Colina, Lido, Capri, and Riviera were apparently hotels or clubs where Mayor, Reynoso, and the other musicians played in the 1950s. Hilton, Tropicana—

Nilda pinched her dark arm and Mayor laughed. "I think," Nilda said, "because Justo and his friends are black, they couldn't play at these places for white people. But he says Héctor had a friend who made the arrangements."

"Harry Devlin," Seeley said.

"*Sí, Señor Devlin. Como usted, un abogado americano. Héctor*—"

Lourdes said, "*Justo*—"

"Héctor was the bandleader." Nilda caught up with Mayor's words. "Sometimes he would sing, but also he had a woman singer, one of his girlfriends. Lourdes sang for Héctor."

Lourdes shook her head vigorously, and Seeley didn't know whether it was to deny that she was once Reynoso's girlfriend or simply to tell Mayor that this was nothing to share with strangers.

Nilda translated, her earnest delivery an implicit rebuke to Lourdes's excitability. "Don't start on that! Just tell this lawyer from America how your friend Héctor makes trouble with Minint." The skeptic's eyebrow aimed at the door, and Seeley understood that the reason Mayor closed it had nothing to do with keeping out noise or smells from the hallway. La Seguridad.

"Again, she worries about the security police," Nilda said. Concern filled the girl's voice, too.

To Lourdes, Seeley said, "Why are the security police interested in Reynoso?"

She didn't wait for Nilda to translate. "Politics!" She said in English, and then in Spanish, "*¿Qué otro problema hay?*"

"Do you know where he is?"

Again Lourdes didn't wait for Nilda. "Villa Marista."

"Villa Marista?"

A noisy, overfed fly circled the glasses of lemonade, but none of the three Cubans noticed. Nilda's solemnity now seemed more like sadness. She said, "In the Sevillano district. The security police take people there for questioning. Before they lock them in prison."

Seeley said, "Tell Mayor it is important that he sign these papers. This is why Héctor traveled to America, so that he and the others could sign the papers and get their music back. If he signs, there will be no more trouble."

"Lourdes says Héctor is a troublemaker. That there will only be trouble."

Seeley said, "Tell her these notices are private. This is just about a business contract between a composer and his publisher. No politics."

While Nilda translated, Lourdes regarded Seeley as she might a particularly slow child. Mayor touched Nilda's arm and whispered to her.

"He says he wants you to give him the paper. Show him where to sign."

The form that Seeley removed from his inside jacket pocket was damp from the humidity.

Nilda said, "Lourdes wants to know why he can't wait until you find Héctor."

Seeley didn't know if the source of the conflict between husband and wife was that Lourdes was once Reynoso's lover, that she was white and Mayor black, or whether it was a simple struggle for household power, but he was tired of the bickering in a language he didn't understand. "Tell her only one person gets to sign this form and, so long as he's alive, that's the person who wrote the music. Tell her that it is her husband's decision, and that under American law Mayor and his friends have only a few months to get their rights back."

Mayor reached across the table for the papers. His look turned shy. "¿Tiene usted un bolígrafo?" Seeley handed him his ballpoint, and while Mayor signed, Seeley explained to Nilda that they also needed a witness but that she was too young.

"No. No. No," Lourdes said, when Nilda asked her to sign as a witness. In their half hour together, the arched eyebrow had not relaxed once, and Seeley decided that what he thought was an expression of skepticism was in fact a small but apparently permanent disfigurement.

Seeley looked at the closed door. "Tell her that if she won't witness her husband's signature, I'll have to ask one of the neighbors." When Nilda translated, Lourdes glared at him fiercely, then grabbed the pen from her husband and let Seeley show her where to sign.

Mayor spoke a few words to Nilda. "He wants you to give him the forms for the other composers. He says he will get them to sign."

"Tell him, thank you, but I'll take care of it." If Reynoso was in trouble with the security police for organizing the composers, Seeley didn't want the same to happen to Mayor.

"He says he knows them. He says he can do it quicker than you."

"I'm sure he has better things to do with his time."

Even before Nilda translated, Mayor laughed, but without conviction. "He says in Cuba, time is the great national treasure. It is the only thing for which there is no rationing. In the U.S. you have a few months. Here we have a lifetime."

"Tell him I'm grateful, but I'll take care of this."

The wrinkles deepened. "Justo wants to know what else he should do."

"Tell him to call me if he hears from Reynoso." He took a business card from his jacket and handed it to Mayor. "Tell him I'm staying at the Nacional."

"Now we go to the drugstore," Nilda said to Seeley. "Auntie's *migraña.*"

Seeley didn't expect dust in humidity this thick, but it rose all around them as they searched for a taxi. The streets were as busy with bicycles as with cars, some carrying two or even three passengers on handlebars, crossbars, and rear forks. At an intersection, Nilda abruptly danced into the street to hail an ancient dark green

Plymouth. Two passengers were already inside and Nilda gestured for Seeley to take the front seat while she joined the others in the back. She gave the driver a street name, then turned to the two middle-aged women next to her. *"La farmacia,"* she said, and immediately quizzed the women on their destination.

While Nilda and the women talked, Seeley went over the exchange in Mayor's apartment. If the security police were involved and Reynoso was in fact a political prisoner, would the other composers be as staunch as Mayor, or fearful like Lourdes? What could he offer but a stranger's promise—an American's promise—that once they signed they would be safe? Exhaust fumes drifted up from a hole in the Plymouth's floor. The futility of coming to Havana felt as dense as the heat. For the first time in months Seeley craved a drink, a freezing cocktail shaker filled with gin. He clamped his jaw shut, as if that would protect him.

The taxi swerved to avoid a pothole, then plunged into another the size of a crater, lifting Seeley from the seat to the ceiling. Nilda whooped and, for the first time on their outing, smiled. Minutes later, the car turned onto a wide boulevard lined with storefronts, some shuttered, others dark behind chicken-wire glass. *"Aquí,"* Nilda said, and the driver drew up next to a Dumpster the size of a freight car, leaving them barely enough room to squeeze out. When Seeley took out a bill, Nilda pushed his hand away and gave the man a few coins. "Americans always pay too much." She put a damp slip of paper—the prescription—in Seeley's hand and led him into the pharmacy.

"This is a foreigners' store," Nilda said when they were inside. There were no customers and the shelves, where there weren't wide gaps, displayed a confusing array of goods. For some, like talcum powder, there was only a single brand for each product, but for others, like ear swabs or bandage strips, three or more different packages had unfamiliar names and descriptions in Spanish, Arabic, and French. One plastic box showed bandages colored khaki, as if they were intended for use with camouflage gear; on another, the bandages were in the shapes of camels, giraffes, elephants, and

lions. But where was the shampoo? The toothpaste? Entire catego-
ries of goods were missing from the shelves.

At the back of the store, next to the pharmacist's counter, a
rack of children's plastic sunglasses in pink, yellow, and lime green
sported characters from old Disney cartoons. The man at the counter studied the prescription, then disappeared between two rows of
tall wooden shelves into a back room. Moments later, a lively argument broke out in the back, followed by high-pitched laughter.
The clerk returned, tossing a small brown bottle from one hand
to the other. This time Nilda didn't object when Seeley paid.

The Plymouth had dropped its other passengers and was waiting at the curb. Nilda gave the driver an address and climbed into
the back while Seeley held the door for her. She had turned quiet
and Seeley wondered how often she got to travel in taxis. After a
few blocks looking out the side window, she said, "If you work for
Héctor, you must be a famous lawyer."

"Only in my own neighborhood."

"Do you work for American singers?"

"Sometimes," Seeley said. "If they have to go to court."

"Hannah Montana?"

Seeley smiled. "Not yet." Did Nilda know that this was a fictional
creation, a dated adolescent fantasy?

"Do they give you CDs, the musicians you work for?"

"I never asked," Seeley said. He now understood what the
questions were about. "Can you buy Hannah Montana CDs in
Havana?"

"Sure. All my friends have them."

Seeley folded some bills from his pocket and closed the plump
hand over them. "Why don't you buy some Hannah Montana
CDs. Maybe before I leave you can play them for me."

Nilda returned to the window and, after they passed more
blocks of tenements and a fenced-in park with swings and see-
saws, she said, "I can help you find Héctor."

Seeley had made Dolores no promises about finding her uncle.

He wondered what Dolores told Amaryll, and what Amaryll told Nilda. "Do you know Héctor?"

"Everybody knows Héctor. He's on the television. I saw him two days ago."

"On television?" This wasn't possible.

"No, by a hotel in Parque Central. He was talking to some men."

"Why didn't you say this at Mayor's?"

Nilda said, "Look, this is where Auntie lives."

The neighborhood was less run down than Mayor's and Amaryll's building was five stories of stucco in several shades of pink; as the painters exhausted one supply of pigment, they had simply continued with another. Balconies of ornately figured ironwork circled each floor, and the doors and shutters were the same dark green as the small forest of palm trees in the park across the street. When Seeley got out of the car, he thought that he could detect the faintest smell of sea beneath the reek of automobile exhaust and diesel fumes. Even the heat seemed to drop a degree or two.

Nilda called up to the third floor, and when the French windows opened Seeley was aware of a sensual blur of motion, flesh, and color: the graceful movement to the balcony rail of long tawny legs; a wild abundance of scarlet bougainvillea spilling out of a blue ceramic pot; dark slender arms gathering up a straw basket; the basket descending from the balcony, dancing like a fish at the end of a line. Nilda placed the prescription bottle in the basket and Seeley watched, transfixed, as the basket made its slow ascent. It could have been a scene from a fairy tale: the lovely maiden, a prisoner in her tower, stealthily collecting succor from her loyal niece. By the time Seeley took in the tall woman in white shorts and sleeveless blouse reeling in the basket, Amaryll was already studying him.

Seeley knew that women judged other women's beauty by standards different from men. But Dolores's judgment on Amaryll was breathtakingly right by any standard. She was beautiful. The dark hair, pulled back severely into a ballet dancer's knot, so tightened the fine planes of her face that Seeley could imagine a pale blue vein throbbing beneath the surface of her temples. The sullen set of her lips betrayed the relation to her solemn niece and the languor of her pose was a dancer's. Her poise, when she balanced the basket on the rail and removed the brown bottle, touched Seeley with the force of a long-forgotten memory, and a sudden pulse of longing astonished him with its intensity.

Nilda returned to where Seeley was standing. "Auntie's more fun when she doesn't have *la migraña*."

"I'm sure," Seeley said. He tried not to think about the lovely figure on the balcony. "When you saw Héctor outside the hotel with the men, did it look like he was their prisoner? Did he look worried? Afraid?"

"Oh, no," Nilda said. "He was talking with them. They were laughing."

Seeley looked up to the balcony, hoping that a glance from Amaryll might reassure him of her niece's trustworthiness as a witness, but she had already gone into the apartment and closed the French windows after her.

7

Amaryll's message at the front desk, that she would meet Seeley in the lobby at 10:00, left him time before breakfast to walk through the Nacional's grounds. The turquoise of the hotel's free-form swimming pool was shades brighter than the sunstruck straits below. On a chaise at the edge of the pool, a lone sun-bather meticulously applied sunblock to one leg, then the other. The vegetation along the winding path was weedy, and the only blooms of any size were brutal, thick-stemmed flowers the color of jonquils, but in place of the frilled collar were petals splattered with what looked like dried blood. There was a low hum of mos-quitoes, and the blossoming heat promised to be as hellish as yesterday's.

Seeley went into the breakfast room with less of an appetite than when he'd set out. Photographs of past guests at the hotel decorated the menu—not only Winston Churchill, but a B-list American film actor and an English fashion model best known for her cocaine escapades. Before Seeley could read the menu, a stocky man approached from the lobby. He had a farmer's slow-gaited walk, and the sort of open face that Seeley might expect to find gazing out from a greeting card scene of Christmas carolers.

"Lynn Metcalf, Mr. Seeley." A boyish smile flickered across the pink, scrubbed features.

"You're with the hotel." The untucked white guayabera might

be local, but everything else about Metcalf, from the shirt's starched and ironed pleats to the hopeful expression on the broad face, was straight out of the American Midwest. Seeley just didn't want company.

"I represent your government here in Cuba. The State Department." He reached for the wallet in his back pocket but Seeley waved it off. The U.S. Interests Section occupied an entire square block on the Malecón and was visible from Seeley's hotel room behind a small forest of flagpoles, half of them flying the Cuban flag, the others empty. The building's cold war architecture was as graceless as the Russians', except with more glass. Large as it was, the structure seemed oddly shrunken and fearful, a cornered, cowering animal, butt up against the seawall.

"May I?" Not waiting for a reply, Metcalf took a chair. "How are you enjoying Cuba?"

"What's the State Department so afraid of? You have guards every twenty feet around your building."

"That's standard," Metcalf said. "We have a Swiss landlord, but the U.S. Interests Section is staffed like any other American embassy. You could say that we're here, but we're not here." The tentative smile twitched wider, revealing a dimple on either side. "Like Americans who don't get their passports stamped at the airport."

Seeley wondered if Metcalf knew, or was guessing. "Do you have a problem with that?"

"No," Metcalf said. "No problem at all." Embarrassment erased the smile. "My chain of command ends with the secretary of state. If someone's presence in Cuba violates any laws, that's for the Justice Department. I came to welcome you to Cuba and to offer—" He broke off when a waiter appeared.

Seeley ordered toast and coffee, Metcalf nothing. When the waiter left, Metcalf said, "I'm here to offer to be of help to you in whatever way I can."

"Why would I need help?"

The dining room bustled with tourists, and scraps of German and French as well as Spanish buzzed around them. At two pulled-together tables, several Asian businessmen dressed identically in dark blue suits, white shirts, and striped ties whispered and handed papers across to each other.

"I can help you get around," Metcalf said. "See people, get your business done."

"How would you know anything about my business?"

Metcalf tapped thick fingers on the white linen. "We received a cable that said—"

"You don't really send cables, do you?"

"E-mail," Metcalf said. "They're more secure, but we still call them cables. My understanding is that you're here to help some Cuban musicians get back their rights."

"Composers," Seeley said. "They're musicians, but they're also composers."

"We can help you locate them." The gray eyes avoided his.

Hobie had alerted his State Department friends that Seeley was coming, but why? Now that he was here, why would Hobie care, or State? Seeley said, "I already have their addresses."

The white-jacketed waiter set down Seeley's toast and coffee, and Metcalf pointed to a small glass-covered jar. "That's guava jam. How good is your Spanish? We can lend you one of our translators."

"I already have one." Did Metcalf know about Amaryll?

"Our people have all been thoroughly vetted."

"I'm sure every one of them is a patriot."

Metcalf said, "Well maybe there are other details—sending faxes, secretarial help, whatever you need."

"Can you tell me where I can find a composer named Héctor Reynoso?"

"Your client, you mean?"

"He's not my client until he signs some papers. I was told the security police are holding him."

"I'm sure that's not true," Metcalf said. "We know that Reynoso's organizing these . . . composers to get their music back. In fact, we have supported his efforts. But that's no reason for the security police to be concerned. He's going to bring hard cash into Cuba's economy. I'm sure the government here is very pleased."

"But you can't tell me where to find him."

Metcalf reached across the table. "May I?" He took Seeley's unused spoon, dipped it into the small jar, and with a quick pink tongue tasted the jam. "You must really try this." He dipped again. "You know, when you finish your business here, you should visit the rest of the island. Santiago de Cuba is beautiful. That's the great mistake tourists make. They think Havana is Cuba."

"I have to be in Boston for a trial."

"That's too bad." Metcalf's expression betrayed no orders from Washington or Beijing to sabotage Seeley's trial. "Your business here is very important to your government. We wouldn't want you to leave before you got all of your composers to sign."

The coffee was strong, almost bitter, and Seeley poured a second cup from the metal canister. "Why would anyone in Washington care who owns this music?"

"Because it's important to the composers." Metcalf toyed with the spoon but left the jam jar alone. "These songs are, what, fifty, sixty years old. By getting the rights back, you're helping to restore the country's cultural heritage. *La cultura.* Your government is deeply interested in the welfare of artists."

"The United States has the worst record for supporting artists of any country in the civilized world."

"As I said, it's also going to bring dollars into the economy, and not just for Mr. Reynoso." Metcalf's veneer of good humor was beginning to wear at the edges.

"I thought Washington was more interested in keeping money out of the Cuban economy."

"The details are unimportant," Metcalf said. "Let's just say that there are elements in Cuban civil society that would benefit from this, and your government is glad to do them a favor. Getting these people their rights back can help advance our objectives here."

"Which are?" Why would Hobie, who had fought against his working for the Cubans, now want to help them?

"The objective of the United States in Cuba is to promote peaceful transition to a democratic system of government based on respect for the rule of law, individual human rights, free speech, and free and open markets."

"I didn't think people actually talked like that."

Metcalf put down the spoon and smoothed the unwrinkled tablecloth. "This is not a situation in which disrespect for authority—the authority of your government or of the Cuban government—is going to help you or your business here." Seeley wondered if Metcalf detected his dislike for authority on his own or if Hobie had given this information, too, to his friends in the State Department. "Don't mistake our friendliness, or the Cubans', for naïveté."

"The Axis of Evil," Seeley said.

"An unfortunate phrase." Metcalf smiled, this time without the dimples. "But I would recommend taking care if you use the telephone in your hotel room. As you may have discovered, only Cuban cell phones work here." He was writing a telephone number on the back of a business card. "This is my home number if you need me after hours."

"Will you be listening in, too? You didn't say who told you I was here, or why."

"What faith would you have in your government if it couldn't keep track of traveling Americans?" He handed the card to Seeley. "Call if you need help. But whatever you do, don't come to our offices. They'll have to log you in, and that could prove embarrassing."

"Because I'm not here."

"Exactly."

Waiting in the crowded Nacional lobby, Amaryll could have been a statue among the milling guests, she was that still. It wasn't her height that set her apart, but the self-possession. The sleeveless white shift, austere against caramel flesh, made the tourists' bright patterns and khaki shorts look like thrift-shop castoffs. Seeley knew that Cubans were allowed in tourist hotels only as employees, which was why yesterday Nilda had waited outside. But Amaryll's posture was of someone to whom the rules did not apply.

"Amaryll Cruz," she said extending a hand. Her voice was pleasantly low, the hand cool, and there was a floral fragrance about her, so faint that Seeley thought he might be imagining it. Certainly, this was the woman from the balcony, but so little of her seemed the same that it disconcerted Seeley to observe at her temple the pulsing blue line that from the sidewalk yesterday he only imagined.

"Did I scare Nilda away?"

"I promised Dolores I would take you to your meetings." Amaryll took the list of addresses from his hand and studied it. "We can start in Centro. That's where you went with Nilda."

The car, parked beneath a palm tree twenty yards down the hotel driveway, was a charcoal husk; it could have been a bombed-out shell on the evening news from Kabul or Peshawar. In front of it was a restored Ford convertible from the 1950s, in back a Chevrolet Impala, both cars in color combinations that had never been seen on the factory floor. Amaryll said, "You don't mind?"

"Mind what?"

"Dolores said that in New York City you drive around in a big limousine." The town car that had taken Seeley to Dolores's apartment in Queens was hardly a limousine. "This is fine," he said. "I appreciate your taking me."

"Russia's gift to Cuban transportation," Amaryll said, pulling open the driver's door. "The Ladas that were so broken-down they couldn't sell them to their own countrymen, they shipped here."

When Seeley climbed in, the stiff synthetic covering on the

passenger seat bent like cardboard. Amaryll's head grazed the ceiling and, slouching so that his would not, Seeley found his knees jammed against the bottom of the plastic dashboard. The slot for a radio was empty. "What else did Dolores tell you?"

"She said you work for artists."

"Only when I'm lucky."

"Do you win all your cases?"

"Most of them. Why?"

Amaryll switched on the ignition and, instead of the cough and sputter Seeley expected, the engine rumbled noisily, but easily into life. "It makes no sense that a rich American lawyer would work for Héctor." Her voice rose over the engine noise. "Héctor is famous only in Cuba. He doesn't have money like a rock star." She put the car in gear.

Seeley wanted to explain that wealth and fame had no connection to why he was representing Reynoso and the others, but he didn't know how to say it in a way that wouldn't sound self-serving. It bothered him that Amaryll's opinion of him mattered that much. "They're artists. They need help getting their music back."

"How do you know that's what they want?"

No one so far had asked him that. "How can they not want to have control of their works?"

"Do you want me to ask them?"

"No," Seeley said. "Just tell them that if they sign the form, they'll get their music back in a month or two. Tell them that if they want me to negotiate with the publishers for them, I can get them more money than whatever the publishers are sending them now."

"You are someone who rescues people."

Seeley heard teasing, not admiration, behind Amaryll's words. "I try to help people who need it."

Amaryll was smiling when she turned to him. "Do you think that is going to make me fall in love with you?"

"That wasn't my intention."

She said, "It is every man's intention."

"Maybe in Cuba," Seeley said.

Amaryll laughed. "Especially in Cuba."

"Then maybe I made a small mistake coming here."

"No," she said. "I think you are someone who makes only big mistakes."

On the balcony, Amaryll's beauty had been a fleeting impression, like a painting glimpsed through passing figures in a museum. Now, so close, her head turning left, then right as she maneuvered in the city traffic, she was a puzzlework of features in the corner of Seeley's eye: high cheekbones; full, pensively set lips; large, dark eyes. Beneath each eye was the slightest gradation of flesh that could be yet another fine angle of bone or the weary slash of too many sleepless nights. The thin dress rose negligently above long legs, as she worked the clutch and brake.

Over the noise of the car, Amaryll said, "Thank you for the pills." She touched her forehead. "You don't know how hard it is to get medicine in Cuba. Do you know the organization Médecins Sans Frontières?"

"The French group," Seeley said. "Doctors Without Borders."

"Well, here in Cuba we have doctors without medicine."

Seeley smiled, and when she looked over at him, he sensed that she was testing him, although he didn't know for what. He said, "I appreciate your taking the time," before remembering that he had already told her that.

"I have no classes now, so I'm free. Only tomorrow afternoon, I have a private student."

"What do you teach?"

"Dance." The dancer's posture on the balcony yesterday; her statuesque presence in the Nacional lobby. "Do you know the ENA?" When Seeley shook his head, she said, "The Escuela Nacional de Arte. I teach there. Students come from all over Cuba. Before Fidel, it was the Havana Country Club. Richard Nixon played golf there when he was your vice president. We are on holiday now."

"But not your private students?" For no good reason, Seeley felt jealous of her time.

"You are surprised, there are rich Cubans who can go on holiday and pay for dance lessons for their children. Mostly they are government officials. Military. Even some famous musicians. But not like Héctor." She lifted a hand from the steering wheel and rubbed a thumb and two fingers together. "My private students want to be admitted to ENA. If you do not graduate from ENA you have no performing career in Cuba. It is my *negocio*."

Amaryll caught his puzzled look. "Even today, with Raúl's reforms, everyone in Havana has one." She nodded in the direction of a bicycle pulling a canopied cab. "Like that fellow, or that woman over there selling peanuts. The man who makes this car run. You work for the state, but if you want to eat, you have a *negocio*. Raúl talks about private enterprise, but we will have *negocios* forever." Abruptly she swerved the car to the curb and switched off the engine. "This is where we start."

Onelio Bustamante's second-floor apartment looked out onto a courtyard where shirtless boys swatted at a black rubber ball with what looked like a broom handle. Barrel-chested, animated, and almost as dark as the boys' rubber ball, Bustamante introduced Seeley to a much younger wife and an elderly couple who, Amaryll explained, were his in-laws, as well as two young girls whose relationship Seeley didn't catch. In no time, Bustamante had switched off the television, pointed Seeley and Amaryll to places on a low couch, and ordered the girls to carry chairs from the other room, and his wife to bring a bowl of oranges. The musician's right leg was inches shorter than the left, evened by the built-up sole of a high-laced boot; as he crossed to take one of the chairs, his foot swiveled ninety degrees.

Amaryll said no more than a few words, and Bustamante was nodding and answering *Sí, sí, sí*. She explained to Seeley, "Héctor told him everything about these papers of yours before he went to New York. He knows you are going to get his songs back for him." As she spoke, a smiling glance from Bustamante took in his entire family.

To Bustamante, Seeley said, "Have you seen Reynoso recently?"

Amaryll translated and when Bustamante shook his head, Seeley made a quick decision not to tell him that Reynoso had disappeared. He gave Amaryll a blank form, and she handed it to the musician, Spanish side up.

Again, the old man looked about at his family and, from the wide windowsill, his wife brought him a pair of eyeglasses. Bustamante studied first the Spanish side of the form, then the English, before turning back to the Spanish. The glasses were old-fashioned aviator frames, and Bustamante pulled them low on his nose and spoke rapidly to Amaryll. She answered deliberately, as if to slow him. Her concentration was intense, eyes meeting the composer's, and then shifting to his wife's when she asked a question. From the number of times Reynoso's name came up, it was obvious that the three were talking about him. Amaryll's responses seemed to check Bustamante's enthusiasm, and he became thoughtful, sharing frequent sidelong glances with his wife, occasionally giving Seeley a puzzled look.

When Bustamante said, "*¿Dónde está Héctor?*" Seeley heard the same worry in the musician's voice as he had in Lourdes's yesterday. Before Amaryll could translate, Seeley said, "I don't know where Reynoso is."

Bustamante turned to his wife, and the two spoke heatedly, interrupting each other, their voices rising. Finally, looking at the floor, Bustamante held out the unsigned form to Amaryll. She pushed it away, her own voice growing agitated, but Bustamante repeatedly thrust the form at her until she took it.

Seeley knew what happened, but asked anyway. "Why won't he sign?" Amaryll shook her head and signaled Seeley to follow her as she rose and let Bustamante and his wife lead them to the door. In Spanish, she said something that brought nervous smiles from the couple. For Seeley, depending on a translator was like walking down an unfamiliar street, blind, and he resented the loss of control. There was a chorus of *chau* from the people in the room. Someone turned on the television, and the door closed behind them.

Outside, Amaryll said, "Someone told them the security police have Héctor. They're afraid of what could happen to Onelio if he signs."

"Did you tell them about the money?"

"It would make no difference." She continued walking past her car. "There are three more addresses in the neighborhood. We can walk." When Seeley hesitated, she said, "I told Onelio to think about it. Maybe he'll change his mind."

Amaryll's long easy strides matched Seeley's. At one apartment, even more crowded with family than Onelio's, the composer was away, visiting a friend in the country, and Amaryll left her telephone number. At another, Seeley discovered that the name on Reynoso's list was the sister of the long-dead composer, and not the legally required widow or child. At the third apartment, the composer was having a late lunch with his family but, like Onelio, he wouldn't sign until he knew that Reynoso was safe. At each stop, Seeley observed Amaryll's effect on people. He didn't know if she was famous as a dancer, but everyone, men and women, gave her the distance they might to a celebrity. In the old men's eyes, he thought that he also saw a wistful light.

Their route brought them back to the car, and when Amaryll asked if he was hungry, Seeley said no. The heat had again dulled any appetite. "But if you are, we can stop."

"No," she said. "Let's go see Linares Codina."

Although Seeley's shirt had soaked through, and perspiration glazed Amaryll's cheeks, her white shift was as fresh-looking as when they started out. She opened the door. "You can see how a wealthy Cuban lives."

Inside, the car was a furnace. Seeley slid down in the seat and angled his knees to avoid the dashboard. As Amaryll pulled away from the curb, he remembered what he wanted to ask her yesterday. "Nilda told me she saw Reynoso with two men in front of a hotel."

Amaryll frowned. "It is a mistake to listen when Nilda tells you what she thinks she sees. She has eyeglasses, but she won't wear them." She stopped to search for a word. "*La vanidad.* She thinks eyeglasses make her look ugly. One time she told me she saw Paul McCartney and Ringo Starr eating ice cream at Coppelia."

"You don't seem worried about Reynoso."

"Of course I worry!" The response was fierce. "I worry about all of them. To be an artist in this country is not easy."

They were on a busy boulevard lined with low buildings, storefronts, and shuttered apartment-house windows. The storefronts stared out blindly from behind rusty gates and windows masked with cardboard, giving no clue if the business was open or closed, its shelves filled with merchandise or abandoned.

"Fidel says culture is like an iceberg. The artists are at the top, but hidden below are all the people who support them. The technicians, instructors, even publishers. He says everyone is equal in the effort."

Irony is hard to detect behind a foreign accent, and Seeley wondered if it was this beautiful woman's flaw that she actually bought Castro's line about equality among workers. "I'm sure the publishers I work for would be comforted to hear that."

After a silent two blocks, Amaryll said, "Of course, what Fidel says is all nonsense. Even when I was a child, I knew that these composers were special. I put them on a . . . what do you call it . . . a stand?"

"A pedestal. Like a statue."

"I fell in love with the old music, Héctor's music and Justo's and the others', when I was still a girl. When it rained, my best friend and I—you know Dolores—would stay inside my family's apartment and listen to the old records, over and over. It was my father's collection, but he didn't care if they got scratchy. He loved for us to play them. For the whole time, we made up dances, and we danced like we were ballerinas." As Amaryll described how her rainy-day recitals progressed to dance lessons, then study at the ENA and a career at the Ballet Nacional cut short by a knee injury, she absently fingered the antique-looking pendant that hung from a thin gold chain at her neck. It was an ivory fish, no longer than a fingernail, but extraordinary in the delicacy of its detail: gills, eyes, even scales.

Seeley made a guess and, when Amaryll stopped speaking, said, "A gift from your father."

"My *amuleto*." She touched it. "My father told me it was carved in the same place in Africa where the music and dance come from." She touched it a last time and returned her hand to the wheel. "Anyway, it protects me from serious harm."

They were driving through a poverty-stricken shantytown, the only vehicle on the rutted dirt road. Under rusting corrugated roofs, dwellings that were little more than lean-tos, painted in glorious shades of purple, vermillion, lemon, and turquoise, rose up a hillside. Wooden stairways snaked between and around them. Gallon-sized cooking-oil cans had been flattened and nailed to patch holes in the wood. There were no street signs or numbers, and twice Amaryll had to stop for directions before locating Linares Codina's shack nestled atop a dirt mound.

Linares, the widow of musician Rubén Fornet, was barely larger than a raisin, but the large dark eyes that looked out from under the halo of white hair made it easy for Seeley to imagine the attractive young woman she had been many years ago. Amaryll introduced Seeley and explained why they had come. The welcoming smile gradually disappeared as the two talked. "¿Dónde está Héctor?"

Light filtered into the room through plastic bags that, drawn taut and anchored with twine, served as windows. The floor was no more than tamped-down earth, but the place was immaculate.

When Linares crossed to the corner of the room that served as her kitchen, Amaryll said to Seeley, "Héctor told her he would bring an American lawyer to explain this to her, but he told her that he would come, too. She wants to know where he is."

"Tell her I can answer her questions."

Amaryll gave him a cold look. "Then tell her where Héctor is."

Linares returned with a plate of hard candies as multicolored as the shanties on the hill. "*No, gracias,*" Seeley said when she held it out to him. In the kitchen corner, a stove and propane tank rested on a concrete pad; next to them were two commercial-sized kettles. The thick scent of sugar mixed with the loamy smell of soil, and Seeley felt for a moment that he would be sick. Amaryll frowned when he handed Linares the blank form, but when the candy maker let it lie on her lap, she took the form from her and read, pausing at each sentence to ask the old woman if she understood its meaning. Linares nodded, but Seeley was sure that she wasn't listening.

"*¿Firmo Héctor este documento?*"

"She wants to know if Héctor's signed."

Seeley said, "Tell her he will. In the meantime, he wants everyone else to sign."

"You don't know that." Amaryll's voice was sharp.

"Why else would I be here?" The heat and the smells of sugar and damp earth in the small room were becoming unbearable. Seeley said, "Tell her there will be money. She can retire from the candy business."

Again, Amaryll's anger flashed, but she said nothing. Linares started in on a story that from her repeated gestures toward the kitchen corner Seeley guessed was about her business. When she finished, her hands were clenched at her sides, the lively eyes depleted.

Seeley had never felt more helpless. He rose. "Let's go." Amaryll kissed Linares on the cheek, and they left.

In the car, Seeley said, "Why didn't you tell her about the money?"

Amaryll's knuckles were white where she clenched the steering wheel. "The great American luxury. Choice." The small car bucked forward. "You buy this brand of soap or that brand. You vote for one political party or another. You sign a legal paper or you don't. In Cuba, you make the wrong choice and they lock you up."

"Does she really think that if she signs the form, she'll go to prison?"

"What do you think Linares was telling me back there? Do you know that she needs a license from the government to sell her candies? But that would cost her half of what she earns, maybe three dollars on a good day, so she prays that no one asks to see her license. Last week, two policemen stop her and they ask, 'Do you have a license?' 'No', she says. So what do these brave men do, these boys who are young enough to be her grandsons? Do you know that a policeman in this country gets paid four times what a surgeon gets? They take her to the station, where a captain asks the same question. Who would it hurt if they let her go? But, no, the grandsons must enforce the law. This is going to cost her three months of her pension."

"And you? You don't think you'll go to prison for driving me around?"

"I worry about them. I don't worry about myself."

Seeley recalled what Metcalf told him at breakfast. "Because you know the government wants the composers to get their rights back. The country gets its culture back and the government gets American dollars."

"Government?" Amaryll laughed. "That is an American fantasy! There is no government here. Fidel is a ghost. Raúl is the ghost's brother. There are just the police, who make Linares Codina's life a misery, and the security police, who Onelio and the others worry about. The rest is just stories about the revolution that the old white men at the Plaza de la Revolución tell to each other. That and their dreams. But no government."

Minutes later the car turned into the Nacional's palm-lined

drive. The doorman saw them, but didn't step out from the shade of the portico. Amaryll switched off the engine and Seeley said, "Can I pay you for your time?"

Amaryll shook her head. "It is good for me to practice my English. You never know when I'll need it." Before Seeley could ask why, she tapped the plastic dashboard. "But you can pay for the Champagne this runs on."

Seeley reached into his pocket, folded three twenties, and handed them to her. "That's why you entered the lottery, isn't it? The *bombo*. You took a chance on going to America but, even before your name came up, you knew you wouldn't go."

Seeley didn't know if it was the beginning of a smile or a frown that played on her lips. "You are so smart, Mr. Lawyer. Tell me, what was my reason?"

"You wanted to see what it felt like to have a choice."

"Very good." Her expression remained ambiguous. "You are starting to think like a Cuban. Tomorrow morning at ten?"

"Are you sure you want to do this?"

"I told you, I have a special affection for composers."

But not, Seeley decided, for lawyers. "Dolores said you have nothing to do with men."

Amaryll looked out the side window, as if making a decision. "What else do you want to know? Have I ever been married? Yes. Am I married now? No. Do I have a boyfriend? No. Do I like men? Of course. But I also like my solitude. What else?"

"Americans?"

"It depends." A smile formed on her lips and, like a ripple on water, instantly disappeared. "Are you seducing me?"

"I never learned how to do that."

"Good. That's a start."

Years ago, Seeley spent two days preparing an icily glamorous Hollywood actress for cross-examination in a lawsuit against her agent. He sat no farther from the beauty than he was from Amaryll now. Next to Amaryll, the star would look like a buffed and painted mannequin. "Can I take you to dinner tonight?"

The question seemed to fluster her. After a long moment, she said, "Not tonight. But thank you. Maybe some other time?"

"Sure." Seeley said.

In a swift movement, she leaned across to kiss his cheek and Seeley was again aware of the faint, thrilling fragrance of flowers. When he returned the kiss, it surprised him, although it shouldn't have, that her cheek tasted of salt.

8

Seeley was up at daybreak. Waiting for coffee from room service, he watched the morning sun transform the straits first into a molten pool, and then a sunburst radiating splinters of carmine, ruby, and coral. The air conditioner slumbered like a pale beast beneath the window; the plastic knob, sticky as flypaper, swiveled uselessly when Seeley turned it for cool air. Amaryll wouldn't arrive until 10:00. Unaccustomed to waiting with nothing to do, he wondered how they did it, the men standing on Havana's street corners and in doorways, talking or just looking about, with no intention, it seemed, of moving on.

He picked up the ringing phone. "How are you doing down there?" Girard's hearty voice was a rasp across his nerves. "What's happening with your musicians?"

Seeley counted: Reynoso was still missing; Mayor had signed his form; the others, so far, had not. He said, "The list is getting shorter."

"That's good, because Butler has a client he wants you to meet."

"He'll have to wait. I'm not finished here."

"Then, when?"

Never, Seeley thought, if I don't find Reynoso. He remembered Metcalf's injunction to be careful using the hotel telephone, but dismissed it. Why should he deprive a Cuban intelligence clerk of the opportunity to sift the tea leaves of Boone, Bancroft office politics for a conspiracy against the revolution?

"Butler said it's important for you to see them no later than tomorrow. We need the work, Mike. We've been talking about laying off a dozen associates in corporate."

Clients always make their concerns sound more urgent than they are, but something was off-key about Butler's impatience. Also, Seeley hadn't any more believed the banker when he said that his clients wanted him because he was the best copyright lawyer in New York than if he told him that St. Boniface was as elite a prep school as St. Paul's. No, whether Butler had work for his partners or not, from Seeley he wanted something else. Seeley let his mind leap. "All Butler wants is to conflict me out of working for the Cubans."

"They gave us a quarter-of-a-million-dollar retainer. Daphne made a point of telling me she thinks it's important for you to meet with the client."

"Daphne's selling the firm's integrity cheap." She also should have known that a quarter million dollars was just Butler's opening offer.

"Why would anyone pay a quarter of a million dollars just to take you away from your Cubans?"

"For the same reason there's a State Department guy here who wants to be my personal assistant and watch everything I do."

"What does that have to do with Evernham's?"

"Hobie. Butler. The State Department. Put the pieces together."

"And come up with nothing. You're imagining things, Mike. Maybe if you come back here and meet with them, you'll find out who they are. I don't think Evernham's is fronting for the CIA."

"No," Seeley said, "the State Department." Even as he spoke, Seeley knew that he couldn't reconcile Metcalf's offers of help with Hobie's efforts to block his contacts with the Cubans.

"If the State Department wanted to keep you from working for a bunch of Cuban musicians, they wouldn't do it by giving a quarter of a million dollars to a private bank to give to us."

"This is small change for them," Seeley said. "Their coffee budget is bigger."

"The only people who have a conflict are the publishers, and you already got their waivers. Give me one concrete reason why anyone else would want to conflict you out of this, and I'll tell Butler you can't see his client."

Smart as he was, Girard was definitive proof that law practice sharpens minds by narrowing them. If there's no conflict, how can there be a problem? "I'll talk to Butler when I get back. A couple of days, no more." Before Girard could object, Seeley said, "How was the wedding?"

The telephone went quiet, as if the connection had been broken. Finally, Girard said, "Clare seemed happy."

"If I remember," Seeley said, "she seemed happy at our wedding, too."

"She told Maisie that her mistake with you was that a woman should never marry her father." Over the course of their marriage, Clare complained that Seeley was as distant and controlling as her father, the senior partner at the Buffalo law firm where Seeley and Girard had started their careers. "Clare told Maisie the trick is to marry your brother, someone you'd want for a friend."

"So that's who she married? Her brother?" Seeley speculated on the kind of man Amaryll would marry. Clare possessed the fortitude and forbearance that New England women's colleges fed their young women with the morning oatmeal, qualities that served her adequately through nine years of marriage to a man consumed by alcohol and work. Amaryll, Seeley suspected, would have kicked him out in a week. Or murdered him.

"What should I tell Daphne?"

Seeley said, "Tell her that maybe I'll stay down here and open a branch office. The reformers will kick out the Castros and we'll start doing business with Cuba again. There'll be all the work a corporate lawyer could want. We can be the first American law firm with an office in Havana."

"I'll be sure to tell her."

It was a measure of the distance between them that Seeley

wasn't sure if Girard knew that he was joking. And, he asked himself, if the distance had grown, which one of them had moved?

One of her friends had borrowed the Lada, so Amaryll picked four addresses on Reynoso's list that were in Vedado, within walking distance of the hotel. They started on the Malecón, below the Nacional, where the brackish, fecund scent of the sea overwhelmed Havana's other smells. Old men fished off the seawall, some with no more than a nylon fishing line wound onto an electrician's spool, others with surprisingly opulent gear of fiberglass and chrome. None, though, appeared to have brought a sack or a bucket to hold his catch. When Seeley mentioned this to Amaryll, she said, "What does that tell you?"

"That they have no hope," Seeley said. "Or that they're not fishermen."

"Or both," Amaryll said.

Vedado was as different from Centro as a resort from a slum, at least if the resort is old and slipping into ruin. Trees shaded the once-grand houses, and there were patches of grass, but behind the bright potted flowers on doorsteps and balconies, gap-toothed shutters hung askew and lathing rotted where the stucco had fallen away.

Amaryll said, "This is where the American gangsters and their girlfriends lived before the revolution."

"Like Westchester," Seeley said. She waited for him to explain and, when Seeley glanced at her, he realized that she hadn't stopped studying him since he brought the prescription to her two days ago. "Nowhere," he said. "A place outside New York."

At the first three addresses, the ceilings were high, but the rooms were divided into apartments so cramped that Seeley felt more comfortable standing. He reminded Amaryll to tell the composers that by signing the form they would not only get their music back, but great wealth as well. The exchanges with the men and their families were long and animated, but no one even asked to look at Seeley's form. Without Reynoso, Amaryll reported, the composers would not sign.

Faustino Grau had toured Europe, the United States, and Asia in the 1990s with Compay Segundo y Sus Muchachos, and his apartment, Seeley and Amaryll's last stop in Vedado, occupied the entire second floor of a rambling colonial pile. Grau's wife told them that the musician was out, but would be back in a few minutes. "You must wait. Faustino wants to talk to you." Hands held open in front of her added urgency to the plea. "He calls and calls your telephone number, but there is no answer."

"Whose telephone number?"

"The U.S. Interests Section. The number the man from your office gave him." She seemed surprised that Seeley didn't know. "I forget his name."

Seeley saw no reason to tell her that he wasn't from U.S. Int. "Metcalf?"

The wife studied the carpet. "No, not that. He was a nice young man . . . from the cultural attaché." The hands were up again. "He gave Faustino his telephone number, but now Faustino calls five, six times a day, and still he will not answer the telephone. You wait. Faustino will be here soon."

If the State Department was so committed to getting the composers their music back, why wouldn't someone there pick up a ringing telephone? Metcalf had said nothing about the cultural attaché's interest, but then Seeley had done little to encourage the official to tell him anything about the department's operations in Cuba.

After forty minutes sipping sweet lemonade and studying the framed gold records on the wall, Seeley handed Grau's wife a termination form. "Ask Mr. Grau to read this. If he has any questions, I can answer them when I come back tomorrow."

Amaryll reached to take back the form, and when Seeley grabbed her wrist she said, "You don't know what he'll do with it."

"What can he do? Read it? Sign it? That's why we're here."

"Tomorrow," Seeley said to the wife as they left.

They had made an almost complete circle from the Malecón, through the leafy Coppelia ice cream park coming out onto Calle Veintitrés, a busy commercial thoroughfare a few blocks from the Nacional. Amaryll hadn't spoken since they left Grau's apartment and Seeley took advantage of the silence to try to understand why the composers would draw so direct an equation of cause and effect between Reynoso's disappearance and their own safety if they signed his forms. "If signing the forms is going to bring money into the country, why should the government have a problem? Why should they worry?"

"These are old men," she said. "They are full of fears."

"Who do you mean, the composers or the men in power?"

"Both." She had given the same answer to his question about the fishermen.

Skinny dogs trotted about as if they owned the sidewalk. Bodies—old, young, light, dark—jostled around them. Slender black girls in impossibly high heels and brightly colored spandex linked arms with fleshy sunburned men in shorts; the iconic image of Che glowered from the men's souvenir T-shirts. Long brown legs marched lockstep with doughy white ones. The girls were barely older than Nilda, the men two or three times their age. It occurred to Seeley that this was the reason for the driver's disapproving look when he climbed into the taxi with Nilda.

"Whatever you are thinking," Amaryll said, "there is no prostitution in Cuba. The government says so."

"This is the same government that you told me doesn't exist?"

"You listen, don't you? You are not at all like a Cuban man."

"*¿Puedo ver su identificación, por favor?*" The policeman, in pearl-gray shirt and dark blue pants, had come up behind them. He touched Amaryll's elbow and led her across the busy sidewalk to the curb. Watching, Seeley had the same helpless feeling as when Nilda gave directions to the taxi driver. The policeman was young and he self-consciously adjusted his navy baseball cap while Amaryll searched in her bag for her identification card. When she handed him the card, he read the information into an old-fashioned walkie-talkie radio, then placed the radio back on his hip where he continued to touch it, like a youngster with a new toy. The officer surveyed the broad street before looking at the identification card again, this time examining both sides. Like the men in doorways, he waited.

Minutes later, a squat black Renault sped down the opposite side of Calle Veintitrés, suddenly swerving into a perilous U-turn that shot it across four lanes to the curb a half block ahead of where they stood. Amaryll saw the car at the same moment Seeley did and, when the door opened, instantly stiffened. The driver was white and small-framed, in a close-fitting black suit; in the glare of the sunlight, the narrow black tie against his white shirt cleaved like an open wound. When he reached into the Renault and collected a straw hat from the passenger seat, Seeley made a bet with himself. Most men handling a fine straw hat will use a light touch, as Reynoso had. But plainclothesmen and prosecutors—the man surely was the police—invariably plant a hat firmly, as if sealing an indictment. The man slammed the car door shut and gracefully set the hat on his head.

The young policeman drew up straight as the driver approached and greeted him with a casual salute and what sounded to Seeley like the word *lieutenant*. When he handed over the identity card, the lieutenant returned it to Amaryll without looking at it. After a few words between the two men, the young policeman walked to a doorway and waited.

Even in her flat sandals, Amaryll was an inch taller than the lieutenant, and it struck Seeley that the difference, as well as her color, made the man a danger to her. The officer leaned forward, his face just inches from Amaryll's, but her posture remained rigid, as if she was resisting an unwelcome force. She saw Seeley start across the sidewalk toward her, but signaled him to stop, keeping the hand behind her so that the lieutenant couldn't see. He gestured vigorously with both hands, moving them first up and down and then sideways, as if he were describing a box. Whatever Amaryll said about her countrymen, this was a woman who made choices—to stay in Cuba when she could have left; to help Seeley; to stand up to a white police lieutenant. The exchange between the two was a battle, one that Seeley sensed Amaryll was losing.

The lieutenant turned from Amaryll and for the first time looked directly at Seeley. The deeply tanned face was a pinched assemblage of sharp planes that made Seeley think of knives tossed in a kitchen drawer. A thick mustache did nothing to soften the angles, and the hooded eyes that studied Seeley were curious and in no hurry. From this distance, the straw hat looked identical to Reynoso's snap-brim with its bright ribbon band, and for a moment Seeley considered the possibility that Reynoso was dead and that the lieutenant had appropriated his hat for a trophy.

When the lieutenant turned back to Amaryll, he started to gesture again, but she must have said something, because he grabbed her by the shoulders and shook her fiercely. Seeley's reaction was a reflex, and in the next instant he was behind the lieutenant, wrestling a firm grip on each wrist, then wrenching the man's arms behind him. The officer fought back with his entire body, and grappling his arms felt to Seeley like twisting heavy cable. In a single surge of strength, he lifted and threw the lieutenant away from Amaryll and onto the curb. It happened so fast that Seeley didn't once take a breath or stop to consider what he was doing. Amaryll came next to him, still erect, even composed. But her arm brushed Seeley's just long enough for him to feel a wildly beating pulse.

The young policeman had come from the doorway, one hand on his holster, the other reaching down to help the lieutenant, uncertain what to do. Angrily waving an arm, the lieutenant ordered him away and sprang to his feet on his own. Amaryll spoke, but the lieutenant ignored her. He didn't appear to be physically injured, but Seeley wanted to see his eyes to measure what moral damage he had inflicted. The lieutenant didn't look at them, or at the pedestrians walking by. Taking quick strides, but with a limp, he returned to the black Renault and climbed in.

"You are a lucky American," Amaryll said.

"No one's ever called me that." Seeley knew that he should be in custody now, and guessed that the fact that he wasn't had nothing to do with being American. There was a history between Amaryll and the lieutenant, and the only reason he hadn't been arrested was that, serious as his offense was, the lieutenant did not want to have to explain his own relationship with Amaryll to a superior at the station house. Seeley didn't know if, for him, that was good or bad, or whether he would be safer in custody.

"Do you have any idea what you just did?" Like her pulse, Amaryll's voice raced.

"I stopped a policeman from abusing a citizen."

"He isn't the police. The one who called him was the police. PNR. The *teniente* is security police. Minint. If you were a Cuban he would have ordered the other one to shoot you dead right here on the street."

Seeley looked down the block. The Renault hadn't moved. He had no feelings about what he had done other than that it was right. It was the image of forced intimacy between Amaryll and the lieutenant that he couldn't erase. "How do you know him?"

"Everyone in Havana knows Lieutenant Piñeiro." When she turned Seeley's wrist so that she could read his watch, her hand was still shaking. "If you want me to help you, don't ever do anything like that again."

"I was worried about you."

"If you need to worry, worry about yourself, not me. I can take care of myself." She looked at the watch a second time. "I have to go. I have to meet my student."

"He was threatening you." Seeley realized how inadequate he must appear to her.

"I was right about you."

"How's that?"

"You are someone who makes only big mistakes. This city is not a safe place for you." Her words had slowed to normal, and she fumbled a slip of paper from her bag. "Here is the address for Gil Garcells." Garcells was their last meeting for the day. "It's a restaurant. He wants to meet there. You can walk or take a taxi. You don't need me. He's a big-time rock star. His English is as good as yours."

"Tell me what the lieutenant wanted."

"I don't need your help," Amaryll said. "I'm here because my best friend asked me to take you around, and because I want to do whatever I can for these composers, but right now I have to leave." She glanced down the street. The Renault was still there, Piñeiro behind the wheel. When she turned back to Seeley, her voice softened. "You really should leave Havana."

"I can't go until I get these people to sign, and I can't do that until I find Reynoso."

Her stare was flat, pitiless. Then she turned and walked off in the direction of the Renault. She hesitated when she came up behind the black car, and Seeley thought for a moment that she was going to get in, but then she quickened her stride and continued on down Calle Veintitrés.

Garcells's fingers tapped the hard plastic tabletop as if he were tabulating the numbers, dates, and ticket prices that he was barking into the cell phone. He switched the phone from his right hand to his left to shake Seeley's hand across the restaurant table. His English had no accent and a cigarette wobbled on his lips as he spoke. Soft-looking, the musician was as pale as an albino. The V of an emerald shirt that looked like silk held his wraparound sunglasses.

"You have to do better than that," Garcells said into the phone, his eyes staying on Seeley. "Across the board, I need another fifteen percent. More on the concessions." He snapped the phone shut and signaled to the waitress standing two tables away. The ceiling-high palm next to her, like the others around the near-empty room, was made of plastic. "Do you want a drink? The tourists love mo-jitos. A beer?" When the waitress came, Garcells touched the half-empty bottle of Beck's in front of him and Seeley asked for orange juice.

"The lady who called said you were a lawyer. But if this is about me copying some other guy's song, I swear to you I didn't. Maybe I took a phrase here or there, a note or two, but I didn't copy anyone else's music. God's honest truth. Everyone does it."

"This isn't about copying." Not once in his practice had See-ley met a plagiarist who admitted it. "I want to talk with you about getting your grandfather's rights back from his American publisher."

"Oh." He squinted against the smoke from his cigarette. "You're the guy Héctor got from La Yuma."

"Yuma?"

"It's what we call the United States." Garcells tilted the long-neck bottle to his lips, swallowed, and put it down. "Héctor said he was going to see a lawyer in New York, but Héctor says a lot of things." He grinned and wagged his head. "I don't always listen that close. But it looks like this time Héctor took care of business."

"My information is that you are your grandfather's only surviv-ing heir. There's no widow or children or other grandchildren."

"Zero," Garcells said. "So I get Grandpa's royalty check. That's right, isn't it?" The waitress arrived with Garcells's beer and Seeley's orange juice. When Seeley slipped the form across the table, Span-ish side up, Garcells turned it over. "The English side is where all the tricks are, right?"

"There aren't any tricks, but if you want your lawyer to look at it, that's fine." Seeley dropped his business card on the table and got up to leave. It was only partly a bluff; he'd already had enough of the musician. "Call me at the Nacional when you're ready to sign."

Garcells raised a hand for him to stay. "Bottom line, after your cut, how much are we talking about?"

"It depends on how popular your grandfather's music is. And I don't get a cut, just a fee for my time."

"Grandpa is *muy bienquisto*. Everywhere I go on tour—Europe, Asia—all they want is Buena Vista, the old songs. The Euros love grandpa's music. 'Son de la Loma.' 'Lágrimas Negras.' Not like Héctor's. Héctor's songs are antiques. I don't know where he gets all the old stuff—*comparsa, conga, habanera, trova,* even *punto* from out in the country . . ."

While Garcells went on, Seeley thought about the dreams that occupied last night's fragments of sleep. Do dreams have sound? These were crowded, not with music, nor even with Havana's sun, water, and palms, but with blocks of color that translated the city's music into a language of shapes and hues that he could understand. Still, he awoke feeling even more a foreigner.

"'Guantanamera,' for God's sake," Garcells was saying. "These venues want me to play 'Guantanamera'!" The fine white-blond hair fell forward, obscuring his eyes, and Garcells swept it back with a hand. "But my own music?" He shrugged. "Only here do people want to hear my music. But, of course, here there is no money." Again, Garcells drew on the longneck bottle. "What about the mechanicals?"

"That depends on how many people want to make covers." Seeley could have been talking to Joel Simkin or another music-industry lawyer. Mechanicals—mechanical license fees—are what a record company pays when one of its acts records someone else's song. "Right now the statutory rate is nine cents a track."

"And the sync rights and ancillaries? Television's got to be a gold mine for Grandpa's music. Movies. Advertising. I saw an article in *Billboard* that the Hispanic market in La Yuma is huge. Video games. Do you handle licensing deals?"

This wasn't why Reynoso traveled to New York and got himself abducted, or why Seeley came to Havana. "Let's take it a step at a time," Seeley said. He handed Garcells a pen. "If you sign this, we can get the music back, and then I'll see if I can find you a licensing lawyer."

When Garcells took the pen, Seeley counted three narrow gold chains on his wrist. The performer handed back the signed form, beaming. Seeley didn't return the smile, and Garcells said, "Is something wrong?"

"Some of the others seemed to think they'd get in trouble with the government if they signed."

Garcells laughed. "If you knew all the euros I bring into this country, you'd know that Raúl worries about my good health more than I worry about his."

Seeley said, "The others are concerned because Reynoso's missing."

"You mean he disappeared? Héctor's always disappearing! That's what he does. He goes looking for action. Here. Caracas. La Yuma." Garcells snapped his fingers. "He disappears."

"The others think the security police have him."

"The security police have Héctor? No way! He met you in New York, right? He came to your office? What Cuban do you know that gets in and out of Yuma so easy? Gets in and out of Cuba?"

"So where is he now?"

"Ha!" Garcells smacked the table, and waved away the waitress who had mistaken his finger snapping for a call. "Héctor's a *fantasma* the way he flies around. Every time I think of him, I pray I could travel like that. The government lets me go to Europe because I bring back money and tourists. Your country won't let me in. Do you know how much money I could make in Yuma? But Héctor? Everywhere! He flies like a bird."

"And you don't know where he is now."

"Have you been to his apartment? Maybe he's there." Garcells shrugged and again brushed back the pale hair. "Or up the street." He nodded in the direction of the Malecón. "The U.S. Interests Section. How do you think he gets to fly back and forth? The Americans know where Héctor is. He's as tight with them as the peel on a banana. He's their Cuban poster boy. They're cooking up some kind of tour for Héctor and his friends."

"He didn't tell me about a tour."

"Héctor acts like he's just another easy Cuban, but he keeps a lot to himself. I only found out about his tour from my agent. When you see Héctor, tell him, whatever gigs he's arranging in America, this tour of his, Gil Garcells wants to be part of it. Tell him to get me on his visa."

Seeley handed a copy of Boone, Bancroft's engagement letter to Garcells. The performer's manner instantly turned cold. "How many more pieces of paper do you have there?"

"It's just a formality if we're going to represent you."

"I already have a lawyer."

"Then let him look at it."

Garcells took back the signed termination form. "Maybe I'll have him look at this one, too."

"If you're having second thoughts, that's not a bad idea."

"No second thoughts. I'm just being careful."

As Seeley got up to leave, Garcells wrote a number on a napkin. "Call me tomorrow. I'll tell you when you can pick up your papers."

When Seeley took the napkin, it felt not only damp, but soiled. He remembered his morning conversation with Girard about meeting Evernham's client. If I don't stop judging my clients, Seeley told himself, it won't be long before I have no clients left.

9

If Reynoso was bringing back money from his foreign travels, he wasn't spending it at home. His apartment was on the top floor at the end of a long hallway of sagging doors. Some bore postcard-sized blue-and-white stickers, NOSOTROS APOYAMOS LA REVOLU-CIÓN, and on a couple of them someone had made an effort to peel off the slogan. Reynoso's door had not even a shred of a sticker. There was no answer to Seeley's knock. The jamb was deeply splintered, and when Seeley knocked again the latch disengaged so that the door opened at the slightest turn of the knob.

Late-afternoon sun burned through the skylight. A couch in one corner of the large room looked like it also served as a bed; in another corner were the bare rudiments of a kitchen. There was a sour, dandery smell of dog, but Seeley saw no sign of one. On a chest-high bookshelf running the length of the opposite wall, most of the titles were Spanish, but a few were in English. Winston Churchill's *Memoirs of the Second World War*, its jacket creased and torn; David Kennedy's *Freedom from Fear*. Reynoso was interested in the European and American history of his own lifetime. Record albums filled the lower shelves, and when Seeley pulled one out, it gave off the scent of old cardboard and vinyl. The labels on the 33⅓ albums were unfamiliar—Fonomusic, Caribe, EGREM.

Three stairs led up to a glass-paned door beyond which wood and wire chicken coops were stacked haphazardly, two and three high. The cages meandered across the tar and gravel roof in the direction of another apartment. Seeley opened the door onto the roof and when it slammed shut behind him a squall of feathers and a frenzy of screeching rose from the cages.

"¡Hola!" It was a woman's voice from the next apartment. "¿Estan ustedes buscando a Héctor?" The woman was as thin as a child and fair-skinned, as was the man sitting at her side. The man's hair was longer than the woman's, which was cut like a boy's. When Seeley came close, the man's arm went around her shoulder.

Seeley said, "Do you speak English?"

"I said, are you looking for Héctor?" From their almost identical features the two could have been brother and sister. The woman introduced the man as Rubén and herself as Gisela. They were sharing a bottle of beer and Seeley declined her offer of one.

"Are those Reynoso's chickens?" Even if they were, Seeley knew that didn't mean Reynoso was the one who fed them. He wanted evidence not only that Reynoso was in Cuba but also that he was not in custody.

"They're ours," Gisela said. "Héctor says he doesn't mind their company." She took Rubén's hand. "Rubén is a poet. I am a journalist. But Rubén drives a taxi and I do some translating for a Canadian publisher. Chickens pay better."

"And the pig?" Seeley nodded in the direction of the rough gray beast tethered to a ring that protruded from the apartment wall. It was snoring loudly, half in, half out of the shade.

Rubén said, "We call him Uncle Sam."

"Very inspiring," Seeley said. He'd had little but toast and black coffee since he arrived and the lack of food and sleep was making him light-headed. "Have you seen Héctor? The lock on his door is broken."

"That's been broken for years," Gisela said. "No one—"

Rubén cut her off. "Why do you want to know?"

Gisela said, "He's probably away somewhere. Héctor travels a lot. Why do you want him?"

As a rule, Seeley didn't give up even the most innocent client information, but if that was his only way to help a client, he would. "I need to get some composers to sign a legal document, but they won't without Reynoso."

Gisela ignored Rubén's cautionary hand on her knee. "Why is it so important to get these documents signed?"

"To get them back the rights to their music."

"Rights?" Gisela said. "You mean, property rights? There is no private property in Cuba."

Rubén said, "An American talking to people here about rights, you can only make trouble for them. For yourself, also."

Gisela looked at Rubén and a complicated, unspoken message passed between them. Seeley recalled the tense exchange between Mayor and Lourdes two days ago. In America couples fight over the wife's spending too much money at the mall or the husband at the neighborhood bar. In Cuba they argue over an invisible boundary: if one of them crosses it, the security police detains them both.

Seeley said, "When was the last time you saw Héctor?"

Gisela brushed Rubén's hand off her knee. "A week ago, maybe nine, ten days." While she spoke, Rubén looked out over the neighboring rooftops crowded with white satellite dishes. "He's not in Havana."

Rubén gave her a black look, rose, and went to the pig.

"Rubén thinks I shouldn't talk to you. He thinks the best neighbors are deaf and dumb."

"Why do you think Reynoso's not in Havana?"

"His dog," Gisela said. "Gordita. If Héctor's in Havana, he leaves Gordita in the apartment. But when he goes away, his sister comes from Camaguey to take him. She came last week."

"Do you have her telephone number?"

Gisela looked over at Rubén but said nothing. From the court-yard six stories down, came the thwack of a ball against the side of the building and the cries of young boys. Seeley thought about Faustino Grau's visitors from the U.S. Interests Section. "Have any other Americans come looking for him?"

"The government loves tourists for the money they bring in." Gisela rubbed thumb and index finger together, the impoverished country's universal gesture. "It's why they don't stamp your passport if you tell them not to. They want you to go to the tourist places like Old Havana, Varadero, Cayo Coco, but they don't want you talking to anyone the Ministry of Tourism hasn't approved."

"You're saying, if you talk to Americans, you get in trouble."

"Rubén thinks so." Gisela's voice dropped to a whisper. "Myself, I think it is more dangerous for you to talk to us than it is for us to talk to you."

"But who would know that we talked?" Seeley glanced around the roof to make his point.

From where he crouched, his hand on the pig's snout, Rubén said, "I told you nothing good would come from talking to an American."

"You're telling me Reynoso is political."

"Héctor? Never. He lives for only one thing. His music. Music is his entire being. Not his reason for being. His *being*. Politics, food, a roof over his head, even friends"—Gisela waved them away with her fingers—"nothing. Night and day, all he thinks about is music."

She turned to watch Rubén disappear into their apartment. "Some nights," she said, "maybe Héctor is lonely, he calls over to Rubén and me to come and listen to old records. Usually Rubén leaves after an hour, but I will stay until two, three in the morning listening to the music with Héctor. He won't touch a drink or a cigar, not even a sip of water. He is in another world. All of the excitement about Buena Vista—you know Buena Vista?—all of that made Héctor happy and sad at the same time. He was glad that the world got to hear some of the old music, but he knew it wasn't the best music, only the most popular. The best music, he told me, was on the old records. Not just his music, but his friends' music, too."

"Did Reynoso tell you about getting his music back from the publisher?"

"Nothing," Gisela shrugged. "He never talked about that."

Of course he did, Seeley thought. No one stays up until three in the morning talking about his dreams without saying how he's going to bring those dreams to life. Why was this fearless woman afraid to talk about this?

"He talked about his tour of America. The tour means more to him than anything in his life." Gisela's eyes were moist. "When Héctor comes back, I'll tell him you are looking for him."

Seeley reached into his pocket for a business card, and handed it to her. "Tell him I'm staying at the Nacional." He glanced over at the pig and, in the window behind it, saw Rubén watching.

In the taxi, Seeley sprawled across the lumpy back seat, fatigue seeping through his bones. He retraced Gisela's words, stopping where she said that Reynoso never spoke of reclaiming his music. He sensed that he was missing an important connection between that fact and Reynoso's American tour but, mind and body, he had no strength to probe further, and for the rest of the trip to the hotel the connection eluded his exhausted stabs.

As soon as he smelled the cigar smoke, Seeley knew who was on the other side of the door to his hotel room; he had been expecting him since their encounter on Calle Veintitrés. All he wanted was to drop onto his bed and sleep, if only for an hour or two. He did not want to deal with the lieutenant. He opened the door and went in.

Piñeiro had the room's only chair tilted back precariously, his crossed feet resting on the bed. The television was on, but with no sound, and in a soft voice he said, "These telenovelas make more sense with the sound off."

After the run-in on Calle Veintitrés, the lieutenant's composure startled Seeley. He expected comrades, guns, revenge. But Piñeiro was alone and his speech was musical, almost lazy. "I apologize for the intrusion, but I thought this would respect your privacy more than meeting in the lobby."

Seeley looked at the bed, but decided that to stand would concede less authority to Piñeiro. His next thought was to throw the lieutenant out. Instead, he said, "Where is Héctor Reynoso?"

"The musician?"

"Composer," Seeley said.

Piñeiro tapped the cigar delicately against the edge of the ashtray on his lap. Of heavy glass in the shape of a star, it looked like a relic of the 1950s. "Reynoso is not important. You have no need to see him."

"Of course I do. He's the reason I'm here. Why are your people so afraid of an old composer that you have to lock him away?"

"This is none of your business."

"But you know where he is."

"If you are so interested, ask the PNR. It is their job to look for missing persons. I only work for the Ministry of Interior."

"Why should I trust the police?"

"A good question." Piñeiro's laugh was small and hollow. "In Havana no one trusts the police. Not even the tourists." He studied the glowing end of the cigar before placing it in the ashtray, and the ashtray on the bed, as if he were preparing to do something that needed his hands free. The trim black suit and starched white shirt, the polished shoes resting on the bed, all exaggerated the poverty of the room's furnishings—a chenille bedcover laundered too many times, bruised chair legs.

Seeley nodded in the direction of the ceiling. "Are we being recorded?"

Again, the empty laugh, but this time the amusement almost reached Piñeiro's eyes. "Our Ministry of Tourism would never let us wire a guest's hotel room. They have much more influence on this island than the Ministry of Interior."

"But somehow you got into my room."

Piñeiro shrugged. "A courtesy of the hotel." He looked about as if searching for something. "I am sorry you must stand. Would you like this chair?"

It was good to know that the lieutenant was uncomfortable looking up at him, but Seeley didn't want a chair. He wanted the bed. He wanted to sleep. On the television screen, a woman's breasts strained at a too-tight blouse as a man shook her by the shoulders. This must be the way Latin men communicated with women, but Piñeiro didn't appear to notice.

Seeley said, "Why are you here?"

"Good. You have decided to talk about something important. Our intentions, yours and mine." Piñeiro tried the cigar, which had gone out, and took his time striking a match to relight it. "Why did you come to Cuba?"

"I told you. I am looking for Héctor Reynoso."

"Reynoso! Reynoso! All I hear from you is Reynoso!" The lieutenant's face erupted into a dangerous crimson, and the fine cheek bones worked like blades sharpening against each other. "Why did your government send you here?"

"My government didn't send me here."

"Of course it did. You are lying." The artery at Piñeiro's neck throbbed. "I want to know the reason."

"I am here as a lawyer working for a private client."

"*Sí, sí, sí.*" Piñeiro used the words to calm himself. "This ridiculous story you told Señora Cruz. This make-believe scheme to make Cuban musicians rich."

"What makes you think the American government sent me here?"

"How can I think differently? Your employer, Señor Harriman, is an employee of the U.S. State Department. That makes you an employee of the State Department."

"Mr. Harriman is my law partner. He is the chairman of my department, but he isn't my employer." Even as he spoke, Seeley realized how unconvincing the words would be to someone who knew nothing about the separation of private business from government control, or the traditions of equality in American law firm partnerships. "And he no longer works for the State Department."

Piñeiro just stared at him.

"Why else would I be talking to these composers?"

"A *charada*," Piñeiro said. "A cover, a masquerade for the real reason you are here. What is that reason?"

"I told you, to help these people. They sold their music to American publishers, and now American law gives them the chance to get their music back."

"From who?" The cigar tilted upward, so that when Piñeiro drew on it the tip became a fiery third eye. "From who do they get these rights back?"

For the first time it occurred to Seeley that the lieutenant knew something that he did not. "I told you. From the American publishers."

Piñeiro's eyebrows lifted over scolding eyes. No, Seeley thought, the lieutenant knew nothing. He was just an ignorant man whose job made him suspicious of all Americans. Seeley said, "The composers sold their music in the nineteen forties and fifties, and now they have the right to get it back."

"Of course, Mr. Seeley, I know all about your American law. What is wrong with this story, this story your government has made up for you, is that the American publishers have not owned this music for fifty years. Long ago, they lost whatever rights they had. Fidel nationalized these rights along with everything else—the distilleries, the sugar refineries, the tobacco factories—"

"Those are businesses. This is music. You can't nationalize an artist's work." *Expropriate*, the lawyer's brain whirred, not *nationalize*. When you take over a company it's nationalization, but when government seizes property it's expropriation. Seeley caught himself. It made no difference what Piñeiro called it. How could he have overlooked this? If the lieutenant was telling the truth, the publishers in fact owned nothing.

"Private ownership is not a highly regarded concept in Cuba, Mr. Seeley." Piñeiro crossed one slender leg over the other. "Land. A sugar company. A song. They are all the same. For music we have here a special law that cancels all contracts with foreign publishers. American publishers. After the revolution, Musicabana took control of this music for the Cuban people. Then EGREM. Today EMC. This is to protect *la cultura* from foreign influence."

EGREM, Seeley remembered, was one of the labels in Reynoso's record collection. "You're wrong. The American publishers are still collecting the money for these songs." Even as he said it, Seeley remembered Simkin's refusal to tell him who the company was sending royalties to.

"Please," Piñeiro said. "You are wasting my time with your lies. Of course the American companies collect the money. They collect it for the people of Cuba. Do you think your government would let EGREM or EMC, Cuban companies, collect money in America? Of course you don't. You already know all this."

Piñeiro's voice grew soft again. "No lawyer of your experience would travel to Cuba in violation of your own country's laws without first asking about who owns this music. So you knew when you came here that the people of Cuba own this music, not your American publishers. And since you knew that, what else can a reasonable man like myself conclude but that you are in truth here as an agent of your government. This ridiculous story of yours is, I must tell you, a very poor *charada*. Someone less generous than I am would consider it an insult to the abilities of our internal security."

If the State Department knew about the expropriations, which surely it did, why hadn't Hobie said something, or Metcalf? And why had his music publisher clients, who also knew, said nothing? Why had they made it so easy for him to take on Reynoso and the others as clients?

"Do you know how the Russians get people to confess?" Piñeiro was out of the chair, pacing the narrow strip on the other side of the bed. "They came here to train us. Their interrogation technique is very *sutil*. They leave the suspect alone in a locked room with no food, no water, just bottles of rum, and then they wait until he confesses. It can take days. But always they get the man's confession."

"And this is what you're going to do to me? Pour rum down my throat?"

"No. I don't want a confession from you. I want the truth. Why did your government send you here?"

"I already told you, no one sent me."

"Don't test me!" In a single swift movement, the ashtray was in Piñeiro's hand, and in the next it was flying directly at Seeley's face. Ash flew, Seeley ducked, and a glass edge scored a gash in the wall behind him. "You come to our island to do injury to the revolution and when we catch you, you tell this *patética* story of composers and their rights because you think we are so stupid that we will believe it."

The cigar was dead again, and Piñeiro threw it behind him to the floor. "What is truly despicable is that you have involved in your activities an innocent woman, a person with no politics."

Seeley remembered the glimpse of intimacy along with danger between Amaryll and Piñeiro on Calle Veintitrés. Amaryll, this dancer who put composers on a pedestal, had to know about the government's seizure of their contracts. And yet, Seeley thought, she came with me to visit the composers, participated in his *charada*. The nastiest part of a conspiracy is that once you start believing in it, any facts will fit, whether they belong or not. Seeley didn't need more facts. He needed sleep. "Amaryll has nothing to do with this."

"How am I to believe that? Señora Cruz—"

"Is doing this as a favor for a friend."

"We are back to your foolish, insulting lie." Piñeiro stared at Seeley for a long time. "If you see Señora Cruz again, ask her about her husband."

"Husband?" Seeley's heart froze. She told him that she was married once, but not now.

"He is one of those men, like you, who cannot take instruction. A man who always must test the authorities."

Seeley distrusted the lieutenant's reserve. He would have preferred the honesty of violence. "If I was such a threat to the revolution, I'd think you would arrest me."

"Eventually, yes, you will be arrested. However, I am a patient man, one who prefers to wait and watch. We have already watched you visit Reynoso's apartment and examine his shelves. We watched you talk on the roof with his neighbors. We will watch some more. But, once we arrest you, we cannot turn back. It will be like a machine that cannot be stopped, and the only object of this unpleasant machine will be to make you tell us why you are in Cuba."

Maybe it was the straw hat, which Seeley was convinced was Reynoso's, or his reflexive dislike of government officials, but Seeley found himself nodding in the direction of the television. "Turn that off before you leave. And pick up your cigar."

The dark eyes widened for a moment, followed by the vacant smile. Piñeiro switched off the television, retrieved his cigar, and, without another word, left the room, which made Seeley wonder, once again, what Piñeiro had in mind for him. Seconds after the door closed, Seeley was on the bed and fast asleep.

At two in the morning, there were no cars on the Malecón. The streetlamps could have been stage props for the scant light they shed, and in the surrounding darkness Seeley could make out figures here and there, but not faces. Fragments of salsa, jazz, and bolero floated out from the side streets. Peter, Paul and Mary sang "House of the Rising Sun." Couples embraced on the seawall. Improbably at this hour, the air was rich with the fragrance of roasting pork. Across the straits, Miami was a faint purple aura, a thumbprint against the horizon. An indifferent tourist, Seeley usually found pleasure wandering the streets of a strange city at night, navigating the precarious edge between solitude and loneliness. But the hour or two of sleep after Piñeiro left had done nothing to lift the weariness. Was it the yearning for a safe place where he could put down his head and sleep that made America seem so far away?

Bottles and empty drink cans surfed the current lapping at the seawall. Farther out, a few late fishermen—*neumáticos*, Amaryll had called them—bobbed in inner tubes the size of truck tires. A yacht that was half the length of a football field appeared to levitate above the black water on its leisurely passage across the straits; a dazzling apparition in the moonlight, it belonged more to Havana's storied past than to its present. Harry Devlin, compact and tanned and looking as much the mobster as any of his old clients, flickered into Seeley's mind. If Castro had in fact expropriated the composers' songs, Devlin, the composers' friend and patron, would have been among the first to know. But if Devlin knew that the publishers no longer had any legal rights for the composers to retrieve, why hadn't he told Seeley this on the phone? Why had he sent Reynoso to him?

This is what I do, Seeley thought. Anyone who reads a newspaper or watches the television news knows that revolutionary governments expropriate private property. Any modestly competent lawyer would have checked out ownership of this music before flying off to Cuba. Give me a case with no real victims, a case like my trade secret trial in Boston where the worst that can happen if I lose is that money moves from one company's bank account to another's, give me that kind of case and I will scour every law book and every pile of documents to ensure that no law or fact stands in the way of my client's victory. But bring me a flesh and blood victim like Héctor Reynoso and I don't want to know about obstacles, much less search for them. Obstacles will only distract me from my client's cause. And when I finally collide with the inevitable brick wall, which all too often I do, why do I think that I can clear the wreckage simply through the force of my will?

Of all the mistakes he had made in his career, none punished Seeley more than his abandonment of the Chinese journalist. Jun Wei had entered Seeley's life almost as an afterthought, at the end of a conversation with a PEN lawyer who called to thank him for helping another writer in whom the human rights organization had taken an interest. The lawyer, Jay Fisher, told Seeley that the

Department of Homeland Security had put Jun, in America on a green card, on the fast track to be deported back to China because of two convictions for shoplifting.

Seeley asked what she had stolen.

"You won't believe this," Fisher said. "A couple of ballpoint pens. Some stenographers' pads. Things journalists use. The DA's office told her that if she'd take a misdemeanor plea they'd let her off with probation, so she signed."

"They can't deport someone for shoplifting."

"The world's changed since Homeland Security took over immigration," Fisher said. "Deportation's mandatory."

"But why her? How many immigrants don't have a misdemeanor on their records? Who pushed her to the front of the line?"

"I didn't ask. She writes freelance about human rights in Tibet. Suppression of the Falun Gong. She has a blog. People follow her on the Internet. But nothing that should upset Homeland Security."

"Where were the convictions?"

"Here, New York City. Why should that matter?"

"Get her a pardon," Seeley said. "A governor's pardon will wipe the convictions off her record. Without convictions they can't deport her."

"I wouldn't know where to begin."

"I'll take care of it." Seeley had never sought a pardon before, but how hard could it be to learn the procedure? He would have a free day between trials at the end of the month, and he was sure that someone at the firm had a political connection to the governor's office that could get him an early hearing before the pardon advisory board.

"Are you sure you want to do this? Jun's a sweet girl," Fisher said, "but she's a handful."

"How's that?"

"She calls me every day. She thinks she's being followed by Chinese security agents."

"Maybe she is."

"Come on, Mike—"

"If she's writing about human rights in China, who else would be interested in her? Where is she now?"

"Upstate. Syracuse. She's some kind of visiting writer at the university."

"Tell her not to go out alone. Tell her she should always have someone with her."

"She's young, Mike, but I think she figured that part out."

Seeley's trial was over the afternoon before the pardon hearing, and he met Jun at the small hotel in Midtown where he had booked a room for her. Over dinner at the quietest, darkest restaurant he knew, Seeley asked questions while she ate. Were there any convictions, or even arrests, on her record other than the two for which Homeland Security wanted to deport her? How many articles had she published? What was the political reaction to them? In the candlelight, Jun's face was pensive, and frightened. She had only one question. "Will I really have to leave America?"

Seeley wondered how someone so knowledgeable about the cruelties of a totalitarian regime could be so innocent about the brutality of a democratic one. "Are you still being watched?"

"I didn't see anyone on the bus from Syracuse, but I don't know."

"When I leave you at your hotel, I want you to go to your room and stay there until I call you from the lobby in the morning. The hearing's at ten o'clock, so I'll be there at nine. Order breakfast from room service but stay in your room."

In his rooms at the University Club, where he had moved after Clare filed for divorce, Seeley sipped at a glass of iced gin and proceeded page by page through the briefing book on pardons that he'd had an associate at the firm assemble for him. This was his first look at the surprisingly spare procedures for requesting a pardon. The associate had also collected case studies of pardons granted and not granted, and a handful of law journal articles about strategies to employ in requesting one. After a five-week patent trial, Seeley was exhausted, but the gin kept his edge evenly honed.

By four in the morning, Seeley knew that the still-thrashing residues of overwork from the trial, as well as anticipation of the pardon hearing, would make the two or three hours of sleep he needed to get through the ten o'clock hearing all but impossible. He emptied the ice from his tumbler into the sink, poured gin to the rim of the glass, finished it in three gulps, then filled the glass again. At last, at the bottom of the third glass, he passed out, falling back across his bed, not remembering if he had set the alarm, and not caring.

Sunlight stirred him awake. Even before his eyes could focus on the bedside clock, a suffocating sense of dread descended over him. It was twenty past nine. After a full minute spent getting the hotel telephone number from information and another two brushing his teeth while the phone rang unanswered in Jun's room, Seeley shaved and dressed with shaking, panicky fingers and, running all the way, was at the hotel by ten past ten. As he waited on the lobby phone for Jun to answer, he asked the man at reception if he had seen her.

"The Chinese girl? She was here an hour ago, looking for someone. Then some friends came and they went off somewhere."

"How many friends?"

"Two."

"Both of them Chinese?"

The man nodded. A sour taste of metal rose in Seeley's throat, and he understood that he would never see Jun Wei again. He applied for a visa and, without offering an explanation, the Chinese government turned him down. Weeks later, the *Times* carried the news that Jun was imprisoned somewhere in Gansu Province in China's vast interior, but by then she had already taken up permanent residence in Seeley's chattering chorus of recrimination; a ghost that haunted Seeley's thoughts and dreams.

So completely did Jun Wei's abduction consume Seeley that when the partners fired him for this last of his drunken blunders, it barely registered. He retreated to Buffalo and to the solo public interest practice that he'd dreamed of even before law school. He abandoned alcohol, as if that would balance his abandonment of Jun, and hadn't taken a drink since. But alcohol was his compass to navigate hard cases, to steer him clear of the always threatening snowdrifts of boredom. Without it, he lost his edge. Seeley's practice in Buffalo's old Ellicott Square Building barely paid the rent, but that wasn't why he left Buffalo when Daphne invited him to rejoin Boone, Bancroft. He returned to New York City because he wanted his old office back and the life that it implied. But he wanted more than that. If he was ever to expel the ghost of Jun Wei, he had to start there, where he had abandoned her.

A guitar struck up in a dark colonnade, and when Seeley turned in the direction of the music the street filled with a swarm of ghost-white figures. They could have been emissaries from the white yacht, they flew by so swiftly. Seeley's first thought was that it was a procession of nuns, but as they passed he saw that the women were not in coifs and habits, but white dresses, pant suits, shorts, T-shirts, and shawls, and that each held a long-stemmed white flower. As the music of the guitar receded in one direction, the backs of the women disappeared in the other. Seconds later, the Malecón was still. It was as if the women had not been there at all.

10

In the morning, Seeley's first call was to Metcalf, waking the foreign service officer at the home number he'd written on the back of his business card. "You never answered my question about where I can find Reynoso."

"Oh." Metcalf was still waking up. "You mean when we talked at the Nacional. Well, no, I suppose I didn't."

Seeley waited.

"We're in regular contact with Héctor. He's perfectly safe."

"I need to see him."

"That's an entirely different question."

"Without Reynoso, I can't get the others to sign."

"I'm not sure I can—"

"Then I'm going back to New York."

"You . . ." A hand over the receiver muted Metcalf's throat-clearing. "I said it was a different question, not that we can't do it. Don't go anywhere. I'm tied up all day but I can meet you at three."

Metcalf was stalling.

"I need to see him now."

"That's impossible," Metcalf said. "I have appointments until two-thirty. I can meet you at three." He gave Seeley the address of a restaurant, El Salvador, in Habana Vieja.

"There's another problem—"

"We can talk about it at three." The line went dead.

•

Even in the best law firms, truly gifted young lawyers are rare and partners fight for their time. Elena's readiness to drop everything to work on Seeley's projects was not going to help her prospects at the firm, and when she told him that she had stepped out of a deposition with one of the other partners to take his call, he felt a stab of remorse.

"Did you find Héctor?"

"Not yet," Seeley said. "I can use your help on something."

"You need me in Havana?"

"I do, but there's a rule that only one Boone, Bancroft lawyer can violate the Trading with the Enemy Act at a time. I have a research project for you, maybe eight or ten hours' work."

"No problem. The deposition will be over in a couple of hours. I have a small project for Barry, getting a copyright transfer searched and recorded in the Copyright Office, but I don't think it's a rush."

Barry Maxon was a trial lawyer like Seeley, but he had no copyright experience. "Who's the client?"

"A company called Saddle River Equities. They're new."

If there was no rush, why had Hobie assigned the work to Barry rather than wait for Seeley to return?

"So I have plenty of time for whatever you need."

Seeley related what Piñeiro had told him about the nationalization. "I need you to find out if the Cuban government expropriated Héctor's music. The others' too."

"A government can't steal an author's work!"

"In fact it can, but I'd like to think that if they did, we can get the music back. Track down the expropriation orders. They'll be in Spanish, but they shouldn't be hard to locate." That would confirm Piñeiro's story, if it was true. "Next, find all the cases you can on expropriation of copyrights. If we're going to file a lawsuit, we need to know what the case law looks like. See if there are any

Cuban cases. There are also four expropriation cases involving Russian writers." *Trafimov, Babenko, Gortikov, Gennadiev.* Seeley could have been sitting in Felix Silver's office, the made-up folk tune was that vivid in his memory. "The government seized the writers' copyrights to shut them down. Felix Silver represented the writers."

"Did he win?"

"All four cases. But they're more than twenty years old. I need to know what the law is today."

"Who should I bill my time to?"

Boone, Bancroft required its associates to measure out their lives in tenths of an hour, billing every six minutes of their workday to one client or another, but Reynoso was still not a client.

"For now, bill it to your new client. Saddle River Equities. We can move the time to Reynoso as soon as I sign him up."

"When do you want this?"

"Tomorrow morning. Call me by nine." Seeley heard an intake of breath on the other end of the phone. "If the case law's against us and we can't get a federal court to overturn the expropriations, I'm just wasting my time trying to get the music back. There's no reason for me to spend another day here. When you finish, make sure you call the car service to take you home. No taxis or subways."

"*If* I get home." It wasn't an objection. She even managed to make it sound lighthearted. "I finished the draft motion for the Boston case. Do you want to see it?"

"Sure. Fax it to me at the hotel. I'll work on it here."

Seeley promised himself that when he got back to New York he would explain to Elena why he was the last partner at the firm to whom she should want to hitch her future.

Nilda's cheeks dimpled as she pulled at the straw, the serious eyes not once leaving the glass. A banana was next to the tumbler on the metal tabletop. They were in the dimly lit snack bar in the Nacional's basement. "Auntie said I should tell you that she had something she had to do."

Only a woman aware of her effect on men could escape with so thin an excuse. Seeley said, "Her telephone was busy."

"It isn't Auntie's telephone. It's the lady's downstairs. Everybody in the building has a line to it." Nilda swirled the tall glass and sucked at the remains of the milk shake. "You think Auntie has a boyfriend." It wasn't a question, and she didn't wait for an answer. "Auntie says everyone in America has their own phone. Even kids."

Seeley said, "Do you think about America? Going there?"

Carefully, Nilda peeled the banana, working from the bottom up to the stem. "Auntie says if you tell people your dreams, they won't come true."

"Does your auntie dream about America?" The unsteadiness in his voice surprised him.

"I don't know. If she does, she doesn't talk about it."

And if she doesn't talk about it, Seeley reasoned, then she must dream about it. Except that when her name came up in the lottery, she turned down the chance to leave.

"Auntie gave me your list. Do you want to go?"

Unless Metcalf could produce Reynoso, and unless Elena's research gave their challenge to the expropriations a chance of winning, Seeley had no reason to talk to another composer. "Not today."

The transparency of Nilda's disappointment reminded Seeley how young she was. He said, "How's Hannah Montana?"

"I bought three CDs." Like the skipping feet, her exuberance clashed with the solemn expression. "Two Hannah Montana, one Justin Bieber."

"You're going to break the embargo all by yourself." Seeley took a folded bill from his pocket to hand to her. "Buy yourself some more CDs."

She put her hands in her lap. "Auntie says I shouldn't."

"This is for the taxi."

She shook her head, grave as ever. "I took the bus."

"Then the bus."

Seeley reached over and pushed the bill into a banana-sticky hand. "I won't tell your auntie, if you won't."

Seeley remembered Amaryll saying that Nilda was nearsighted, and it occurred to him that maybe she wasn't solemn at all, just a young girl intently focusing on the blurred world around her. "Why aren't you wearing your glasses?"

She showed no surprise that Seeley knew about them. "They're just for reading."

Either Nilda was lying about this, or Amaryll was.

"You know, Auntie doesn't have a boyfriend. She told me to tell you she was sorry for being rude yesterday." Nilda handed him a scrap of paper folded as small as a postage stamp. "She wants you to come to dinner tonight. Eight o'clock." She nodded at the paper Seeley was holding. "That's the address. Auntie likes you, you know. She doesn't invite men to dinner."

"Why do you peel your banana from the bottom up?" In a city where entire families travel on a single bicycle and flocks of white-clad women suddenly appear, then disappear, at 2:00 in the morning, why should this be unusual?

"Everyone peels them that way. How do you peel yours?"

"From the stem down."

"You get strings that way." Nilda unrolled the peel. "See, no strings."

She was right; there were none of the usual spidery threads. The message was so obvious that Seeley decided to ignore it.

At midafternoon, El Salvador cabaret was empty except for a waiter slicing fruit at the bar across the cavernous room. The place looked like it was in business long before the revolution. Apparitions of bare-shouldered women and slick-haired men in tuxedos danced in the peeling, gold-veined mirrors. At the other end of the room from where Seeley sat, spotlights hung from a low gantry, waiting for a white-jacketed band to climb onto the stage with trombones, trumpets, guitars, and conga drums, and for a sequined singer with an hourglass figure to join them.

Metcalf arrived and pulled out the chair opposite Seeley. He had on a tie and a light cotton jacket today, and when he took off his straw hat, the circular crease that it left in the thatch of fine hair glowed like a halo in the shadowy room. For a long moment, Metcalf looked at Seeley and, when Seeley didn't speak, he said, "Your government is going to be very disappointed if you leave without getting the forms signed. What's this other problem you said you wanted to talk about?"

"Why didn't you tell me Castro expropriated the music?"

"Would you have stayed, if I did?" There was cunning in the bland face that Seeley hadn't seen before. "Who told you?"

"I found Lieutenant Piñeiro parked in my hotel room. He didn't believe me about why I came to Cuba. The Ministry of Interior thinks I came to Cuba to start a counterrevolution."

"We can handle Minint." The caroler's pink cheeks tightened. "There's a saying here. 'As Fidel breathes, Minint breathes.'"

"And when Fidel stops breathing?" Seeley had the same mixed feelings about Castro that he would for any leader who jabbed one finger in the paunch of the world's greatest superpower, but with his other hand abused his own countrymen.

"The State Department's legal advisor takes the position that Castro's expropriation of American properties in Cuba is illegal and therefore of no effect."

"That's a great comfort," Seeley said, "but I doubt that whoever gives Lieutenant Piñeiro his orders is a careful student of the legal advisor's opinions."

The waiter came to the table and nodded at Metcalf as he might to a regular customer. *Café helado*," Metcalf said.

Seeley said, "A beer. Beck's." He could have been answering a question about the weather, not ordering his first alcoholic drink in more than a year.

Metcalf's usually bland expression showed surprise, and Seeley wondered how much Hobie had told the State Department about him.

"No Beck's," the waiter said.

"What do you have?" Gin, not beer, had been Seeley's problem, and a cold beer might do more than just ease the restlessness and irritability that had dogged his time in Havana; it might restore the edge to his dulled judgment. The waiter's list was short, and Seeley ordered Cristal.

Worry replaced Metcalf's surprise, and Seeley said, "What did Hobie Harriman tell you about me?"

"I've never met the man."

"But you know who he is."

"Hobie Harriman? Of course, everyone at State knows who he is."

"But he didn't pass on a message about me? About a trial I have in Boston in less than two weeks?"

Beads of perspiration gave a shine to Metcalf's upper lip. "My briefing said only that you are very smart and very stubborn."

"And?"

"And something of a hothead."

"Not the kind of qualities the State Department admires." Seeley's fingers tapped on the tabletop. His anxiety for the waiter to return felt all too familiar. "Was that Reynoso's problem? That he was a hothead?"

If Metcalf noticed Seeley's use of the past tense, he didn't let on. "Héctor is a colorful man. Also a complicated one."

"I can't get the composers to sign without him. And if I can't get them to sign, there's no reason for me to be here."

"I told you," Metcalf said, "it won't be easy—"

"If you can get him in and out of Cuba and America like he was a diplomat, you should be able to arrange a meeting in the city where he lives." Seeley pushed back his chair, as if to leave.

Metcalf's soft hand restrained him. "Of course we know where Héctor is. He's right here in Havana. But getting you together with him won't be that . . . straightforward." The waiter was approaching, and Metcalf leaned in to speak. "Héctor has been, let us say, somewhat too *public* about his contacts with us. With Raúl's reforms, the situation here has never been more dangerous, and when this place explodes, the blame's going to be on America."

The drinks arrived, and Metcalf tilted the glass of iced coffee toward Seeley in a silent toast, giving him the same curious look as before. When Seeley tipped the longneck bottle to his lips, the beer was ice-cold and, as it rolled over his tongue, it possessed for an unlikely instant the bright edge and aftertaste of a fine gin martini. The impact was immediate, and from deep inside him a voice cried, *Yes!* In the golden mirrors, shadows appeared that had been invisible before. "You abandoned Reynoso," Seeley said.

"Of course not. Héctor's too important to our interests." For Seeley, that was the wrong reason not to abandon someone, but Metcalf ignored his frown. "We can't let the Cubans find our fingerprints anywhere near Héctor."

"But you have no problem with me chatting up his friends."

"You're a private individual. That's why we're willing to help you. I can't promise you that my successor will be as helpful as me."

The maneuver was obvious, and ordinarily Seeley would have overlooked it. But scant sleep and cold beer on an empty stomach made him attentive. "You're leaving Cuba."

"I'm retiring," Metcalf said.

The man couldn't be more than fifty, Seeley thought. Fifty-five at most. He didn't accept that he was retiring. "Where to?"

"Clear Lake, up in California. Fish every day. No bureaucracy to fight."

"Except Fish and Game." Seeley contrived a knowing look. "Clear Lake's a fine spot. I've had good luck with western muskie there." Seeley didn't fish, had never been to Clear Lake, and didn't know if, outside of *Field & Stream*, a muskie had ever been seen west of the Mississippi. "What about you?"

"Well . . ." Metcalf faltered and looked about, as if the waiter could help him. "I guess we'll just have to see." He turned back. "Your government is asking you to stay."

"You have to do better than that," Seeley said.

"You can be prosecuted for traveling to Cuba illegally."

"That's still not good enough." Seeley drew back from the table and, as if he were connected to him, Metcalf moved forward.

"Have another beer," he said.

Seeley had emptied the bottle and not realized it. The voice inside him that said *yes* the first time said *yes* again, but he knew that a second beer would turn into a third and that, in time, gin or vodka or rum would replace the beer and that, before he was done, he would be staring at himself in a mirror, debating the easiest way to kill himself. "One's my limit," he said. "Piñeiro thinks I'm working for you." I already said that, he thought. One beer, and I'm repeating myself. "He thinks I'm here to overthrow his government."

"You have no reason to be concerned for your safety. You're an American lawyer, and you are here working for a client."

What was it Elena had said? *I'm an American lawyer. What can they do to me?* Seeley said, "The next time the lieutenant knocks on my door I'll be sure to flash my bar card."

"We can put you on the payroll as a consultant," Metcalf said. "That will give you diplomatic immunity."

Never trust a bureaucrat when he starts improvising. Seeley slammed down the bottle. "You're not listening to me!"

Metcalf jerked back and the waiter looked up from the orange, green, and yellow mounds of sliced fruit in front of him. "What do you want?"

"I want a meeting with Reynoso."

Metcalf's lips became a narrow line. "I'll set it up when I get back to the office." He gulped down the rest of his iced coffee.

"It has to be tomorrow, or I leave. After that the composers and their families can take care of themselves."

"Do you know the Christopher Columbus Cemetery? The Cementerio de Cristóbal Colón. Go there tomorrow and you will find Reynoso." Seeley must have started because Metcalf smiled. "Don't worry. Your musician is upright and in good health. I'll have him meet you by the 1942 baseball monument. Call me from outside the hotel tomorrow and I'll let you know the time. But remember, the 1942 monument, not the one from 1951."

Seeley said, "I also want a letter from the State Department."

"Of course, saying that you didn't come here illegally. That you are working for us—"

"No. I want a letter that I can submit to a federal judge stating what you told me before, that it is the position of the United States government that Cuba's expropriation of the composers' property is illegal and without effect."

Metcalf said, "I don't have the authority to order such a letter."

"Of course you don't." Seeley tried to remember the level of Hobie's last position there. "This has to come from someone at the level of assistant secretary or higher."

"When the time comes, if you get into litigation and you need a letter, I'm sure we can write one directly to the judge."

"But you'll be retired by then." Why did it seem to Seeley that eager as Metcalf was for the composers to sign he was indifferent to them actually getting back their rights? "It doesn't make much sense to get them to sign these forms and take their chances with the security police if in the end the government owns the music and they don't."

Metcalf colored. "You have no idea how important the welfare of these people is to me."

"To you, yes. But to your employer?"

"I'll send a cable requesting the letter tonight."

"And you'll make sure that Reynoso is at the cemetery tomorrow." Seeley lifted the Cristal bottle to his mouth before he remembered that it was empty. The beginnings of a hangover pecked at the back of his eyes. This, from a single bottle of beer. His own *migraña*. He remembered Amaryll's invitation to dinner, but the thought didn't give him the lift that it did earlier. A gray premonition of dread wrapped around him like a blanket. Regret, Seeley thought. Misery and regret are once again going to rule my life.

•

The Nacional's business center was on the hotel's second floor. A framed display of black-and-white photographs showed Fidel Castro entertaining one foreign dignitary after another in the hotel ballroom. In all but one picture, the visitor's eyes were fastened on the charismatic Cuban. Only in the photograph of Castro with the president of China did the foreign leader look not at his host, but outward, over the photographer's shoulder, at Cuba.

Inside the business center, Seeley gave his room number to the receptionist, who directed him to a booth among the several along one side of the room. For Barry Maxon, who knew nothing about copyright law, to oversee the work of this new client, Saddle River, made no more sense now than it did ten hours ago when Elena first told Seeley about it. But if the business center had a functioning computer, Seeley could at least find out who Saddle River was.

The accordion door wouldn't latch and the computer was a relic from the nineties. Seeley typed in Boone, Bancroft's Web address, punched the tab for the firm's new business center and entered his passcode. New business files were open to partners and associates alike, as well as to their secretaries, but Seeley felt like a burglar breaking into a sleeping household.

A message flashed in red across the screen: PASSCODE NOT RECOGNIZED.

Seeley entered the numbers a second time, then a third, with the same result.

When Seeley returned to Boone, Bancroft five months ago, and the IT staff took a week to assign him a new passcode, he used his secretary's code to clear conflicts and check on new matters coming in from old clients. Trying to remember her code, he studied the keyboard for inspiration, but when he typed in 9152, the same red message appeared.

9512. Same result.

9521. Black-lined columns and entry boxes jumped onto the screen, as welcoming as banners.

Seeley was typing *Saddle* into the space designated for new clients when the accordion door slid open and alcohol fumes poured into the booth, followed by a man's head, red-eyed and rooster-necked. "Do you speak English?" The accent was Australian.

"A little," Seeley said.

"I'm having a hell of a time getting funds wired from my bank in Melbourne. The people here don't understand a word."

Seeley said he was sorry that he couldn't help, waved the man out, and shut the door. He checked his watch. Even if he caught a taxi to Amaryll's apartment right now, he would be late. He finished typing *River* and hit Enter. NO CLIENT BY THIS NAME.

If Elena was working on a project for Saddle River, that meant the company was a client, and if it was a client, someone had run its name through a conflict search. Seeley reentered the company's name in the box for conflicts and the screen at once filled with columns of company names. Saddle River was the first in the left-hand column. Seeley glanced at the top of the page. The conflict had only cleared yesterday, which was why the company wasn't yet in the new client database. He scrolled to the bottom. In the space where the client's address and other contact information, including the names of its officers, would ordinarily appear was only "c/o Evernham and Company" with the private bank's address on Broadway. Across from that, in the space for "Responsible Attorney," was not Barry Maxon but Hobart Harriman.

Seeley now understood why Barry, not he, had been assigned to Saddle River's copyright work. Seeley had told Ike Butler that he had no interest in taking on anonymous clients, so Hobie passed the work on to another partner. But that did not explain why Boone, Bancroft had withdrawn his passcode, or tell him who was trying to keep him out of the firm's system. And who was Saddle River?

11

Larger than life, Amaryll's shadow danced on the walls of the candlelit room. Seeley's gaze traveled from shadow to dancer and back. On the CD player, a trombone battled a bank of saxophones; drums insinuated themselves as a beat more than a sound; a familiar male voice that Seeley couldn't place joined the trombone, jousting against cries from a chorus of women. The source of Seeley's discomfort was not the straight-backed chair but the excruciating intimacy of observing Amaryll, no more than an arm's reach away, so completely absorbed in the music. He felt that he was watching the most private of acts. Drifting lazily against the musical mayhem, at a sustained, spiraling note from the trombone, she suddenly turned still. When the saxophones faded, Amaryll reached behind her to lower the volume on the player.

She said, "That made you uncomfortable, didn't it?"

The candles gave off a lavender scent and the flickering shadows lent an impermanence to the room. The dark hair that Seeley had only seen pulled back into a dancer's severe bun, was down now, falling in curls over Amaryll's shoulders, amazing in its thick abundance.

"That was beautiful."

"You *were* uncomfortable!" Amaryll laughed. "A Cuban man would have jumped up and danced with me. Even if he was shy, he would have moved with the music. But Americans . . . *Ay! Ay!*

Ay!" The serious, compelling woman of the car and the composers' apartments was gone. In her own home, Amaryll was light,
almost girlish. Still laughing, she said, "Would you like another
slice of watermelon?"

Seeley shook his head. "This was wonderful. Everything." Incredibly, Amaryll had created dinner on a two-burner hot plate
and a stove smaller even than the one in the candymaker's shack.
Roast chicken, its flesh moist under crisp golden skin, white rice
that soaked up the juices, new peas, their emerald-green skins
brightened by the thinnest imaginable slivers of lemon. Dessert
was watermelon, the old-fashioned kind with seeds, but ruby-red
and sweet.

"Did you know whose voice that was on the CD?" Her smile
teased him. "That was Héctor. Your client. A CD, but an old recording. 'Havana Rum.'"

"Very romantic."

"Not really." Amaryll was still giddy from the performance.
"It's a *melodía* for a famous brand of rum, an advertising song."

"A jingle." As Seeley suspected, the reason that Reynoso gave
for wanting his music back, to rescue it from commercials for frozen tacos and shaving cream, was a deceit. "Are you sure?"

"Everyone knows this. He wrote it for Bacardi in the 1950s. My
father told me that for a time it was more popular even than dance
music. Day and night it was on the radio."

"Reynoso told me he and his friends wanted their songs back
so that companies couldn't use them like that."

Amaryll said, "The man who ran Bacardi was a great supporter
of *la cultura.* Of Fidel, too." She studied Seeley, gauging his reaction.
"A musician like Héctor had to look out for himself. Nobody re-
members it today, but in the forties and fifties, if you were dark"—in
a swift, graceful gesture, she touched the skin of her forearm—
"you couldn't play in the cabarets where the tourists went, where
the money was."

Except, Seeley thought, that Devlin opened those doors for

Reynoso and his friends, even before the revolution. "I thought Castro changed that. Black and white, equal treatment."

"Equal treatment, yes. After they closed the clubs, black and white musicians could starve together. That was years before I was born. By the time I went to ENA, no one was playing the old music."

"So Reynoso wrote jingles."

"Ay, how tasty the cane is, honey," Amaryll sang softly. "Bring your cart over here." A wink mocked the song's lubricity. "Héctor wrote that to get volunteers to work on the sugar harvest. There's a story that Fidel himself asked him to write it."

Amaryll continued humming the tune as Seeley looked about the room. Instead of framed pictures, an artist had painted scenes the size of movie posters directly onto the plaster, like frescoes. On two walls, the views were of orchards dense with oranges, grapefruit, and lemons; brilliant blossoms cascaded and monkeys flew between the trees. Across from Seeley, next to the French windows, a man and woman elegantly dressed in the style of the forties sat at a café table set with coffee service and a flask of brandy, observing a calm Caribbean Sea.

Amaryll said, "You shouldn't be hard on Héctor. You are too much of an idealist, a romantic. The only room for romantics on this island is in the prisons. Héctor is like the rest of us. He had to be practical. He did what he had to do to survive."

"And the others, his friends—they also don't care how their music is used?"

"I told you," Amaryll said, "they are afraid." She took the other chair from the table and sat opposite him. With the volume turned down on the CD player, the music had a muted, fogged-in quality; there was none of the vocal or percussive drive of "Havana Rum." "Even if they believed you, that you can get their music back for them, they think that if they sign your papers, they will be questioned by the security police. Maybe go to prison."

"That didn't stop you from coming with me to translate."

"You mean, am I afraid? Of course I am." This was a change

from her earlier bravado. "But I promised Dolores I would go with you. You should be afraid, too. They say there is an American in prison now, just for visiting with Cubans."

Seeley remembered his partner Thatcher Burleigh saying the same at the executive committee meeting. Cuban news in New York is only a rumor in Cuba.

"I promised Reynoso."

"Dolores is my best friend."

"Reynoso is my client."

"And, for a promise you make to a client, someone you don't even know, you don't care if these people get hurt, or if you get hurt." The dark eyes glistened with emotion. "Do you have any idea what it is like in a Cuban prison?"

"No one is going to prison." Even as he spoke the words, Seeley knew how irresponsible they were. What did he know of how political oppression worked in this country? Nor was there anything he could do to protect these people.

As quickly as the tears of protest filled Amaryll's eyes they disappeared. "Let's not be so serious." She rested her hands on her lap, and smoothed the cotton shift. "What else are you doing with your time in Havana?"

"Waiting to see my client. A man at the U.S. Interests Section told me he could arrange a meeting with Reynoso at a cemetery here."

"Cementerio de Cristóbal Colón."

Seeley nodded. "I feel like one of those men who wait in the doorways day and night and do nothing."

"The women also wait, but they don't have time for doorways. They stand in line for food. Then they wait so they can trade the food for medicine for their children. Next, they stand in line for the children's doctor. They wait for the water to come so they can wash the family's clothes. Cubans have much experience with waiting. Five hundred years. Waiting for the Spanish to leave. The Americans. The Russians."

"It's been a long time since the Russians left."

"Yes, but the Americans are always here. We are never allowed to forget that you are just across the water." This wasn't the gay woman of minutes ago, or the intently engaged dancer. Fatalism hooded her words. "It is in the interest of the people in power to keep the American enemy close. Without the American oppressor, the revolution ends. So you understand why we wait."

"For Castro to die."

Amaryll shrugged. "Who knows? He still writes essays in *Granma*. Or does he? His name is there, but no one knows. Where there is a ghost in the room, everyone is careful not to disturb it."

"And Raúl?"

"We are a people who are born with the habit of waiting in our bones."

Seeley told her about the swarm of white-clad women on the Malecón.

"Las Damas de Blanco," Amaryll said. "They are the mothers and wives and sisters of dissidents who are in prison. On Sunday after church, they march to protest the men's imprisonment."

"This was at two in the morning."

"I don't know about that. Nilda wants to be a Dama." She bit her bottom lip, as if she regretted what she said. "A little girl's *vanidad*. She thinks dark people look *atractivo* in white."

"She told me she only needs her glasses for reading."

"My niece!" Amaryll laughed. "You know nothing about young girls, how proud they are of their looks." Behind the high spirits, Amaryll was hiding something.

"And your ex-husband," Seeley said. Piñeiro had spoken of a husband even though Amaryll told him she was no longer married. "What about him?"

"Virgilio? Who told you about Virgilio? Dolores? No, Nilda."

Seeley said nothing. He had no desire to invite Piñeiro into the room.

"All these questions!" Amaryll said. "You are like that lawyer on the television. Perry Mason."

"Except not as successful," Seeley said, thinking, Cuba is where old television shows come to die. "What about Virgilio?"

"It was the lieutenant who told you." Her look was dark, and Seeley wondered how she knew.

"Your lieutenant came to see me in my hotel room." Why did he say *your* lieutenant? "He said I should ask you about your husband."

"It is nothing. The lieutenant is playing tricks with you. What else did he say?"

"He wants to know why I'm in Havana. He doesn't believe I came to get the composers to sign the forms."

"I told you it was a terrible mistake for you to attack the lieutenant. I am worried that he did not have you taken to prison."

"Do you still think about leaving?"

"Everyone on the island thinks about leaving."

You are like Reynoso, Seeley thought. You won't give me a direct answer. "And you?"

"All the time."

"But you stayed even when you could have left."

Again, the soft smile. "Do you dance?"

The question was so unexpected that Seeley's first thought was that she meant ballet. "Never."

She rose and took his hands. "Of course you do. I watch you. You move like an athlete." She went to the CD player and turned up the volume. "It is impossible to be in Cuba and not to dance."

Seeley pictured himself as one of those heavy sunburned men with their young Cuban girlfriends. "But only the Cubans make it look good."

The tempo of the music on the CD player was slow, painfully so. There was a cello and a voice, but the two sounds were indistinguishable. Lacking the form of words, the voice became the cello and the cello, the voice. A breeze came through the open French windows. "This is sacred music," Amaryll said. "It is from the same place as Héctor's music and the others'. This is the music that the slaves brought with them from Africa five hundred years ago. It is how our *antepasados*—our ancestors—explain to us who we are."

The music was unlike any that Seeley had heard before, a sound that belonged to an African jungle where the canopy of foliage admits no light, and even the birds and monkeys are silent as they move from branch to branch. The cellist's bow traveled across a single string, producing neither rhythm nor melody, only a sinuous trajectory of line; a doomed man's sorrowful sigh. The music filled the room with a melancholy and longing so profound that Seeley couldn't breathe.

"The music sounds like water, doesn't it? Like a moving stream. But if you listen closely, with a Cuban's ear, you will hear the struggle in it. Always a struggle. From the very beginning, the slaves who were shipped here to work in the mines rebelled. All of the time, there were uprisings. More slaves came, thousands every year, and when the mines gave out, they put them to work in the sugar factories and then on the plantations. But the black uprisings never stopped, or the force that the whites used to put them down. That is the reason you don't hear the old music like this in Cuba today. Not even Héctor's."

Amaryll reached out for Seeley to join her and, when he didn't, she shrugged, then swayed against the music as she had earlier, her narrow smile mocking him. "It would be so nice to travel to America with you."

The words were Amaryll's, but it felt to Seeley as if he had spoken them; as if her desire to leave, and his desire for her to do so, were one. This incredible woman, this woman whose secrets he could never hope to share, was opening a door. He didn't know which frightened him more—the possibility that whatever this was that they shared would shrivel into something small and sad the moment they left the island, or that this was a woman for whom he might do anything, give up everything.

"Beautiful, no?" Amaryll's voice was a whisper. "'Música Nocturna.' This is by Ibrahim Valdéz."

From one of their visits, Seeley remembered Valdéz, a bachelor in his eighties, a quiet, diffident man in shirtsleeves and suspenders. Seeley rose and crossed to Amaryll. Her fingertips when she touched the back of his neck were cool, and with just two fingers she gently guided him into the music. This close, her hair wasn't black, but blue-black, and the vein at her temple was no more than a shadow. Seeley touched the small of her back and, as she moved, he realized that under the light shift she wore nothing. It startled him how fragile this tall, vibrant woman felt. Her lips, when they touched his, tasted obscurely of watermelon, and then a second time, when she opened them, tasted of nothing so much as her.

She glanced over his shoulder, then turned so that he, too, saw the clock on the shelf. It was 11:50. "You have to leave in ten minutes."

"Your coach turns into a pumpkin."

"Pumpkin?"

"Squash. An old fairy tale. Cinderella."

She said, "America is a land of fairy tales."

"What happens at midnight?"

"No fairy tale. The CDR lady."

"CDR?"

"There's one on every block. Maybe you didn't see her when you came in, but she saw you, and now she waits for you to leave." Amaryll drew back so that only their fingertips touched. "Don't move," she said. "Be completely still. Listen to the music."

Seeley had the sensation of unfolding like a leaf; growing larger, illuminated. The feeling was as alien, yet as inborn, as time travel. Like a climber grasping for the rock above him, he could find no purchase on the moment nor, he realized, did he have any desire to do so. If Amaryll suddenly dissolved into the dense air and was swept off over the balcony it would not astonish him, nor would it surprise him if he followed.

"This is the most subversive music of all," Amaryll said. "It makes practical people dream."

After that, they stood listening, fingertips touching, and when the music ended they remained still, silent, studying the depth in each other's eyes.

Finally, Amaryll spoke. "Stay until morning." It was as much a question as a command.

If she could dismiss the CDR lady, Seeley thought, so could he. "I thought you'd never ask."

Later in the night, when she was above him, the miniature ivory fish swung from the thin gold chain and glowed in the candlelight.

"Do you ever take it off?"

"My *amuleto*?" Amaryll said. "I think that with you I must always keep it on."

12

Like many experienced lawyers, Seeley had a well-calibrated instinct for the shape and structure of legal doctrine. Given no more than a handful of clues from an unfamiliar body of law, he could quickly fill in the rest, much the way a backwoods guide can plot terrain from a few salient landmarks. But American foreign-relations law was alien to Seeley's intuitions, an incoherent jumble of politics, diplomacy, and statecraft. He had researched the field when he helped Felix Silver with the Russian writers, but that was more than twenty years ago, and he didn't trust his knowledge to be current.

Elena called while he was on his second cup of coffee, and her voice, even after what must have been a long night in the library, was bright. "Most of the Cuban cases are about sugar refineries or distilleries. There aren't any decisions on Cuban copyrights. The closest cases are the ones you told me about, the cases involving the Russian writers, but they won because the government was trying to suppress their works. Is that what Cuba's trying to do to Héctor?"

"These are old songs. There's nothing political about them. I'm sure this is just about money. It usually is."

"Then maybe money was part of the Russian cases, too. I can look at the case files to see if there's anything about it in the briefs."

"How much time have you billed so far?" Seeley had told Elena to bill her time to Saddle River, but now that he knew who the partner in charge of Saddle River's engagement was, he worried that too many hours logged to the company's account could draw Hobie's attention before Seeley had a good explanation.

"A little over ten hours."

As Seeley guessed, Elena spent the night in the office. "Forget the case files. There wasn't anything about money in the briefs."

"How do you know?"

"I was Silver's research assistant when he filed the cases. Go home, get some rest, and then I want you to start drafting the complaint. You know who the plaintiffs are. Reynoso. The others."

"And the defendants?"

"The Republic of Cuba and some John Does." The Does were a placeholder. Inevitably, there would be other defendants, along with the Cuban government, and Seeley would add their names once he knew them.

"Did you get the motion I faxed to you for the Boston case?"

"You did a good job with it. Thanks. I need to make a few changes, and I'll fax it back to you."

"What about Héctor?"

"I'm seeing him in a couple of hours." Seeley still distrusted Metcalf's promise to produce Reynoso, but no one had called to cancel the meeting. "Now go home and go to bed."

Seeley got out the map the desk clerk had given him and located the Cementerio de Cristóbal Colón. Then he took a termination form from his briefcase and a sheet of hotel stationery. If Reynoso wouldn't come with him to see the others, he could write a note asking them to sign.

How neatly the tumblers would fall into place if Reynoso was alive and Metcalf had in fact arranged a meeting. In no more than a day or two, he would be back in New York with the signed forms and there would be a draft complaint waiting on his desk asking a federal judge to declare that the compositions belonged to the composers who wrote them, and not to the Cuban government that stole them. *One, two, three*: the composers sign the forms; the judge returns their rights to them; the publishers hand them back their music. For the first time since Reynoso walked into his office, everything would be under control.

The Cementerio de Cristóbal Colón was a paved-over parking lot for the dead, acre after acre of granite, marble, and concrete slabs, interrupted only where weeds forced their way between the cracks, or strips of grass marked ancient divisions. Mausoleums the size of suburban homes fought for space with turreted chapels and intricately sculpted tombstones. Under an immense tree in full leaf, a three-quarter figure of an anonymous baseball player in cap and uniform emerged from the monument where Metcalf told Seeley that Reynoso would meet him. Head cocked, the player gazed over the ranks of gravestones, scouring the horizon for some long-ago home run. According to the plaque on the monument's granite base, the memorial was not just for players, but for PLAYERS, UMPIRES Y MANAGERS DE BASE-BALL PROFESIONAL 1942. Equality had come to Cuba long before the revolution.

Seeley considered the lineaments that Reynoso had acquired since their meeting in New York: the humble artist indignant over the misuse of his works, but coy about the true reason for wanting them back; the winking, hand-clapping friend of the U.S. State Department who shuttled easily between Cuba and America planning for his dreamed-about tour; the composer who shaped his music to the demands of powerful patrons in and out of government. Which one was Seeley going to meet today—or would there be an entirely new Reynoso?

"*Buenos días, Señor Seeley.*"

Seeley turned. Even in the morning heat and sun, Justo Mayor had on his seaman's toque.

"Where is Reynoso?" And, Seeley thought, who is going to translate?

A grin creased the unshaven face. "This is a fine place for old musicians to come, wouldn't you say?" Mayor pointed to an unseen, distant gravestone. "They are all here. All the famous ones. Chano Pozo." He made a quarter turn, his arm still outstretched. "Ibrahim Ferrer. There," he pointed. "There. There. All the old guys. Buena Vista Social Club." The inflection, oddly, was British. "Soon enough, Justo, too."

"And Reynoso?"

"Ah, Héctor, that is a complication. But I am sorry for my English. The other day . . . our visit . . ." Mayor's head waggled side to side. "My wife understands little English, so in her presence I speak Spanish. It promotes domestic peace. Also," he smiled again, "I sometimes learn more if visitors don't know that I understand what they are saying."

Seeley remembered Nilda telling him, in Mayor's presence, that the musician's wife ran the household. "Metcalf sent you."

"I know Mr. Metcalf, but no, Mr. Metcalf did not send me." Mayor drew closer to Seeley. "It was Héctor who told me to meet you here."

"I don't believe you. The security police have him. You said so yourself when you called his niece in New York."

"You are wrong. I talked to him."

"Then why didn't he come here himself?"

Mayor tugged at the front of his cap. "Héctor says you think he is a man of no *importancia*. No property." He pointed in the direction of Chano Pozo's grave. "Do you know Albert Korda—"

"The man who took the photograph of Che." If Reynoso were in fact alive, Seeley didn't understand why he would be sulking.

Mayor nodded, impressed. "Korda's buried over there, past Chano Pozo. They put Che's portrait on peso notes, but give Korda a centavo for his work? Never."

"And you think I don't care about Reynoso's work?"

"It doesn't matter what I think. It is what Héctor thinks." The old composer's face was inches from Seeley's and, like the last time, a sweetish scent of tobacco and rum rose off him in a humid cloud. "Héctor says you betrayed him."

"Why would I come to Havana to do that?" The smell of rum made Seeley dizzy. "I have never betrayed a client. Why would I start with him?"

"He calls you a *puerta de vaivén*. A swinging door." The sudden bitterness in Mayor's voice turned the words into a profanity. "When you visit the composers on Héctor's list, you have all the legal papers, but it is a *charada*. You tell them not to sign. You make up a story that the security police will arrest them, like they arrested Héctor. That the Americans will never give them their money—"

"You know that isn't true. At your apartment, it was your wife who told you not to sign, not me."

"I know only what the others told Héctor." He pulled the toque low on his forehead. "They said you—"

"Not me," Seeley said. "I didn't even talk to them—"

"Well, the woman who talked to them for you. She translated your words."

Amaryll. Why would she deceive him or the composers like that? What was it she told him? *When I was a small girl, I put composers on a pedestal.* And now that she was a woman, who occupied that pedestal? "Reynoso told you this?"

"Who else?"

"When did you see him?"

"Yesterday afternoon. No, the day before. At his apartment."

"Was his dog with him?"

"Gordita?" Justo's look was puzzled, impatient. "Of course. Gordita is always there."

Two days ago, when Seeley went to the apartment, Reynoso's neighbors, Gisela and Rubén, had told him that the dog was at his sister's in Camaguey, halfway across the island. "When you saw Reynoso, did you have much time to talk?"

"Of course. We are old friends. We had a glass of rum or two. We listened to music."

Mayor was lying. But why? "What did he tell you about what

happened? The people who took him from New York. Who kidnapped him?"

Mayor stopped, caught. "I didn't ask him."

"Why? If you care so little about how your old friend disappeared, why did you call his niece in New York?" If Mayor was lying about Reynoso, maybe he was also lying about Amaryll.

Mayor said, "You think I am making this up."

"And if I went to Reynoso's apartment now?"

"He will piss on your shoes and shut the door."

"There is a misunderstanding," Seeley said. "I can fix it."

Mayor's expression was dark. "Héctor doesn't want you to talk to the musicians."

A shadow passed over them and, when Seeley looked up, a giant bird, coal black and with a wing span larger than a hawk's, swooped onto a mausoleum roof, coming to rest on an iron cross. "If I leave," Seeley said, "who is going to get the composers to sign?"

"Héctor will. Or me."

"You don't have the forms."

"You left me a copy. My wife can make more."

The reluctant wife. "You don't know where to send them."

"We have lawyers here. Cubans. They will know how to do it."

"Reynoso told me no Cuban lawyer would help him. Why are you doing this?"

"For the same reason as the others. Money." Seeley waited for the universal gesture, but Mayor's thick-veined hands stayed at his side. "We are not like Gil Garcells, who goes on tours and sells CDs and lives like an American. After all these years, it would be nice for us to see some money. The widows, too. I would like to buy some good shampoo for my wife. Pretty handkerchiefs. Soap. Héctor, I don't know what his reason is. Héctor is very . . . complicated with all of his politics. But for us, it is about the money."

"I can go with you. Your friends are going to ask, where is the American lawyer."

"You think too much of yourself," Mayor said, puffing out his chest to mimic Seeley's pride. "Nobody has a wish to see you."

"And if I can get Reynoso to explain to you that this was a misunderstanding?" Seeley realized that he had fallen into Mayor's trap, believing that Reynoso was free and not in custody. Standing in this vast Cuban graveyard, the difference between the two states of being seemed curiously small.

Mayor wasn't listening. He nodded toward where the giant bird was perched and said, "Over there is a marker for William Morgan. Do you know him? He was an American, but he came here to fight with Fidel in the revolution. He even brought his own troops. After they drove out Batista, Morgan supported Fidel, but he was no communist. Morgan hated communists. He was a capitalist all day long."

Seeley waited for the lesson that Mayor would pluck from a gravestone. "How old are you, Señor Seeley?" When Seeley didn't answer, Mayor said, "Thirty-three. Señor Morgan was thirty-three years old when Fidel had him shot by a firing squad." He squinted or winked, Seeley didn't know which. "People said Morgan was CIA, and that's why Fidel executed him. Myself, I think he was just a revolutionary who liked private property. He was still a young man, many years younger than you, I would say."

The latch was still broken, and when Seeley pushed open Reynoso's door, a stench of piss and excrement flooded out. Seeley's first thought was the dog, but the smell from the apartment was acutely human, as was the still shadow that lay across the bare wood floor. Seeley forced himself to enter. As if it had levitated there, Reynoso's narrow body hung inches from the ceiling, tethered by a loop of electrical wire to the brown-painted pipe running the width of the room. Head cocked, arms at his side, palms out, Reynoso looked like he was asking, *Why?* Directly under him, a chrome-and-vinyl kitchen chair that Seeley didn't remember from the first visit lay on its side.

Close enough to touch the body, Seeley didn't. Reynoso had not died easily. The shrewd thoughtful eyes now belonged to a fish, glassy and protruding; purple patches suffused the bloated skin; where the frayed electric cord throttled the musician's swollen neck, the skin was black and crimson. Seeley gagged at the odor. He thought of Reynoso's courtly manner, the trim straw hat with the gaudy ribbon, and it sickened him that the last earthly act of this elegant man had been to foul himself. The scolding angle of Reynoso's head reminded Seeley that if Mayor was telling the truth, the composer died thinking that Seeley had betrayed him. He tried to convince himself that this was not the same as Jun Wei. Unlike Jun, when Reynoso disappeared he had gone after him. Why then did the chorus chattering inside Seeley's head insist that he had abandoned Reynoso?

Sunlight filtered through dust motes. The composer's books and record albums were as Seeley found them three days ago, neatly stored on the wooden shelves. At the other end of the room, where the steps led to the roof, the glass-paned door was bolted shut. Outside, the chickens were silent in their coops. The quiet was obscene, Seeley thought, criminal. Where was the wailing? The requiem? The eruption of outrage?

A bone-hard finger tapped at Seeley's shoulder and he spun, heart racing. The bald head was level with Seeley's chest, and when the man stepped back to view the hanging body, he crossed himself rapidly and as quickly averted his eyes. "*Usted no debe estar aquí.*" When Seeley shook his head, the man repeated, louder, "*¡Usted no debe estar aquí!*"

"I don't understand," Seeley said. He pointed to himself. "*No español.*"

The gnome's frightened eyes looked about and his face reddened with determination. "*¡Aquí!*" The man went to the stairs leading to the roof, unbolted the door, and threw it open. "*¡Aquí!*" From the doorway, Seeley watched the man walk, then half run to the apartment at the other side of the roof. The chickens shrieked and flew up in the stacked cages, hurling themselves against the wire mesh. The racket brought Rubén to his door, and Seeley went out to meet him.

It is odd what you notice at such moments, Seeley thought. The pig was no longer by the wall, and suspended from the ring to which the animal had been leashed was an open burlap sack filled with chicken feed. The man spoke to Rubén in hurried Spanish, the poet watching Seeley over the man's shoulder as he listened. The two Cubans turned and walked together to Reynoso's apartment. Rubén cupped both hands around his eyes to peer in. They talked and, after a minute, the short man went back down the stairs into the apartment.

Rubén returned to where Seeley waited. His face was stricken and a tremor warped his voice. "Already, people are there. Not the CDR man, but he's coming, I'm sure." He placed his hand at the small of Seeley's back and prodded him through the doorway into his own apartment, and then to a small room that looked out on the roof. "I don't know if this is political, but if they find an American in Héctor's apartment, they will make this *político*. The security police will come. You will be safe here."

Across the roof, Seeley could make out figures moving in Reynoso's apartment. Rubén was not a stupid man. He knew as well as Seeley did that when the police came Seeley would be no safer in his apartment than in Reynoso's. This was the first place the police would search. But Seeley had to know who was last with Reynoso.

Seeley said, "What do you mean it may be political?"

"Before he went away, Héctor told Gisela he was afraid the government was going to cancel his tour. I think maybe they did cancel it, and that destroyed Héctor's will to live. So . . ." He lifted his hands chest-high, palms up.

"You can't believe he killed himself. He's wasn't someone who would do that."

"You met Héctor, what, once? What do you know about him? That tour was his dream. It was his whole life. Gisela is too patient. Night after night, she listened to his great plans, and even after she left, you could hear him, into the early hours of the morning, playing his guitar, trying to bring this fantasy of his to life."

The callused fingertips, Seeley thought. Reynoso told him that he had stopped performing, not that he no longer played. "He didn't kill himself."

"Then you tell me, how did he die? You think the government set this up so he couldn't travel to America?" The formerly silent husband paced back and forth across the room, fabricating lies, but why? "The government doesn't work that way. It would simply revoke his exit permit."

"He hired me to get his music back," Seeley said. "His friends' music, too. I don't know anything about this tour, but I know how much he wanted the music. No man with a passion like that kills himself."

Rubén hovered in the doorway, blocking his exit. Then Seeley understood. In this building, on this block, Rubén was the CDR man. It was Rubén who told Minint about his earlier visit to Reynoso's apartment. Surely Gisela hadn't told them, and there was no one else.

A cell phone rang. Rubén fumbled the phone from the back pocket of his jeans and, as he did, a slender black cylinder fell out and clattered onto the floor. A six-inch blade sprang from it.

Confusion momentarily stopped them both, Rubén deciding whether to answer the phone or to pick up the knife; Seeley wondering why a poet would carry a switchblade. "Raúl," Rubén said, darkening in embarrassment.

Seeley's first, improbable, thought was that the president of Cuba was on the phone, then he remembered that a decree from Fidel's brother had made it possible for Cubans to buy cell phones. It would take a poet and taxi driver some time to save the hard currency to purchase one, unless the phone was a gift from his government.

Rubén flipped open the cell phone, but his eyes darted between Seeley and the floor, choosing between lifting the phone to his ear and retrieving his knife.

The PNR would be in Reynoso's apartment by now, and the security police would be here next.

In a single, lunging movement Seeley swept the cell phone from Rubén's hand and, in the same uninterrupted arc, let it fly across the room so that it crashed through the window, landing in a far corner of the roof. Torn between going after the phone or the knife and trying to stop Seeley from leaving, Rubén shot him a frantic look. In that brief interval Seeley was out the door.

Another door was at the end of the corridor and beyond that a treacherous plunge of stairs that Seeley took two, three at a time. Lightbulbs were out or missing, and Seeley tripped and stumbled, twice sliding a half flight down. Music and the odors of cooking leaked into the passage. Once again, the quiet and banality of daily life seemed monstrous. Paint peeled off the walls in sheets. At the bottom of the stairs a wooden door blocked his way. Seeley rammed through it, destroying the latch, and coming out into a dirt courtyard.

Other than a few chickens pecking at weeds, the courtyard was empty. Across the barren, littered space, a narrow archway opened out to the sidewalk. The street was as quiet as when Seeley had arrived. He gave himself some seconds to catch his breath. Rubén had recovered his cell phone by now. There were no flashing police lights, but that would quickly change. Seeley went through the arch to where men lounged in doorways and others played at their eternal game of dominoes. From there he went into the street in search of a taxi.

13

The policeman's baton aimed at the taxi and waved it to the curb.

Seeley had seen no sign that Piñeiro's men were following him, but his first thought was that the police had somehow tracked him from Reynoso's apartment to the U.S. Interests building, a half hour and miles away. "Keep driving," he said.

The taxi driver turned and shook his head. "He wants your passport. Do you have one? Everyone must show a passport at U.S. Int."

Seeley paid and got out. Stout bollards ringed the massive building, and behind them, a ten-foot fence of iron spikes rose from a low concrete barrier. When Seeley handed his passport and visa to the policeman, the man gave back the visa without looking at it, but browsed through the passport as if it were a magazine. At the identification page, the officer's eyes went from the photograph to Seeley and back several times. This was more than a screening for locals who wanted to leave the country. Seeley remembered giving his business card to Gisela at their first meeting, which meant that Rubén, too, knew his name.

The policeman fidgeted with the radio on his belt, adjusted his beret, and returned the passport to Seeley. "Over there." He pointed his baton in the direction of the glassed-in kiosk guarding the American building.

Behind the smoked glass, the guard was no more than a shadow.

Seeley bent to speak into the louvered metal disk. "My name is Michael Seeley. I'm here to see Lynn Metcalf." The soldier leafed through a binder, and when he ran a finger down the page Seeley thought of the lobby guard at Evernham's doing the same. The guard's voice was as distant and disembodied as the clerk's in a subway token booth. "You're not on the visitor list." Seeley detected a trace of the deep south in the hollows of the man's voice.

"Just call him, and tell him I'm here." The shadow shook its head and Seeley dug in his pocket for Metcalf's card. Leaning into the window again, he said, "I met Mr. Metcalf at a party at the Chinese cultural attaché's." He didn't know if China had an attaché in Cuba, but the guard wouldn't know either. He added a dollop of southern syrup to his voice. "Mr. Metcalf told me I should come here if I ever needed him."

The empty voice said, "You will have to step away from the facility, sir."

Finally Seeley found Metcalf's card and slid it through the slot at the bottom of the window. The guard pushed it back without looking. "You may have met him, sir, but he didn't put your name on the list."

"Probably," Seeley said, cutting back on the syrup, "that's because he didn't know that someone would steal my wallet. I had to borrow money from a tourist to get a taxi here."

"I'm sorry, sir, but—"

"Well then, maybe you can tell me what an American citizen who has had his money and credit cards stolen, who doesn't have the fare for a taxi back to his hotel, what he's supposed to do?"

"Look," the guard said, "I'd really like to help you—"

At that note of hesitation in the guard's voice, Seeley slid his passport through the slot, but the guard pushed it back. "All I'm asking is for you to call Mr. Metcalf and give him my name. No one's going to court-martial you for doing that."

A second, then another passed before the shadow of a hand reached for the telephone receiver and the voice said, "Wait over there, sir, away from the facility."

The policeman with the baton was occupied with another visitor. His detention of Seeley had been no more than a routine screening, after all, but Seeley still felt exposed, at risk, and minutes later the sight of Metcalf lumbering down the gravel path from the building to the rear door of the kiosk was a relief. Metcalf showed the guard his identification, signed a form and gestured for Seeley to slip his passport through the window slot. This time the guard didn't return the passport, but buzzed him through the iron gate. A second guard in the lobby unlocked the double door. When they were a distance from the guard, Metcalf said, "You weren't really robbed, were you?"

"Héctor Reynoso is dead."

Metcalf touched Seeley's elbow. "Let's wait until we're in my office."

An elevator took them to the fifth floor. Behind floor to ceiling glass, ranks of workers, mostly Cuban women, sat at computer screens in a fluorescent-lit room. The glass walls stopped at Metcalf's office. Inside, the desk, chair, and file cabinet were government-issue gray steel, and there was a sagging couch upholstered in orange vinyl. Metcalf closed the door and took the chair. Seeley glanced at the couch and decided to stand.

"I told you not to come here."

"You didn't hear me," Seeley said. "Reynoso is dead."

"You don't know that. Just because he didn't show up for your meeting at the cemetery doesn't mean he's dead."

So Metcalf knew about the switch. Seeley's annoyance at the guard in the kiosk had only been a pilot light. Now it flickered into rage. "I found Reynoso hanging from a pipe in his apartment. Someone tried to make it look like a suicide."

"Oh." Metcalf ran a thumb across his upper lip, as if smoothing a mustache. The Christmas caroler's face showed no emotion. "Did anyone see you?"

Seeley felt an angry twinge in his shoulder, as if it were only an instant ago that he turned Rubén's cell phone into a shattering missile. "That's it? *Oh?* Of course people saw me. He had neighbors. Friends."

"But no police? Good. You're still free to talk to the composers. You can get the forms signed." Metcalf caressed the invisible mustache. "I know, it's unfortunate, but sometimes these things happen."

Seeley leaned over the desk and, grabbing Metcalf by the shirt with both hands, pulled him from his chair. "I need to know who had a reason to kill Reynoso."

Metcalf was impassive, a dead weight in Seeley's hands. "You don't know that it wasn't suicide. Maybe he was depressed because we had to cancel his tour."

"That's what his next-door neighbor said, but he's an informer for Minint. What are you?" He let Metcalf drop back into the chair.

"Then maybe it was Minint." The bureaucrat picked a paper clip off the desk and twisted it back and forth. "The security police. They weren't happy about Héctor organizing the tour."

"This wasn't about his going on tour." About this much, Rubén was right. "If it was about the tour they just would have turned Reynoso and the others back at the airport." For the first time he had Metcalf's full attention. "This was about the music. Someone doesn't want these people to get their music back."

Metcalf looked over at the double picture frame on his desk. The wallet-sized photographs were of a blond child of three or four squinting into the camera and a woman in glasses. The pictures were old, or the woman was much younger than Metcalf; the eye-glass frames were jeweled and her hair was a lacquered beehive. "Minint," he said, this time with even less conviction.

"No, not Minint," Seeley said. "What reason would they have?" His rage at Metcalf's coolness over Reynoso's death, the thumb caressing the invisible mustache, still burned. Metcalf knew that it wasn't Minint. Just to rattle him, Seeley said the first thing that occurred to him. "It's the State Department that doesn't want the composers to have their music back." As soon as the words were out, he knew that he was right.

"That's ridiculous! You know that's not true! I've done everything I can to get those forms signed. I came to see you at the hotel. I set up your meeting at the cemetery with Reynoso."

"And sent Mayor instead."

The fingers playing with the paper clip froze. Metcalf said, "You tell me what more I could have done."

"If the State Department really wanted the forms signed, it would have sent you to see the composers. Others. Mayor. But instead, they grounded you and, to get the letters signed, you have to rely on a private citizen who's here illegally and doesn't even know the language."

"You have no idea how much these composers and their families mean to me. If the law says they're entitled to get their music back, then they should get it back."

There was something profoundly wrong here, a fissure hidden beneath the State Department's stone-smooth surface.

"My wife's an artist, you know." Metcalf's voice was jumpy, uneven. "Nothing that would impress someone from New York, of course. Just a medical illustrator. But she's a damn fine artist."

Seeley knew that it wouldn't last, but for the moment he almost liked Metcalf. Outside the window, a squat vessel, like a tugboat, crossed the straits. "Why did the State Department back off from this?"

Metcalf shook his head. "You mean getting the music back from the publishers?"

"You're on your own, aren't you?" Still watching the tug, Seeley said, "This started off as a State Department project but when they dropped it—what was it, two weeks ago? Three?—you kept it going, as if the department was still behind it. When you came to my hotel and told me how much the American government wants to protect artists, you were already freelancing."

Seeley turned and the paper clip in Metcalf's fingers snapped.

"What else could I do? I was detailed here to be liaison for Héctor's American tour. I was already working with him when he told me there was a way for him and his friends to get their music back from the publishers. An American lawyer told him about it."

"Harry Devlin."

"My boss in Washington thought it was a great idea. I told Héctor I'd do anything I could to help him and the others. Find a lawyer for him, make arrangements, talk to the publishers. But he said Devlin already gave him the name of an American lawyer. You, I suppose. And he went off to see you."

"Reynoso is dead because the State Department set him up to get his music back. His friends' music. Then it pulled its support. It left him out there, all by himself."

"No, Héctor is dead because he wouldn't listen to me. He was like you. He had to do this his own way. He thought he was smarter than anyone else. I told him to slow down, but he wouldn't listen. He had to get those forms signed now."

"Because," Seeley said, "he knew that six months from now most of them would be worthless." Seeley strung the events together. Reynoso came to him for help even though, without the composer knowing, the State Department had already withdrawn its support. Hobie maneuvered for Seeley to drop Reynoso, and Ike Butler tried to get him to represent some anonymous companies, one of which Hobie brought in as a firm client. "When your boss pulled you off from this project, did he tell you why the department changed its mind?"

"Washington changes its mind all the time," Metcalf said. "If you want your calls returned, you don't ask why."

"But it didn't matter if they ignored you. You cared about these composers."

"I still do—"

"Did the name Evernham's ever come up? Saddle River Equities?"

"Never." Metcalf removed a blue bandanna handkerchief from

a trouser pocket and used it to wipe his damp fingerprints from the desktop. "How many signed forms do you have?"

Unfeeling as it was, the man's doggedness was impressive. "Two. Mayor and Garcells. I left a form with Faustino Grau's wife. Garcells is showing his to a lawyer."

"You haven't made much progress, have you? I hope you're not billing these people by the hour." Metcalf tucked the handkerchief into a jacket pocket. "I want you to stay here until all the forms are signed. As I told you, we can protect you."

"What do you mean, 'we'? You mean 'you.' What have we been talking about? You're all alone on this."

"What can I give you to stay?"

Seeley said, "I want you to arrange a visa for Amaryll Cruz. My translator." The words surprised him as much as they did Metcalf.

Metcalf started to answer, stopped, then started again. "And if I do, you'll stay and get the rest of the signatures?"

"Not just a visa. I want you to get her out of Cuba. Safely. No rafts, no leaky boats. An air ticket."

"I can get a visa. But we can't get Cubans off the island."

"Of course you can. You got Reynoso in and out, anytime he wanted."

"Only because the Cubans were cooperating."

Seeley gave no thought to details. "I'm sure you'll find a way to get them to cooperate again. Bring me the airline ticket when you bring the visa. Keep the date on the ticket open."

Metcalf said, "Most men come here, they have their little affair with the local beauties, but they go home alone."

Seeley didn't know if his motive was to save Amaryll for himself, or simply to save her, but it wasn't a question he was going to explore with Metcalf.

Metcalf tried on a smile. "This sweetie of yours must be very special in the sack."

"Is that why you stick with your girlfriend over there?" Seeley nodded at the portrait frame on the desk. "Because she's so special in the sack?"

Metcalf flushed. "That's my wife."

"I know that," Seeley said. "But before you made that crack, I was beginning to like you."

"Why is it so important to get her off the island?"

"Because she's in danger."

"From who?"

"From whoever arranged Reynoso's murder. She went to see the composers with me. They're going to think she's involved."

"Not everyone wants to leave this island. How do you know she does?"

Things had changed since the *bombo*. Amaryll had said it herself: *I want to go to America with you.* "She told me."

"A visa will take a week, maybe two."

Reynoso's death changed everything. However thin Metcalf's promise of protection was, Seeley thought that he could finish in two days, three at most, in time to get to his trial in Boston. He said, "You have forty-eight hours to get a visa, an exit permit, and a plane ticket. Otherwise, I'll be on the Air Canada flight out of here on Friday."

"And you'll get the forms signed?"

"I said I would. You can also find out why the State Department changed its mind about helping the composers get their music back."

"Why should that matter?"

"Because whoever made that decision is responsible for Reynoso's murder."

"I'll call a guard to collect your passport and show you out." Metcalf rose. "You're not someone the State Department wants walking around this building on his own."

14

The CDR lady filled a ground-floor window of Amaryll's apartment building, hands clasped, arms resting on the sill, her head moving only to watch Seeley's approach. So absorbed was Seeley with whether Amaryll had betrayed him with the composers that, until this moment, he hadn't considered if she knew that Reynoso was dead. When he came into the courtyard, the CDR lady was already at the door, arms folded across her ample chest. The pose was that of a Russian peasant, and it occurred to Seeley that the country's last sponsor left behind more than graceless architecture. He said, "I am visiting Amaryll Cruz."

"*No es posible.*" The scowl was the familiar expression of smug officialdom everywhere, the suppressed anger of people who know that their authority is entirely borrowed.

Seeley held thumb and index finger an inch apart. "Just for a minute," he said, starting in.

"She has a visitor." The woman's plump finger pointed upstairs, then tapped her wrist where a wristwatch would be, even as her eyes asked Seeley if her English was correct. "*Usted no debe estar aquí.*" The woman drew in a breath, giving her rounded features a beaky aspect. "*Peligroso. Es muy peligroso.* Danger."

"Danger for who?"

There was a movement in the hallway behind her, and a man, almost skeletal in a sleeveless undershirt, came to the woman's side. A machete hung loosely from one hand, and he was covered with dust, as if he had spent the day working with powdered stone. Still watching Seeley, the woman half turned and spoke a few words to the man, who nodded but didn't leave. To Seeley, she had nothing more to say, but remained in the entry, unmoving, until he left.

Across the avenue, Seeley found a doorway in a shuttered storefront outside the line of sight from the CDR lady's window but in direct view of Amaryll's apartment. The dark street teemed with life, and the usual clots of men lingered on corners and in doorways. A bicyclist with a passenger on his handlebars swerved to avoid the domino players at their table, half off, half on the sidewalk. At the intersection, the occasional automobile headlamp lit up the crumbling masonry of the building on the corner. Television chatter streamed out open windows. In Amaryll's apartment, behind the open French windows, a dim light was visible through the curtain.

Seeley stepped into the great symphony of waiting that was Havana's street life, a musical score marked less by expectation than by loss. Héctor Reynoso. Jun Wei. What other lives had he ruined in his headlong drive to . . . to accomplish precisely what? What object justified the wreckage that he caused? Clare, whom he married and then abandoned to nine years of alcohol and overwork, belonged on the list of victims. Who else?

Seeley had not once been unfaithful to Clare, but less than a year after they married an incident occurred that, without his realizing it at the time, wrenched their relationship more deeply than any casual infidelity. He had filed a patent infringement lawsuit in Chicago for a British client, the manufacturer of railroad coupling devices, and at the company's request traveled to its London headquarters to prepare its executives and lawyers for the motions, depositions, and discovery orders that would follow, and to meet with potential expert witnesses. At the end of three days of meetings, Seeley declined an invitation from one of the lawyers for a weekend of golf in the country. He had caddied as a boy, and the experience of carrying two leather bags eighteen holes in 90-degree summer heat ruined any taste he might have had for the game. Instead, he took a train to Swansea to explore the Welsh country-side and visit what he was told was a lively community of artists.

The countryside was breathtaking, the art amateurish, and the days passed quickly and pleasantly, but the train back to London, suffused with the Sunday melancholy of a weekend winding down, was congested, gray, and damp. Seeley left the crowded first-class compartment to see what space there was farther back, but in every car passengers were shoulder to shoulder. Looking into second class, there was barely room to stand.

As Seeley turned from the second-class door, a shard of bright-ness in the scene stopped him. At first he mistook it for a reflec-tion off the glass, a bending of light among the crush of bodies, but when he looked again he saw the girl, seated on the wooden bench that ran the length of the second-class car. Initially, it was the contrast that arrested him, a luminous Renaissance angel set between two heavy, raw men in caps and coarse worker's woolens. The girl's downcast features possessed such a fair, long-lashed beauty that Seeley was unable to move from where he stood. She looked up and, without curiosity or even intention, her eyes locked on his. It was as if she expected him to be there between the cars, waiting for her. After what could have been seconds or hours, the conductor touched his elbow and told him to move along; passengers were not allowed to stand between the cars. Feeling foolish, Seeley left.

Back in his compartment, Seeley told himself that what he had seen was in fact an illusion, a daydream, a trick of light on glass, for when he tried to remember the girl's features he could summon no more than fragmentary impressions—pale skin, an elegant neck, dark hair falling onto rounded shoulders, deep blue eyes—all of it as innocent as grace itself. When the train arrived at Paddington Station, Seeley waited by the side of the first-class car for her to pass, the feeling of loss already growing inside him. But she didn't appear, even after the train had completely emptied and backed out of the terminal.

Seeley had done nothing like this before or since; it was what a boy in the throes of an adolescent crush might do. Each evening of his remaining three days in London, he took a cab to Paddington Station to wander through the main hall and out along the tracks among the arriving and departing passengers. He looked into the cars destined for Wales. The possibility of seeing the girl again was, he knew, meager, but he consoled himself that the chances of finding her in the railroad station were better than they would be at one of the overpriced restaurants to which his client would have taken him for dinner. Nor did the thought stop him that if, against all probability, he encountered her, he would be capable of doing no more than he had on the train. For what did he have to offer? She was only a girl, and he was an American with a client expecting him in the morning and a wife in New York awaiting his return. Should he meet her in the flesh, he would be as dumbstruck as he was the first time. He wanted only to see her once more.

In the years since, if Seeley was in a railroad station, he would at times catch himself looking for the girl. Or it could be in a theater or a restaurant that a pale profile, the angle of a neck, would send a thrill through him, but then a head would turn and he would see his mistake. The girl surfaced in his dreams. Over the years, the image, so indefinite to begin with, grew inconstant. Sometimes her hair was long, other times short; once, even, it was light-colored. Eyes changed color, too. What persisted was the same unshakable gut-grip of loss that consumed him in Paddington Station. He felt it now, watching Amaryll's window.

Silhouettes moved behind the curtain, then disappeared. Seeley thought of the dancer's shadow on the frescoed walls. The light went off and he guessed at a stalker's emotions—exhilaration, humiliation, rage, power—and compared them to his own. He hated himself for being here, in this darkened doorway watching a woman's window, hoping to discover . . . what? I am better than this, he told himself. This is not who I am.

A half hour or more passed before the light went on again, and twenty minutes later a figure came out from the courtyard. The domino players turned, then went back to their game. For a breath-catching instant, even in the dark, Seeley was certain that he recognized the figure, but he felt the man's presence as a physical, not a visual sensation. When the man brought the lighter to his cigarette, Seeley's heart contracted into a fist. The lieutenant stopped at the domino table and said a few words, producing barks of laughter, before continuing on to where a black Renault was parked.

Seeley waited for the Renault to leave. The window of the ground-floor apartment was empty, and he crossed the street to the courtyard, moving quickly so that the CDR lady, if she was still about, would have no chance to intercept him. He took the stairs two, three at a time. Half-open doors exhaled the residues of the night's cooking. Amaryll's door was closed, and when it opened to his second knock, Seeley thought that he had come to the wrong apartment. The woman at the door was a stranger. Against the faint incandescent light, Amaryll seemed inches shorter, as thin and fragile as she felt to him when they danced, the vein at her temple a vague blue outline.

She drew herself up, and the prison gate behind her eyes slammed shut. "Do you know about Héctor?"

"I was there," Seeley said. "I found him."

"This is terrible . . . a terrible thing."

"The lieutenant told you."

Amaryll shot him a fierce look and leaned out to survey the hall, bending deeply and unsteadily, as if in pain, but when Seeley moved to catch her, she instantly drew back. She studied him for a long moment, then stepped aside to let him in and briskly shut the door. "Why are you here?"

The apartment was a hothouse. She had shut the French windows, and the dim light was from a single bare bulb hanging from the ceiling. Neither the scent of lavender from the extinguished candle nor the smell of the lieutenant's cigarettes could mask the venereal reek of sex that filled the room. At the sight of the sheets crumpled at the edge of the bed, Seeley braced himself for anger, but a feeling of sadness welled up instead. He had visited homicide scenes soaked with blood, the walls still pulsing with violence, but he had never stepped into a room thicker with emotion than this one.

Amaryll rested a hand on the back of the chair that had been Seeley's at dinner and, glancing down, looked surprised to discover that the other hand was holding a knife. She put it on the table, her fingernails streaming red, and Seeley's first thought was that she had slashed a wrist. He would not have expected a vanity like nail polish from her. That was the sort of demand someone like Piñeiro would make.

She said, "I asked why you are here."

"What claim does the lieutenant have on you?"

"I will not be questioned! What claim do you have on me?"

"Why do you sleep with him?"

"You have no right to ask that!" Her eyes were liquid with anger. "Is this what you do in America? Spy on women? Watch at their windows?" Her breathing was uneven, choked with fury. "For what? So that you can save them? Save them from what?" The storm was easing; her breathing slowed. "I think that maybe they need to be saved from you."

"You lied when we went to the composers." There was a moral equation here. If Amaryll could sleep with the lieutenant, she could also betray him. "You said you were translating for me, but you told them not to sign. You told them there wouldn't be any money. You said they would get in trouble with the security police. That's why you agreed to take me around. To lie. One of Metcalf's translators would have told them the truth. Nilda would have told the truth."

Amaryll ran her index finger along the knife's edge. "And now you are going to tell me why I would do that."

"It was just another service you provide for the lieutenant."

Seeley expected another outburst, but Amaryll's voice was a whisper. Scarlet nails rested on the knife. "Who told you this?"

"Justo Mayor. He came to meet me at the cemetery, not Reynoso." The switch didn't seem to surprise Amaryll any more than it had Metcalf. Seeley said, "The lieutenant told you about Mayor at the cemetery."

Amaryll exploded. "You are wrong about me. Do you think that all I do is talk about you and your affairs? That everything is about you?" She played with the knife blade, testing it with the flat of her thumb. The finger hesitated. "If that is what you want to believe, I won't stop you."

"What should I believe?"

Amaryll shook her head. "You understand nothing about life in this country."

Seeley didn't see the hand move, but he felt the knife's edge under his jaw.

"Do you want to know what it is like to live here?" Her voice was again a whisper. "This is what it is like. A knife always at your throat. This is how every one of the composers lives. Even Garcells, but he won't admit it."

"And you lied to them because you thought that signing the forms would put them in danger."

"What I thought doesn't matter. It is the position you put them in."

"The ones who signed knew what the risk was." Whatever Garcells knew, greed had overcome his misgivings. Seeley thought of the back-and-forth between Mayor and his wife. "They were completely informed."

"Did they know that someone was going to assassinate Héctor?"

Until now, the word in Seeley's thoughts was *murder*, not *assassination*, but finally here was something on which he and Amaryll could agree. "No," he said, "they didn't know."

"Of course they didn't!"

Seeley felt a prick like a needle, then the pressure of the knife's long edge. He imagined blood leaking onto the deadly fingertips. "And that's why you sleep with the lieutenant. So the knife doesn't cut." He could easily disarm her, but he lacked the will to do so.

"You know nothing about what it is like, always to be a victim, to starve so that the fat white men in the palace can eat. Does Raúl look to you like he's missed a meal in the last fifty years? Any of the other old white men around him? Look at Linares Codina. You work at a *negocio* to get enough food for yourself and medicine for your grandchildren, but if you don't pay half your earnings for a license, they arrest you and you pay a fine. And if you complain? Prison. Fidel talks for hours, but if someone speaks a single word of complaint? Prison. Especially if you are dark-skinned."

"You won the lottery. All you had to do was leave."

"*Ay! Ay! Ay!*" She waved the knife at him. "Do you know how much I hate this island? There is not a minute in the day that one side of me doesn't burn to escape. But the other side of me fights to stay. Both at the same time. You have no idea what it is like."

Seeley nodded in the direction of the bed. "What does the lieutenant have over you?"

"Over?"

"Some kind of power."

Amaryll looked at him curiously. "You cannot fix this. I made a mistake yesterday, letting you stay." She rose. "Now you must go."

Seeley said, "You didn't tell me why you lied to the composers."

Amaryll rose and walked to the door. "You would not believe me if I did."

Try me, Seeley wanted to say, but in this city of lies, large and small, he didn't trust himself to recognize the truth.

15

The chrome on the Cadillac convertible parked in front of Garcells's villa sparkled in the early-morning sun and the tucks and seams of the red leather upholstery glistened. The musician answered the door in bare feet. Today's silk V-neck was pale cream and matched the car outside.

"Did you show the forms to your lawyer?"

"Not yet," Garcells said. "Why?"

"Reynoso's dead—"

"I know. My agent called."

"Did your agent tell you that he was murdered?" Seeley hadn't yet grown comfortable with Amaryll's word, *assassinated*.

Garcells led Seeley into the brutally air-conditioned living room. The furnishings, all whites and beiges, leather and metal, could have come from a spread in a glossy shelter magazine. Plate glass looked out on a Japanese garden that was twice the size of Reynoso's entire apartment.

"Does that change things for you about signing the form?"

"Why should Héctor's being dead make a difference?"

"I think he was killed to stop him from getting his music back."

"Or to stop him from going on tour." Garcells had gone to a small antique desk, the only piece of furniture in the room with any character, and from a drawer took the papers Seeley left with him.

"If I file that form," Seeley said, "I think you're going to be at risk."

Garcells took the papers to a couch and made an elaborate show of lighting his cigarette with a tiny gold lighter.

Seeley ignored the nod in the direction of the couch opposite, and remained standing.

"You mean I should be afraid, like the old guys you talked to?" His laugh was harsh. "There's nothing Minint can take from me. I don't have a pension." He put the papers on the coffee table in front of him, and when he threw his arms across the back of the couch, the gold bracelets jangled. "With all the money I bring back to this island, they're not going to kill, what do you call it—the golden goose."

The musician pulled on his cigarette and, concentrating, let wobbly smoke rings escape through pursed lips. "It's the same as in Yuma. They can't touch a celebrity. Maybe a little slap on the hand if I do something that really pisses off some official. But the government knows better than to try to hassle me. The fans won't let them."

Seeley wondered if the reason for the performer's nonchalance, a reason Garcells himself wouldn't mention, was that he was white and the others black. He knew that he shouldn't let his dislike for the man influence him, but he also knew that arguing with Garcells would be a wasted effort. He handed him a pen. "We need someone to witness your signature."

"Nico!"

In seconds, a slim boy in a white cotton jacket and an unknotted black bow tie came into the room. Garcells said a few words in Spanish and nodded in Seeley's direction. Nimbly moving his fingers, the musician manipulated Seeley's pen so that it jumped from one side of his hand to the other, then back, as the boy watched. Pink rabbit eyes studied Seeley from under white eyelashes. "Does our visitor look like a frightened man, Nico? He thinks I shouldn't sign these papers to get back Grandpa's music. What do you think?"

Seeley didn't like people who showed off in front of the help. He forced a smile and looked in the boy's direction. "Does he let you drive the Cadillac?"

Garcells said, "Maybe I should get my Cuban lawyer to do this for me."

"It's your money. Or your grandfather's. Do what you want."

Garcells righted the pen and signed at the bottom of the papers. He handed the pen and pages to the boy, pink fingers brushing against thin brown ones, and Seeley showed the boy where to sign. The signatures he dated himself.

Garcells rose. "Am I all done?"

"Finished," Seeley said.

"Where were you? Why didn't you answer my telephone calls?" The questions started as soon as Faustino Grau opened the door, even before Seeley could get out his name. "All week I have been waiting. No, longer. First you come after Faustino like mosquitoes, *buzz, buzz, buzz,* you never stop. Then, not a word. You will not even pick up the telephone." The breathless complaint carried them through the hallway and into the living room with the framed gold records on the wall. "I have forgotten my manners. Would you like something to drink? *¡Limonada?*" Grau stopped long enough for Seeley to remember the oversweetened lemonade from his last visit and say no.

A small man, almost elfin, Grau made his way around the chairs, stroking the sateen here, touching the mahogany there, as deliberately as if he were deciding which one he might purchase. Thick drapes muffled the din of traffic outside. Grau was fastidiously turned out: a paisley silk cravat tucked into a sweater-shirt that looked like cashmere; velvety dark-green corduroys that broke elegantly at the cuff over tasseled loafers. When finally the composer selected an oversized wing chair, his feet barely touched the floor. He gestured for Seeley to take the chair across from him.

"From the beginning, your people at U.S. Int."—Grau pro-

nounced it *Youzint*—"would not leave me alone, so I say, yes, Faustino will do what you ask, even though for me the money is small." For emphasis, tiny, fine-boned fingers pinched together like a bird feeding its young. "Then Héctor disappears, and now no one will pick up the telephone so that I can say, 'Take me off your list. Faustino Grau does not want to disappear like Héctor Reynoso.' So now you are here and I tell you: take me off your list!"

"Reynoso's dead."

"Yes, of course I know that. Héctor was *impulsivo*. That is why you must take my name from the list."

In a city with an overtaxed telephone system, word of Reynoso's death had spread rapidly. "Did you talk to Lynn Metcalf?"

"Who? Is she in the cultural attaché's office? All of the people who came to see me were men. They climbed over themselves like monkeys to get Faustino to join the tour. A week later, they don't know who Faustino Grau is. But no one named Metcalf. I would remember."

"This is about Reynoso's American tour?"

"Of course it is. Why else do you think Héctor is dead?" Even as the headlong rush of words slowed, the tips of the tiny shoes danced on the hardwood floor. "Are you telling me U.S. Int. doesn't know this?"

Seeley said, "I don't work for U.S. Int."

The feet went still. "How can you come here, come into my home, and fail to tell me you are not with U.S. Int.?"

"I was thinking the same thing myself." Repeated blasts of an automobile horn filtered through the drapes, and Seeley wondered if it was the taxi driver he'd instructed to wait. "I left some forms with your wife on Monday."

"Ah, yes." The toes got to work on the floor again. "Those papers to get my music back. You want me to sign them."

"When I left the papers, I didn't know about Reynoso."

"And you think his death has something to do with these papers? Of course not! His trouble was with the tour."

Why were these people—first Garcells, now Grau—making it

so hard for him to protect them from their own greed? Seeley caught himself. What did he really know about cause and effect in Cuba? Maybe they were right, that it was the tour that had condemned Reynoso and not his effort to get the music back. But he needed more facts.

"Tell me," Grau said, "when I get my music back, will I be able to sell it again?"

"You can even sell it back to your publisher," Seeley said. "This time, they'll pay you what the music is worth. But there's a risk—"

"How much money will I get?"

"I'd only be guessing. I don't know how popular your music is."

"Very popular. More popular than Héctor's music. Everywhere, people love my songs."

"Do you get money now? Royalties?"

Grau rocked back and forth. "EGREM used to send me money. They got dollars from the American publisher and paid me in pesos. It never added up to much. But for many years, I have not seen even a peso. How long must I wait for the money?"

"Two months, three at most."

"And all I must do is sign your papers? Can I do that here in Havana? Sadly, right now it is not possible for me to travel to New York. So you will tell me what I must do."

"First, I want to know why you think Reynoso's tour got him killed."

"And you will tell your friends at U.S. Int.—you have friends, there, yes?—you will tell them to remove my name from the list?"

Seeley nodded.

Grau relaxed into the chair, his feet now dangling like a marionette's. "What do you know about this music? Mine, Héctor's, the others'?"

"I've heard it," Seeley said, although the word *music* was too earthbound for a sinuous, melancholy line drawn by a cellist's bow through the dark treetops of an African jungle. The night at Amaryll's felt like it belonged to another lifetime.

"That is all you can say? 'I've heard it'? You think I am speaking of Buena Vista. Tourist music. No, I am speaking of music that is older than Cuba itself. The music that the slaves brought here from Africa. Of course, we have employed our talents to keep the music authentic, so if you perform my music or Héctor's for a Cuban he will hear only a single sound: Africa. He will hear the voices of the jungle and the plains, the pain of the slaves on the ships that brought them here, the pain that their great-grandchildren still suffer. That is why you can go everywhere, but you will not hear this music performed on the island. In homes, maybe, or in a small club in the early hours. At a funeral for one of the old composers. This is why Héctor is dead and another one of us, a foolish man, is in prison. For wanting to perform this music in public."

"You mean Maceo Núñez?" The one name on Reynoso's list without an address.

"You know Maceo?"

"Why should performing the music be a problem?"

"Only a Cuban would understand."

That had been Reynoso's answer in his office, and if Seeley had only pressed him for its meaning he might have saved others as well as himself from a good deal of trouble. "That's not good enough. You have to tell me why."

"Ask your friends at U.S. Int. I am sure they are thinking of little else today."

"No, I want you to tell me. If I'm going to stick my neck out getting signatures and filing these forms so all of you can get your music back, I want to know that this wasn't why Reynoso got murdered."

"You are in no danger," Grau said. "The two things are completely different."

"Tell me how."

Grau studied him silently. "Do you promise you will get my music back for me? Get me my royalties?"

"So long as what you tell me makes sense."

Grau gripped the arms of the wing chair as if he were in a plane taking off. "Race," he said. "At the very bottom, this is not about music. It is about race."

When Seeley didn't respond, Grau said, "Race is the single fact that will destroy the revolution. Every day we are told that the Americans are plotting the counterrevolution, but that is the lie our leaders tell in order to survive. No, it is race that will destroy the ruling class, and they know it." His look turned dark. "Ask yourself, who has political power in Cuba? How many blacks do you see running the government? You Americans look at Cuba and what do you see? A communist tyrant. But a black Cuban looks at the ministry offices in the Plaza de la Revolución and what does he see? One white oppressor after another. Batista, at least, was a *mulato*."

Seeley remembered Nilda pinching her dark forearm and reporting that the conflict in Justo Mayor's household was between a black man and his white wife. Only a white man, Grau, could be telling him this. "Why should that be a reason to stop the tour? People in America hear these songs every day."

"Of course they do, but they only hear watered-down arrangements, elevator music, and by who—Puerto Rican groups, Mexicans. Is this *la cultura*? No, Minint worries that if Héctor and the others—me—if we perform this music in Yuma, it will not be popular tunes that your countrymen hear. They are going to hear the original Afro-Cuban music. *Son. Nueva trova*. Minint is afraid that the tour will light a fire. And today, with television, the Internet, that fire will travel like a hurricane, even to a backward island like this one. How long have you been here?"

"Not long."

"Have you watched the life on the streets? The men waiting on corners? Did you notice their color? The government will tell you that only a third of the island's population is black, but everyone knows that it is much more. So many whites went to Miami that the blacks now outnumber us. Sixty percent, maybe seventy.

On the street corners, what do you think these men are waiting for? Work? I promise you not. There is no work. They are waiting for the spark that will light the fire."

And, Seeley thought, if Minint feared that Reynoso was organizing his friends to protest the cancellation of the tour, then Piñeiro suspected that Seeley had come to Havana to help him, to win a propaganda victory for America. And if the protest should lead to something more violent, who in the State Department would complain? But if this were so, why hadn't the security police put him on a plane out of Cuba, just as they abducted Reynoso on a plane coming in?

"If your government was so concerned, why did it let the plans for the tour get this far?"

"Money," Grau said. "What else? Foreign royalties. American CDs. Cable. Except for the tourists it brought in, Buena Vista never made a peso for the government."

"What changed?"

"You really don't know?" Grau was incredulous, and once again Seeley felt that he was shrinking.

"Your president. You elected a black man president. When this music is played in America, who do you think is going to light the fire of counterrevolution? I don't mean your president will himself put a match to the gasoline, but if Cuba's greatest enemy, a country with as long a history of racism as Cuba itself, if this country can elect as its leader a man whose ancestors came from Africa, what does that tell blacks here about their own dream of racial justice? That is why Minint will not let this music travel. Minint is afraid of the hope that it will raise in people's hearts. Minint is afraid of the revolution inside the revolution."

What was it Amaryll said?—*This is music that makes people dream.* For the first time since arriving in Havana, Seeley's hopes for the composers lifted. When he attacked the Cuban expropriations in federal court, any judge who cared about free speech would strip the music from the Cuban government and return it to the composers, just as the courts had given their works back to Felix Silver's Russian writers.

Now Seeley understood why Reynoso was so fearful coming into his office that morning. The composer had risked everything. "Reynoso wanted his music back so that no one but the people who created it could control its performance."

Grau slid forward so that the soles of his shoes rested flat on the floor. "I don't care about Héctor's reasons. All I need to know are my own." He rose, walked to the hallway, and called to his wife to bring the papers Seeley had left with her. While they waited, Seeley said, "Will you come with me to see the others? Explain to them why it's safe for them to sign."

"I am a busy man," Grau said. "I don't have the time."

"Then just a phone call. How long could it take?"

Grau's wife came into the room and, when she saw Seeley, smiled. "It is good to see you again. I told Faustino you would come back, that the American State Department would not forget him."

Grau answered the question still hanging between him and Seeley. "No visits. No telephone calls. I already told you, you do not understand Cuba." A thought stopped him. "This Lynn Metcalf you asked me about. Is she at U.S. Int.?"

"Yes. But she's a he."

"Do you know him?"

Seeley nodded.

"You must tell him to take my name off the tour." Taking a book from the table next to him to use as a surface, the composer signed both documents. He rose and handed the papers back to Seeley, who gave them to Grau's wife to sign as a witness.

"As you can see," Grau said, his gesture taking in the elegantly furnished room, the gold records, the wife. "I am not Héctor Reynoso. I have a great deal to lose."

16

Seeley had asked the taxi driver to wait, but the car was gone and in its place at the curb of the broad boulevard, its engine running, was an American station wagon, dark green with faux wood panels on the side, impeccably restored from the 1950s. Seeley looked into the vehicle, but the two men in the front were too engaged in conversation to notice him. He walked to the busy intersection where there might be a taxi stand. Off the boulevard, business bustled at open-air storefronts. *Mulatos* and *mulatas* were here and there on the crowded sidewalk, but most of the flesh that thronged past Seeley was dark brown, even black. He could have been in a marketplace in Lagos or Nairobi, Grau's revolution slumbering restlessly inside the revolution. When he turned right at the cross street, Seeley saw that the station wagon had moved forward two or three car lengths.

From nowhere, the flat of a hand shoved Seeley into an open doorway, and, before he could recover, a second thick body joined the first. The two men hustled him farther into the dim hallway, next to a reeking staircase, and an iron grip jackknifed Seeley's wrist upward, sending a bolt of fire through his shoulder. While the first man levered Seeley's arm, the other emptied his jacket pockets and sorted through the contents. Seeley's useless cell phone detained the man briefly; after exchanging looks with his partner, he jammed it into his back pocket. Wallet, passport, and visa he gave back to Seeley, but he added Garcells's and Grau's forms to the ones still unsigned and tapped them on a thigh to square their edges. Next, with the care of an industrious clerk, he tore the forms first into lengthwise strips, and then crosswise, until they were confetti on the hallway floor.

One man pulling Seeley by the elbow, the other by his pinioned arm, the two marched him out the door and across the sidewalk to the open panel door of a rusting van and, at a grunted signal, heaved him, resisting furiously, inside. None of the pedestrians stepping off and on the sidewalk around the van appeared to notice.

The van's interior was stripped to the metal and smelled of sweat and old grease. Candy wrappers littered the floor. The man holding Seeley scrambled into the van after him and pulled the door shut, while the other walked around to the driver's seat, climbed behind the wheel, and, grinding gears, rolled the vehicle over the curb and onto the street. Empty beer bottles pitched about, colliding. Blocks passed as Seeley looked for his chance. Seeley's captor breathed heavily. This had been a workout for him, but the man's grip on his wrist was unyielding. He had positioned Seeley in the corner, trapping his other arm between his back and the bench seat. Even if Seeley could work his hand free, there was no means of escape. Where the door handle would be was no more than a protruding knurled stub.

Just to see if he could start something, Seeley said to the one holding him, "Who do you work for? Who sent you?"

Neither man answered.

More storefronts and faded tenements sped by. The van bounced through a pothole, and when the driver half turned and spoke a few words to his partner, Seeley saw his chance in the sudden brown and white animal blur low along the curb. "Look!" Seeley cried. "¡Animales! Look!" Twenty feet ahead, the blur turned into a pack of gaunt, yelping dogs that shot into the street in front of the van.

The vehicle swerved, throwing Seeley's seatmate to the other side of the cabin. In that instant Seeley freed his arm from behind him and thrust himself over the front seat, catching the driver's neck in the crook of his arm and squeezing with all his strength. The grip on his other arm tightened as his seatmate worked to right himself. Using the driver's neck for leverage, Seeley pulled himself further over the seat back, slipping his hand from the driver's throat to clutch at his eyes. The van leaped again, this time pitching the other man against the far window. The concussion must have dazed him, because Seeley's other hand was now free. Keeping one hand over the driver's eyes, Seeley grabbed the steering wheel with his other and aimed at the parked car directly in the van's path. In the next second he saw the two children playing in the back of the car. Fighting the sightless driver for control of the wheel, Seeley hurled his weight into it, swerving the van back toward the street. Car and children disappeared behind him.

The steering wheel, slick with perspiration, slid through Seeley's grip as the blinded driver fought to pry Seeley's fingers loose. Seeley wrenched the man's head back, and there was a short, choking gasp before the man's hands dropped away. Now blind and out of control, the driver forced down the gas pedal, rocketing the van forward. Seeley searched for another immovable object to bring the ride to an end. His seatmate, now recovered, clawed at Seeley's back. A street lamp came into view, but passed. At last, what he was praying for heaved into sight: a gray, overflowing Dumpster the size of a whale. Seeley braced himself against the driver's seat and, straining to steady the wheel, headed directly at the mass of steel.

The collision threw him back onto the floor. When Seeley's vision cleared, the puckered soles of his seatmate's running shoes rested inches from his face. The crash had forced the panel door open, and the man's head and torso hung out of the van like disgorged cargo. Accordioned against the dashboard, the driver groaned, his mouth a bleeding gash.

Seconds later, hands grappled under Seeley's arms, pulled him onto the sidewalk, and steadied him to his feet. In a dazed response from his long-ago football days, Seeley flexed his shoulders, arms, and knees, finding some aches, but nothing broken. He immediately recognized his rescuers as the two men from the green station wagon. Slender and of medium height, in black trousers and white shirts, neither wore a jacket or tie, but the appearance of each, right to the closely trimmed mustache, stamped them from the same mold. When he finally caught his breath, Seeley said, "You work for the lieutenant."

The taller of the two waited for his partner to snap handcuffs on Seeley before answering. "We have been watching you," he said with the same clipped briskness as Piñeiro. "Believe me, this is to protect you."

"From who?"

The station wagon was parked alongside the wrecked van, squarely in the thoroughfare, and the men were as indifferent to Seeley's question as they were to the horn blasts and cries from other drivers. The taller man helped Seeley into the vehicle while the other, the driver, waited for a break in the cars and bicycles navigating around him before putting the vehicle in gear and making a U-turn.

The man beside Seeley said, "The lieutenant thinks you are headed for trouble."

"Nothing I can't handle." The words sounded absurd, even to Seeley.

The officer must have been amused, too, because his smile, unlike Piñeiro's in the hotel room, showed genuine pleasure. "The lieutenant says you are like a toy, a little armored car. Your boss winds you up and you go bumping around, here, there, here, there, knocking on doors, pushing doorbells."

Seeley didn't have to ask who Piñeiro thought his boss was. "Why does he think I do this?"

"Ay, that remains the great mystery for the lieutenant. First, he thinks that he knows what you are doing, and then you do something else, and he must change his mind, and he no longer knows. I can tell you, man to man, this is making him crazy."

Seeley ignored the false familiarity, but heard the truth in it. If Piñeiro thought that he was in Havana to stir up the musicians over the tour, his visits to Mayor and Bustamante had confirmed that. But the visit to a widow like Linares Codina could only have confused the lieutenant. Seeley looked into the rearview mirror, where the silent driver was watching him. This wasn't like Gisela and Rubén on the rooftop, one voluble, the other guarded; this was the police game, the talkative, friendly cop and the quiet one who listened and made notes.

"And what will the lieutenant do?"

"What can he do? He will keep watching until you make another mistake, or until he grows tired."

"Another mistake?"

"Your two friends back there."

"And then?"

His seatmate shrugged pleasantly.

Seeley said, "Who do they work for, the two men?"

"Maybe if you didn't crash their van, we could have followed them and found out."

Seeley heard the implicit reprimand for interrupting their surveillance. "You could have stayed with them."

"The PNR will see to them. Our orders are to keep you away from trouble."

"Where are you taking me now?"

The man turned to the window and didn't speak again until the station wagon pulled into the driveway of the Nacional. The driver came around to open the door, but his partner restrained Seeley, holding on to the links of the handcuffs until the driver could unlock them. "It will save face for you if we remove these before the doorman sees."

At the reception desk, when Seeley asked for his room key,

the clerk's gestures were bright and overwrought; he pointed out the elevators as if Seeley hadn't been using them for days. Either he had seen Piñeiro's men with him or more trouble was coming— probably, Seeley thought, in his room—and to his surprise he missed the company of the two security police.

The room was in shreds. Bedding and linen were in a pile on the floor, clothes had been tossed all about, bureau drawers hung off runners. In the bathroom, Seeley's leather shaving kit was overturned on the shower drain, its contents in the sink. He recognized the stench of sweat and grease hanging in the humid air. This had been the first stop for the men in the van, and Seeley knew what he would find next. His briefcase, kicked under the bed, was empty. Mayor's termination form was missing, as was the remainder of Seeley's supply of blank forms and Elena's draft motion for the Boston trial that he hadn't finished revising. The thugs were thorough, if not discriminating. Also gone was Reynoso's list of composers, which explained how the two men found him in Grau's neighborhood.

Seeley told himself that if he hadn't relied on Amaryll, but accepted Metcalf's offer of a translator, the forms would all have been signed days ago, and none of this would have happened. He would be back in New York and his motion in the trade secret case would be filed as would his complaint against the Cuban government for its expropriation of the music. Once again, he felt that he was missing something, the single thread that connected the day's events. It was as if the city's loathsome heat had clogged his ability to perceive and to reason. He craved the iced glass of gin that would slice through it all like a diamond blade.

17

Unless she was traveling, Daphne was invariably the first lawyer in the office, and when the telephone in Seeley's room rang at 7:00, he knew who it was.

"You need to get back here, Michael. Have you seen all your composers?"

"Almost all." He didn't have the will to tell her how little he had accomplished and, remembering Daphne's fondness for Reynoso's music, instead painted quick sketches of several of the musicians, including Garcells.

"Is that Jorge Garcells's son?"

"Grandson."

"What about Héctor Reynoso?"

Seeley picked over his words, balancing Daphne's feelings against the likelihood that the security police were listening in. "He died."

There was a sharp intake of breath on the other end. "How old was he?"

"I don't know. There aren't many details. This isn't a big town for news." If Daphne thought that Reynoso died of natural causes, that was fine. Seeley just wanted the call to be over. "Maybe I'll know something when I see you."

"That's why I called. You have a client waiting to meet with you."

Seeley said, "Saddle River Equities."

"Why, yes. How did you know?"

"I can't come back yet. I still need to get some forms signed."

"Without Héctor, what reason do you have to stay?"

"I promised to get the others' forms, too." The promise was to Metcalf, not Reynoso, but Daphne didn't need to know that, any more than she needed to know that most, so far, hadn't signed.

"Hobie agreed to hold Saddle River off until you get back. But if you're not here by tomorrow, he's going to ask the executive committee to revisit its decision about letting you work for your Cubans."

"Because now there's a conflict with my Cuban clients."

"As a matter of fact," Daphne said, "there is."

"Since when does a new client conflict out an old one?"

"When the new client's been referred to us by a bank like Evernham's. You know very well we've leapfrogged clients before. We've done it for you. And your Cubans aren't even clients. I looked. There aren't any engagement letters."

"Has Evernham's brought any other clients to the firm?"

"I'm sure there will be others."

"But right now, only Saddle River. Doesn't that tell you something, Daphne? Hobie brought in Saddle River for only one reason: to conflict me out of working for the Cubans."

"That's ridiculous. You have no reason to—"

"Who signed Saddle River's engagement letter?"

"Ike Butler."

"But not whoever runs the company. Don't you want to know who's behind Saddle River?"

"That's Evernham's business. We're a law firm, not a detective agency." There was a thoughtful silence, then Daphne said, "It may be a couple of days before I can get the executive committee together. Ed and Darryl are out of town."

Seeley smiled. The absence of committee members hadn't stopped her from calling a meeting last week. A year ago, when Daphne summoned Seeley to her office to dismiss him from the partnership, he sensed a surprising depth of affection coming from her. She was giving him room to breathe. He heard the tapping of her keyboard.

Daphne said, "Thursday afternoon at four o'clock."

"Meanwhile," Seeley said, "tell Evernham's to find another law firm."

"Saddle River is a high-value client, Michael. Long term, we need clients like that. We also need relationships with banks like Evernham's."

"High value," Seeley said, "but not long term. The only reason Saddle River retained us is to stop me from representing the Cubans. Once I get these forms signed, their work is going to disappear, and there aren't going to be any more clients coming from Evernham's."

Hobie and Butler moved in circles where law, finance, and political power clasp hands in polite exchange, where obligations are acquired and discharged not over days and weeks but generations, and not just in boardrooms and law offices but on the squash courts at St. Paul's. Seeley had no doubt that the sudden appearance of Saddle River was part of such a transaction. For him to ask if this was a favor Evernham's was doing for Hobie, or one that Hobie was doing for the bank, would not even begin to peel away the layers.

Daphne said, "I hope you're planning to be with us for the long term, Michael. That means we need to see you Thursday at three." Seeley thought she was going to hang up, but she said, "And, about Héctor. I'm sorry. I really am."

"Thanks, Daphne. I'm sorry, too."

The address that Metcalf gave him for Reynoso's funeral service was not far from the *farmacia* where Nilda had taken Seeley on his first day in Havana. The echoing, low-ceilinged room was crowded with cafeteria tables, and Seeley's first thought was that he had come to the wrong place and that he would miss Metcalf, who had promised to bring Amaryll's visa and air ticket. Steam tables and stainless-steel counters ran along one side of the room, and behind them women in aprons and shorts dished out food to a shuffling line, mostly of men. Then Seeley saw the rows of folding chairs at the front, arranged as for a service. On one chair, pulled away to face the others, a man picked at a guitar, his head just inches from the soundboard. Seeley recalled how Reynoso tilted an ear when he clapped his hands.

At the tables, Seeley recognized some of the musicians he visited with Amaryll. Most nodded as he passed, although not in a friendly way. Mayor, coming off the food line, was without his seaman's toque today, and the egg-bald head gave him a vulnerable, almost frail appearance. Searching the room for Metcalf, the sight of a familiar face in the foreign setting caused Seeley a moment's confusion. At the table in the farthest corner, watching him, was Harry Devlin. This was Havana's logic: instead of one composer in the cemetery, another; instead of one American at a composer's funeral, a second.

"It's nice to see you, Michael." Devlin reached a welcoming hand across the table. He was going on ninety, but the lawyer's deeply seamed cheeks were pink with health; the youthful blue eyes hadn't lost their cunning and the handshake was like oak. "Surprised?"

"I'm getting used to people I know showing up among the dead."

"Yes, it is too bad about Héctor, but . . ." Devlin narrowed his eyes against the smoke from his cigarette. "This isn't nearly as grand as the Biltmore Ballroom, is it?" The Biltmore in downtown Los Angeles was where Seeley first met Devlin, at a benefit for the Artists Rights Alliance. "The casket's upstairs if you want to pay your respects." Devlin indicated a winding iron staircase diagonally across the room.

"I'll go up later." Seeley didn't want Metcalf to have to look for him.

"You missed the excitement an hour ago. The culture minister came and gave a little eulogy. What a true hero of the revolution Héctor was, how vital a part he was of *la cultura*." Devlin's phrasing had lost none of its music, the Celtic rhythms with which he once seduced juries in courtrooms around the country.

"Reynoso told me he wanted his songs back so that he could stop frozen taco companies from using them in their ads. Then I found out he wrote advertising jingles himself."

"You mean 'Havana Rum'?" Devlin laughed. "I guessed you'd find out. I told Héctor that protecting the music from Madison Avenue was the only way we could be sure you'd take him on as a client."

Seeley resented the easy condescension with which the old lawyer let him know that he had tricked him. "Why didn't you tell me Castro expropriated the music? Even after I get all the forms signed and delivered to the publishers, the Cuban government is still going to own the music."

"I figured if I told you about that, you wouldn't take this on." Devlin must have seen Seeley's rising anger because a practiced look of self-reproach replaced his smile. "All we needed was for you to take the first step—"

"And then you thought I'd be hooked, that I'd challenge the expropriation."

"Isn't that what you're going to do?"

Devlin's sudden seriousness was a warning light. No good could come from telling him that an associate in New York was already drafting a complaint challenging the Cuban government's ownership. "If you really have a conflict that stopped you from working for Reynoso, you know you can't ask me about his legal affairs." It felt good to have Devlin on the defensive. "You didn't tell me what your conflict was."

"I do some work for American interests here." The steel-wool eyebrows shifted in anticipation. "Also, as I told you, I do work for the Cuban government in the U.S."

"Where's the conflict with Reynoso?"

"Suffice to say, Michael, I represent interests adverse to Héctor."

"Adverse enough to kill him?"

Again, the laughter sounded genuine. "I forgot how direct you are. No, just the usual adversity. You'd be amazed how much American business there is in Cuba, even with the embargo. Where do you think Cuba gets most of its grain?"

"What other companies do business here?" Seeley didn't picture Devlin representing an American grain processor.

"This goes way back. American companies have been trading here since the beginning of the revolution. Who do you think kept the Cubans in business before the Russians? Che Guevara was running the Central Bank. Where do you think a dreamer like that raised the cash to keep the country going? From the same men who owned the hotels and casinos in Batista's day."

"I thought Castro shut them down."

"For a month, maybe. They made a big deal about it, but it was mostly show. Angry crowds wrecking the casinos, knocking over slot machines, scooping up the silver. The revolutionaries knew even less about running casinos than they did about banks, so they let the old operators come back and operate them. They didn't kick out the last of them until the Russians came." Devlin stubbed out his cigarette in a flimsy tin ashtray embossed with Camel's humpbacked logo. "This is a fascinating city, isn't it?"

"Endlessly," Seeley said.

Devlin didn't seem to hear. He was thinking about the old days. "Of course, it's far from what it was in the 1950s. Believe it or not, in many ways it's better today." Abruptly, he stared at Seeley, "Just not for an American who doesn't know his way around."

"How mixed up was Reynoso with Americans? Today, not fifty years ago."

"Today or fifty years ago—they seem pretty close for an old fellow like me. People today believe a lot of nonsense about those times. The nightlife. The glamour. Jack Kennedy, when he was a senator, spending a lost afternoon in a suite at the Comodoro with some doped-up cabaret dancers. Sinatra humping showgirls in the Tropicana men's room. All of that was true, of course. Did you know, I was there the night Dizzy Gillespie sat in with Chano Pozo?

"But there was another side to Havana. Extortion. Kidnapping. Girls forced into prostitution. Torture. Shootings as casual as a penny arcade. The American hard guys were like boys on a high-school outing. They did things here they'd never do in the States. And they got away with it because the men who ran things—Meyer Lansky, Phil Gronek, Santo Trafficante—always made sure to split their take with Batista and his crowd. That part hasn't changed." The frosty eyes studied Seeley. "It gets warm here in Havana. Politics and business have a way of melting into each other."

Across the room, a second man pulled a chair from the front row and joined the first, positioning a set of bongo drums between his knees. The drums' shell was a glossy lipstick red, and Amaryll's murderous fingers danced over Seeley's thoughts. Devlin reached for the cigarette package in front of him, and Seeley quickly rested his hand over the lawyer's. He said, "You're telling me that Reynoso's trying to get his music back put him in the middle of business and politics. That's why he's dead."

Devlin had to know that Seeley's hand was there to test his reaction, and his pulse didn't quicken. "You're asking the wrong man. I'm just an American who loves the old Cuban music." He lifted the quart bottle that was on the center of the table, examined it, then put it down. The clear liquid had a faint greenish tint and there was no label. At the Biltmore benefit, where they first met, Seeley had just sworn off alcohol. Devlin had observed him staring at the filled wine goblet in front of him and told Seeley that when he came to an event like this, the first thing he did was turn over his wineglass. That way, he said, the waiter doesn't make a mistake and neither do I.

Devlin shifted in his chair and surveyed the room. There were at least two hundred people, smoking, talking, laughing, and a haze of blue smoke hung below the ceiling. A second guitarist joined the two other musicians at the front, but in the din, Seeley could barely make out the chords. Several tables away, Mayor, his back to Seeley, passed a half-empty bottle to a neighbor.

"Just watch," Devlin said. "Before we leave, those three over there will be an entire band. Trombones, trumpets, congas, timbales, cowbells. Singers. You don't hear the old music like this in Cuba today."

A man approached the table and asked if he could take one of the chairs. The cigar between his lips was as thick as a tree limb. As an afterthought, the man nodded at the unopened bottle of rum. "*¿Me permite?*" A movement behind Seeley momentarily distracted Devlin from the question. "*Claro,*" Devlin said.

Seeley turned to see Metcalf approaching the table, a large envelope in his hand. He exchanged looks with Devlin, but neither spoke. Seeley said, "Do you know each other?"

"Only by reputation," Metcalf said.

"Which is?" Seeley pulled out a chair for Metcalf.

"Statecraft is a professional discipline." Metcalf ignored the chair. "Mr. Devlin is an amateur, but he thinks he can practice it like a professional."

Devlin said, "Would you like me to leave?"

The attitude that filled the space between the two men was taut as a line, and although it seemed to Seeley that Metcalf was the only one pulling on it, with Devlin you could never tell. Seeley said to Metcalf, "Is there anything you don't want him to hear?"

Metcalf handed the envelope to Seeley. "There's everything you asked for."

The envelope was unsealed, and looking in without removing them, Seeley examined the visa and one-way airline ticket to Miami. "What about the third document?" The exit permit was missing.

"They'll be holding it at the airport," Metcalf said. "And you'll stay in Havana until you're done?"

"That was our agreement."

Devlin placed a hand on a chair back to invite Metcalf to sit. "Do you like Cuban music, Mr. Metcalf?"

"I don't get much chance to go to clubs." Metcalf glanced anxiously around the room. It was plain that he didn't like being seen with Devlin. "I need to get back to the office." He gave Seeley a last look before turning and disappearing into the crowd.

Devlin smiled. "Our man in Havana."

Seeley wondered about the hostility between the two men. "Reynoso is in a casket up there because the State Department led him on, then dropped him. Is that your client—the State Department?"

Devlin gave him a pained look. "I have never worked for the United States government in my life, and at my age it's safe to say that I never will."

"But you work for the Cuban government."

"Like you, Michael, I have devoted a good part of my career to leveling the playing field between the world's haves and have-nots."

"And that's why you're here now—to level the playing field?"

"No, I'm here to pay my respects to an old friend." Devlin looked around. "Also, I came to listen to my favorite music. What did I tell you about the band?" Three more men had pulled chairs from a table and were setting up their instruments, a bass and two saxophones. "If you want to pay your respects, you should go upstairs before they take the casket away."

"You know a lot about Cuban funerals."

"These days, funerals are about the extent of my social life."

The circular stairway took Seeley to a room with a ceiling even lower than the one below. Velvet drapes of a deep green entirely covered the four walls, giving the room the feel of a severely compressed stage set. Recessed spotlights illuminated small knots of men, some in military uniforms, others in dark suits. They looked more prosperous than the ragged crowd downstairs and, for some reason, the phrase went through Seeley's mind, *blood on their hands.*

Music floated up from the room below. Under the floral sprays, the pine casket looked cheaply made. Someone had positioned Reynoso's ribboned straw hat over where his head would be, and when Seeley touched the crown, no one noticed. Seeley thought of Gisela's memories of the long nights in Reynoso's apartment, listening to the old music and to his plans for the American tour.

A wreath hung from a wooden tripod next to the casket. The dense arrangement lacked any fragrance, and the note attached with a gold ribbon was no ordinary card but a letter-sized proclamation richly printed on heavy stock, its border also embossed in gold. At the bottom, in lavish strokes from a felt-tip pen, were several indecipherable Spanish words and, beneath them, in the same loose hand, but in script three times larger, *Fidel Castro.* In the signature, the *F*'s circling cap was a sombrero brim, its body a dagger. The cross in the *t* flew out over the *o*, abruptly stopped in a meaningless flourish, then swept down and back to underscore the full name.

There was a movement at the stairway, and Mayor entered with the men from his table downstairs. Seeley started in his direction, but the old musician stopped him with a glare so cold that Seeley instantly understood the lesson that Mayor learned from Reynoso's death: it is not safe to be seen with Americans. Mayor and his companions circled the coffin and Seeley returned down the stairs.

The band had grown to two dozen or more musicians. Two men and a woman faced off against each other, transforming the harmonies into a raucous sexual challenge. To their side, a man and a woman sang, their lips just an inch or two from touching. Seeley recognized the composition at once.

Devlin was at the table where he'd left him. "'Havana Rum,'" Devlin said. "One of Héctor's best songs."

Seeley took the chair across from him, and Devlin said, "You know, when I told Héctor to see you about getting these notices to the publishers, I didn't think you'd come to Havana. If you remember, I warned you not to."

"And I told you that after Reynoso disappeared I had no choice. You didn't give me a single good reason not to come."

"Well, then, I'm sorry I got you mixed up in this."

Was it the music or his own thoughts that had made Devlin remorseful? "Mixed up in what?"

"Whatever deal you made with Metcalf to stay here, you should break it. Metcalf would do the same, you know. Break a promise if it served his interests."

"You don't even know him." It wasn't Metcalf that Seeley was thinking of but Amaryll, and he asked himself if arranging for the visa and exit permit had been a mistake. How could he have fallen in love with someone so faithless?

Devlin said, "If Héctor's dead because he was organizing his friends to get their music back, you're putting yourself in the same position he was in."

"Faustino Grau doesn't think that's the reason."

Devlin shrugged; he didn't care what Grau thought.

"I have it under control," Seeley said.

Devlin nodded to where the bottle of rum had been at the center of the table. "Are you still off the booze?"

"Sure," Seeley said. A single beer to get his edge back didn't count.

"Keep sober. Stay alert."

"Alert for what?"

"I already told you. I'm sorry." A small man, Devlin had shrunk even deeper into himself while Seeley was upstairs. Regret was not part of the man's makeup, but now it defined every aspect of him. The apology seemed directed not to Seeley alone, but to the room. It may have been the angle at which he held his head or the slant of the light, but the lawyer's flesh was translucent, his jaw pure bone, the embodiment of a brittle mortality.

Seeley said, "Your client had something to do with Reynoso's murder."

Devlin's eyes widened and thoughts moved like shadows behind them. "Think about it. Property. Politics. Greed. Fear. But mostly fear. Layer on layer, over and over. It never stops." His eyes widened. "Look," he pointed across the room. "They're bringing the casket down."

Mayor and another man, each with a shoulder under a corner of the coffin, were at the top of the curved staircase. The crowd saw them and fell silent, but the band, which had been playing against the din, lifted its volume so that the music filled the large room. The pallbearers, each with a steadying hand on the casket, made their careful way down the stairs. No men in uniforms or dark suits followed. From below, a man cried, *hoooahh!* A pair of hands shot into the air and clapped, in time not with the music but with the footfalls of the men coming down the stairway. Other hands went up in ovation, *hooahh, hooahh*, so that by the time the pallbearers crossed the room on their way out to the street, everyone in the place was on his feet clapping and hooting, whether for the band, or for the memory of Héctor Reynoso, or for the momentary joy of being alive and well fed.

Devlin took his seat. "The musicians will keep playing," he said. "If the burial were at Cristóbal Colón, they'd go there. But it's in Camaguey, where Héctor's family is, so they're going to stay right here. They could play into the night." And Devlin, it appeared, was going to stay for as long as they did.

There would, Seeley knew, be no further conversation about Reynoso, the notices, or the wellsprings of Devlin's remorse. Seeley realized that he was gripping Metcalf's envelope as if it were a prize wrested from a nightmare.

"God," Devlin said, his eyes now closed. "How I love this music!"

18

Four in the morning is an hour for inventories, mostly of loss. Reynoso. The cold looks from Mayor and the others at the memorial gathering. Daphne was going to retire and Seeley's partners in New York were going to fire him once again. The air conditioner hissed, rattled, and fell silent. On the night table, the envelope with the visa and ticket glowed silver-green in the moonlight. Seeley had gone directly from the memorial gathering to Amaryll's building, but she wasn't there. No, the CDR lady told Seeley, arms locked across the broad peasant chest, he could not go upstairs to wait. *¡No es posible!* Seeley returned to the Nacional. Through the evening and into the night and early morning, he tried every half hour, sometimes every ten minutes, but either her number rang busy or no one picked up. He imagined Amaryll's expression when she opened the envelope and slid out the documents. At 4:30 he gave up calling.

He dozed and awoke before dawn, tried the telephone once more, then showered and went out. A taxi was at the bottom of the Nacional's driveway, and Seeley shook the snoring driver awake. When he arrived at the apartment building at 7:30, the CDR lady wasn't at her window, and the door in the entryway was unlocked. Seeley went up the stairs and down a hallway still thick with last night's cooking smells, but magically silent at this hour. Only after he knocked on the door did it occur to him that Amaryll might not be alone.

After some minutes, the door opened. Amaryll looked behind her, but said nothing and let him in. She was in jeans and a white T-shirt, her hair wild from sleep. Seeley's earlier visits to the apartment had been at night, when the only light was from a flickering candle or a dim, bare bulb. Now, the early light streaming through the open French windows revealed just how bare the room was. Other than a clock, the CD player, and pile of CDs, it could have been an anonymous hotel suite. There were no photographs or pictures or books, not even magazines; none of the ordinary accretions of daily life. The frescoes painted into the plaster only underlined how like an empty box the room was. This was the dwelling of someone who was prepared to leave at any moment.

Seeley handed her the envelope, which he had sealed, and Amaryll used the watermelon knife to slit it open. Her expression as she examined first the visa, and then the air ticket, was slack-jawed, eyes darting, as if she were seeking escape. The blue vein at her temple throbbed. "How did you get this?"

"Someone I know in the State Department. The exit permit is at the airport."

"What did you have to do for this?" There was wonder but no excitement in her voice. The set of her mouth confused Seeley. Was she displeased, or just wary?

"A man there owed me a favor."

A breeze came through the open window, carrying Havana's street sounds—cries, car horns, barking dogs, the ever-present music—and the fragrance of strong morning coffee.

Amaryll went to the window and looked out for a long moment before closing it. She came back and sat at the table, each hand gripping an edge. When finally she looked at Seeley, her eyes were filled with tears.

Without her saying anything, Seeley knew. If he was honest about it, he knew even when he was ordering Metcalf to make the arrangements. "You're not going to leave, are you?"

"It is not possible."

No es posible. That should be the slogan for my time here, See-ley thought. Nothing in this country is possible, for me any more than for the Cubans. "Of course it's possible," he said. "You can get on a plane this afternoon, or tomorrow, or whenever you want."

"You think this is why I slept with you. Because you were my ticket to Yuma." Her voice was hoarse and there was a miserable twist to her mouth.

"You don't believe that any more than I do." Seeley had never seen a face so beautiful turn so utterly wretched. "You told me you wanted to go to America."

"You didn't listen. It was a fantasy, something Nilda would make up." She played with the knife, pressing the flat of the blade against her palm, first one side, then the other. "When I spoke, you heard your dreams, not mine. No matter how much I care for you, it does not mean I will give up everything that is important in my life so that I can be with you."

At four in the morning, Seeley's list was just a catalogue of loss. Now he actually felt the weight of his hopes shear away, like the wall off a building. He trembled at the force of the concussion: his hopes for Reynoso and the other composers; for his law practice; for saving Amaryll or even seeing her again. He wished for the pain of a physical blow to obliterate his feelings. Why should it surprise him yet again that at the far side of whatever he was seeking lay nothing but pain?

Amaryll pressed the knife point into the pad of a fingertip. "You have no idea what it means to live in an occupied country. The Spanish. The Americans. Twenty years later, you can still smell the Russians. An occupier is like a demon that comes into your room at night and steals your soul. The Tourism Ministry turns Habana Vieja into Disneyland, and what do they restore? Colonial buildings! The architecture of our occupiers!"

This was nervous chatter; Amaryll was hiding something. Her eyes asked for his understanding. "Do you know what a curse it is to cut people off from their soul, to see their soul crushed into the dirt?" She put the knife down, "Héctor was wrong to dream of an American tour. Bringing his music to Yuma would be like putting milk into water. *La cultura* cannot exist away from Cuban soil. It is why those of us who can leave here, stay. Héctor, Justo, Faustino. All of us. *La cultura* is all that is left to being Cuban."

Seeley said, "I don't believe you. If *la cultura* was so important to you, you wouldn't have played the *bombo* with Dolores. I think you're afraid to go to America. You painted a perfect world for yourself here"—his gesture took in the frescoes—"and you're afraid that the real world won't be like this, that no one in America will know you."

"I don't care what you believe." The red nails flew at him. "I will not be challenged! This is not one of your stupid trials. This is my life."

Hopelessness rose unbidden inside him, a gray mass separating from the bottom of the sea. Why had living become so hard?

Amaryll's face was inches from his, "You know nothing about me or about Cuba." She held his eyes with hers for what felt like minutes. She was deciding whether and how to tell him something.

Finally she said, "Do you know that they put political prisoners in the same cell as murderers? As rapists? Do you know what the noise is like? Day and night it is like the roar of a great machine. Or the stench? For two hundred men, maybe three hundred, the bathroom is one"—she raised a finger—"one hole in the floor. Or the insects? Flies, lice, mosquitoes, every minute of the day."

"Why are you telling me this?"

"You asked me about Virgilio? My former husband? He is in a prison like this. This is why Nilda wishes to march with Las Damas de Blanco, to protest his imprisonment."

Seeley thought, This was why a girl who skipped so exuberantly should have such a solemn face.

"You would understand Virgilio. He is like you, someone who has no respect for the authorities, someone who, to protect a com-

plete stranger, would attack a lieutenant of the security police on
the street. That is why he is in prison, for the crime of insulting
officials in public. He was a writer for one of our newspapers that
appears and disappears." Her voice turned clinical, almost frigid.
"Did you know, if you are a prisoner who talks back to the guards
there are special penalty cells for you, where they leave you alone
in the dark."

"And Virgilio talks back to the guards."

"What do you think? Isn't that what you would do?"

"And this is why you stay here?" Incredibly, Seeley was jealous
of Virgilio. "What can you possibly do to help him?"

"Some payments cannot be put in an envelope. I think you are
not very smart if you don't know."

As much as Seeley wanted to blame his craving for a drink
on Amaryll's intransigence, her impiety, he knew that the blame
wouldn't stick. In Los Angeles, when he was first trying to stay
sober, Devlin told him the sad truth about his drinking: You don't
need a reason or a cause, Michael. You drink because you're a
drunk.

Seeley said, "How does your husband feel, knowing that you
sleep with the lieutenant to protect him?"

Amaryll winced, as if he had slapped her, then struck back at
him with her open hand.

It could have been a feather. He wished for a blow with pain
behind it.

"Of course Virgilio doesn't know. Piñeiro is only a lieutenant,
but he has the influence to keep Virgilio out of solitary." She
looked at the documents on the table, as if seeing them for the first
time. Pushing the knife aside, she slipped the papers back into the
envelope, and offered it to Seeley. With the other hand, she touched
the back of his wrist. Her fingers, always so remarkably cool, burned.

If Amaryll spoke, Seeley didn't hear the words. "Keep them,"
he said. "I have to leave." In three long strides he was out the door.

Bodies clogged the sidewalk, unmoving, and Seeley pushed his way past them onto the street. The few cars only honked and zig-zagged around him. Where in a neighborhood of strangers and collapsing tenements does a foreigner find alcohol at eight in the morning? Seeley's thoughts skipped ahead to the Nacional, but even if the bar was open at this hour, the thought of a bartender measuring out one thimbleful of gin at a time infuriated him. He didn't need a drink. He needed a quart of gin. Gallons. He dug in a pocket, grabbed a fistful of bills, thrust them to the sky and cried—"Taxi!"—but no car stopped. There was an electric snap of ozone in the heavy air, and from the sidewalk a sound like laughter.

Minutes passed, or hours, before a battered sedan, garish in its rusty orange primer, slowed alongside him. Three women, plump as pigeons, were squeezed into the back, and the driver stuck out his head. Like the car that took Nilda and him to the *farmacia*, this one had a yellow placard on the dashboard announcing it-self as a taxi. "Take me to a liquor store," Seeley said to the man at the wheel. "Gin. Whiskey." The women stared at him through the open window, and it occurred to Seeley that he must look like a madman.

The driver looked at the money in Seeley's hand, but didn't understand.

"Rum," Seeley said, and the women answered, "¡Ron! ¡Ron!" Voices batted back and forth, the women's drowning out the driv-er's objections. Heads wagged. A pair of hands gestured, bringing an imaginary bottle to generous, painted lips.

The driver shook his head. "*Solamente con la libreta.*" The women, as crazed now as Seeley, sang to the driver while pointing out the window, "Manrique y Lagunas." The driver, vanquished, waved Seeley into the passenger seat next to him. The women in the back clucked at their victory.

Seeley's knees pressed against the dashboard and he jammed his right foot to the floor, as if that would speed the car on to Manrique y Lagunas. To himself he whispered the two names—he guessed that they were streets—hummed them to the beat of the taxi's laboring engine, trying to distract himself from his scouring obsession.

"¡Clooney!" one of the women cried, and Seeley grappled at the word's meaning. "¡Clooney!" the woman in the middle said, "¡George!" clapping hands. The other two joined in. "¡Clooney! ¡George!" Then, hands still clapping, it was back to "Manrique y Lagunas."

Finally the taxi pulled to the curb and the women got out, but offered a last chorus of "Manrique y Lagunas" from the sidewalk. Minutes later, Seeley pumping the imaginary gas pedal the entire way, the taxi stopped at a half-curtained storefront with a line of customers snaking out the door.

"Manrique y Lagunas?"

"*Sí*," the driver said.

Seeley was out of the car. "*¿Ron?*" Seeley handed the driver a bill.

"*Sí, ron.*" The driver tapped his palm with a finger. "*Pero, solamente con la libreta.*"

"*Ron?*" Seeley said to a tiny woman at the end of the line. In the early morning heat, she had on a dark sweater over her cotton house dress. The woman studied him, frowned, and raised an empty liter bottle. "*¿Dónde está su botella?*" She held up a tan booklet the size of a small diary. "*¿Dónde está su libreta?*"

Bottles of all colors and sizes hung from dark hands, waiting to be filled; ration books waited, too. Seeley shaded his eyes to look past the line into the storefront. He felt the anxious pulse of nightmares: arriving in court without his papers or at international departures without a passport. He calmed himself. Bottles and ration books were details. Even in a foreign country, he could talk his way around them. Another, more alarming thought crept in. What if, in this country that staggered from one shortage to the next, the rum ran out before he got to the front of the line? He felt in his pocket for more bills and closed his fist around them. "*¡Hola!*" he cried, borrowing Gisela's greeting from the roof. People inside the storefront turned. He waved the bills in the air. "¡*Ron!* ¡*Hola!*" People stared and giggled, but pressed against each other to let him pass.

Two men in T-shirts, white aprons over their jeans, stood on either side of a metal cask the size of a wine barrel. "¡*Ron!*" Seeley held out the bills. The taller man continued with his customer, but the other looked down the line as if he would find there the reason for Seeley's presence. "¿*Tiene usted la libreta?*"

"No ration book," Seeley said. "*Ron.* Money." When Seeley thrust the bills at him, the man turned and whispered to his partner. Both glanced at Seeley and shook their heads. The partner said, "Go to the foreigner's store."

"The foreigner's store? Where? ¿*Dónde?*"

The men shrugged and went on serving their customers. The line edged toward the counter, pushing Seeley to the side. The madness in the taxi, the jostling in the storefront, had been a distraction, but now the craving for alcohol and oblivion returned stronger than before; it absorbed every particle of his consciousness. He went out a second door into the street. Manrique, not Lagunas. A hand tugged at the sleeve of his jacket. The man, thin and dark as coffee, with a narrow weasel's face, cradled a flat, pint-sized bottle in his other hand. Was the bottle tinted green, or was it the liquid inside that filled the bottle to its neck? The man must have seen him in the ration store. "How much?" Seeley said.

"*No, por acá.*" Pulling Seeley by the sleeve, the man led him to a covered arcade, away from the sidewalk traffic. Crimson paint peeled from the columns, revealing raw concrete. There was a barnyard smell about the place. The flat bottle, when the man handed it to Seeley, was cool.

Seeley held out some bills. *No,* the man shook his head. The gray eyes were watery but acute, and they fixed Seeley with a look of such profound compassion that, as with the women in the taxi, Seeley realized how desperate he must appear. He tried to push the bills into a worn and frayed shirt pocket, but the man ducked and darted off, as if they were playing at a game of tag.

The cap was off the bottle in a second and Seeley tilted the neck to his mouth, drawing hard at the opening, engorging the liquid, taking it down in gulps with a violence that sent a racking shudder through him. He was aware neither of taste nor smell, only a damp fire engulfing mouth and throat. He lowered the bottle, screwed on the cap, unscrewed it again. He drank. But where was the numbness? When would it come? He took another long pull from the neck.

Outside the arcade, the street and sidewalks warmed in the morning sun, but Seeley remained inside. He saw nothing but the bottle, and only when the liquid dropped to its last quarter inch did the claw tearing at his insides finally loosen, making way for the familiar, blessed ache. Thank God! The talon, the howling dog retreated. Seeley knew from experience that he could manage the ache that replaced them. He could breathe. He stepped out from the arcade and, legs still shaky from the shock of his own transformation, walked in the direction of the Malecón.

Seeley soon lost awareness of time, and for the next several hours he explored the seawall and the streets that spiderwebbed out from it. At the corner of Neptuno and Padre Varela, tucked between two buildings, he discovered an open-air market, the stalls piled with masses of green, yellow, and red—fruits and vegetables that he didn't recognize, bloody but unfamiliar cuts of meat. In the corner of the market was a tiny refreshment stand with a display of bottled soft drinks on the counter and, on the back shelf, a row of half-pint bottles with the same unmistakable yellow-and-red label that Seeley had seen all over Havana. Beneath the brand HAVANA CLUB, the red sun at the center of the label drew him forward like a magnet. The girl took a bill from the fistful that Seeley held out and gave him some coins in change, but with a stern shake of her head refused to sell him more than one bottle.

Two blocks away, at Neptuno and Lealtad, Seeley came upon

the rubble-filled ruins of a building that seemed more private and secure, and more inviting, than the others that he passed. All that remained of the building was a portico, three fine stone columns in fading shades of blue, and a lintel, still intact. Embedded like a giant fossil in the brickwork of the neighboring apartment house was a collage of plaster, paint, and shreds of flowered wallpaper. When Seeley returned to the refreshment stand and showed the girl the empty bottle, she consented to sell him another, and a routine began. At the bottom of another half-pint, Seeley found himself narrating his progress through the day. FOREIGN VISITOR DISCOVERS ANCIENT RUINS.

For long, meditative intervals, Seeley stopped at the seawall, sipping at the current half-pint of Havana Club, losing himself in the patterns formed by the peacock sheen of marine fuel on the surface of the water. When, on another trip to the market, Seeley found the refreshment stand shuttered, none of the earlier panic returned, only the calm certitude of a native and, in what seemed like no time, he located a hole in the wall—literally it was that, a four-by-four opening in the concrete brick—from which a gray-haired man, who could have been Reynoso come back to life, sold him half-pints of Bucanero rum but, like the girl at the refreshment stand, no more than one bottle each visit, no matter how much money Seeley offered him.

Dusk fell and it occurred to Seeley with alarm that his perspiring body had all this time been sweating alcohol; that he could go on drinking like this forever, the ache filling the hole inside him so long as he continued feeding it, but not bringing him even close to the crest of the wave that would sweep him away. In this heat-drenched, perspiring city, had he once seen a drunk passed out in a doorway or on a park bench?

He blinked and it was night. Reflections of lavender and rusty orange swelled and shrank on the water. A lamp went on in the lighthouse. Inside him, dread beat with heavy wings. He could not get drunk.

His travels from the seawall to the ruins brought him closer to the Nacional, then farther away from the hotel, but the thought of being trapped inside his room sickened him. The moon lit the ruins. Somewhere in his explorations, Seeley had acquired a folding beach chair of pitted aluminum and shreds of plastic webbing, and over the course of the late afternoon he had tucked under the concrete rubble three more half-pints of Bucanero. He reclined in the chair and studied the label on the bottle. At its center was an ornately framed portrait of a gay buccaneer, louche in a wide-brimmed, ostrich-feathered hat. FOREIGN VISITOR INTERVIEWS PI-RATE OF THE CARIBBEAN. He snapped off the foil cap.

FOREIGN VISITOR ATTEMPTS TO DECIPHER PUZZLE. Reynoso could not have entered the United States without help from the State Department. Nor could he have left Cuba without the cooperation of officials here. But whoever had the influence to authorize Reynoso's movements to and from the island lacked the power to keep him alive. Or had someone simply changed his mind about the composer? What did it mean that after Seeley spoke with Metcalf, it was Mayor, not Reynoso, who appeared at the Cementerio de Cristóbal Colón? And what explained Harry Devlin's presence in Havana? Unlike Seeley, Devlin traveled nowhere unless a client was paying his bill. But if that was so, who was Devlin's client?

Seeley sipped at the bottle. Over the course of the day, he found the rum's cloying taste increasingly repellent—licorice and sweet unnameable spices that made him think of nothing so much as Christmas cakes. But to switch would be disloyal and possibly dangerous for, thank God, the rum was at last doing its work. The wave was finally approaching, the ache receding, and a foglike stupor was filling the hole that still gaped inside him. Had anyone ever observed that the neck of a half-pint rum bottle resembles the snubbed barrel of a revolver? FOREIGN VISITOR COURTS OBLIVION.

Seeley's eyes fell shut. In the instant before he slid over the top of the blessed wave, a lineup of sports players appeared before him, each one instantly recognizable: Reynoso, Metcalf, Hobie, Butler, Devlin. Each man held flat against his chest a black-and-white portrait of one of the others. Linking the men and the pictures, like the diagram for a football play, was a kaleidoscope of Os, Xs, and arrows. EX-FOOTBALL PLAYER UNCOVERS MUSIC, MURDER MYSTERY. As quickly as it appeared, the picture dissolved, overtaken at last by Seeley's dreamed-for dreamless sleep.

19

The dog, yellow teeth bared, growled and tugged at Seeley's shoe; the misery that filled its eyes could have been Seeley's own. Hangovers are the same everywhere, and although Seeley never before awoke in an open lot strewn with bricks and chunks of plaster, the sense of irreparable loss was no different from the parched awakenings of so many mornings in his past. Trying to rise from the broken beach chair, jerking back his leg to shake off the dog, his spine exploded in a fireworks of pain. The Doberman's black ears pointed at him like obscene fingers.

"Por favor, su tarjeta de turista."

Over the policeman's shoulder, a violent blue light rotated on the roof of a white sedan. In English, another voice said, "Please, your tourist card. The visa." Like his partner, the policeman was young, in blue pants, gray open-necked shirt and navy beret. The Doberman's leash was wrapped twice around his wrist but, even squinting into the sun, Seeley could see that the man was exaggerating the effort it required to restrain the dog.

A second flashing sedan jumped the curb, scattering the pedestrians at the edge of the ruins, before coming to a stop. More blue-and-gray officers arrived on motorbikes.

Seeley reached into an inside jacket pocket, then the other, but the visa was not where he carried it. His passport was missing, too. The old anxious dream of forgetfulness had followed him into life. The English-speaking officer whispered into the walkie-talkie strapped to an epaulet as he unbuttoned a shirt pocket and lifted out a blue-jacketed passport. He flipped it open to the photograph page and, after studying it for no more than a second or two, returned it to the pocket. He said a few more words into the radio before snapping it off. To Seeley he said, "You will come with us."

Seeley's insides clenched against the sickness rising in him as he struggled up from the beach chair. Had they taken the passport while he was passed out, or had they retrieved it from a thief? When he tried to stand, his legs and feet were numb. The first policeman leaned in and snapped handcuffs on his wrists. Even with the two officers guiding him by his elbows, Seeley repeatedly stumbled and fell on his way to the car. Climbing in, he nicked his head on the sedan's low roof.

The car shot off the sidewalk and onto the street, giving Seeley an instant's view of a gaunt, unshaven stranger reflected in a storefront window, and then of the second car, blue lamp flashing, followed by two motorbikes. There was little room in the back of the car, and Seeley's cuffed hands behind him forced his shoulders forward against the driver's seat. Neither policeman spoke and, from his trip to the hotel with the security police, Seeley knew that it would be useless to ask where they were taking him, or why. Lawyers create authority through words, police through silence.

After several blocks, the driver turned into an alley, bouncing the sedan over ruts and potholes to where other police cars were parked at angles alongside a cinder-block building. The blue-lit car that had followed them gave a high *whoop, whoop* as it sped past, followed by the motorbikes.

Threads of oily carbon rose in the humid air. Policemen loitered outside the building. More were inside in an airless room that, even before the work day began, was filled with the accused. If, as Amaryll had told him, Cuba's official position was that there are no prostitutes on Havana's streets, it was only because, in their short skirts and glittering rainbow tops, they were inside the already-steaming station house. There were old people, too, men and women. Seeley thought of Linares Codina, the candy vendor in her immaculate dirt-floor shack.

There were no chairs or benches, and the English-speaking officer directed Seeley to stand by the door while his partner talked with a man in khaki at a desk across the room. Thirst ate into Seeley's thoughts. His wrists, damp with perspiration, chafed in the handcuffs. To occupy himself, he marked in his mind the locations around Havana of the people whose signatures he needed on the termination forms and plotted the shortest course that would encompass them all. He could, if he moved quickly, get to every one of them in a single day. Next, he played at guessing which of the two officers had his passport.

The khaki officer made a telephone call, then another and, after he hung up, the blue-and-gray officer came to where they were standing and exchanged rapid sentences with his partner. Neither looked at Seeley, but it seemed that both were pleased with the result of the phone calls. A question had been authoritatively answered, and it was not going to result in Seeley's release.

Other officers made detours to chat with the two guarding Seeley, examining him like a specimen before moving on.

A hangover can turn seconds into hours. Seeley no longer trusted his sense of time, and with his hands locked behind him he was unable to look at his watch. Ten minutes could have passed, or forty, when two men in olive-green uniforms came through a side door. Other than Piñeiro, were there any police in Cuba older than thirty? Seeley's English-speaking policeman called over to the men in olive green. After a short exchange, one set of handcuffs was traded for another that pinched even tighter, and the officer who spoke no English—Seeley had guessed wrong about which shell the pea was under—unbuttoned his shirt pocket and handed Seeley's passport to one of the new men. The tourist card, Seeley decided, was long gone, and he wondered if he would ever need it again.

•

At the sight of the white two-story building, Seeley knew that this was no ordinary jail. The structure at the end of the winding gravel driveway was a ramble of porches, balconies, awnings, and porticoes. Trees lined either side of the drive, and the shrubs and hedges that framed the lawn in front of the building gave the appearance of a formal garden. As one of the officers who accompanied Seeley on the ride from the station house held the door for him to get out, Seeley sensed about the grounds the eternal quiet of a monastery or convent.

Inside, the foyer walls were of dark, elaborately carved wood depicting a menagerie of birds, fish, deer, and stags dancing about cornucopias of tropical fruits. From behind a lime-colored desk, a large man greeted the officers and, with an effort, rose and removed a loop of keys from the hook on the side of the desk. The man must have weighed as much as the two policemen together, and Seeley wondered what sort of *negocio* fed him so well. The big man led them down a corridor to the last in a row of banded metal doors, where he selected a key and turned a lock, then a second key and another lock. Seeley winced as the handcuffs came off. The rush of blood to his wrists felt like bee stings, and he rubbed one, then the other, to relieve the numbness.

The heavy door slammed and the bolts shot back into their chambers. Hospital-white tile covered the walls and ceiling of the windowless room. The wood-plank floor was the same blinding white, and the buzz from the fluorescent ceiling fixture could have been a swarm of mosquitoes. It might have been a doctor's examining room, except that a worn footstool was the only furniture and, other than the open box of latex gloves on the floor, there were none of the usual medical paraphernalia. *Doctors without medicine.*

Seeley speculated on the origins of the building. There were too many small rooms for it to have been a house, or a school, and he returned to his first impression of the place. Who was it who told him that the government detained political prisoners in a

former monastery—Mayor? Dolores? Whatever brought him here,
it was not being drunk in public.

The bolts snapped back and the door opened three or four
inches. Seeley's guess that it was another prisoner jarred him; until this moment, he hadn't regarded himself as a prisoner. A light-
skinned youth in jeans and T-shirt slid in as the door closed
behind him. Like an offering, he carried in his outstretched arms
a folded garment of bright yellow and on top of that a pair of paper
slippers. "*Por favor, quítese la ropa, los zapatos, el reloj.*" The boy gestured at his own clothing to make Seeley understand and, as Seeley undressed, the boy stretched on a single latex glove. In his
despair, Seeley had to laugh. What fantastic weapon do the security police think an American lawyer would secrete within himself? Of course. Legal documents! An incendiary indenture rolled
tight as a suppository; once loosed, it would explode like a firebomb
in his captor's face.

The boy looked sympathetic and Seeley, his tongue thick with
thirst, said, "Water. *Agua.* Can I have water?" The boy shook his
head politely, even sweetly, before gesturing for Seeley to turn.
Light fingers moved quickly, delicately, and after he finished, the
boy handed Seeley the slippers and yellow overalls, collected Seeley's clothes, shoes, and watch from the floor, then pounded once
on the door to be let out.

Seeley walked about the cell, counting seconds, then minutes, to keep track of time. He sat on the footstool, which was
unsteady, then stood in one place and, when he tired of that, in
another. The counting of seconds and minutes had a hypnotic effect and, as the hours passed, the hangover receded. Unexpectedly
even his thirst abated. Seeley became aware of an involuntary
hunch around his shoulders and wondered if it was the result of a
night spent unconscious on the wretched beach chair or of something deeper, a prisoner's diffidence of spirit, a shrinking back
from the walls and ceiling of his cell.

Another guard arrived. Wordlessly, he snapped on handcuffs

and led Seeley back down the corridor, across the now empty reception area, to an unmarked door. At a knock, the door opened to men, some in uniforms, others in jeans or trousers and open shirts, talking among themselves. None seemed to notice as the guard walked Seeley to a banquet-sized table and pulled out a chair. He waited for Seeley to sit, then removed a cuff from one wrist and locked it to a table leg. The air was thick with cigar smoke and people drifted in and out. The mechanical hum of an air conditioner drowned out their talk. The place could have been a university common room. Maybe it was the uniforms, but beneath the civilized chatter Seeley sensed a potential for violence, as would erupt if someone prodded a sleeping lion.

Lieutenant Piñeiro was in a corner, smoking and talking with a woman and another man. The woman, a bottle blonde, was thick and plain as a dumpling. When Piñeiro saw Seeley watching him, he said a few words to the others and gestured to the guard to bring two more chairs to the long table. Piñeiro positioned one of the chairs so that it was directly across from Seeley, but he remained standing and rested a foot on the seat. The blonde took the other chair and from her bag removed a ballpoint pen and what looked like a child's plastic-bound notebook decorated with polka-dotted flowers.

"Your name." Piñeiro trimmed the ash of his cigarette with a long fingernail, letting it drop to the stone floor. He had on the same black suit and tie from their first meeting, but the face seemed even sharper than before, as if he had not eaten since then. Seeley felt his blood rush at the physical presence of authority, and any fragility or encumbering diffidence from his time in the cell instantly dissolved. "You know my name."

"Your nationality. The date and place of your birth."

"You have my passport. The information's there."

"Ah, yes, the passport that you told Cuban immigration not to stamp."

Seeley remembered the name of the detention facility for political prisoners. "You don't take people to Villa Marista for pass-port violations." The lieutenant's noncommittal nod told him that he had guessed right about where he was. "I have the right to appear before a judge." Seeley didn't know if Cuban law gave him that right, but it was something to say.

Piñeiro dropped his cigarette to the stone floor and let it smolder. "The government has seventy-two hours to present you to a judge." The child's notebook was open, but the blonde had so far written nothing.

Seeley nodded in the direction of the figures still moving about the room, indifferent to what was happening at the table. "Why are they here?"

"To guarantee your physical well-being. You should worry only when they disappear."

"Why are you holding me?"

"*Disturbio público*—public nuisance."

"You mean sleeping in public?"

"*Borracho*, like a common drunk." Piñeiro clucked his disapproval. "And homicide."

"Whose?"

"Héctor Reynoso. You were there."

Piñeiro's casual manner puzzled Seeley. He had been more intense in the hotel room, when less was at stake. Seeley said, "I thought he killed himself."

"No, you only tried to make it look like he did. Before you ran away."

"Why would that be a matter for the security police?"

"Because you are a foreigner involved in the death of one of Cuba's leading musical figures. This is an attack on *la cultura*." The two words had a different sound coming from Piñeiro's lips than they did from Amaryll's, something to be feared. Piñeiro's eyes stayed on Seeley's to make sure he understood. "This is an attack on the revolution."

No, Seeley thought, remembering Grau's lecture on race and

the politics of Cuban music, it was Reynoso's music that was the attack on the revolution.

The woman picked up the flowered notebook and clicked the ballpoint pen. Now Seeley saw where Piñeiro was going to take his questions. This would, after all, be the same as in the hotel room. He tried but failed to moisten his tongue. Talking had brought back the thirst. His head throbbed.

"Your purpose in coming here was to stir up Cuban musicians to oppose the revolution. What are their names?"

The woman's pen hovered over the open notebook.

Seeley said, "Without their permission, I cannot disclose who my clients are."

"Héctor Reynoso was your client."

"Why ask if you already know?"

"Then you admit Reynoso was your client?" Piñeiro smiled, but it wasn't pleasant.

"No, I'm telling you that whether he was my client or not is a confidence that I cannot break." Technically, Héctor Reynoso never was his client, but Seeley would not help the lieutenant.

"Gil Garcells told us that he met with you and signed your piece of paper."

Seeley waited.

"Who else signed?" When Seeley didn't answer, Piñeiro removed a folded letter-sized sheet from his inside jacket pocket and handed it to him. On it, typed with an old-fashioned carbon ribbon, were the names of the composers, widows, and children, with the exception of one: Justo Mayor. How could Piñeiro, who seemed to know about Seeley's every movement in Havana, have missed the meetings with Mayor at the composer's apartment and later at the cemetery? Unless Mayor was working for Minint, and Piñeiro didn't care if Seeley knew. Seeley handed the sheet back to Piñeiro.

"A noble American lawyer," Piñeiro said. "An idealist. A romantic." The smile, more taunting this time, was to tell Seeley that he had borrowed the words from Amaryll. Seeley's first reaction was anger at Amaryll for sharing her observation with the lieutenant, but then he realized that she did it to protect him. Only a romantic would come to Cuba for the reasons he did, and not on a mission to undermine the revolution.

There was a stir at the door, and the blonde looked over, then Piñeiro. For the first time, the people in the room became still. An erect, gray-haired man filled the doorway, but didn't enter. The khaki uniform was expertly tailored so that with a small effort on the man's part a modest paunch would disappear beneath a barrel chest. A rainbow of bars, medals, and ribbons glittered above the pocket. The man's hands were empty, but his posture suggested a riding crop in one.

Piñeiro crossed to the door. As the two men spoke, the superior stayed close to Piñeiro, forcing the lieutenant to look up at him. Seeley noticed that the man's chest expanded even more while they spoke, but shrunk when Piñeiro turned to come back to the table. The officer went away and the blonde picked up her pen and pad.

Piñeiro stopped at an elaborately carved cabinet beneath a black-and-white portrait of Fidel, the only picture in the room. "Do you want something to drink?" The words carried over the hum of the air conditioner and the conversations that resumed after the officer left. "We have rum. Evidently, you like our rum." He raised his voice. "White? Or dark? Gin. Vodka. We still have a good quantity of vodka." This brought a laugh from some others close by.

Seeley had no desire for alcohol. Whatever demons drove him yesterday, they were now asleep. What he needed was a pitcher of ice water, but instinct told him that getting out of here unharmed required that Piñeiro see no sign of weakness. Piñeiro called to the guard and directed him to remove the handcuff from the chair and replace it on Seeley's free wrist. The blonde closed her notebook and rose from the table. This must have been a signal to the others, because the room quickly emptied and the guard, the last one out, closed and locked the door behind him, leaving Seeley and Piñeiro alone.

From nowhere, a fist hard as bone smashed the ridge below Seeley's eye. Thrown off balance by the blow, and without the use of his hands to steady himself, Seeley slipped from the chair, but refused to let himself fall. Piñeiro was completely still, as if nothing happened. Seeley heard heavy breathing and at first thought that it was his own, but then he saw that it was the lieutenant, and that the hand at Piñeiro's side was still clenched. Seeley felt a trickle of blood run down his cheek.

A small brown notebook appeared in Piñeiro's other hand. "Who is Nick Girard?"

"No one. My law partner." As Metcalf warned, Girard's telephone call to the hotel had been intercepted, as had the others. "You're going to get in trouble with the tourism ministry, tapping hotel telephones."

A thin, even shy smile appeared under the mustache as Piñeiro consulted the notebook. "Daphne Hancock?" He pronounced it *Han-coke.*

"The same."

"Elena Duarte?"

"She works at my firm."

"A Cubana?" Seeley shrugged. It was none of Piñeiro's business, but that was why he was asking. These were his real questions, the ones to which he didn't know the answers. The other questions, like the bare fist, were to get Seeley's attention. Piñeiro's expression turned sly. "Saddle River Equities?"

"I can't answer that."

Piñeiro rubbed the notebook page with his thumb. "Saddle River Equities. A corporation registered in the Netherlands Antilles."

"Why is your government interested?" If Piñeiro would explain that to him, Seeley might understand why he was here.

Piñeiro ignored the question. "If you tell us about this Saddle River Equities, who owns it and why they sent you here, we could release you in, what, no more than an hour or two. Truly, at once."

"Don't you think I want to get out of here? Do you really believe that if I knew who Saddle River was, I wouldn't tell you?" Like it or not, Saddle River was now a client of the firm. But it wasn't confidentiality that held Seeley back, for what, really, did he know about the company? It was a client of Evernham's and, if Hobie was the partner in charge of the engagement, there might be a connection to the State Department, too. But if the Lieutenant had listened to the wiretap of his call from Daphne, he already knew all that. What was so consequential about this shadow corporation and its hidden owners that Piñeiro, if he wasn't lying, would detain and then release him just to know who they are?

"Would it help you to speak if you had a glass of water? You must need one very much by now. I am not a drinker myself, but I am told that alcohol has a way of—what is the word—"

When Seeley didn't answer, Piñeiro said, "Dehydrate. Yes, alcohol will dehydrate you. So tell me, why are you here?"

Seeley's dislike of authority was ingrained and rarely personal; it was the simple fact of authority that he resented. But for Piñeiro, the dislike was more than that. The lieutenant's corrupt advantage over Amaryll was despicable. Seeley would for the right reason give up what little he knew about Saddle River and Evernham's to anyone who asked. The bank and its client were, he suspected, little better than the lieutenant himself. But to a monster like Piñeiro he would tell nothing.

It was night before two guards took Seeley to a long bunkerlike structure across the lawn from the main building. Hour after hour, Piñeiro had paced the common room, asking Seeley questions that grew wordier and increasingly complex, punctuated by odd little stories and parables about the revolution and Sierra Maestra, as if the lieutenant had himself been there. As the afternoon, then the evening, wore on, he repeatedly cursed Seeley in Spanish, but didn't once strike him again. It would have made no difference to Seeley if he had. Always, the questions came down to two: Who owns Saddle River? Why did you come to Cuba? In Seeley's experience, the moral disfigurement that made officials like Piñeiro such lousy investigators was their blindness to the possibility that ideals, not greed, could drive human behavior. When Amaryll told the lieutenant that Seeley was a romantic, Piñeiro doubtless thought her a fool for being so easily duped. The lieutenant was incapable of accepting the truth, that Seeley came to Cuba for the single purpose of helping some old composers get back their music.

The cell in the bunker was barely six feet by nine. As in the examination room in the main building, the white tile that covered the walls and ceiling was blinding under the fluorescent lamps. A pallet with neither sheet nor mattress hung from two chains anchored to the wall. Across from the bed, a half-inch pipe extended over a hole in the plank floor, dripping a narrow trickle of water into the hole. Before the guard could remove the handcuffs, Seeley was on his knees in front of the pipe. He let the water slide down his throat until the reek coming from the hole made it impossible to continue.

There was no window, only a louvered metal vent where the wall met the ceiling. Although it was about a foot square, the vent let in little air, and the heat was several degrees more intense than outside. Seeley had visited American prisons where the din of human cries was unrelenting, day or night but, oppressive as that was, he would have welcomed it now. The only sound after the guard slammed the door and shot the bolts was the steady electric buzz of the fluorescent lamps.

Seeley kicked off the paper slippers, leaned back on the pallet, and pressed his feet flat against the opposite wall. Then, placing his palms against the wall behind him, he slid forward and pushed back with his arms so that, parallel with the floor, he could inch first one foot, then the other, up the wall. Next he did the same with his hands, gradually making his way up to the vent. He shut his eyes against the fluorescent glare and moved another inch, but his feet, slippery from the effort, slid across the glazed tile. Unable to find purchase in the narrow ribbon of mortar, he crashed to the floor.

He tried several times more, sometimes coming close to the vent, other times falling well short. Once, when he was suspended like this in midair, a panel in the door slid open and a pair of puzzled eyes studied him. Seeley winked, as if to say this is something that Americans do to amuse themselves, and the panel slammed shut. Finally, when he thought that he could not manage another ascent, he made it to within inches of the ceiling and, overjoyed, pressed one hand even harder against the tile to lock his arm in place and reached for the vent with the other, working his fingernails between the flange and the metal frame in which it was seated. To his amazement, the vent instantly came loose in his hand and fell to the floor.

Seeley reached through the square opening and clasped the rough stone of the outside wall. His other hand followed, and he chinned himself to the opening and crooked his head against the ceiling so that he could breathe the night air. He hung like this for minutes, resting at arm's length, then pulling himself up to breathe. The cinder track circling the lawn glowed in the moonlight, and beyond that, through a thin curtain of trees, was what looked like a baseball field. He thrust an arm out to test what freedom felt like, then, exhausted by an effort that had dissipated the last residue of his hangover, and careful to avoid the vent that had separated from its louvers when it struck the floor, he let himself down.

Sleep under the buzzing fluorescent came in what Seeley guessed were five- and ten-minute patches. In the half-waking state between, his thoughts drifted to his youth and to another white-tiled place, the neighborhood barbershop, jammed with exotic appliances and the mysteries of manhood: plastic combs standing in jars marked STERILIZER and filled with ice-blue fluid; hair tonics of every possible consistency and hue lined up like liquor bottles on a tavern's mirrored back bar; lather that foamed out of a whirring black box far too compact to hold such a bottomless supply. Even as a boy, Seeley was well-known in the neighborhood for his prowess at sports and his troublemaking, and two or three of the white-jacketed barbers would have a hearty word for him when he came in, and others whispered to their customers. Now, thinking about this time, Seeley saw that it was his introduction to the fraternity of men, with its fragrances of aftershave and powder, its warm, ritualized bonds, a closeness he experienced nowhere but in that wondrous place, not even later on the football field or playing squash with Nick Girard. What had severed that youthful union?

Seeley's ears pricked at a new buzzing in the cell, higher-pitched and more insistent than the fluorescent. A needle stung his neck, then his arm. He looked up. Mosquitoes swarmed through the vent opening. Seeley cried out, slapped his face and arms, but finally gave up. He laughed, because he knew that otherwise he would cry. Even if he could repair the vent, he lacked the strength to climb the wall again tonight. How little I change, he thought. Every time I try to make my life better, I only make it worse. He let the day's events, then yesterday's, pass through his thoughts, and continued back to his first day in Cuba and his last days in New York. Like so many pages of a legal brief, he let the days make their inescapable case: he had no problem that he had not created for himself. This, he supposed, counted for wisdom.

20

A day and a night passed without a second summons to the common room. Seeley had no contact with his jailers other than a tin plate of rice and beans handed through the shuttered slot in the evening and, in the morning, two chunks of crusty bread, also on a tin plate. To Seeley's wonder, the bread was as tasty and well-baked as any he'd eaten. A jar of weak, unsweetened lemonade came with each meal. The mosquitoes disappeared after the first night.

Seeley occupied part of his time plotting the Boston industrial espionage trial, starting with his own opening statement, moving on to the points his adversary would make, proceeding methodically through each witness on direct and cross-examination, and then mentally outlining his closing argument. Freed from the usual office interruptions, the power of his concentration startled him. Inside the bare tiled walls he discovered an edge of acuity that he thought he could only acquire from alcohol. I should reserve a room here, he thought, and then it occurred to him that he could still be here long after the trial concluded.

He spent as much time as he could physically bear at the vent-hole at the top of the cell, hanging from one hand, then the other, cheek against the ceiling, neck and shoulders twisted to survey the narrow patch of green outside. Only once did figures occupy the empty space. At dawn three guards appeared, walking alongside and behind a man so much larger than any of them that he could have belonged to a different species. The parade took no more than seconds to cross the venthole's narrow field of view, but even in the breaking light Seeley could make out that the giant, black as a shadow, was not only handcuffed but shackled at the ankles. For the next several hours, whenever his strength allowed, Seeley lifted himself to the hole to watch for the giant's return from the direction of the baseball field. He came to believe that his own survival depended on seeing the man again, alive.

At midmorning the cell door opened and the guard ordered Seeley out. His eyes traveled from Seeley to the venthole, to where Seeley had swept fragments of the broken vent under the pallet. At first confused, the guard called to his partner waiting in the corridor, "*El prisionero americano trató de escaparse.*" The second man came in, had a joking exchange with the first, then slipped the handcuffs on Seeley and steered him out of the cell.

On the wide lawn, a half dozen workers, shirtless and in shorts, squatted, pulling weeds. From beyond the line of trees at the edge of the villa's grounds, a bat cracked against a baseball, followed by cries from the players. Again Seeley thought of the black giant who disappeared under guard into the woods, but he felt better prepared for Piñeiro than he was the last time.

The heavily curtained common room was half in shadow, a blessing after the fluorescent-lit cell. The air-conditioning was off, and the sour, muddy smell of dead cigars hung in the air. The guard led Seeley to the table where two days ago he and Piñeiro had sat. While one guard watched, the other removed one handcuff and then, to Seeley's surprise, the other. When the door closed behind them, there was no click of a dead bolt. This was not Piñeiro's doing. The lieutenant's gray-haired superior in the well-cut uniform had arranged this. No handcuffs; an unlocked door; workers lifting their eyes from the weeds to witness a prisoner shot while trying to escape.

A crack separated the doors of the liquor cabinet. Seeley considered the possibility of a hidden camera and decided not to move; he refused to give Piñeiro the pleasure. Instead, he studied the portrait of Fidel and, recalling the pastel-tinted photographs in his office, considered the monumentality that black-and-white photography confers on its subjects. In color, El Comandante would be just another scraggly-bearded man on the street. The iconic photograph of Che, *Guerrillero Heróico*, would be unknown today—Che himself might be forgotten—if the film in Korda's camera had been Kodachrome. How many tyrants owed their reign to the compelling abstractions of black and white?

The door opened, and Harry Devlin came into the common room. Seeley waited for him to cross and take the chair opposite. "A lawyer who makes prison calls. Very impressive."

Devlin was smoking a panatela, not his usual cigarette, and he drew on the cigar until the tip glowed red. "You mean, that they let me see you?"

"Why are you here?"

"I thought you might be glad to have a visitor. Has anyone from U.S. Int. come by to see you?" When Seeley didn't answer, Devlin said, "I didn't think so."

"Can your client get me out of here?"

"Do you have any idea how lucky you are?" Devlin's smile turned the lines at the corners of his eyes into creases. Decades of trying cases before juries had erased any boundary between real and feigned delight. "You really don't understand, do you? Your drunken binge probably saved your life."

"I'll be sure to add it to my gratitude list next Thanksgiving."

"It was the PNR that took you off the street, the civilian police. You wouldn't believe it to watch them, but they're meticulous about keeping records. Before they turned you over to the security police, they put you on their books for being drunk in public. That means there's a paper trail. Minint has to account for you."

"Accounting for me doesn't mean keeping me alive."

Devlin examined the cigar as he turned it in his fingers. "You think they're going to release you and then shoot you as if you were trying to escape." Seeley didn't know whether to be comforted or alarmed that Devlin had read his thoughts. "Don't worry. This isn't like a spy novel. If the Cubans wanted to kill you, you'd already be dead."

"What do they want?"

"You already know. There's a lieutenant in the security police who thinks you have something of value to share with him. Unless you can convince him he's wrong, they won't let you leave."

"But whoever you're representing has the influence to get Minint to drop its interest in me."

"Not influence," Devlin said. "Access. That's all we have. Access and the opportunity to make a reasoned, factual argument. I hope you realize the Cubans will let you die here, and your government won't lift a finger."

"You just said they don't kill Americans."

"I didn't say kill. I said, let you die. On the other hand, Fidel and Raúl aren't going to live forever. Someday the Cubans may find it useful to have you in custody, a body for them to bargain with. You're not important enough to Washington to trade for the Cuban Five, but you could be a down payment."

Business as usual. On one day the State Department strikes a bargain with China to settle a trade secret lawsuit; on another it exchanges prisoners with the Cubans. And in between it makes a deal that sacrifices a handful of impoverished composers. Now Seeley understood why Devlin was here and not U.S. Int. "The State Department's trading favors with Cuba. That's why they abandoned Reynoso and the others. It had no problem helping the composers until Cuba said to cut them loose. You're working for the Cuban government. Just like when you helped them with Bacardi."

"Cuba doesn't need me or the State Department to do what it wants."

"Then who?" From a dusty ruin, a blackout fragment flashed through Seeley's thoughts of men lined up on a playing field, each holding a larger-than-life picture of another: Butler to Hobie to Devlin.

"You also give my client far too much credit."

Immediately, Seeley saw his mistake, and felt incredibly foolish. He had thought that when Hobie tried to stop him from representing the Cubans it was just another errand for his friends at the State Department, like trying to get him to settle the Boston trade secret case. "Not too much credit," he said to Devlin, "if your client has Evernham's as its banker."

Seeley was right that Hobie and Evernham's brought in Saddle River to conflict him out of working for Reynoso and his friends, but not for the reason he had first thought. It was a perverse consolation that Piñeiro, hammering away at him all afternoon— "Who is Saddle River?"—similarly believed that the company was a U.S. government decoy. But, no, the State Department wasn't using Saddle River Equities to get its way in Cuba. Saddle River was using the State Department, and Devlin was its lawyer in Havana.

Seeley thought of the ransacked hotel room. The forms shredded into confetti. "Saddle River hired the thugs who stopped me when I left Grau's apartment."

Devlin looked about as if inspecting for listening devices, his expression mild. "I don't believe I said anything about a company called Saddle River."

"They arranged Reynoso's murder."

Devlin drew on the cigar so strenuously that, head-on, he appeared to be holding an ember between his lips. Like a signal flare, the reaction confirmed what Devlin would never tell him in words. "Really, Michael, I think you've been alone in your cell too long. It's given you unhealthy thoughts."

"That cell could be the safest place for me right now. Minint may let me die there, but they're not going to kill me."

"And you actually believe my client wants you dead?"

"They obviously wanted Reynoso dead."

"You don't know that. But, as I told you, if someone wanted you dead, you would be."

"How did Saddle River get the rights to the music?" By now Elena would have completed a draft of the complaint challenging Castro's expropriation of the Cuban music. If Saddle River had somehow acquired the music from the Cuban government, Seeley would have to file and serve the complaint immediately, not only against Cuba, but against Saddle River, too. Otherwise, the composers and their families would have no hope of getting their music back. "Even if Saddle River has Evernham's as its banker, it doesn't just walk up to the Castros and say, sell me the music you stole from the Cuban people."

Devlin shrugged. "I really can't say."

"Not can't. You mean you won't say. Who's behind Saddle River?"

"I can't answer that, Michael, but surely you have discovered in your law practice that the questions 'How?' and 'Who?' usually have pretty much the same answer." Devlin put down the cigar. "Of course, I have told you nothing about my client. If you think about it, I haven't even told you who my client is."

"If your client didn't want Reynoso and his friends to get their music back, why did you send him to me?"

"I already told you," Devlin said. "I had a conflict."

"You're lying."

"Héctor was a friend. I wanted him to be represented. I'm sure you've done that for clients yourself dozens of times."

"Sure, but I never dropped one client for another. You were already representing Reynoso when your new client came to you. Reynoso wouldn't have known he could get his rights back if you hadn't told him. That's when you cut the composers loose and sent them to me."

The blue eyes, when they connected with Seeley's, were acid.

Seeley said, "How could you do that? Just drop your old friends like that?"

Devlin reached across and, with a gentleness belied by the sudden movement, touched the swelling beneath Seeley's eye left by the lieutenant's blow. "Think of the most obvious, most mundane reason you can, and you'll have the answer."

The only reason that occurred to Seeley was also the least probable. "Money."

Devlin nodded. "People see a lawyer who's had a long and celebrated career, and they think he has more than enough to retire on. That if he still works, it's for the pleasure of it, and not because social security won't cover even a tenth of his expenses. In my best years, through the sixties and seventies, lawyers, particularly solo practitioners like me, didn't make the kind of money they do today. While the others were putting away money to retire on, I was still paying child support and alimony to two ex-wives. I made some ill-advised investments. I'm going to be ninety next November. People don't want to worry if their lawyer will still be breathing at the end of the trial. So, sad and shameful as it is to say, I need the work. I need the money."

"Reynoso's friends are going to have plenty of money when they get their music back." *When*, Seeley tried to convince himself, not *if*.

"Maybe, but first they need to win the expropriation case against Cuba. You can hold out that long. I can't."

"You still haven't said why you sent them to me."

"Héctor knew that he could get his music back. You're right. I was the one who told him. He was going to get a lawyer anyway, so I sent him to you."

"And you were secretly hoping he would get the music back."

Devlin said, "I never bet against a client."

"Why did you come here?"

"To Villa Marista? To see how sober you are."

Seeley realized that, instead of looking at Devlin, his gaze had drifted to the thumb-sized crack between the liquor-cabinet doors. "I've been locked up for three days. I'm completely sober."

"Do you honestly believe that? Look at yourself."

Seeley followed Devlin's eyes and saw that his grip on the edge of the table had turned his knuckles white.

When Devlin leaned in to him Seeley could smell the tobacco on his breath. "No one who's sane and sober flies to a strange city illegally, without knowing a word of the language, looking for a man he met only once, and for how long—fifteen minutes, twenty? You're the first on the scene to find Héctor dead; a local beauty gives you the brush-off; and it's still morning when they kick you out of the ration store, but you manage to get loaded anyway. Even if you didn't take a single drink, I wouldn't call that sober."

"This is different."

"Why, because there's a woman?" Devlin circled a lit match around the tip of the panatela, which had gone out. "I never thought of you as someone who would turn into a peckerhead over a woman he just met."

Who told Devlin about Amaryll?

"There is no woman like a Cuban woman anywhere in the world." Devlin's eyes were watery, and Seeley didn't know if it was from the cigar smoke or his memories. "Smart as hell, too. She'll latch onto an American fellow, twist him around her finger until he can't think straight, and then get him to take her back to Yuma."

The word sounded strange coming from Devlin. Seeley said, "She won't leave Cuba."

"I wouldn't want to think about how much trouble you've created for her." Devlin's opaque gaze abruptly swung open like a secret door, giving Seeley a glimpse into a soul cauterized by endless compromise. The door as swiftly closed. "That's what your problem is, Michael. You push and push. You don't know when to stop."

Seeley said, "You're afraid I'm going to hold you responsible for what you did. For what your client did."

Devlin rose. "I'm sorry, Michael, but I can't let them release you, not with the kind of crazy fantasies you have knocking around in your head. You're too much of a risk. Truly, I'm sorry. You can consider this my amends to you."

"Amends means change," Seeley said, "and I don't see you changing."

Devlin's features collapsed another fraction. "Well, then, I hope you can forgive me."

Before Seeley could speak, the old lawyer was across the room and at the door, calling to the guards in Spanish to take Seeley away.

21

The clang of metal striking metal in the corridor jarred Seeley awake. From the blue-black sky outside the venthole, he knew that it was night. In the confused passages between scraps of sleep, he had been thinking about fear, tracing its vein through his life, surprised at the length of it, from the fear that he could not protect his younger brother from their father's beatings, to the concerns for clients like Reynoso and Jun Wei, to the fear that his own incarceration would never end, that he was condemned to spend day after day with nothing—not work, not even a book or newspaper—to distract him from his own dark thoughts. It disturbed him that he could locate no moral divide between the fear that he felt for others and the fear that he felt for himself. He added prison cells to airports as places that made him philosophical.

Bolts shot back and the cell door swung open. Seeley rose from the pallet to meet the guard, but when he reached the door there was only the receding clatter of boots racing on concrete. The guard was gone and the door at the end of the corridor was open. Even as he thought of the shackled black giant who went into the woods and didn't return, his own fears dissolved. Action had always been his antidote. He walked to the end of the corridor and at the open doorway turned left. The guard station was unattended, but a small mountain of cigarette stubs overflowed a tin ashtray and the acrid smell of smoke was fresh.

Seeley tested the door to the outside and found it unlocked. He thought of what Devlin said. If the Cubans wanted to kill you, you'd already be dead. The lawn, when Seeley opened the door, was a desert in the moonlight, and the cinder track that encircled it sparkled like a ribbon of broken glass. The villa was dark, except for a single lit room on the top floor. Who would be awake at this hour? In his two days here, why had he seen only that one other prisoner? Casually, as if he had decided to take a stroll around the grounds, Seeley went down the steps, across the track and onto the lawn. Dew immediately seeped through the paper slippers. If the iron gate at the foot of the driveway wasn't open, he could easily scale it. But, even if he got past the gate, how far could he go, an American who didn't speak the language, in neon-yellow overalls, with neither passport nor money?

From the direction of the trees bordering the baseball diamond, there was the rattle and hum of an engine switching on. The word *clockwork* slipped into Seeley's thoughts. Gravel crackled and a dark sedan with its headlights off—the chrome ornament on the hood made it a Mercedes—crossed the cinder track onto the lawn, then suddenly accelerated, skidding to a stop just feet from where Seeley stood. The driver stepped out and moonlight flashed for an instant off wire-rimmed glasses. Neatly groomed in a dark suit, white shirt, and solid tie, the man came toward him, but Seeley walked around the car to look into a side window. The car was empty.

"I am from the Swiss Embassy," the driver said to Seeley's back. "My instructions are for you to please come with me." The words had a French accent but a German cadence, charming but meant to be obeyed. Swiss, Seeley thought, but that didn't mean that the man was from the embassy or was here to help him.

"Why should I get in?"

The man glanced at his watch. "This is not a problem."

"Maybe it's not a problem for you—"

"Please. I have been fully advised. If you wish to leave, you must come with me." No more than a few seconds passed, but the driver checked his watch again. "You must come now. The guards will return and the gates will close."

"What is the name of the security-police lieutenant who put me here?"

The driver was at the passenger side, holding the door for See-ley. He visibly stiffened as he climbed in himself. "The Swiss Embassy does not deal with local officials at the rank of lieutenant." To Seeley's thinking, the attitude put the driver in the Swiss diplomatic corps as definitively as a sash across his chest. He followed him into the Mercedes, and was still closing the door when the car skid-turned across the lawn and sped through the open gates at the end of the driveway.

"Where are my clothes? My passport?"

The Swiss switched on the headlights, and the dashboard cast a glow across his features. "My instructions are only to deliver you."

"Deliver me where?"

The Swiss didn't answer but increased his speed, letting the few cars on the road fall back into the darkness.

Against the black landscape, the image of Reynoso hanging from the pipe in his apartment burned in Seeley's memory like an effigy. Eleven days and over a thousand miles later, the squash-court chatter hadn't subsided. If he hadn't taken the composer on as a client, Seeley told himself, Reynoso would still be alive. He would be alive if Seeley hadn't come to Havana to look for him. If he was honest with himself, Seeley would accept that Reynoso had himself set his execution in motion long before they'd met. But that kind of honesty was beyond his reach.

The road became a highway and the Swiss pushed the Mercedes harder, past mile after mile of weed-choked fields and low clusters of cinder-block buildings as broken as their empty window frames. Seeley glanced at the billboards, but none were those he remembered from his long-ago ride into Havana. He said, "This isn't the road to the airport," but the driver didn't respond.

Not once during Seeley's three days in Villa Marista had Amaryll left the periphery of his thoughts. In the past, boredom had sooner or later ended every one of his relationships with women. An affair could last for weeks or months but at the end every one succumbed to his indifference. His marriage to Clare lasted nine mostly empty years. Life with Amaryll would not have been like that. She wouldn't let it. He promised himself that he would change.

The driver slowed and turned onto a narrow road, the Mercedes swerving and juddering in ruts the size of tractor tires. There was a wooden shack, its door hanging open and, two hundred feet further on, a black Suburban parked beneath a canopy of trees. Within a sharpshooter's distance were two battered Renaults, baby blue and tiny as minnows. The Swiss pulled alongside the Suburban but watched the Renaults; he was unhappy that they were there. "You asked where I was delivering you? Here. I am delivering you here."

Seeley said, "The Renaults are Minint." One visit to Havana and he was an expert on the security police.

"This cannot become an international incident." Nerves had made the Swiss talkative. "According to my briefing, you are not even in Cuba."

"That fact has been a source of great comfort to me. Who's in the Suburban?"

"I'm sure you will find your clothes there. Also your passport." The Swiss glanced at his watch and again looked in the direction of the Renaults.

Seeley said, "Turn around and pull close to the Suburban." The Swiss did as directed, and when the Mercedes was less than a door's length from the larger vehicle, Seeley squeezed out. A smoked glass window lowered, and Seeley looked down into a blond-stubbled face that surely would never grace an American Christmas card. Metcalf's eyes were bloodshot, his lips raw. He glanced at the bruise below Seeley's eye, but only said, "Get in." When Seeley opened the front passenger door, Metcalf said, "No, the back. Your clothes are there. You can change."

The Mercedes was moving before Seeley closed the door, but

the Renaults stayed. Metcalf glanced at the rearview mirror. "They want to be sure you leave the island." He put the Suburban in gear and, palming the steering wheel one-handed, hot-rod style, turned onto the dirt road back to the highway. In the side-view mirror, the two Renaults followed.

"Your suitcase is on the floor behind you. Your briefcase, too, but it's empty."

"You can always trust a lawyer with an empty briefcase." Seeley pulled his belt to the last hole. Even his wristwatch was loose when he strapped it on. In his own clothes, in a big air-conditioned American vehicle that still smelled of the factory, he already felt better.

"I got you a seat on a charter to Miami. I booked a connecting flight to La Guardia. You'll be in New York by two this afternoon."

As at their meeting in his office, Metcalf was saying *I*, not *we*, and Seeley hoped that this morning the official was not operating all on his own. "What time does it leave?"

"The plane to Miami? Eight-thirty."

Seeley looked at his watch. They had two hours. Without knowing what he would do there, he said, "Take me to Amaryll's apartment."

"That's not possible." Metcalf's foot went down on the gas pedal as if to show his resolve.

"Because the people in the Renaults wouldn't approve." Was Piñeiro in one of the cars?

"You'd only make more trouble for her," Metcalf said.

"More?"

"You're a person who makes trouble just by nodding to someone on the street."

"I don't have any signed forms." He was sure Metcalf already knew that, but he needed to say it.

"It doesn't matter anymore."

"Of course it matters."

"Let's just say the State Department has been persuaded that this is a good time for you to leave the island."

Seeley said, "Who got the State Department to change its mind about the composers? To stop helping them?" When Metcalf only clamped his jaw shut, Seeley said, "Who's behind Saddle River?"

"That's so many levels above me, I'd get a nosebleed just thinking about it." Metcalf glanced at him in the rearview mirror. "They moved up my retirement date. In two weeks, I'll be pulling in those western muskies by the boatload."

Seeley smiled. "You found out."

"That there's no such creature as a western muskie?" Metcalf's attempt at a smile was grim, and in the bright sun he looked haggard. "I didn't think there was, but you have a convincing way about you." He looked over the seat. "That's not a compliment, by the way."

"It is to a trial lawyer."

Seeley lifted the briefcase from the floor behind him and set it against the door for a pillow. Then he put up his feet and in less than a minute was fast asleep.

Daylight streaming through the Suburban's open window woke Seeley to the far-off racketing of a helicopter and the industrial smell of aircraft fuel. The vehicle was at the edge of the tarmac in an area enclosed on three sides by a fence of crenellated metal roofing and spiraling concertina wire. Seeley checked one side-view mirror, then the other. Parked in the enclosure next to a cluster of dwarf palm trees was one of the Renaults. On the other side of the fence, fifty or sixty yards away, a medium-sized commercial jet had its stairway down and hatch open. Luggage rode a conveyor belt into the hatch, and figures moved in the cockpit. Sunlight glinted off two smaller aircraft parked at the edge of the runway. The terminal, its paint a shabby white, was smaller and older than the one at which Seeley had arrived.

"Here are your boarding passes." Metcalf handed an unmarked manila folder over the seat back. "If you want to know what else your government's done for you, I just took you through customs and immigration while you were sleeping."

Seeley opened the manila folder. Inside were his passport and two boarding passes, one for each leg of the trip.

"You're cleared through to New York. Someday maybe you'll be asked to return your government's favor. You're on your way in twenty minutes." Metcalf opened his door and climbed down.

"Why didn't you come to Villa Marista?"

"My instructions were: hands off. Everything was handled through back channels. It's why the Swiss picked you up. He was going to bring you here, but I insisted."

"Why would you do that?"

"To apologize." Metcalf was looking past Seeley to the opening in the fenced enclosure. "I'm sorry about Villa Marista."

"Don't be," Seeley said. "It saved my life. If the police hadn't pulled me off the street, I'd still be drunk now." He turned to follow Metcalf's gaze. A charcoal-painted Lada had stopped inside the gated area, and Amaryll stepped out, a red legal-sized envelope under her arm. She looked over at the airplane still loading baggage on the tarmac, then at Seeley.

"I'm sorry I made things hard for you," Metcalf said. "The least I could do was give you a chance to say good-bye." When Amaryll approached, Metcalf backed away.

She was wearing the same white shorts and blouse as when Seeley had first seen her on the balcony, her hair drawn back and her posture tall, but now something was missing. If she was a woman who wore makeup, he would say it was that, but she wasn't. She said, "I wanted to see you before you left."

"Why?" The residue of their last meeting stirred the old empty ache inside him. What was he thinking when he asked Metcalf to drive him to her apartment?

"So I can thank you." Amaryll hesitated, unsure. She nodded

toward where Metcalf stood several feet away. "He told me what you did to get the permit and visa for me. That was brave of you, to promise to stay here and get your forms signed. Also, you were kind, not telling me you did this and making me feel that I owed something to you."

"Why would that matter?" Seeley noticed that the slight gradation of flesh beneath her eyes was inflamed, as if she, too, had suffered through more than one sleepless night. Then he realized what was missing. "Where is your *amuleto?*" The tiny ivory fish and its thin gold chain were gone.

She shrugged. "It is only a superstition, that it would protect me."

"Like *la cultura,*" Seeley said. "The past can make you a prisoner."

When Amaryll nodded, Seeley pushed down the hope that rose inside him.

"You were right about Virgilio," Amaryll said. "If he talks back to the guards, he must take responsibility for what happens. It is not my job to protect him, like a little boy. So you see"—she held her hands open in front of her, like a magician promising nothing up his sleeves—"I must be honest with you. Other people, I don't care what they think. But with you I have to tell the truth about myself."

Seeley drew in a breath to calm himself. "There is nothing to stop you from coming to America."

Amaryll looked directly at him. "Only you."

"What do you mean?"

"You are someone who lives only to rescue people. Like when you tried to save me from the lieutenant on Calle Veintitrés. That is the spirit that drives you. It is a wonderful spirit. *Heróico.*"

Across the tarmac, passengers were climbing the stairs onto the plane.

"But you can't live like that," Seeley said.

"No one saves someone just to set them free." Amaryll shifted the red vinyl envelope from one hand to the other. "You are a man who takes hostages. Why should I live like a prisoner in America when I can live free here?"

"That wouldn't happen."

"You mean you would change? I don't think so. You don't even understand why you do these things. You think it is because you are a good person, which you are. But really the reason you do it is to make yourself feel big."

"Not big," Seeley said. "Whole." Over the long days and nights alone in his cell at Villa Marista, he'd learned more than that mosquitoes bite.

"So then you understand why I can't come with you."

The doors of the Renault opened and a man and a woman got out. Seeley couldn't see if their uniforms were Minint green, but such fine distinctions no longer mattered.

"I can change."

Amaryll's chest rose with her breath. "Can you really promise that?"

In trial or in negotiations, to get his way with an adversary, Seeley had shaved the truth too many times for another half-truth to matter. But this was different. "No," he finally said. "I can try, but I can't make that promise." Seeley wanted more than anything to sweep Amaryll onto the waiting plane, as if that had been the single reason for his presence in Cuba, but in the same instant he understood that was impossible. The collision of thought and feeling staggered him. Painful as it was, the moment would pass if he let it. "You knew I couldn't make that promise even before you came here."

Amaryll looked down, and her shoulders dropped. "No. I thought about it, but I didn't know how honest you would be with yourself."

"And if I lied? Would you have come to America?"

"Now," Amaryll said, "we will never know."

Metcalf had moved to where Seeley could see him. He pointed

at his watch and then at the plane. The stairway was empty, every-one onboard.

"You know," Amaryll said, "when we went to the composers and I told them not to sign, it wasn't because the lieutenant told me to. He never even talked about them." She looked straight at Seeley, her eyes holding a curious smile.

"I know that," Seeley said. "You did it to protect them from the security police."

"I also did it to protect you. An American can get in trouble with Minint trying to organize Cubans."

"I suppose I should thank you," Seeley said. Against his will he, too, was smiling because he saw the symmetry of their plight.

"So you tell me," Amaryll said. "How does it feel to be a vic-tim? Someone who needs to be rescued?"

"It feels like shrinking," Seeley said. "Not great, but I'll get over it."

"Maybe," Amaryll said, "but not if I was there every day to re-mind you of it."

"So," Seeley said, "we're the same."

"For us to be together would be like a never-ending dance, you trying to lead me, me trying to lead you. I am a practical person. The only romantics on this island are in prison or getting on an airplane. Some things cannot be fixed. Even by you."

Amaryll's eyes blurred and Seeley's first thought was that she was crying. But her eyes were perfectly clear. The tears were his. Blinded like that, he at last saw why she had come and under-stood the price that she had paid. "It was you who got me out of Villa Marista."

"You would have done the same for me. More. Whatever it required."

Seeley started to speak, but she pressed a cool finger against his lips. "If you want to thank me, you can take care of this."

She tucked the red envelope under his arm, then turned and walked back to her car.

Metcalf touched Seeley's elbow. "You have to go."

Seeley went to the Suburban and lifted out the suitcase and the empty briefcase.

Amaryll got into the Lada and slammed the door closed.

This, Seeley thought, is as close to a love story as my life will ever come.

22

Havana's rhythms pulled Seeley backward, Manhattan's forward. Like Amaryll, he felt torn in two, and even with all that he now had to do in New York, a part of him wanted only to be back in the heat and stench of Havana's streets, in the composers' apartments, on the Malecón at 2:00 in the morning, even shuttling drunk between the produce market and his makeshift home in the ruins. He evened up the documents on his desk, as if that would square the dislocations in space and time.

Seven hours ago, he was on a Havana–Miami charter with a Catholic men's group that was returning from a week in the Cuban countryside delivering supplies to hospitals. The airborne scene was straight from some hellish painting: drunken, red-faced men jamming the aisles, their voices growing louder, the hilarity more forced, as they drank from the bottles of rum they'd brought on board, each working to outdo the others with tales of his adventures.

Even before he snapped on the seat belt, Seeley had unzipped Amaryll's red vinyl envelope, releasing a petroleum odor not unlike the aviation fuel outside, but sweeter, almost voluptuous. The smell took him back to the blotchy purple ink of the quiz sheets that the nuns at St. Boniface handed out to their classes. The twenty or so sheets in the envelope had the same slippery feel as that long-ago mimeograph paper. Seeley removed one. The first paragraph was in Spanish, but the words were familiar, and the second paragraph, in English, confirmed that it was a copy of the termination forms he had brought to Havana. The remaining sheets were identical, except for the signatures at the bottom. Justo Mayor, Onelio Bustamante, Faustino Grau, the others. He pictured Bustamante, eyes on the floor, head moving side to side disconsolately. The composers, widows, and children who were too frightened even to touch the papers that Seeley offered them had somehow been persuaded to sign. Even the signature of Maceo Núñez, the imprisoned composer, was here.

Stapled to the back of each form was a half sheet of the same flimsy mimeograph stock, and Seeley saw at once who collected the signatures. The half sheets were attestation forms, and all but Mayor's were signed by the same two witnesses: Justo Mayor and Amaryll Cruz. While Seeley was in Villa Marista, they were out meeting with the composers and their families. If they had asked, Seeley would have told them that one witness was enough.

"Mike?" Elena came into his office. Her smile disappeared at the sight of the black-purple bruise below Seeley's eye, but she said nothing and placed a small stack of papers on his desk. Seeley quickly paged through it. On top was the complaint that Elena had drafted to overturn Castro's expropriation of the Cuban composers' music. Beneath the complaint was her memorandum analyzing the four cases invalidating the Russians' expropriations of the dissident writings, and last were copies of the cases themselves.

Trafimov, Babenko, Gortikov, Gennadiev. The cases seemed less weighty now than when he had described them to Elena over the phone in Havana. They were, after all, only decisions of two trial courts, the lowest courts in the federal judicial system, and lacked the authority of an appellate ruling. As much as it meant to Seeley, the fact that Felix Silver had litigated the cases would mean nothing to the trial judge in his own case. Even if Seeley could persuade the judge to rule for his clients, he knew that it could take as much as a year for the court to issue its ruling, long after the composers' termination rights expired. He was counting on the Russian quartet to accomplish a far speedier result: to convince Saddle River and its banker that it would be a waste of their money to defend the lawsuit.

Elena must have seen Seeley's worried look. "I can still look in the case files to see if there's anything that helps us."

More research wasn't going to help his case. The complaint was going to have to stand on its own. "If there were anything else, I would have seen it when I was working for Silver. We can always amend the complaint if we have to."

"Did you get the termination forms signed?"

"Some people did. Not me. The publishers will have them first thing tomorrow." Seeley wanted the signed forms to reach the publishers before he filed the complaint, and he had already left them at the firm's delivery desk downstairs. He had also printed out the motion in his trade secret case, and revised it a second time, to be faxed to Dane, Perry, his local counsel in Boston.

From the instant the charter flight lifted off the runway at José Martí, Seeley dreaded what he had to say next. "You need to get hold of a blank form and bring it to Dolores to sign."

"Dolores—why?"

"For Reynoso's music."

Elena instantly made the connection, but to Seeley's surprise, she took the news as coolly as Metcalf had. "How? He seemed fine when he was here."

"Maybe that's the problem. He should have stayed here." Which story should he tell? The official tale of suicide? Grau's story that the Cuban government wanted to stop Reynoso from organizing protests over his canceled tour? Or the story that Seeley himself had pieced together during his exchange with Devlin at the Villa Marista, that Saddle River had arranged Reynoso's murder. "The security police weren't pleased that Reynoso was organizing the composers to go on tour."

"Politics can be a dangerous business in Latin America."

Business can be a dangerous business, too, Seeley thought, which is why he was certain that Saddle River was responsible. He lifted the complaint from the top of Elena's pile.

"When do we file the complaint?"

"Tomorrow morning," Seeley said. He would review and revise Elena's draft before he left the office, hand it to the night staff for typing and proofreading, and arrange for a courier to file it in court and serve it on the defendants before noon.

"I didn't know where you wanted to file, so I left the space for the court blank."

Silver had filed two of the Russian cases in federal district court in Washington, D.C., and two in the district court in New York City. "Right here," Seeley said, "Southern District." A letter from the State Department asking the court to strike down a foreign expropriation order might impress a federal judge in Washington more than one in Manhattan, but Seeley was far from sure that Metcalf, now only days from retirement, would produce the promised letter. Also, he knew more judges in the Southern District than he did in Washington, a fact that could help bring Saddle River and Evernham's to the settlement table.

Seeley studied the caption listing the parties at the top of the draft complaint. Héctor Reynoso was the first named plaintiff, and Seeley pencilled in "Estate of" before the composer's name. After Reynoso were Justo Mayor, Gil Garcells, Onelio Bustamante, and the others. As defendants, after the Republic of Cuba, Seeley had instructed Elena to add the names of the publishers to ensure that, if the case went to trial and he won, the publishers would be required to turn the music over to the composers and not to the Cuban government.

Elena watched Seeley write "Saddle River Equities" in the space between Republic of Cuba and the publishers.

"We're suing Saddle River? Why?"

"They're our only real adversary. Not the Cuban government or the publishers. It's Saddle River that claims to own the music.

The publishers are just collecting royalties for them." This was why Joel Simkin and the other publishers' lawyers wouldn't tell him where they were mailing their checks.

"Do you know that for a fact?" Elena probably hadn't intended the edge in her voice, and she colored.

"Do I know it absolutely? No. But just because Castro stole the rights in the 1960s doesn't mean that he owns them today. Cuba's always needed hard currency. If someone with cash offered to buy the music, why wouldn't Castro sell it?"

Seeley also guessed that the sale was long ago. The Castros surely understood that if they sold off the country's African heritage today, they would have an uprising on their hands far more violent than anything incited by Reynoso's tour. But when and how had Saddle River acquired the music? The security police knew no more than Seeley did, which was why Piñeiro had hammered at him hour after hour at the Villa Marista, his questions rambling, but in the end always coming down to one: Who is Saddle River?

Seeley said, "Why do you think Evernham's wanted us to represent Saddle River? To stop us from working for Reynoso and his friends. If we got them back their music, Saddle River would have nothing."

"They could have other reasons. Maybe they bought someone else's music from the government and just don't want you challenging how Castro got the rights."

"I didn't know about the expropriations until I got to Cuba. Saddle River couldn't know I was going to attack them." Seeley caught himself. Elena's questions were beginning to irritate him, even though in her place he would ask them, too. He reminded himself that she was on his side, maybe the only person in the firm who was. "All Evernham's knew was that I was going to file termination notices. Whatever else happened, so long as I didn't file, the publishers would keep sending checks to Saddle River."

"But they're a client of the firm. How can we sue them?"

"It will certainly raise eyebrows."

"You could," Elena started to speak, stopped, then said, "You could get a report from the Copyright Office to see if this really is the music they claim to own."

Seeley was sure that what she had started to say was that the district court judge could subject him and the firm to penalties for naming a party as a defendant without first determining that there was a factual basis to do so. He said, "I already ordered a report, but it's going to take two weeks."

"So, wait until then."

"We have to file now. If we don't, Saddle River is going to file against us first, wherever they think they have the home-court advantage. Also," Seeley said, "we have a trial beginning in Boston in five days. I need you to go up there tomorrow morning."

If this turned into a professional catastrophe, Seeley wanted Elena to be as far away as possible. "You need to get together with the people at Dane, Perry." Seeley's local counsel in Boston were overseeing the pending motions in the industrial espionage case, filing papers, and making formal appearances. Apart from keeping Elena away from the disaster that the suit against Saddle River could become, the work in Boston would be good training.

"How are you going to try a case in Boston and run this lawsuit at the same time?"

"If I'm right," Seeley said, "Saddle River's going to fold their hand as soon as they see our complaint. The case will be over by tomorrow night."

"And if you're wrong?"

"If I'm wrong, trying cases in two cities at the same time is going to be the least of my problems."

23

Elena had put in another late night. The termination notice for Reynoso's compositions, signed by Dolores Moncada, was on Seeley's desk when he arrived just after 7:00, and he put the document in his secretary's in-box for a courier to hand-deliver to Joel Simkin.

Simkin and the other publishers' lawyers wouldn't be in their offices for at least another two hours. Seeley picked up the deposition of one of the Chinese researchers in his Boston trade secret trial and continued marking it for cross-examination. When Seeley asked the scientist about the instructions his superiors had given him in preparation for his visit to the Waltham laboratory, the man had a whispered exchange with his lawyer before finally answering that if he received any instructions, he now forgot them. Lies this transparent were not going to work in front of a Boston jury. Seeley's thoughts wandered back to Saddle River, to Hobie, the State Department, and Evernham's, and he asked himself if their deceptions would be any more durable.

The canned music while Seeley waited for Simkin to come on the line was tinny and thin as water. Here is one of the largest music publishers in the world, Seeley thought, with a library of thousands of Latin compositions as well as rock, country, folk, and blues, and this is the gruel they play for telephone music. He caught himself. When had music ever mattered to him before?

Simkin came on the line. "We just got your termination notices."

"There's another one coming, from the Estate of Héctor Reynoso."

"I saw the obituary in this morning's *Times*," Simkin said. "You never know about people, do you? Did you think he was someone who would take his own life?"

"I try not to think too hard about my clients' personal lives." It had taken almost a week for the news to get from Havana to New York, more than enough time for Minint and the Cuban propaganda machine to shape the story. An obituary writer for the *Times* wouldn't question the official version of Reynoso's death, and Seeley could only guess at the arrangements that had been made for the police to classify as suicide what they doubtless knew was the murder of a Cuban national arranged by an American company.

"How long have you been sending Reynoso's royalties to Saddle River Equities?" When Simkin didn't answer, Seeley said, "When was the last time you sent money to a company that acquired its rights from a totalitarian government?"

"You know from our last call, I can't tell you who we send our checks to."

The answer was as good as a title report from the Copyright Office confirming that if Saddle River itself hadn't bought the music from Castro, somewhere along the chain of ownership it had acquired the music from someone who did.

"We're part of a public company, Mike. We have shareholders to answer to. You can be sure that whoever's getting the checks has uncontested rights—"

"Why did you waive the conflict and let me represent the composers?"

"Our trial counsel told us—"

"I thought I was your trial counsel."

"This came up last year when you were off in Buffalo. The lawyer we retained told us that if we sued to overturn the expropriation, it would be a long shot at best. So we figured that since the terminations were coming up, once the composers got their music back, they could sue. They'd be a lot more sympathetic as plaintiffs than a bunch of New York music publishers and they'd have a better chance of winning. We thought that if we let you represent them, sooner or later you'd realize you had to sue the Cuban government to get their rights back for them. Then we could negotiate new publishing deals with them. A walk in the park for you."

"Like a week in the Alps," Seeley said. He decided not to tell Simkin about his time in Villa Marista. Ross-Fosberg was a paying client, and he needed clients that paid their bills if he was going to rebuild his pro bono practice. "Why would it matter to you if the composers got their rights back? Every six months you write a check. Why should you care if the check is to a Cuban composer or to Saddle River?"

"You know, Mike, that's one of your biggest problems. You honestly believe that you're the only lawyer in New York who cares about artists. Do you think I would have set you loose on this if I wasn't sure that you would do the right thing? Did you even consider that maybe we want these writers to get their songs back because they're the rightful owners?"

"Then you'll be glad to know," Seeley said, "that after I get the judge to rule in favor of the composers, and you and I sit down to renegotiate their contracts, I'm not going to ask you just to triple the royalties. I'm going to want the composers to control the licenses, too. No commercials for frozen tacos, no jingles for toothpaste, if they don't want them."

"I'm sure your clients will be very happy with any deal you make for them." Simkin's voice turned weary. "So will we."

"That's good, because there's a complaint coming your way. It names you and the other publishers as defendants along with the Republic of Cuba and Saddle River Equities. I want to make sure that when the judge overturns the expropriation you can explain to your shareholders why you're sending money to the men who wrote the music and not to Saddle River."

"Sue us." Simkin's good nature had returned. "It should be a novel experience, being sued by our own lawyer."

"If it's a comfort," Seeley said, "you won't be the first."

"Did your client really kill himself?" Girard had read the *Times* obituary, too.

"No," Seeley said, weighing how much to tell Girard of what he knew or at least suspected. "He was murdered because he was helping his friends get their music back."

They were in Girard's office, eating pastrami sandwiches delivered from the Second Avenue Deli across town. Girard was the descendant of Beacon Hill bluebloods and Western New York's old Dutch stock, and his deeply informed taste for Jewish delicatessen was one of a handful of discreet passions. Only Second Avenue, he insisted, brined the meat and spiced and smoked it correctly. Seeley's own appetite had picked up almost as soon as he left Havana.

"I thought that's why you were down there. To get them their music back." When Seeley nodded, Girard said, "That means his friends are in trouble, too."

"They were only in danger until they signed. All the notices were delivered this morning. They're safe now. The only people who are going to profit if they die are their heirs."

"How can you be sure? This is politics. These governments line people up and shoot them just to warn the others not to misbehave."

Seeley said, "The Cuban government may have helped with the cover-up, but it didn't kill Reynoso."

"Then who?"

Girard was going to find out soon enough. "Our new client," Seeley said. "Saddle River Equities."

"That's crazy!"

"I didn't say it wasn't." Seeley quickly laid out the indicting facts: Evernham's offering up Saddle River as a client to prevent Seeley from representing Reynoso and the others; Hobie getting his State Department friends to order the U.S. Interests Section to back off from helping the composers recover their music; Devlin's presence at the memorial service, and his virtual confession at the Villa Marista. It was only when Seeley got to how Saddle River acquired the rights to the music that his footing became less sure, and he stopped.

For all of his bearlike, shambling manner, Girard had as quick a legal mind as any Seeley knew. Seeley had seen him sift through eighty single-spaced pages of a corporate acquisition agreement and in minutes identify for his client the weak points in the financing arrangement and the flaws in its tax structure. "You don't know that Saddle River owns the music," Girard said. "And if they don't own the music, none of this makes any sense."

"They own it," Seeley said. "Why else do you think Evernham's gave us a half-million-dollar retainer?"

"A quarter million," Girard said. The tone was offhand, but he reached for his invisible squash racquet to swat away the unpleasantness around him.

"They would have paid half a million. More. This music is throwing off tens of millions of dollars a year for Saddle River. How much work has the firm done to earn the retainer?"

"Barry Maxon was working on something—"

"How about all the other clients Evernham's promised?"

"We're meeting with them. These are courtships. They take time."

"But no one's signed up, have they?"

Girard swung the racquet back and forth, punishing the air in front of him. "Say you're right—and I'm not saying you are—where are you going with this?"

"I want Saddle River to sign the music over to the composers."

The racquet stilled. "And how are you going to persuade them to do that?"

"By filing a lawsuit against them."

"You can't sue our own client."

"They won't even file an answer. They're going to drop their claim as soon as they read the complaint."

"Because you know something that all of their lawyers and investment bankers forgot to tell them when they bought the music." The racquet fanned the air again. "No investor buys an asset that size without doing an ownership search. Either they bought the rights from Castro, or whoever they bought them from got the rights from Castro."

"And how did Castro get them? By stealing them from the composers. That's what countries like that do. But an American court won't recognize that kind of ownership." Seeley told him about the four Russian cases. "The case law is against them."

"And you think Hobie hasn't figured a way around this? I'm sure his friends at the State Department have something."

"Maybe he doesn't know there's a problem, or maybe he's waiting to see if I found out they don't have clear title to the music. Either way, as soon as he sees the complaint, he's going to advise Saddle River to walk away from this."

Girard said, "Hobie's been campaigning to get you fired from the firm. He's talked to everyone on the executive committee. He even tried to lobby me."

The last time Seeley was fired, Girard had disappeared. "What did you tell him?"

"That it's you who should be running the litigation department, not him." Girard looked out the window. "I think you'd do a great job. The litigation partners all respect you, and the associates, God help them, worship you. But why is it that everything you touch has to turn into an opera?"

Girard didn't care if he ran the litigation department. He just wanted to lock him into the routine of responsibility. Seeley said, "You think I should sacrifice my principles."

"No, I think you might want to reconsider your principles if they wreck so many lives."

Girard was thinking about Clare, not the Cubans. Seeley said, "There are people in Cuba depending on me."

"Your partners are depending on you." Girard put down the racquet. "These people are strangers. You've seen the last of them."

The plain finality of Girard's words jarred loose the old hopeless ache. Mayor, Bustamante, Grau, and the others were now just names on a legal document. He was not going to see the Cubans again. "That's why I have to do this."

Girard went to the other side of his desk, crumpled the sandwich bags and tossed them in the wastebasket. The squash racquet had swept all misery away. "You haven't told me what Havana was like."

"Like New York," Seeley said, then remembered Nilda peeling her banana from the bottom up. "Except upside-down."

Seeley locked the office door, shut the lights, and turned off the telephone. He lowered the blinds. He could have been an office worker preparing for a nap, or to take his own life. From the center drawer of his desk, he removed the pale blue airmail envelope that he had found tucked among the signed forms in Amaryll's red envelope. *Michael Seeley* was written on the front, in the same forceful hand as the signature on the witness forms, and he slipped out the tissue-thin sheets. He put his feet up on the desk and read, not because he hadn't already memorized every word, but because it was the only salve he had to ease the pain of Amaryll's absence. Even so, it was like reading a letter from someone who died.

> *Dear Michael,*
>   *If you have the forms in your hands now, it means that you are free and in America, and I am very happy for that. You will also know that I went with Justo to see the musicians. Justo came to me because I had your list of names. He needed a witness and he said that because I told the musicians not to*

sign when I went with you, it was important now for me to
tell the musicians why they must sign.

I knew it was a mistake when I told them not to sign
because it is always a mistake to stop people from making their
own decisions. And this is an important decision, not only for
the composers, but for Cuba. It will restore this music to
the heart of the people. Reinaldo Arenas, who was a
counterrevolutionary and also a great Cuban writer, wrote
that dictators will try to destroy art wherever they find it
because art touches the realms of human thought and
emotion, which they cannot control.

Which is more important, the artist or the work? Now,
with your help, the composers will get their music back and the
government cannot stop the performance of their art here or in
America. So this was right for me to do. I am not brave.
I am a single woman living alone in a crazy country, often
frightened, and that explains what I do. I am not an idealist
like you, not a romantic. I am a practical person, or mostly
practical. So, because I could not live with myself if I did not do
what is right, it was practical for me to go with Justo. I will stop
now because to write English is harder than to speak English.

Lieut. P. is an ambitious man, and I explained to him why
it would be bad for his career if you remained at V.M. If he
does not arrange for you to be released, or if he cannot do that
quickly, I will send the forms to the American Metcalf so that
he can send them to the people who need to have them. I will
also give Mr. Metcalf this letter, and hope that he will get it
to you.

Lieut. P. told me about the many empty bottles you left
on the Malecón. You cannot run away from your darkness
like that, but I am putting a small gift in this envelope to
protect you.

Yours,
     Amaryll

*Oh yes, Nilda does not stop talking about the American. She
found you very charming.*

From the bottom of the envelope, Seeley lifted out the thin chain
and let the ivory fish swing freely. He had become a Cuban fisher-
man, a tiny finned creature dancing at the end of his golden line.
God, did he miss her!

Knuckles as hard as a prison guard's baton rapped at the locked
office door.

"Michael!" It was Daphne. "We need to talk!"

Seeley returned the letter to the envelope and the envelope
to his desk drawer. The *amuleto* he slipped into his pocket.

24

Daphne filled the doorway. "Were you planning to defend Saddle River as well as sue them?" She studied the empty wall where Seeley had removed the colored photographs and could have been deliberating whether the nail holes needed to be patched and the office repainted for a new occupant. "Hobie called. He's furious. If it matters, so am I."

It was Daphne's dominating presence, not her authority as chairman, that cowed even the most senior partners in the firm. The nuns at St. Boniface, who were a good deal tougher than Daphne, never succeeded in disciplining Seeley when he was a student there, which was probably why Daphne didn't intimidate him.

Seeley said, "The lawsuit's not going anywhere. As soon as Saddle River sees it can't win, they'll drop their claim to the music."

"And you don't think Evernham's regular lawyers, the ones who they're going to return to, thanks to you, didn't take the law into account when they advised Saddle River to buy the music? This isn't some local savings and loan society, Michael. I'm sure they did their due diligence."

"Hobie's a backslapper, Daphne, a Washington operator. He's not someone who pulls case reports off the shelf and reads judicial opinions."

"This isn't about cases and statutes. Foreign affairs is a chess game, and Hobie knows how it's played." Daphne paced the office, one foot placed carefully in front of the other, like a decorator measuring for new carpet.

Seeley said, "This is federal court, not the United Nations."

"You need to find other counsel for your Cubans, Michael. If you can't find someone to take the case pro bono, tell them we'll pay their fees. But I want you to find someone good, and I want them to substitute in for you immediately."

Seeley said, "Did Hobie tell you who owns Saddle River?"

"We've been over this."

"How many corporate shells have you worked for where you didn't know who the principals were?" Daphne was proud of her success in advancing Boone, Bancroft toward the first tier of New York law firms where it could be selective about its clients, and it disappointed Seeley that she would be so indifferent about this one. "There's a lieutenant in the Cuban security police who has nothing on his mind but who's behind Saddle River."

"Is that how you got that shiner? Holding out on the police?" Daphne was at the window, and she opened the blinds. "What happened to you down there? I've seen you do some crazy things, Michael, but nothing like this."

Seeley joined her at the window. Thirty-one stories down, two men in hard hats watched a third man jackhammer the pavement.

When he didn't answer, Daphne said, "Let me worry about who our clients are. The media's going to feast on this. Man bites dog; lawyer sues client. Don't make the partners regret bringing you back into the firm, Michael. Don't make me regret it."

When Seeley turned from the window, Daphne seemed suddenly to have aged. The erect bearing was gone. This close and in the bright window light he could see every wrinkle behind the careful makeup. He was going to miss her when she stepped down. "You promised me an executive committee meeting."

"That was about representing the Cubans, not suing a client of Evernham's."

"I'm still representing the Cubans."

"Four o'clock," Daphne said. "Hobie will be back from Washington. I want this resolved by the end of the day." She was partway out the door, then stopped. "I want to hear what Hobie has to say. I can't believe he didn't do his homework on whatever cases you found. But if he didn't, I'll need to reconsider if he's the lawyer who should run this firm."

Seeley said, "Nick would be a better chair."

"Except," Daphne said, going out the door, "he doesn't want the job."

Seeley dialed Elena's extension, expecting her secretary, but after two rings, Elena herself picked up.

"I thought you'd be on your way to Boston."

"I had some personal things to finish up. I'm catching a plane tonight."

There was a coolness that Seeley hadn't heard before. He said, "Do you have time to do some research on who owns Saddle River? Corporate records, trusts if there are any, offshore filings."

"Sure." The warmth was instantly back in her voice. "How far do you want me to go?"

"As far as you have to," Seeley said. "I want to know whose bank account those royalties are landing in." He anticipated her next question. "Bill your time to me. I'm your new client."

The others were in the conference room when Seeley arrived, the hundred-dollar bills already tucked into wallets and pockets. "Ed's in a board meeting in Atlanta," Daphne said from the head of the table, "but Darryl's on the speaker." Hobie was again at Daphne's right, and Seeley sidestepped the chair that Girard pulled out for him so that he could directly face the chairman and her chosen successor from the far end of the table. None of the partners seemed pleased to have their workday interrupted.

"Is that you, Mike?" Valentine's voice came from the starfish-shaped speaker on the center of the table. "How was Cuba?"

When Seeley said, "Good to hear you, Darryl," the voice said, "I was afraid this was going to end in pain."

Strike one ally, Seeley thought. Daphne's enthusiasm for Cuban music wasn't going to secure her support either.

Daphne got out one word—"Evernham's"—before Hobie interrupted. "Evernham's is a substantial client with—"

Daphne waved him off. "It makes no difference what work we do or don't do for Evernham's or its clients. Right now, we have a conflict because Michael got it into his head to sue Saddle River."

Hobie's eyes roved the table, making contact where they could, lining up his troops. He knew just what each partner on the executive committee wanted from the firm and how to arrange for him to have it in return for his vote when Daphne stepped down.

Daphne turned back to Hobie. "Michael seems to think that there's some question about who owns Saddle River."

Hobie shrugged, and when he leaned forward over the table, the gap between his suit jacket and shirt collar yawned. "I can't imagine why their ownership should be an issue."

On his way to the conference room, Seeley had stopped at Elena's office to see how far back she had been able to trace the company's flesh-and-blood owners, but the lights were off.

Hobie said, "I can assure all of you that Saddle River owns every song in the Cuban catalogue."

Daphne moved her chair back so that she could watch both Hobie and Seeley. Darryl's voice came from the speakerphone. "I thought you said the Cuban composers owned the music."

"They do," Seeley said. "The government stole the rights from them fifty years ago, and Saddle River somehow got the rights from the government."

Darryl's voice crackled over the line. "So Saddle River owns the music."

"Not under the case law," Seeley said.

Girard, his eyes half-closed, watched Hobie.

"No American court," Seeley said, "is going to uphold ownership based on theft. In every one of the relevant cases, the judge expressly refused to recognize claims based on expropriated property."

Hobie leaned forward to survey the table. A smile creased the basset face. "You mean the *Trafimov* case? *Babenko? Gortikov? Gennadiev?*" He pulled his jacket forward so that it snugged against his shirt collar. "I read your girl's research memorandum. I didn't know she was doing work for Saddle River." As the attorney in charge of the Saddle River engagement, Hobie had reviewed Elena's time notes and the notes had led him to her memo. "I'm glad to have her on board," Hobie said. "She's a bright girl."

Hobie was too confident.

Seeley said, "The fact that the cases are about Russian books, not Cuban music, makes no difference. The legal principle is the same."

"You're absolutely right," Hobie said. "Russian literature, Cuban music, it makes no difference and, so far as writing goes, I give your girl an A+. But in the research department, she gets an F."

Seeley's heart seized. Elena had missed something. Daphne put a finger to her chin. The partners looked at Seeley's end of the table. Static played on the speakerphone. Seeley waited.

"Your girl should have looked at the case files. The other filings in the Russian cases."

Twice Elena had asked Seeley if he wanted her to look at the files, and both times he'd said no.

If, to the others, Hobie's smile appeared benign, to Seeley it was brutal. Hobie rocked in the swivel chair, taking a sadist's pleasure in repeating the case names, as if he, too, had composed a folk tune. "*Trafimov, Babenko, Gortikov, Gennadiev.* If your girl had looked into the case files, she would have found that in every one of these cases the secretary of state submitted a letter informing the court that, in the interests of American foreign policy, the court should overturn ownership claims based on expropriation. That's why the Russian writers got their works back. The law had nothing to do with it. It was the secretary's letter."

So that was how Felix Silver won the four cases. Through Metcalf, Seeley, too, had asked the State Department for a letter supporting his position. But it wasn't the coincidence that struck Seeley; it was the fact that Silver hadn't told him. Had Silver wanted his young research assistant to believe that he had ridden to victory bareback, without help from Washington? And what had been at risk for Silver? The professor had a secure, tenured post at Harvard, not a law firm partnership that could be withdrawn in an instant. Still, Seeley had bought all of Silver's story, and more.

"And . . ." Daphne said.

"I was at the State Department this morning, talking with a friend in the Office of Legal Counsel." Hobie leaned toward Daphne, as if he was confiding just in her. "The secretary of state will not file such a letter in this case. That means the judge is not going to pay any attention to the four Russian cases. He's going to uphold Saddle River's ownership."

Inside Seeley's head, the chorus of recriminations began. He imagined a revolver at his temple; he actually felt the pressure of the trigger against his finger and the barrel against his flesh. This is why suicides aim at their brains and not their hearts: to stop the noise. Of course Hobie knew everything about the cases and the files and the letters. His friends in the State Department's Office of Legal Counsel had briefed him. Seeley said, "We don't know what weight the judges in the Russian cases gave to the State Department letters—"

Hobie said. "They gave them conclusive weight."

"You don't know that," Seeley said. "There's nothing in any of the opinions where the judge said he was resting his decision on a State Department letter." Hobie's blank look told him that, as Seeley guessed, the lawyer had not read the cases. Seeley said, "I'm betting that my judge is going to follow what the judges wrote in these four cases, and not what some State Department lawyer put in a letter more than twenty years ago."

Hobie's pale blue eyes continued their circuit around the table. He wanted every member of the committee to understand the depth of Seeley's recklessness. "I didn't say that State isn't going to file a letter in this case, only that it's not going to send a letter asking the court to overturn an expropriation. *Your* judge, as you call him, is in fact going to have the benefit of a letter from the secretary of state, but the letter will reach a somewhat different conclusion on the issue of ownership than the letters in the Russian cases."

Hobie, the designated successor, rested a hand on the back of Daphne's chair. "This morning, the State Department's Office of Legal Counsel was instructed to draft a letter to the judge—where was it you filed your complaint, the Southern District?—advising him to dismiss your complaint and uphold the Cuban expropriations on the ground of an overriding national interest in the conduct of this country's foreign relations. The letter will confirm that it is in the best interests of the United States for Saddle River to retain ownership of the music. The State Department lawyer who is drafting the letter has considerable experience with these matters, and the secretary will sign the letter tomorrow morning. The judge will dismiss your complaint by the end of the day."

Daphne was on the edge of her chair; she almost seemed amused. Girard looked genuinely perplexed. From the speakerphone Darryl said, "Why would the State Department support expropriation in this case if it opposed it in the others?"

"Diplomatic considerations," Hobie said. "Some deep thinking at State. Long-term strategy relative to Cuba that's different from our strategy with Russia. The Cold War is over. The world has changed."

The banality of corruption in American life was an unceasing marvel to Seeley. This was no bribe to a customs guard in a third world country, not even a corporate kickback to some government purchasing official. No, it was friendships, old school ties, favors exchanged over generations—Butler's *relationships*—that first quietly nudged the State Department to withdraw its support from Reynoso's efforts to get the composers' signatures and, when that didn't work to protect Saddle River's investment, to file a letter in court that would.

Daphne said, "You need to withdraw your complaint, Michael."

My biggest mistakes, Seeley thought, have always been about people. Maybe that was why, against all his instincts, he was now going to trust his partners not to abandon him. He rose and studied each lawyer around the table as he might the members of a jury. It was stagy, doing this, but he knew that it was the only tactic that had a chance of working.

"At the very beginning," Seeley said, "when Hobie tried to conflict us out of representing the Cuban composers, I am confident that he had the best motives, just as I am sure that yours today will be impeccable. However, our peers judge us not by our motives and intentions but by our actions, and as lawyers that means they will judge us not only by the work we do, but by the clients we do it for."

At the edges of the conference room, shadows moved about, the Cuban composers and their families. Héctor Reynoso, Justo Mayor, Onelio Bustamante, Linares Codina, Faustino Grau, even Gil Garcells. They were waiting for Seeley at long last to do something for them.

"Saddle River," Seeley said. "Who is hiding behind that name? How did this person come to own a catalogue of Cuban music expropriated—*stolen*—from its creators by a foreign government? What influence has this person exerted, what crimes has he committed, to hold on to this music? How comfortable are you not knowing the answers to these questions?"

Hobie half-rose. "This is absurd—"

"Can you answer my questions?"

"That's not the issue before us."

Seeley fingered the ivory *amuleto* in his jacket pocket. Again, his gaze surveyed the partners around the table. "Now ask yourself which client best fits your own sense of justice? Who would you be prouder telling your children and grandchildren that your law firm represents—an artist who stands up to an oppressive government, or a moral weakling who hides behind his banker's account books? Which one do you think a federal trial judge will choose?"

As he spoke, Daphne had not once taken her eyes off Seeley. "What do you want, Michael?"

Seeley said. "I need time to do some research. I don't think Hobie's letter from the State Department is going to make a difference, but I need to check out the case law."

Hobie's basset head wagged, but before he could speak, Daphne said, "There's no time. You have a trial starting in Boston on Monday, and we still have a complaint hanging over the head of a new but valued client."

"I'll have the answer for you first thing tomorrow morning."

Girard said, "And if Hobie's right about what the judge will do with the State Department letter, you'll drop the lawsuit?"

"No," Seeley said. "I'll resign my partnership and continue the case on my own."

Daphne extended one placating hand toward Seeley, another to Hobie. "No one is asking anyone to resign. Let's take it one step at a time. Do your research, Michael, and let us know what you come up with."

Girard gave Daphne a curious look and pushed back his chair. Daphne rose. "Do we need a vote?"

On the speakerphone, Darryl said, "I'm with Daphne. Let Mike do the research."

"Anyone opposed?" The others, except Hobie, shook their heads.

Not quite a roar of acclaim, Seeley thought, but he'd take what he could get.

"Fine," Daphne said. "Let's get back to our billable work." Hobie leaned in to whisper to Daphne and she gave him the smallest frown. But when he finished, she turned to Seeley. "I want you to go down to Evernham's and explain all of this to Ike Butler. And I don't want you to badger him about who owns Saddle River. This is to be a mission of peace, not provocation."

Legalities are for lawyers, not businessmen like Butler. Before the banker would advise his clients to drop their claim, he would require more than a research memorandum predicting that a court would follow the case law over a State Department letter. Butler wouldn't tell his client to relinquish its claim unless the department in fact decided not to file its letter. Seeley knew that if Hobie could get his friends there to write the letter, he could also get them to withdraw it. But that meant, whatever Seeley found in the library tonight, he also had to find a reason for Hobie to do just that.

When Seeley stopped at Elena's office, two outsized suitcases, one gray, the other a dull red, blocked most of the doorway. They were made of some indestructible ceramic-looking composite and came from an era before luggage manufacturers added wheels. An immigrant's suitcases, Seeley thought; Elena's mother's and father's.

Elena watched him climb over the luggage. "How'd it go?"

Seeley hadn't told her that there was an executive committee meeting, but even the biggest law firm is a small village. He said, "Can the State Department get a court to overrule its own precedent? Hobie is having them send our judge a letter saying that Saddle River owns the music even though they got it from Castro."

"How are they going to explain away the Russian cases?"

"I don't know that they have to explain anything, just that they're the State Department and that they think the country's foreign-relations interests override everything else."

Elena closed the briefcase that she was filling with files. "Do you want me to stay and do the research? I can go to Boston tomorrow."

Seeley wondered how she was going to carry the stuffed briefcase along with the two suitcases. "Catch your plane. I'll do the research myself." He caught her questioning look. "Believe it or not, I remember how to do legal research. Even with a computer." The prospect of a long night in the firm's library bothered Seeley less than the fear that he would find little case law in his favor.

Elena held out a densely filled legal pad to Seeley. "Do you still want to know who owns Saddle River?" The answer wasn't as important as it was an hour ago, but no associate likes to complete a project only to have the assigning partner ignore it.

"Sure," Seeley said. He flipped through pages crammed on both sides with handwriting and intricate diagrams.

Elena said, "If you sort through all the closed corporations, holding companies, limited partnerships, powers of attorney, and trusts, you'll find that Saddle River is owned by someone named Willis Cushman III. He's the ultimate beneficiary of the trusts. He pockets the royalties. And you already know where he lives."

Seeley had never been there but, by reputation, it was hunt country and old families. Jacqueline Onassis, when she lived nearby, fit right in. "Saddle River, New Jersey."

Elena said, "I did some research. The Cushmans weren't on the *Mayflower*, but they were sailing right behind. Banking, investments. Railroads in the old days. Mines. He's closer to the bottom of Forbes's billionaire list than the top, but he's there. You wouldn't expect someone fancy like that to own a bunch of Cuban songs."

Seeley said, "It's not a hobby. The catalogue is throwing off millions of dollars a year." More, Seeley thought, if to the CDs, radio play, and Internet he added in commercials—Reynoso's frozen tacos. He set the pad back on Elena's desk. What had made him think that Saddle River's owners were disreputable? Willis Cushman was exactly the kind of client that Evernham's would cultivate and that Boone, Bancroft would want. "Are you sure he's the only beneficiary?"

Elena turned to the last page. "Just 'Willis Cushman III et ux.'"

"Et ux?" A possibility glimmered.

"So?"

Seeley said, "Didn't they teach you Real Property at Harvard? No lawyer today uses Latin unless he's trying to hide something."

"The Middle Ages were over by the time I got there."

"*Et ux* means *and wife*. It's short for *et uxor*. Is there a record of who Cushman's wife is?"

Elena had already swiveled to her computer. "If they're as social as they're rich, she shouldn't be hard to find."

As Elena typed in queries, Seeley maneuvered around the luggage to where he could look over her shoulder. What could she possibly have packed in these enormous suitcases? Elena dressed well for a young associate, and she would be in Boston for the two weeks of trial, but the bags reminded him once again of how little he knew about women.

The printer whirred and hiccupped. Elena handed Seeley a page from the Sunday society section of *The New York Times* dated June 1977. Beaming out from the top right column were the plump, flushed features of Willis Cushman III in white tie and, next to him, his radiant young bride. The printer had reduced the size of the page, and the reproduction was poor, but it was easy to see that Mrs. Cushman was dark and attractive—not Amaryll's sleek, Caribbean beauty, but with sharper, even Semitic features. Bride and bridegroom had met at Princeton, where the bride graduated magna cum laude. By the third paragraph of the story, a smile began to spread across Seeley's face, and a wave of relief swept through him, as it had when he stepped into Metcalf's Suburban outside Havana. Evernham's client had far more than money tied up in Cuban music. Devlin was right about the questions *who* and *how* having the same answer. Now that Seeley knew who owned the music, a first-year law student could figure out how they acquired it.

25

The downtown express crammed with morning commuters rocked in the grooves, white flashing past, then black. In the gritty subway window, Seeley caught his reflection holding a slender black portfolio. He remembered Reynoso coming into his office, clutching that old cardboard valise to his chest, and thought of the contemporary history books on Reynoso's bookshelf. Would the old musician have grasped the larger significance of a wedding announcement in *The New York Times*? Would he have observed between the lines of the society-page prose a lesson about what happens when culture, history, and politics distill themselves into a Cuban cocktail?

The wedding announcement had put Seeley in a tipsy mood, and when he called Butler's office to arrange a meeting and got back a three-word e-mail from an assistant that the investment banker was "out," he considered the implicit resonance of the word. Had Butler passed out? Was he out and about? Out of luck? Out of the closet? Seeley left a message with Hobie's secretary for Hobie to set up the meeting.

Hobie was waiting in Evernham's fourth-floor reception area, and when he made a show of scowling and tapping his wristwatch, Seeley instantly distrusted his own buoyant spirits. It had been a mistake to underestimate Hobie yesterday. He had gone to the executive committee expecting to destroy Hobie's objections, but his adversary had out-prepared him. Seeley knew that it was only his partners' trust in Daphne not in him, that saved him.

Hobie noticed the leather portfolio. "Your research?"

"You could call it that."

Hobie nodded to the man behind the reception desk and led the way down the corridor. In the conference room where on his earlier visit Seeley glimpsed the jowly, tanned profile of a former secretary of state, young men in shirtsleeves bustled about with thick loose-leaf binders and stacks of documents. Seeley followed Hobie into the smaller conference room with its view of New York Harbor and the Statue of Liberty. It was only two weeks since he was last here, but Seeley had the muddled sensation of being a different person.

The receptionist had alerted Butler, because the banker came into the room moments later. His expression hardened when he saw that Seeley was in the chair with its back to the harbor light. When, the last time, Butler gave him the chair with the view, Seeley thought it was the gracious instinct of a host, and only later realized that it was a tactical move; backlit by the bright harbor light, Butler had succeeded in obscuring his own expressions in shadow. The banker asked if anyone needed coffee or tea and, not waiting for an answer, took the chair across from Seeley. He ran a hand through his hair. "Where do we stand with this lawsuit? I'm sure Hobie told you how dismayed we were to learn that you would file a lawsuit against a client of your own firm."

Seeley said, "My clients are prepared to dismiss their complaint against Saddle River before the clerk's office closes today." In fact, he had only guessed what his clients would think if they knew what he was doing.

"Well, I'm relieved to hear that, but what in God's name were you thinking?" Either Butler was someone who flushed easily or he was stuffing down anger.

Seeley said, "I needed to get your client's attention. I want your client to know that I will pursue the composers' case against it through trial and appeals if necessary."

At the same moment, Butler and Hobie understood that Seeley would, as he said, drop the lawsuit, but only if Saddle River met his conditions.

Hobie didn't want to hear the terms. "He can't do this, Ike. The dismissal has to be unconditional—"

Butler's eyes narrowed against the harbor light. "What do you want from us?"

"Saddle River has to drop any claim to my clients' music."

Butler looked at Hobie. Did Butler know what Seeley had discovered about his client? Did Hobie know? For the first time, it occurred to Seeley that Butler had disclosed very little to his old prep-school friend.

Hobie said, "This is ridiculous, Ike—"

Butler raised a hand to stop him. His smile, thin as wire, was forced, a parody of courtliness. "What consideration are your clients offering for us to sell such a valuable asset?"

"I didn't say 'sell.' I said, your clients are going to drop their claim to the music." As he spoke, Seeley unsnapped the portfolio. It was of fine French leather, an extravagant gift from Clare that he would never have bought for himself. "And the consideration, as I said, is that my clients will withdraw their lawsuit against your client." He removed a folder and placed it on the table in front of him. "These are quitclaim grants for all of the music." Seeley's final task in the library last night after finishing his research was to make copies from a form book of the document used to transfer copyrights; he filled them out when he got to the office this morning. "Your clients just have to sign these forms giving up any claim to the music, and my clients will drop their complaint."

"Now you've completely lost me," Butler said.

"This is a bluff, Ike. The judge is going to dismiss the complaint."

Butler looked back at Hobie. "Is there a problem with the State Department letter?" There was an unfamiliar note of urgency in his voice.

"Of course not," Hobie said. "The deputy secretary already approved it. If the secretary weren't traveling in the Middle East, she would have signed it already."

Seeley said, "Does your bank play the odds with its clients' investments?"

"That's a strange question."

Seeley said, "I read thirty-one cases last night, going back to a Supreme Court decision in the 1870s. Even if you get your State Department letter, I don't give it better than a thirty-percent chance of persuading the judge to rule for Saddle River."

Some of the cases that Seeley read supported his position, that a judge would ignore the State Department's attempt to interfere with his decision, while others did not; the remaining cases, including the one from the Supreme Court, could support arguments either way. Sophisticated bankers like Butler might not be interested in legalities, but they usually found precise numbers compelling. Seeley had pulled the number out of the air. Thirty percent had a scary, too-slender-to-risk feel to it.

"Don't listen to this, Ike—"

"Did *you* read these cases?" Butler's voice was frigid.

"I read a draft of the department's letter over breakfast," Hobie said. "Its reasoning is strong and its tone is forceful. The judge will have no choice but to follow it."

"Maybe. And only if it's signed." Butler's voice was somewhere between a whisper and a sigh.

Seeley tapped the file folder. "Say Hobie's right. There's only a small chance that he is, but say the judge is a pushover. If he is, we'll take an appeal."

Hobie said, "I promise you, Ike, my partners will fire him before they let him do that."

Once again it struck Seeley that Hobie never referred to him by name; it was as if they'd never been introduced or that he'd simply forgot.

"I don't know why you haven't fired him already. You're the head of his department, aren't you? If one of my bankers pulled a stunt like this, I'd fire him on the spot."

"Unfortunately, it takes a partnership vote to expel a partner."

Seeley wondered if it was an indication of their background or of the quality of their relationship that the two could so easily talk about him as if he were invisible, or a portrait on the wall.

"It's impressive," Seeley said, "the fascination that litigation holds for the public. Newspapers, magazines, news shows. I understand there are entire television programs devoted to high-profile lawsuits."

"And you think our clients have something they wish to hide?"

Clients, not *client*. Butler apparently understood where he was headed. "You tell me," Seeley said. "Do they have anything to hide?"

"Of course not," Butler said. "But our clients value privacy for its own sake. People of their background usually do."

In the corridor, a flurry of white shirts swept by, then another. Butler turned to see what Seeley and Hobie were looking at. It was the young bankers from the other conference room.

Butler turned back to the table. "A competitor of ours is on the ropes. The Fed asked us to make a bid on their wealth-management business. How often do MBAs get to be heroes?"

"Not often enough," Seeley said. The rush of white reminded him of the predawn procession of the Damas de Blanco on the Malecón. Few people understood the arrogance of power and corruption better than those women. They would immediately grasp the implications of the *Times* wedding notice.

Seeley opened the portfolio again and this time slid the copy of the *Times* society page across the table to Butler. Yesterday, it took three paragraphs for Seeley to make the connection. Butler had only to look at the picture. Instead of the angry flush that

Seeley expected, the color drained from the banker's face. Butler said, "Do you find this amusing, Mr. Seeley?"

"Hypocrisy doesn't amuse me." This is going to work, Seeley thought. Butler is going to make a deal to keep his clients out of the news.

Hobie, baggy eyes moving between Seeley and Butler, took the article from the banker and, after skimming it, shook his head. "So Willis Cushman is married to Phyllis Gronek. Do you think he's afraid people are going to find out that he's married to a mobster's daughter? That's ridiculous. Everyone knows Phil Gronek was his father-in-law." Hobie tapped the copy of the article. "It was in the *Times* for God's sake!"

Seeley said, "Everyone also knows that Phil Gronek was a banker, just like Mr. Butler, here." Butler turned crimson, and it pleased Seeley to see color back in the man's face. "Of course, Gronek's clients came from a different background than Evernham's. No Willis Cushmans for Phil Gronek. His clients all had names that ended in vowels. When they built their hotels and casinos in Havana, he wrote the mortgages. He even bought a couple for himself."

"This is old news." Hobie looked at Butler for support, but the banker's eyes were on the fingers tented in front of him. "Everyone knows Gronek's background."

"But do they know how a thug like Phil Gronek came to own a large slice of Cuba's most valuable music?" Seeley watched for Butler's reaction, but now the banker was gazing out at the harbor. "When we depose Mrs. Cushman for the trial, I think we're going to learn that the music was a gift from her father, maybe even a wedding gift. Why don't you ask Mr. Butler here?"

Butler had more important business with the Statue of Liberty, so Seeley recounted what Devlin had told him at the memorial service about the days right after the revolution. "Gronek must have known that one of Castro's first moves when he took power would be to shut down the casinos. But he also knew that they wouldn't stay shut, so when his friends took the night flight out of Havana, he stayed and ran the casinos for Castro. Those casinos helped finance the new government. He ran them until the Russians came, and then he lost them for good."

This was where Devlin's story stopped, but it didn't require much guesswork to fill in the rest. First, though, Seeley had a question for Butler. "Does your bank ever represent companies whose assets have been expropriated?"

"From time to time, yes, of course."

"How do your clients get paid off for their losses?"

"Governments usually have bank accounts around the world. We use our extensive global banking relationships to seize any dollars or other hard currency we can find."

Butler nodded at Seeley's understanding of what happened between Castro and Gronek. Butler was going to help him because it was the only way he could extricate himself. The banker was going to let Hobie bear the consequences for whatever happened with the Cushmans.

"And after the foreign bank accounts are emptied?"

"You look for other assets," Butler said. "By then, there's usually not much left."

"So," Seeley said, "Castro gave Gronek the music to compensate him for his losses on the casinos." Butler's silence told Seeley that he was right. "Back then, the music probably didn't earn as much as the casinos, but there's a nice thing about owning copyrights. There's no overhead and no employees stealing from the house. It was a good deal for Gronek."

"Why would Castro have to give him anything?" Hobie was on his feet, walking around the table. "Why wouldn't he just kick him out?"

"He could have," Seeley said, "but look at what he got instead: an enforcer. Reynoso and his friends may be cultural heroes, but their music is a threat to the people in power. If there's a black uprising in Cuba, this music is going to be the sound track. Even a government like the Castros' knows it can't shut down this music without creating even bigger problems for itself. But if a private copyright owner files a lawsuit to stop the performance of a song, the pressure is off the government. If Reynoso somehow found a way to put his tour on the road, Saddle River was prepared to shut it down by enforcing the copyrights."

"This is ridiculous!" Hobie was furiously flicking the edge of the table with his index finger. "This happened fifty years ago. It has no connection to the Cushmans."

"Of course it does," Seeley said. "This is why Reynoso's American tour was only a dream. The Cuban government wouldn't let it happen. Too many of his countrymen were going to see it on television."

Hobie took his chair again. "This is all very tidy," he said, glaring at Butler. "It looks like the kind of package a private bank would put together."

"I can assure you," Butler said, "Philip Gronek was never a client of Evernham's."

Seeley calibrated the friction between the old prep-school classmates, and considered what he might do to increase it. Any split between the two men could only work to his clients' advantage. It was no more than a guess, but he said, "The transaction was arranged by a lawyer named Harry Devlin. He represented Gronek and the others in Cuba. He also knew the musicians. He helped them get jobs at the hotels and put some of them together with American music publishers."

Butler turned to Hobie. "I didn't tell you, but we retained Mr. Devlin at the Cushmans' request. I believe Mrs. Cushman knew of him from his work for her father. In any event, he got involved too late to be of any help."

"Because," Seeley said, "your client decided it would be more efficient to have an old composer killed than to expose itself by enforcing its copyrights."

"I don't know anything about anyone being killed," Butler said, "and I'm certain the Cushmans don't either. But thanks to you and your lawsuit, the world is going to think that the Cushmans pay their hunt club dues with royalties stolen from starving Cuban composers. You're trying to blackmail us. That's the lowest crime there is."

"It's a class thing," Seeley said. "For blackmail to work, someone has to have a monster of a secret and a great deal to lose. In Cuba, the poor have no secrets and my clients have nothing to lose."

"But you do. Your firm will fire you from the partnership. Hobie just told us that. Fighting for this music is going to be suicide for you."

"Like it was for Reynoso?"

Hobie looked over at Butler. "How much is the Cuban music worth?"

"Capitalized, somewhere between forty and fifty million dollars." Just reciting the numbers seemed to anger the banker.

"And in this economy," Hobie said to Butler, "do you want to be the one who tells the Cushmans to drop their claim to the music and take that kind of loss? That's what Seeley here is asking you to do."

Finally, Seeley thought, he admitted in my presence that he knows my name.

In the cool conference room, Hobie was perspiring. "You're letting him blow this out of proportion, Ike. I can't see why defending a lawsuit should be a problem for Willis or his wife. Or winning one."

Seeley saw Hobie's predicament. He said, "If Butler had told you the music was a mobster's payoff from Castro, you never would have involved the State Department. You wouldn't have asked your friends there to withdraw their support from Reynoso. Even now, you wouldn't be asking them to send a letter to the judge telling him to uphold the Cushmans' claim to the music. So, you're wondering how you can ask them to change the department's position once again, without losing what's left of your credibility in Washington."

Hobie took the carefully folded display handkerchief from his breast pocket and dabbed at his forehead. "Let me talk with Willis," he said to Butler. "You're their banker, but I'm their lawyer, and this is a legal issue. I'm going to advise him to defend the lawsuit. Their claim to the music is good, and the State Department letter will support their claim."

"How certain are you that the secretary will approve the letter?"

"Absolutely certain," Hobie said.

"State has consistently opposed the Cuban expropriations," Butler said. "Why should it take a different position now?"

"The considerations that apply to nationalized distilleries and sugar refineries are different from those that apply to copyrights." Hobie's gravelly voice thrummed with authority. "Copyrights involve a nation's culture, and the secretary believes that the United States government should not intrude itself into another country's cultural affairs."

"Well," Butler said. "I suppose we'll have to see what the secretary does. State certainly didn't seem to mind poking around in the Russians' cultural affairs in those cases you told me about with the dissident writers. The Cushmans are horse people, and they understand odds. Without this letter you're promising, their odds of winning the case just won't be good enough. Certainly not good enough to justify an attack like this on their reputation. If the secretary doesn't sign, I'm going to advise the Cushmans to walk away from the music and let Mr. Seeley's Cubans have it."

Seeley wondered why Butler had so readily accepted his word about his clients' chances of winning the lawsuit, and it occurred to him once again that Hobie had not read the cases.

"You can't do that," Hobie said, and when Butler didn't respond, added, "The letter will be signed and filed in court today. Monday at the latest."

"And if it isn't," Butler said, "you're going to be the one who explains to the Cushmans how your incompetence cost them all this money."

Watching the banker and lawyer scramble, each to cover his own butt, Seeley couldn't restrain a smile.

Butler saw it and said, "You've changed your mind about not dropping your lawsuit?"

"No," Seeley said. "I was wondering, when the two of you were in school together, which one got the better grades."

26

Magically, the high ceilings of the second-floor dining room at the Racquet and Tennis Club transformed the gray Park Avenue light into the ivory of ancient manuscripts and muted the clatter of heavy silver. Lunch for Seeley was bluefish broiled in butter and lemon, the skin charred by the grill so that it was crisp, even brittle. The oven-roasted potatoes were crusty and the spinach well buttered. As he ate, Seeley described the meeting at Evernham's to Girard, who interrupted with only an occasional question for clarity.

When Seeley finished, Girard said, "Would you want to be the one who tells the Cushmans you screwed up and that they have to drop their claim to the music?" He speared a last piece of potato with his fork. "Butler was twisting Hobie's shorts to make sure he gets the secretary to sign the letter."

"Even if the secretary signs and they file the letter," Seeley said, "the Cushmans are going to settle the lawsuit."

"Why would they do that? I don't know them, and I'm sure they care about their reputation, but no one gives up that kind of money without a fight."

"Butler will convince them. He's more worried about Evernham's reputation than he is about theirs. His own reputation, too."

"I don't see Evernham's getting involved in a mess like this."

"It didn't happen all at once. When Devlin told the Cushmans

that Reynoso and the others were going to file termination notices, they knew it was just a matter of time before the composers
attacked their ownership, so they got Evernham's to hire Devlin to
stop them. The retainer from Saddle River was to conflict me out
of working for Reynoso. It was also Butler's down payment to
Hobie to steer the State Department away from helping Reynoso."

"Sooner or later someone was going to file one of those notices."

"No," Seeley said. "There's a time limit on terminations. For
some of the songs, the deadlines expired even before I met with
Reynoso. The window's going to close on most of the rest by the
end of the year. All Butler had to do was hold off the musicians for
a few months. That's why he hired Devlin. Devlin knows the musicians and he knows people in the Cuban government if Evernham's needed help there."

"You're not suggesting that Evernham's was involved with
Reynoso's death."

"His murder."

Girard looked about, searching for his invisible squash racquet.

"I know you want their business, Nick, but don't pretend to be
naïve. A bank like Evernham's will sponsor the invasion of an
entire country to protect its client's interests. Do you really think
they would let some old Cuban composers get a piece of a client's
fortune? That Butler would let them get in the way of his annual
bonus? Hobie may have kicked and fussed this morning, but in the
end he's going to do what Butler tells him to do. Evernham's is the
only client he's brought to the firm, and without them he'll never
make chairman."

Girard drummed his fingers impatiently. "Hobie's not going to
be chairman." He smoothed the heavily starched tablecloth with
the edge of his hand. "After yesterday's meeting, Daphne told him
that she changed her mind. She's not going to retire. My guess is
she had second thoughts about Hobie."

That was why Hobie had been so abrupt with Butler this morning. He no longer needed him as a client. "Then this is just about
the State Department," Seeley said.

Girard had finished lunch and was looking for the waiter. "No law firm in today's market is going to take in a partner at Hobie's level unless he has a three- or four-million dollar book of business. Evernham's won't give him that. No one else will, either. The State Department's the only place Hobie can get a job as big as his ego."

For a moment after yesterday's executive committee meeting, it had occurred to Seeley to settle the Boston industrial espionage case with the Chinese if in exchange the State Department would withhold the secretary's letter, but in the next instant the very thought humiliated him; he had pushed some ethical lines in his career, but never to where it would injure a client. "Hobie's going to have to convince his friends in Washington to change their minds and withdraw the letter."

"How is he going to do that? Tell them he made a small mistake when he asked them to back off from helping the Cubans? That he made another mistake asking them to draft a letter for their boss to sign? What reason would he have even to try?"

"I'll find one." It felt to Seeley like being on the squash court, Girard putting a spin or a slide on every one of his returns.

"I hope you do, because I'm worried about your Cuban friends." Subtly, Girard's tone had changed. He was still sparring, but there was also an edge of genuine concern in his voice. "Think about the headlines if you go ahead with your case here. 'Castro Steals Music from Local Composers—Hands Cuban Heritage Over to American Mobster.' Your Cuban friends are going to be the first to suffer."

"If I drop the case, they get nothing. No music. No money."

"That's what they had before you started this, and somehow they managed to live with it. What you're doing now could make their lives infinitely worse. This is like that Chinese girl, the journalist, all over again."

"I can take care of this." Seeley just needed to make a phone call.

"How many people are involved?"

"Fourteen musicians or their families. My interpreter." Seeley signaled to the waiter to take away his plate and, when Girard ordered coffee and pie, asked for the rice pudding. He reached inside his jacket. "I need to make a phone call."

Girard glanced around the hushed room and shook his head. "House rules."

Seeley strode out of the dining room and when he reached the wide hallway broke into a run, taking the stairs down to the first floor two at a time. The white-tiled men's room with its bright lights could have been a young boy's memory of a barber shop or a grown-up's of a prison cell. He already had the phone out, and scrolled for a number on the screen, before remembering that the phone was a replacement for the one that was stolen from him in Havana. He punched in a number and prayed that his memory was correct.

It took less than a complete ring for Metcalf to answer.

"This is Michael Seeley." He worked to catch his breath. "Are you still planning to retire?" Daphne changed her plans, and Seeley hoped that Metcalf had not.

"Do you mean, has the State Department done anything to make me change my mind?" Metcalf paused to let Seeley think about that. "No. As soon as I pack up here and collect the wife, we're headed to Chicago and then Clear Lake." Seeley waited for a crack about western muskie, but there was none. "Did you deliver the forms to the publishers?"

"It's done," Seeley said. "I need your help."

"Like I told you at the airport, the composers owe you. Me, too."

"This is your desk phone, right? In an hour, can you go for a walk and call me back?"

Metcalf didn't need Seeley to explain that this was not going to be a conversation that he would want to have in his office in the U.S. Interests Section. After he took Seeley's number, Metcalf said, "Do you remember when you asked me who got the department to pull its support from Héctor? I talked with someone in Washington yesterday. They still don't know about my freelancing. He said it was a wealthy couple in New Jersey, that Hobie

Harriman was the go-between. This was two to three weeks ago. Does that help you?"

"Immensely," Seeley said. "I'll talk to you in an hour."

When Seeley returned to the dining room, Girard was standing at the table talking to two men who had greeted him earlier on the way in. Girard introduced them—one was an investor, the other did something in advertising—and after a brief, hearty exchange, the men left. Seeley remembered Girard saying that Clare's new husband was in advertising, but decided that it was not him he had just met.

When Girard was in his chair again he said, "You talked to Hobie?"

"No," Seeley said, "someone at the State Department." Literally that was true until Metcalf packed his bags.

"When will you know if the secretary signed the letter?"

"Hobie said in a couple of hours, when she gets free, wherever she is."

Girard leaned forward. His smile, like his bowtie, was slightly crooked. "That black eye of yours that no one wants to talk about. What went on between you and that woman who translated for you?"

The question startled Seeley. It was as alien to the dining room, where men talked of business, politics, and sports, as a woman herself would be. "I need to go."

"You said Hobie wasn't going to hear from Washington for a while." Girard nodded at the coffee and dessert on the table. Seeley's rice pudding was in a silver goblet finely pebbled with condensation.

Seeley regretted this. Girard had opened a door that he hadn't even planned to unlock.

"Your translator, how'd that work out for you?" When Seeley didn't answer, Girard said, "At the wedding, Clare said she thought you were the kind of man who would be happier with a woman who didn't love you than with one who did."

Seeley sipped at his coffee. "For a woman who just got married, Clare's thinking a lot about someone who's not her husband anymore."

"Like it or not, you're still a part of her life."

Seeley wanted to leave, so he tried to keep the words light. "Women are a mystery."

"That's a large part of their attraction," Girard said. "I can tell you that I'm almost completely certain that Maisie's never been unfaithful to me, but I can't tell you I'm absolutely certain. That will always be part of her mystery for me. Whose fault was it that it didn't work out with this translator—hers or yours?"

Seeley poked at the rice pudding with his spoon. Wasn't this the way friends are supposed to talk? "Do you want to know the truth?"

"About your feelings? It would be a novel experience."

"I never felt this deeply for anyone before." The girl on the Swansea train was a fantasy; Amaryll was real. "There's not a minute in the day that I don't miss her."

Girard studied him. "What are you going to do about it?"

"Nothing. There's nothing I can do." Seeley was finished talking about Amaryll. He possessed so little of her—a letter, a tiny fish on a gold chain—that, foolishly, he had thought that talking would somehow install her as a reality in his life. Instead, she dissolved into the air like a wisp of song. He took a spoonful of rice pudding and tasted the rum in it. It was no more than a flavor on his tongue but, nauseated, he pushed the silver goblet away.

Then Seeley realized what was wrong about the conversation. He hadn't told Girard that his translator was a woman, much less that he had a relationship with her. Only one person could have told Girard about Amaryll, someone who had been having him watched all along. "Hobie talked to you about the Cushmans and their problem even before Reynoso came to see me."

"What are you saying?"

"You were following Hobie's lead from the beginning. That's

why you kept making up reasons for me not to help the Cubans. Why it would be a mistake for me to go up against Hobie. Ten minutes ago, you were telling me I should drop my lawsuit."

"If you think about it, Mike, I was trying to protect you."

"From what? Launching another one of my crusades? No, you weren't thinking of me or my clients. You were protecting your practice. Hobie thought he could get to me through you, and he figured he could get to you by promising you work from Evernham's. He was half-right."

Only Girard's fingertips scratching at the tablecloth told Seeley that his partner was struggling to control himself. House rules didn't permit squash in the dining room, even with invisible racquets. Girard said, "Has it ever occurred to you that the reason people are always letting you down is that you set your standards too high for us ordinary mortals?"

Seeley rose and pushed in his chair. "I have to go."

"Do you know who your real enemy is, Mike? It's not Hobie or me. It's you. You are."

"I spent a night making love to a prison cell full of mosquitoes. Tell me something I don't already know."

27

Ordinarily, Seeley welcomed solitude the way other people seek companionship. But, after the lunch with Girard, the afternoon floated uneasily over pools of loneliness too deep to plumb. The exhibits and depositions for the trade secret trial were on the conference-room table, waiting to be packed into boxes for overnight delivery to Boston, the blue binders for Seeley's witnesses on one side, the black ones for the Chinese researchers on the other. Elena was in Boston. The summer law clerks were off with half of the New York associates on a chartered fishing boat on Long Island Sound. Many of the secretarial staff had started the weekend early, but now and then the clatter of a computer keyboard or the muffled ring of a telephone rose from the warren of cubicles and offices along the hall. Outside, even the jackhammers were still. Hobie had promised to meet Seeley here at 2:30, and it was now almost 3:00. Maybe it was the thought of Girard on the way to his vacation home in Montauk, but Seeley pictured his life as a long, receding tide.

Another half hour passed before Hobie strolled into the conference room. He walked the length of the table deliberately, one hand in a trouser pocket, the other grazing the top of the deposition binders as if each required his blessing. He had exchanged the morning's damp and rumpled shirt for a fresh one, and the handkerchief in his breast pocket was crisply folded. When he reached the end of the table, Seeley said, "Did the secretary sign the letter?"

"She approved it. The deputy secretary has instructed an assistant secretary to sign it."

Seeley felt the words more than he heard them; they could have been sharp stones. "It sounds like the smart people are passing the buck. They don't want to be anywhere near this when it blows up."

"The secretary can't sign every piece of paper that crosses her desk. I promise you, nothing's going to blow up."

Seeley said, "You can't let them file the letter."

Hobie lifted a transcript from the table. "Your Boston trial? It's too bad you didn't get your client to settle. You might have made some friends for yourself at State."

Seeley took the transcript from Hobie and replaced it on the pile. "We're still going to beat the Cushmans in court." It wasn't a bluff. After his long night reading cases, Seeley believed that the State Department letter was only a hurdle, not a barrier, to winning the expropriation cases.

Hobie said, "Did you see who has the case?"

Cases are assigned to federal district court judges randomly and Seeley hadn't thought to check whose docket *Estate of Reynoso v. Republic of Cuba and Saddle River Equities* landed on because he expected the Cushmans to settle long before a judge even read the complaint.

"Lloyd Dickerson," Hobie said.

"Oh."

Dickerson was the most recent judicial appointment in the Southern District and had a reputation as an intensely loyal party man. Seeley didn't suspect a fix; it's virtually impossible to rig a case assignment in federal court. But, however Dickerson got the case, he was going to be more disposed than any other judge in the district to attach weight to a letter from the administration that appointed him. Seeley said, "Whoever the judge is, the State

Department letter's going to backfire. It's going to be a disaster for them."

"I'm sure you'd like me to think that, but the only way you're going to climb out of this hole is to withdraw your complaint."

Metcalf had returned Seeley's call two hours earlier. After a career in government, the foreign service officer had no illusions about how uncomfortable his life would become, even in retirement, if he turned on his former employer, but he agreed to testify in court if that was what it took to get the composers their music back. In return, Seeley promised to keep him out of the case if there was any way he could. But that meant he had to get Hobie to understand the magnitude of the State Department's misadventure in Havana and to accept that unless he got his friends in Washington to withdraw the letter, many of them would be out of jobs. Some could go to prison.

"You know," Hobie said, "that letter isn't just to help the Cushmans. It's also a brilliant tactical move for State. I suppose we should thank you for creating the opportunity to file it." Condescension rolled like a grape on his tongue. "The letter is going to advance American policy in Cuba without alienating the usual constituencies at home."

"What policy?"

"Engagement. The administration has been working hard to develop better relations with Cuba. Loosening travel restrictions for Americans. Toning down our rhetoric on human rights. Not second-guessing the Castros' management of internal economic affairs."

"Like letting them steal their own people's music to hand over to an American gangster. There's no more foreign policy here than there was in the 1950s when the State Department was a front for the United Fruit Company."

"There may be an auspicious parallelism of interests, but nothing more than that. My intervention on behalf of Saddle River just happened to come at a fortunate moment for our client. There is no connection between my efforts on behalf of a client's investment—"

"Their windfall."

"Between securing their wealth through entirely legal means and our government's pursuit of its foreign policy."

"Except," Seeley said, "that your intervention for the Cushmans didn't start with the secretary's letter."

"I don't know what you mean."

Hobie wore dullness the way he did his rumpled suits, as an affectation and a deceit to the unwary. The ruse clawed at Seeley like a vicious, slow-witted animal. Seeley said, "When Evernham's found out Reynoso was organizing his friends to get their music back, and that the U.S. Interests Section was helping him, you got the State Department to drop its support and abandon the composers."

"Of course I did. That's what a lawyer who knows telephone numbers in Washington does for his clients. You really can't be that uninformed. This is how business is done in the capital."

"A news reporter isn't going to need a sharp pencil to draw the dotted line between the State Department and Reynoso's murder."

"That's crazy. There is no connection." Hobie straightened, as crisp as his starched shirt. "You don't really think this is about Cuba, do you?" He didn't wait for an answer. "Cuba's no more than a chess piece."

Moby Dick, Seeley thought. It wasn't the great whale's whiteness or size or ferocity that tipped Ahab into madness. It was the beast's dumb obstinacy. "The United States government sponsored the murder of an innocent man."

Hobie didn't hear. "This isn't about Cuba any more than the Cuban missile crisis was about Cuba. Do you have any idea of the ramifications of what we're doing there? The scale?" He paused to see if Seeley was listening. "What we're dealing with here is China."

Hobie was off in a world of diplomatic make-believe, and Seeley had no idea what he was talking about.

"Who else do you think we're fighting for influence in Cuba? An island two hundred miles from Miami. Cuba is going to be

China's twisting knife in America's side, just like it was the Soviet Union's. Just like Taiwan is the knife that we twist in China's side."

It was going to take a two-by-four across the forehead to get Hobie to confront the disaster that he and his partners in the State Department had created in Havana. "The Cushmans must be grateful. You got the United States Department of State to abduct a Cuban national from Manhattan, fly him out of the country, and hand him over to his country's security police. Why? So that they would lock him away where he couldn't get the others to sign—"

"I don't know anything about that—"

"The U.S. Interests Section and Minint both wanted Reynoso off the streets. Parallel interests, isn't that what you call it? Minint didn't care about the termination notices. They just didn't want Reynoso agitating people about his tour."

Hobie brushed Seeley's words away with a hand. "How could you possibly know any of this?"

With a silent apology to Metcalf for the misery this would carry to his door, Seeley said, "I wasn't getting anywhere with the musicians, so an official at the Interests Section made a date for me to meet Reynoso at a cemetery in Havana. But when this official went to collect Reynoso from where he was being held, he was gone." That was why Mayor, not Reynoso, met him at the baseball monument. When in their phone call two hours ago Seeley asked Metcalf about Mayor's role, Metcalf said only that he was sure Seeley could figure it out for himself. That meant Mayor had been working for Metcalf, and when Metcalf went off in his own direction, Mayor followed. How much higher would Lourdes Gallindo's crooked eyebrow rise if she knew what her husband was up to?

"This all sounds like a terrible misunderstanding."

For the first time, Seeley heard a stumble in Hobie's voice; he finally had his attention. "When you passed on the news to Butler that I was getting some of the composers to sign, he had two thugs clean out my hotel room and try to kidnap me. He arranged for me to get locked up at Villa Marista. It would have been helpful if you briefed a lieutenant there on your plans." In a reflex, Seeley touched the still tender flesh beneath his eye. "The lieutenant didn't believe me when I told him why I was in Cuba. He didn't even know who Saddle River was." Seeley realized that apart from Piñeiro's entirely justified suspicions, the lieutenant had been protecting him from the moment he landed in Havana; at least once, with the thugs in the van, Piñeiro may have saved his life.

"Well, I had nothing to do with any of that." When Hobie pressed his hands together, Seeley noticed for the first time that the fingernails were chewed and uneven. "Ike told me he asked this fellow Devlin to visit you in prison."

"I'll have to remember to thank him when I depose him for the trial."

"You know, we—Evernham's—tried to protect your musician. Devlin was supposed to persuade him to be more cooperative."

"Reynoso was dead before Devlin got there." Seeley looked down through the window. The laborers were back. They hadn't abandoned the street after all, just gone for a leisurely Friday lunch. Once again, a longing for Havana—its noise, filth, and stench—gripped him with an intensity that made it hard to breathe.

Hobie jammed his hands in his trouser pockets and slumped back into the chair. "That wasn't supposed to happen." His neck disappeared into his jowls. "But you have no proof. Even if any of this were true, who would know?"

"I plan to depose Devlin, Butler, and every State Department person I can find before trial."

"What makes you think any of them will tell the truth?"

"That's what a trial lawyer does, Hobie. He gets people to tell the truth even when they don't want to."

"There are client confidences here. You can't disclose—"

"None of this information comes from a client, or anyone who has a reason to lie."

Hobie locked his hands as if in prayer. "Ah, yes, your man at U.S. Int." Hunched down in his chair like this, Hobie looked almost frail. "Why would he want to wreck his career over this?"

"His career's already over. He thinks this is too important to cover up."

"If the State Department is truly as malign an institution as you say, it surely would have no difficulty tracking him down and persuading—"

"I'm planning to call you as a witness, too."

"You can't call a partner in your own law firm as a witness."

"I promise you," Seeley said, "by the time this case goes to trial, we won't be partners. You can figure out for yourself which one of us is leaving the firm."

"You have to believe me. I had no part in arranging any of this." Hobie lifted a transcript off a pile on the table and, opening it at the middle, turned pages as if he might find there the instructions for saving himself. "I didn't know this was going to happen."

Seeley's frustration with Hobie was rapidly turning into exhaustion. It wasn't just the sleep that he lost in Havana and hadn't yet recovered; it felt like a lifetime's accumulation of fatigue pulling him down. Still, Hobie was close to where he needed him. A drink would help me through this, Seeley thought; a juniper foretaste of gin touched the back of his tongue.

Seeley said, "Do you really think the State Department's going to take you back once your friends learn what you got them into? When they realize how big a mistake it was for them to help Evernham's and the Cushmans?"

"This is just a speed bump. We'll get past it." The words were at war with Hobie's damp, collapsing features and wilting suit. The knot of his paisley tie was black where perspiration seeped into it. Fear was turning Hobie inward; he was like an animal curling into a ball to protect itself. "Surely you can't think—"

"You have a choice," Seeley said.

Hobie had pulled himself forward from his deep slouch to lean over the table. His arms were spread-eagled in front of him, fingers arched and splayed as if grappling for purchase on the glass-hard tabletop, a sailor in rough seas grasping at the corners of a life raft. "I can't tell them to shred the letter."

"You don't have to," Seeley said. What he was about to propose was going to shield Hobie and his cronies in the State Department from responsibility for crimes committed here and in Cuba; it was going to protect Devlin, Butler, and the Cushmans as well. Seeley didn't feel good about that. In fact, he felt rotten. None of these people had a twinge of remorse for what they'd done. But if Hobie went along, there would be no need for a trial or for Metcalf to testify. There would be no occasion for news reports that would instantly reach Cuba, putting Amaryll, Mayor, and the others in danger. The Americans would avoid punishment, but so would the Cubans. The Cushmans would lose the music; the Cubans would regain it. The moral balance was crude, and if it defaced the memory of Héctor Reynoso, Seeley knew that he would have to live with that. A chattering ghost to join the others. He said, "They don't have to shred the letter."

Something acute flashed behind Hobie's eyes.

"All you have to do," Seeley said, "is tell your friends in the State Department that the lawsuit has been settled. That means the case is over. If there is no pending case, there's no place for the State Department to file the letter. Tell your buddies they'll have to save their foreign policy master stroke for some other day."

The lawyer's affected confusion dissolved.

Seeley said, "No one but the Cushmans and their banker needs to know the terms of the settlement."

Hobie's expression was bleak. "What terms?"

"The Cushmans sign the music over to the Cubans."

"How are your clients going to pay for it?"

"They're not," Seeley said. "The music belongs to them. The Cushmans have been living off other peoples' property rent-free for as long as they've controlled the catalogue. They should be glad my clients aren't going to ask for back royalties."

"But Ike said the catalogue's worth forty, fifty million dollars."

"I'm sure that if you explain the situation to the Cushmans with the same detail that I described it to you, they'll understand. I think they're going to fight to see who gets to sign the settlement papers first."

"You really can't expect—" Hobie stopped. "How do I know this fellow of yours from the U.S. Interests Section won't talk to the press?"

"You don't know." Seeley hadn't considered that possibility before, but no one at the State Department needed to know that there was a whistle-blower. Hobie surely understood that for him to be able to return to the State Department, he would have to keep Metcalf out of his story. "That's just a chance you have to take," Seeley said. "If you consider the alternative, you don't have a choice."

Choice, Seeley thought. I could write a treatise on the subject. Even in America, it was in shorter supply than Amaryll believed. Two weeks ago he had no choice but to go to Havana, just as he had no choice today but to accept the settlement of his case. Nor did Hobie or the Cushmans have a choice. If the Cushmans didn't hand the music over to the Cubans, one or both of them was going to face criminal prosecution for conspiracy to abduct a foreign national from American soil. The *New York Times* wedding portrait was his only clue, but Seeley guessed that it was Mrs. Cushman, Phil Gronek's daughter, whose idea this was and whose name would be first on the federal indictment.

"You know," Hobie said, "I have friends at Treasury. I expect that they would be interested in your unlicensed travel to Cuba."

"Is that the best you can do? Threaten me with prosecution for illegal travel? No heavy breathers pulling me off the street? Stringing me up from a pipe across the ceiling?"

"I'd think that with your history, the State Bar would be delighted for the opportunity to pull your license."

"I'll take that chance."

"Would you really put a client's welfare ahead of your own?"

"You would, too, Hobie. We just have different ideas about who our clients should be." He handed Hobie the folder with the quit-claims.

Hobie opened the folder. "What are these?"

"The quitclaim grants I brought to Evernham's this morning. Saddle River turns over every piece of music in its catalogue to the composers or their families."

"Surely this isn't necessary. My word should be sufficient. My clients are prominent—"

"I want them signed and on my desk by eight o'clock tonight." This would leave Hobie time to fax the forms to wherever Mr. and Mrs. Cushman spent their summers, and for Seeley to catch a late flight to Boston. The signed termination notices were already in the publishers' hands. Seeley's secretary would file the quitclaims for recordation in the Copyright Office on Monday morning, and in the afternoon she would fax to the court the necessary papers for withdrawing his complaint. The claims of Mayor and the others to the music were now secure. Seeley could negotiate their new royalty arrangements with the publishers when he returned from his trial in Boston.

"You realize," Hobie said, "you're losing any leverage I could have gotten for you at State. You won't be able to track down that Chinese journalist of yours."

It was time to let Jun Wei go, but Seeley knew that he couldn't, ever. "I can live with that. Can you?"

"I'm not the one who screwed up." In the doorway, his posture once again erect, his expression bright, Hobie tugged with up-turned fingers at the hem of his jacket sleeves. "This is about your office, isn't it? All this undermining of my position here. What you really want is your old office back."

"No," Seeley said. "It's just an office. You can have it."

"Well then, Michael, everything considered, I'd say we've ac-complished a fine piece of work. The Cushmans are going to take a financial beating of course, but I'm sure our tax fellows here can help ease the pain for them. And, you know, 'Who steals my purse

steals trash . . .' and all that. We certainly saved the Cushmans'
reputation for them. We also saved the State Department a good
deal of embarrassment. And we restored these musicians of
yours—"

"Composers."

"We got them and their families their music back and, once we
take the publishers over the coals, more money than they've ever
seen. All in all, I'd say we've achieved a . . . *splendid* resolution."

The appraisal was so absurd that Seeley wanted to howl, to
take Hobie by the shoulders and shake him into a size and shape
more approximately human. His anger at the man had the kick of
alcohol. To control himself, Seeley grabbed a handful of binders
and placed them in an empty shipping box. In his fingertips he felt
the awakening pulse of the trade secrets trial, the renewed excitement of battle, even after all these years of trying cases. He and
Elena were going to win in Boston, not only against the Chinese
researchers, but also against their employer who put them up to it.
Sober in his cell at the Villa Marista, Seeley had mastered every
detail of the case, and there was no way that they could lose.

He had almost filled the box before he realized that Hobie was
still at the door. Hobie said, "Don't you agree that this is a fine
result, Michael?"

Seeley was done with Hobie. He recalled the hallway glimpse
of the lawyer humming and scribbling at his desk, a hand curled
over the page, as close to the paper as a schoolboy drawing with
crayons. An impulse of compassion welled inside him. The odd
thought struck Seeley to forgive his partner. If only he could discover his own great trespass, the offense that he had been trying
to right from his first conscious breath, he might even forgive himself. He needed forgiveness no less than the Cubans needed their
music back, and for the same reason: to be restored, to be whole.

"No," he said to Hobie. "Not a fine result. A *splendid* one. Absolutely splendid!"

ACKNOWLEDGMENTS

For their generous help with this book, I am grateful to William Craig, George Fisher, Meg Gardiner, Tom Herman, Alba Holgado, Pam Karlan, Jorge Machado, Armando Menocal, Frank Ratliff, William Ratliff, Keith Reeves, Jon Reichman, Jan Thompson, and Carl Yorke.

Leonardo Padura's Mario Conde novels were a continuing inspiration, and Juan Antonio Rodríguez and William Ratliff's unpublished study *Protecting and Promoting Fidel: Inside Cuba's Interior Ministry* (Hoover Institution Archives) provided valuable insights into the operation of Cuba's domestic security operations.

I am indebted to Thomas LeBien for fine editorial suggestions, as I am to Wendy Strothman and Lauren MacLeod at the Strothman Agency. My thanks, also, to Lynne Anderson for her sharp editorial eye as well as for typing the manuscript, with an assist from Mary Ann Rundell.